MORGAN'S RUN

by

TAMBO JONES

PUBLISHER'S NOTE

This is a work of fiction. All names, places, characters, and incidences are either the product of the author's imagination, or are used fictitiously, and any resemblance to actual people, alive or dead, events or locations, is completely coincidental. Trigger warning: This book contains graphic depictions of physical and emotional child abuse and its psychological aftereffects. Trigger warning: This book contains graphic depictions of physical and emotional child abuse and its psychological aftereffects.

A product of TAMBOWRITES
Cover art and design: Michele Maakestad
Interior fomatting by: Michele Maakestad

TRADE PAPERBACK ISBN: 978-1-951023-13-3

1st Edition: 2017
2nd Edition: 2020

Praise for MORGAN'S RUN

Psychological thriller "Morgan's Run" delves deep into the nature of obsession and the malleability of identity. The novel explores the lasting damage of childhood abuse and asks if one can break free from maladaptive coping mechanisms. Above all, is it ever safe to stop running?
- Jen Danzinger, Executive Producer, Bare.

***

"Morgan's Run" pulls us through the flight from abuse into the fight for a future.
- A.R. Miller, author of the Fey Creations series

***

"Morgan's Run" is a romantic thriller that kept my heart pounding to the very end. Tamara Jones is a first rate, suspenseful storyteller.
- Audrey Brice, Thirteen Covens

For Kelly
The best of us.

ONE

DARCY CAN'T REALLY BE DEAD, Morgan thought, clutching damp tissues and trying not to feel overwhelmed. After spending much of her twenty-seven years running through large cities, she stared at the sedate, wide-open space of rural Minnesota as if it were an alien landscape. She'd been born in Madison, fostered in Milwaukee, ran away to Chicago, to Detroit, Indianapolis. Always cities. A person could disappear in a city, become another bug in the swarm, but everything stood out in the country. One little deviation from the norm brought notice. One little tree. One stone. One farmhouse.

One city girl with nowhere else to run to.

At least until her only friend and website partner had unexpectedly died.

A copy of Darcy's will lay on Morgan's lap, the top page speckled and smeared by her tears. Pages three and four had insisted Morgan visit rural Minnesota and endure an apparently endless sales pitch from Ms. K Bennet, the financial advisor driving her to Darcy's house.

After hearing at least five miles worth of gibberish on the benefits of using the firm to convert annuities to equity instruments—whatever that meant—Morgan sighed and pressed her forehead against the window. God, she wanted to run, to feel pavement and earth beneath her scuffed Nikes, the wind tugging at her ponytail, and hot summer sunshine on her shoulders instead of being cooped up in a leather-scented car with a woman who only cared about selling market indices and accounts.

Bennet insisted Morgan, as the new sole owner of Pony and Mule Web Development, should consider the ease of asset allocation services and integration options on her websites.

"I just write articles and reviews for FrugallyUrban. I don't know anything about the business end," Morgan said, but Bennet continued, assuring her that putting links back to her financial consulting office was simple and would provide added benefits to Morgan's site customers.

Morgan barely listened as they drove past a farmhouse with a partly-built addition off one side; just golden wooden studs, plywood floor, and a roof. Morgan bet pretty much everyone within five miles knew exactly who was building the addition, why they were building it, how much they spent, and who did the work. Then they'd debate the merits of all of those things over coffee in a diner or farmhouse kitchen somewhere. She shuddered.

Maybe a mile, mile and a half past the farmhouse, Bennet braked, slowing to a sedate pace as they passed a large, cheery sign saying *Welcome To Hackberry, Pop. 586* - along with smaller signs for Hackberry Lions, Hackberry Lutheran Church, Hackberry VFW, and a cardboard reminder to donate to the Hackberry Youth Can Drive.

Darcy's hometown. Only she wasn't in it anymore.

Morgan pushed a wayward strand of dark hair aside and rubbed her forehead. *I can't do this. I just can't. Darcy, I'm so sorry, I ca—*

Bennet pulled into a driveway and turned off the car. "We're here. Are you ready to examine the real estate portion of your portfolio?"

Morgan jumped as if slapped and slowly lowered her hand. The house looked exactly like the pictures Darcy had posted—yellow craftsman bungalow with some trees here and there, marigolds and petunias in the flowerbeds, and a swing on the porch. Kids rode by on bikes, their chatter barely heard over the pained slam of Morgan's heart.

C'mon, Darcy, she thought, eyes stinging. *Open the front door already. You're still here. You're still alive. You have to be. You can't leave me all alone with this pushy woman.*

Morgan sat, shaking and staring at the porch swing, until Bennet came around and opened her door.

Bennet offered a hand to help her stand and Morgan took it without thinking. Bennet's palm was warm and sweaty, her grip tentative. The air smelled of fresh-mown grass. Swallowing past the constriction of her throat, Morgan ducked back into the car for her backpack and smoothed her cutoffs before following Bennet. Her feet on the concrete steps made a solid, welcoming thud as she climbed them, and she paused to touch the porch railing. The paint was cracked, but not yet peeling, slightly rough beneath her fingers. Homey. Worn.

While Bennet searched for the key, Morgan looked out to the neighborhood. Houses much like Darcy's all faced the paved highway and clumps of roadside mailboxes on posts. An enormous tractor rumbled by and a pair of little girls on bikes with training wheels resumed riding circles in the road. They couldn't have been more than five or six years old and Morgan watched them as if they were fairies in an old fantasy novel.

They rode around and around, laughing and unfettered by parents. The girls leisurely pedaled to the nearest lawn whenever a car came near, then returned to circles on the smooth pavement. One, with long auburn hair halfway down the back of her sundress, barely needed the training wheels at all.

"Miss Miller?" Bennet asked, her voice frustrated.

Morgan turned, shaking her head. "Yes? What?"

Bennet held the wooden screen door open, darkness beckoning from within. "Do you want to come in?"

Morgan hesitated, then entered. The air felt closed up and stale despite the window air conditioner laboring gamely to her right and another whirring somewhere far off to her left. Beneath the staleness she smelled dog and a faint, faded wisp of Murphy's Oil Soap, surely from the oak floors and trim. Torn storage boxes stood stacked in the corner and a rug lay rolled up against the far wall. A horsey wallpaper border circled the room and horse figurines pranced on every available surface. Horses, horses, everywhere.

Gut clenching, Morgan held her panic tight as she placed her backpack beside the door and kept her gaze away from the fearsome beasts endlessly leaping about.

Bennet pressed a ring of keys into Morgan's hand. "These are for the front door. We couldn't find any for the back." She shrugged slightly and strode past, letting the screen bang closed behind her. "I don't think she ever locked it. Pity. Someone came in and trashed the place. Probably kids. Several valuable items were damaged, and some of the equine statuary was stolen, but we had it tidied up. At least it didn't lower the value of the property."

Some were stolen? Good God, how many horses did Darcy have? Morgan flinched away from the figurines and followed, letting Bennet lead her through Darcy's cluttered, horse-crammed house like an inept Realtor. She pointed out obvious features—Look! There's the stove!—and Morgan soon wished she'd quit yammering. The house had three bedrooms and a full bath upstairs, a powder room, junk room, and home office down, plus a dining room and a sprawling kitchen devouring the back quadrant of the main floor. The whole place felt like Darcy, her lacy blues and purples, clotted with too many horsey knickknacks, braided rugs, and piles of papers, even a battered saddle in the corner of the den. Each cluttered room gave Morgan both a grimace of fear and a welcoming ache in her heart.

Bennet found the door to the basement and, fumbling for a light, pointed down into the dark. "Here's the basement," she said with tired, false cheer. "The light's right here," she said, shrugging. "Somewhere."

"It's okay," Morgan mumbled, moving to the kitchen sink. A clean teacup sat upside down in a dish strainer. A bottle of Lemon Joy and a scrubby sponge in a saddle-shaped holder were placed to the right of the faucet. All were slightly marred by a thin layer of dust. "I can find it later."

Bennet smoothed her blazer and said, "Since you've been Miss Harris's website business partner for so long and you're surely tech-savvy, I'd like to take a moment to explain our online market analysis services."

Morgan shook her head. "Not now, okay?"

"But, Miss Miller," Bennet said, "with today's markets, any moment of hesitation is money lost. You need to consider how to best invest your assets. I know you've only received limited payments from the joint accounts, but once the rest has gone through probate, your remaining funds will be quite substant—"

"She just died," Morgan said, wandering away. "Please. Let me deal with that. I can't talk about money now."

"Your friend died three weeks ago," Bennet said, her voice measured and strained, "and your assets have languished all that time. Fortune favors the bold, after all. She barely waited a full day after her mother's death to aggressively prepare for the financial security you've now acquired but do not seem to comprehend."

Morgan shrugged and took a steadying breath. *I just found out yesterday she'd died. It might be three weeks for you, but it's too soon for me to think about money.*

The pair of windows over a dinged Formica table opened to the back yard, fully fenced in tall, wooden planks. The fence met an ancient garage in the corner with a doghouse built into the closest side. She saw food and water dishes, both overflowing with old leaves and dead grass. She counted six balls piled beside the doghouse, a hunk of knotted blue rope, and something shaped like a giant Cootie toy, without the legs.

"Where's Ranger?" Morgan asked, still gazing out the windows.

Bennet continued to explain how their financial advisors could take her nest egg and expand its earning potential, but she stopped when Morgan turned to her.

"Where's Ranger?" she asked again.

"Ranger?" Bennet asked, her brow furrowing. "I don't know of anyone—"

"Her *dog*." Morgan tried not to let her frustration show. "Ranger's Darcy's dog."

Bennet flicked her hand as if shooing a fly. "Oh. The dog. Off to the shelter, I suppose."

"What? Darcy loved her dog! How could you—"

"Miss Miller, I did nothing of the sort. It's common practice that pets are taken to a shelter to be cared for if no family or friends step forward to claim immediate custody of them. You have much more pressing concerns than a dog. Since you're so prone to distraction, perhaps you should simplify matters and authorize me to manage your accounts on your behalf. I have papers right here."

I might be grieving, but I'm not dumb, Morgan thought, giving

Bennet a quick glance before shaking her head. "No, I'll get to it. Just not now, okay? Maybe in a few days. Next week. I don't know."

Her gaze lit upon bits of Darcy's life: a wire basket of tea packets—surely consisting of Apple, Peppermint, and Blackberry, Darcy's favorites—sitting beside a box of dog biscuits. The pile of notepads with a leash on top. A big bowl of half-eaten dog food on a lucky-horseshoe mat near the back door. A rawhide strip beneath a kitchen chair with a thick, quilted pad on the seat.

Ranger might be locked up in dog jail, she thought, panicking. *Or he might be dead, put to sleep because no one wanted him, because I didn't recognize the accountant's number on my phone. Because I thought it was a telemarketer. Darcy and Ranger. Both gone. Oh, God.*

Her hands balled and she ground her knuckles into her eye sockets. *Not gonna cry. Not gonna cry. Damn it, Morgan you are NOT gonna cry!* She stumbled back until she slammed against the counter. Across from her, in the bowels of the refrigerator, the ice-maker clinked. Otherwise, Bennet and the house were silent, unable to do anything more than watch her.

Eye pain helped Morgan focus, helped her feel more real, more solid. *I can't let Ranger die. I can't.*

She took a breath, a shaky one, and lowered her hands. "Take me to the shelter. I have to get Ranger."

Bennet grimaced in obvious disgust. "Excuse me?"

"You said he was mine in the will. That means he's an asset, right? So I want to go get him."

"First of all, Miss Miller, *dogs* are not *assets.* Second, if he was taken to the shelter, he's surely gone by now. It's been almost a month."

"We have to try."

Bennet sighed, long and deep, then shook her head and

opened her briefcase. "Miss Miller, there is no 'we'. I have flown you in from Baltimore, read you the will, and escorted you to your house and its contents in the belief that you might be interested in my services, but you can't be bothered to unfreeze the bulk of your assets, let alone consider building your quite-promising financial future. Instead, you're wasting my time fretting over a worthless *dog?*"

Fuming, Bennet pulled out a large manila envelope and thrust it at Morgan. "I have no duty, or desire, to drive all the way back to Albert Lea to search the shelter for a dog that surely isn't there, a dog you yourself cannot identify, then bring you and the filthy beast back here in my car. My duties are—"

"I *can* identify him!" Morgan said as she struggled to catch the overstuffed packet, since Bennet let go before she'd gripped it. "He's a, uh, shepherd-retriever mix. Yeah, that's it. Shepherd-retriever mix."

"What breed of retriever?"

Morgan shook her head, confused. *There are different breeds?*

"Does he have identifying marks?" Bennet asked, her voice rising. "White spots? Black feet? Anything to distinguish him from other mutts?"

Morgan clutched the envelope, wrinkling the paper. "I don't know, I've never seen—"

Bennet took a step toward her. "Is he neutered?"

"I, uh... I think so," Morgan said, backing away.

"How big is he? Is he house-trained? Paper-trained? Does he do tricks? Does he wear a collar, and if so what kind and color?"

"Uh. A collar?"

Bennet glowered then stomped to her briefcase and snapped it closed. "You can't identify the dog, Miss Miller. Perhaps if you'd been quicker to answer your phone messages you would have arrived soon enough to save him."

"That's not fair. I had no idea Darcy—"

"You need to answer your phone in a timely manner, Miss Miller. Prompt and open communication is essential for day-to-day life. As is dedicated asset management. Both are skills you obviously lack."

"That's not—"

Bennet continued, undaunted. "Your missing dog is not my fault and I won't be held responsible. He's your dog. You find him."

Morgan blinked at the unexpected anger fluttering in her belly. "How can I—"

"I have to go." Bennet turned and strode toward the front of the house. "Your power and water bills have been paid through the end of the month," she said over her shoulder as Morgan followed her. "I suggest you review them and the other household paperwork in that envelope, assuming you don't lose yourself daydreaming. There are several documents to sign. All are very important. Perhaps you should pay attention to them, since you obviously can't pay attention to me."

"Wait. What documents?"

"They're in the packet along with the checks from the joint accounts." She paused at the door and turned to frown at Morgan. "I am not your friend, Miss Miller. I was hired to fetch you, inform you, deliver you, and explain our services in the hope you would maintain accounts with our company. I've done that. I am not willing to be your personal chauffer, or transport an animal in my car, while you mindlessly stare out the windows. If you need additional financial advice, my card is in the packet." She gave Morgan a final nod and said, "Good day, Miss Miller."

Before Morgan could respond, Bennet shoved through the screen door and stomped across the porch. Muttering, she huffed down the steps to her car, slammed herself in, and drove away.

Morgan stood gaped-mouthed on the porch, manila envelope clenched against her chest. Her mind stumbled, tripping over the same obvious facts. This tiny town had no busses, no cabs, no train stations, and no large towns within jogging distance. After years of nearly effortless freedom wandering from city to city on the East coast, she felt trapped, surrounded for miles by corn and soybean fields, and had no one to help her escape.

She stared, numb, out to the road. *How can I survive in the middle of nowhere when I don't drive?*

Two

MORGAN SAT AT DARCY'S KITCHEN TABLE, listening to the house and wondering what she was going to do. She decided she was thirsty. Yes. Thirsty. Surely Darcy wouldn't mind if she had a glass of water.

Cupboard by cupboard she searched for glasses. Two faded cans of SpaghettiOs sat with the canned veggies and soup and Morgan nearly slammed the door on the rotten things. Instead, she stared at the cans and realized her customary alarm had been tinged with sorrow. *Not this, not again. Oh, Darcy. Why do you buy this nasty stuff? We both know tomatoes make you break out.*

Grimacing, Morgan found a dishtowel to protect her hand and flung the pasta—and the towel—directly into the trash. She washed her hands and resumed her original search, finally locating clean glasses beside the sink. A handful of ice, a little tap water. All set.

Now what?

She leaned a hip against the counter and sipped, her gaze wandering around the messy kitchen as she tried to think. She felt foggy. Slow. Overwhelmed.

The envelope Bennet had left her lay on the kitchen table, silent and accusing. She flipped it the bird then made herself leave the kitchen before her mind wandered away again.

Little beyond horses and clutter caught her eye until she reached the converted office off the living room. A dog bed lay on the floor near the desk and Morgan frowned at it. *Ranger. I have to find Ranger.*

Goal in mind, she plucked her backpack from beside the front door and removed her laptop. Once it had awakened, she opened her browser and... nothing.

Darcy didn't have WiFi. Dammit.

Morgan returned to the office and sat at Darcy's desk to contemplate the wide, gleaming monitor and silvery tower stuck in its cubby. The monitor had a little apple logo with a single bite missing. A *Mac*. *Oh, Darcy.* Morgan knew nothing about Darcy's beloved Macs other than some skinny dude used to run the company and their commercials were kinda catchy. Surely it couldn't be too difficult to get a few minutes on Google.

She bent to turn the tower on. It didn't so much as whirr. She pushed the power button again. Nothing. The screen remained utterly black.

Sighing, she leaned back in Darcy's chair and clenched her fingers into her hair.

"Okay," she said aloud, mostly to reassure herself. "Even if I can't turn it on, there's surely an Ethernet cable or cord or something I can plug into my laptop. Surely."

She retrieved her laptop and knelt on the floor before Darcy's desk. Hopeful, she grasped the Mac tower to remove it, but gasped when the front panel came off in her hand, leaving wires and busted hardware bits dangling. The left side had been shattered and the right was... gone.

I just wanna find Darcy's dog! Morgan crushed back another wave of tears and pulled the rest of the computer from the cubby. It had been smashed into countless pieces, all wadded up and crammed out of sight, but there were four cords coming from the remnants of the back. Power. Monitor. USB. And an Ethernet! Hallelujah!

Morgan cried out in triumph as she plucked the cord free from the busted mess of circuit boards and wires. It snapped easily into her laptop's port and she sat, cross-legged, laptop on her knees, as she opened Chrome.

Still no connection.

She wanted to scream, to cry, to throw her laptop against the wall, but instead she lay on the floor, head cradled in the dog bed, staring at the ceiling as she willed herself to calm down.

My closest friend's dead and I can face that. I think. I'm a vagabond city girl who needs to find a dog I can't identify, decide what to do with a house I don't want, and survive alone without food or transportation in a microscopic town lost in a sea of soybeans. Fine. I'll manage. Somehow. But no internet? God, I can only take so much.

A cobweb spider spun a gossamer cloud in the corner far above her head. It calmly moved from one end to the other, methodical and sure of its actions. It had a plan. A purpose. Business to attend to.

Morgan sat up. *That's what I need. A plan. People communicated and gathered information before the world went digital. Right? They sent letters, made calls. Pen and paper. Telephones. Basic stuff.* She pushed herself to her feet. *I just need a phone book.*

She finally found two in a kitchen drawer. One for Hackberry and several small towns in the cooperative—whatever that was—and one for Albert Lea.

It took a bit of searching, but she located the listing for the county humane society and made the call.

"I'm looking for my dog. Well, he's sort of my dog," she said to the friendly voice on the phone. The voice grew less friendly as Morgan answered questions and explained her plight.

"Ma'am," the shelter worker said, "I'm sorry, but if the dog's been gone a month and you can't even tell me what it looks like, maybe it's better off with us finding it a good home."

"You don't understand. He was Darcy's dog, but Darcy died

and they just notified me about her will. I didn't even know—"

"Ah yah, I understand, but you'll still have to come down and identify the dog, show proof of ownership, and pay all the fees. Otherwise, you'll have to be approved for adoption. Frankly, adoption would be a great deal cheaper if we've had it as long as you say, but if you don't have references and a vet I seriously doubt you'd get approved anyway. I'm sorry."

"But—"

"Ma'am, you'll just have to come down. I can't do anything over the phone. Okay?"

Before Morgan could plead her case again, the line went dead.

She closed her cell and sat at the table where the packet of papers still waited for her. She stared at the envelope for a moment and swept it aside, knocking it to the floor. Everything looked like Darcy, and she'd never see Darcy again. Missing her friend, the only person she'd let past her shields, Morgan laid her head on her arms and wept.

* * *

• *Twenty five years earlier* •

"Oh quit crying, ya fucking baby," a bleached-blonde teenager muttered around her cigarette. She sat at a cracked and stained kitchen table and counted cash and ratty slips of yellow and blue papers into separate piles. "I'm not buying you any goddamn cookies."

Her scrawny mother clenched the upper arm of a toddler dressed only in a saggy diaper, her fingertips digging into the flesh beneath the edge of the little girl's cast. Despite the child's flinch, she crammed a crusty tissue against the kid's nose and told her to blow. "Goddamn it, Liberty Jo! If you can get yourself Hershey Bars and whiskey, you can buy your baby girl some goddamn twenty-five cent animal crackers."

Libbey folded the yellow and blue papers only to shove them into the pocket of her cutoffs. "I need my fucking chocolate to get the taste of dick outta my mouth, and the whiskey's for my headbanger headache. The rest goes to apples," she snapped as she hefted herself to her feet, dangly horseshoe earrings reflecting shards of yellowed light from the naked bulb over the table and her bulging belly peeking out from beneath her tank top. "The little bitch ruined my life, so she don't need no fucking cookies. She's damn lucky I buy formula for her baby brother."

The child wrenched her face away from the awful tissue. "She's barely *two*," the grandmother said, catching the toddler's nose in the messy tissue again. "And I told you it ain't her damn fault you were stupid enough to believe some horny-ass horse trainer. Get her the goddamn—"

"I gave up my dreams for her, and I work fucking hard to pay for her goddamn clothes and diapers and that fucking Care Bear she wanted so much."

"Dreams?" her mother shot back. "Loitering at race tracks isn't a *dream*, Liberty Jo. You're too damn young to be hanging with gamblers and gangsters."

"It's the horses, Ma, and you know it," Libbey said, her expression softening. "I was gonna be a jockey, or a trainer. Anything so I could work with horses. You know it's all I ever wanted."

The grandmother rolled her eyes. "Yep. Blowing gamblers behind the stables is really chasing your dreams."

"At least I get to see my horses instead of wiping a whiny kid's ass!" Libbey yanked the papers from her pocket and shook them at her mother. "She took my dreams, but she ain't takin' everything.

These fucking food stamps are mine and I ain't buying any goddamn cookies! I'm buying apples for my horses!"

"Think, for once in your life, Liberty! Screw the horses. Better to support these kids than spend your little bit of cash on more whiskey and crac—"

"I need the whiskey and rock to cut this headbanger headache," Libbey muttered, cramming the papers into her pocket again.

"Headache my ass," the grandmother said as she pressed the crusty tissue tighter against the struggling child's nose. "You're a filthy drunk and an addict. You know damn well one of these days someone'll actually look at your fake ID and throw your under-aged ass in jail. How will you see your precious horses then?"

"I don't know, but at least I'll get some peace and fucking quiet." Libbey glared at her mother then left, slamming the door behind her.

The grandmother sighed and let the toddler go. "She's something, ain't she?"

The little girl ran for a pile of blankets and crawled in, releasing a mewl of pain when her cast clunked against the floor. She wadded herself with the blanket's ragged, urine-stinking warmth. Her belly grumbled and she lowered her head to her one good arm. A roach crawled from a fold in the blanket, antennae wriggling, and skittered away.

Across the room, the grandmother fished a butt from the ashtray and lit it. She sucked in a drag and stood, shifting her leg aside to give her room to scratch her privates. Cigarette hanging from the corner of her mouth, she limped to the smeared, sagging fridge and rooted inside.

The toddler raised her head as her belly groaned. "Cookie?" she called out.

"We ain't got no cookies. And your horse crazy whore of a

mother ain't gonna buy no more."

"Ungy?" the child tried, quieter, cowering into her soft, fetid cave.

"Goddamn kids are always hungry." She pulled a couple of red-and-white paper tubs from the depths of the fridge and took a sniff.

The child's belly tightened in eager anticipation, grumbling louder.

The woman dumped the smaller tub into the bigger one while the child peeked out to breathe in the heady aroma of KFC gravy. The woman then fished a fork from the dishes at the sink and limped to the TV. She flipped on *Price Is Right* and limped back to the couch.

The little girl watched, her hazel eyes wide and desperate as she crept silently from her blankets and stood. On the TV, a woman hit a button at seventy-seven cents and people cheered. The child braved a step toward the food and saw not only gravy, but mashed potatoes too.

She took another step. Then another.

She stopped, just out of reach, and licked her lips. Cheerios and sour tasting milk had been breakfast the day before. Nothing since.

"Ungy." She licked her lips again then hesitated, but hunger fueled by cold chicken gravy made her take a step toward her grandmother. Then one more. "Ungy. Pwease. Mowgan ungy."

"Fucking hungry kid," grandmother said, and she leaned forward, lashing out, the back of her hand striking the child across the face.

The child tried to flee, but her grandmother's hand was faster. "It's my fucking snack. You can wait 'til supper!"

The second slap sent the toddler to the floor, landing on her already busted arm, and she screeched.

The woman burst to her feet while the child wailed and tried to crawl away. A clear glass horse on top of the TV wobbled and fell, landing heavy and hard on the child's hip, then it fell to the yellow linoleum and shattered. The woman kicked her. "See what you've done? Get your bawling, begging ass TO BED, and just *wait* 'til your mother gets home!"

Good hand covering her butt, she scurried and buried herself in the blankets once again. Her brother woke up screaming and, as the woman plucked him from the box, she kicked the toddler again for making too much damn noise.

* * *

Unaware she was rubbing an ache out of her left forearm, Morgan yawned and blinked blearily past the fading, distant scent of long-dried urine. She'd fallen asleep at Darcy's table as the morning had shifted to afternoon, if the light slanting through the kitchen window was to be trusted. Morgan stood and stretched, spine popping, and realized she was hungry.

Other than some condiments and a couple of unopened packages of cheese, the fridge had been cleaned out. The freezer contained little more than ice, frozen chicken patties, and a single diet dinner.

Morgan eyed it doubtfully, wondering if gluten-free pasta and tasty-tomato-free-marinara would rightly be considered food.

Darcy eats this stuff? she thought, but decided beggars couldn't be choosers. At least it'd shut up her grumbling belly.

It was edible. Barely. A pile of Parmesan cheese and a couple of dashes of Tabasco helped immensely.

A natural list maker, even having a 'things to do to be normal' list when she was a schoolchild, Morgan choked down fake pasta and typed a list on her laptop, just to get her thoughts in order.

Food

Supplies

Internet

Ranger

Transportation

Stupid papers

Just having a plan made her feel better, and she pondered her list as she chewed. She couldn't get Ranger until she had transportation, so she moved him down the list. If she had internet, she could at least locate nearby places to get food and other supplies, so it floated to the top.

Hoping to find information about Darcy's internet provider, Morgan fetched the packet of papers from the floor and unfastened the clasp. A quick search produced no cable or telephone bills.

Surely there's a local WiFi hotspot, she assured herself as she reached for the Hackberry phone book. She flipped through the yellow pages and found a few listings for computer repair. One, from NH Network and Hardware Services, said they offered *friendly, locally-owned service for business and personal computers and systems.* It sounded like just the thing, and the name made her think of New Hampshire. She'd spent some time in Concord and Nashua, and had found them to be nice towns.

Encouraged, she opened her cell and dialed.

A man promptly answered. "It's Nick," he said, sounding distracted, probably dealing with whatever beeped and booped in the background.

"Um. Hi," Morgan said. "I, uh, tried to log on today but I couldn't and—"

"Did you try resetting your router?"

"*Um. Router?*" She'd heard of them, sure, but had only used wireless networks in coffee shops and libraries. Routers had never been a consideration.

"Are you on dialup, cable, or DSL?"

"I honestly have no idea, but it doesn't really matter. If you just tell me where a nearby hotspot is, I'll be fine."

After a span of silence other than faint swishy sounds and aggravated male chattering, he asked, "What's your address?"

"Not sure. I just got here. Hang on." Morgan rummaged through Bennet's papers again, searching for any envelope or document addressed to Darcy, and found a bank statement. "326 Fieldmore Drive in Hackberry."

"Hackberry? You're kidding, right?"

"Uh, not kidding. I can see the sign from the porch. Lions. Lutheran Church. Youth Can Drive. Definitely in Hackberry."

He sighed, apparently too distracted to appreciate her attempt at humor. "I *mean*, there are no wireless hotspots in Hackberry. Private networks, sure, but no hotspots."

Morgan nearly dropped the phone. *No WiFi?* "Then how can I get online?" Someone yelled in the background and she heard a warbling electronic squeal.

All of the background sounds faded away and his voice perked up. "I can install a wireless network in your home or place of business, no problem. I have an opening tomorrow morning. Will that work for you?"

Morgan's hope fell. "Sure. Tomorrow. Okay."

"I'll be there before nine."

The connection clicked off and Morgan stared at her phone. *What the hell am I supposed to do until tomorrow morning?*

Muttering to herself, she wandered the house again, searching for electronics. There was an iPod and dock in Darcy's office. No television, but a stack of about twelve documentary DVDs in the den's closet. The only phone in the house hung on the kitchen wall with a red blinking light over 'messages'. Morgan picked up the receiver. No dial tone. Sighing, she returned it to the hook. She found a CD player mounted under one kitchen cabinet with a bright-pink shuffle hanging from the audio-in jack and a few custom-mixed CDs in a little case in the cabinet above.

The upstairs bathroom had a CD player much like the kitchen, with three more CDs all labeled 'mixed music'. Morgan put one in and skipped through several depressing country songs before turning the dang thing off.

Nothing else in the house was plugged in except the coffee maker, three lamps, and a digital clock flashing 2:17AM. Morgan checked her phone. The clock was only ten hours and twenty-one minutes wrong.

Morgan stared at the flashing numbers with growing alarm. Although she operated their website, Darcy had apparently missed the digital revolution, or had at least decided not to join up. Morgan moved through the house again, quicker, her gaze darting from shelf to shelf, cabinet to table. She found only a few books in the overwhelming clutter—all skinny romance novels with swooning women and bare-chested men on the covers—and some technical web mags. A ragged WordPress guide sat on the corner of Darcy's desk, and the dusty bookshelf in the corner held programming and site-hosting manuals. There were a few basic cookbooks in the kitchen; all were old, battered, and grease-stained.

Morgan forced her hands to unclench. *All alone with no internet. Not even a TV. And nothing decent to read. I am going to go stark raving insane.*

She pulled aside a lacy curtain and looked out the window to the highway. The little girls and their bikes had gone and she saw nothing but the houses across the street, one with a middle-aged man mowing a lawn with a push mower.

She let the curtain fall. *I guess I could take a run. Check out this dinky town.*

Out the back door and through the gate to the alley, then Morgan turned left, smiling at the gravel crunching beneath her feet.

She'd started running when she was in foster care at eight, first in a mindless panic, then also for pleasure.

It relaxed her. Sometimes it burned off the panic before it became a problem.

She reached pavement and turned left again, across the highway and past rows of houses and trees until she ran out of road. A quick backtrack, and she jogged down another street. She let a loose map form in her head as she ran, corner-to-corner and street-to-street, crisscrossing the town.

The small cluster of business and community buildings, a block-sized city park, and maybe only a couple of hundred houses were completely surrounded by fields. She stopped once at the edge of town and sighed at the highway unfurling to the horizon. She wanted to follow it, maybe catch a bus back to the coast, but she had no idea where the highway went, nor how far away real civilization would be. For all she knew, it led further into Minnesota Nowhere and, besides, her worldly belongings were back at the house.

Just settle the estate and put the house on the market, she thought. *Once I figure out how to update FrugallyUrban I can get the hell out of here. It'll be a couple of days. Tops. Sorry, Darcy, but I can't stay here.*

Decision made, she resumed her run.

* * *

Afternoon turned to evening, the air scented from barbeque grills. Still she ran over the same handful of roads until her legs ached and her body cried out in fatigue. She stopped at the local gas station in the hope they stocked bottled vitamin water and was happily surprised to find a small grocery inside. Nothing truly fresh, but a few canned and boxed goods, frozen pizzas and burritos, and hot sandwiches in a cabinet on the counter. The clerk was a skinny blonde college kid who barely glanced up from her cell to ring up Morgan's purchases.

Food procured, Morgan returned to the house to re-hydrate and stretch her twitching muscles while the oven heated and her pizza cooked. She settled on the couch to eat and read one of Darcy's romance novels, but soon gave up. Bodice rippers held no interest for her.

Morgan took her remaining pizza to the kitchen where the last records of Darcy's life lay sprawled across the table. She stared at the mess of documents and considered returning to the book and boredom, but Bennet had said the utilities were paid through the end of the month. July was half over. And she had little money, even less food, and few immediate options beyond what others had deemed worthy of her attention. Bills. Bank statements. Investment options. Stability.

Fuck.

I have to do this. For Darcy. Then I can move on. Morgan flumped onto a kitchen chair and rubbed her aching quads as she contemplated the sprawl of papers. Her head drew back in revulsion and her feet twitched to run again, but she took a breath and reached for a piece of mail.

Power bill. Due on the 27th. $128.78. More money than Morgan had in her online account.

She took another bite of pizza before moving the bill far to the left and picking up the next item, sorting the mess into loose piles of must pay, must read, must sign, and checks to cash—almost nine hundred dollars worth, so far—with most of the stack of papers left in a loose pile beside her.

Morgan boggled at the three checks a moment—she'd never been that wealthy before—then resumed her methodic sorting. She'd categorized almost half of the stack when someone knocked on the door.

Morgan swallowed her mouthful of pizza and stood, eyes widening. Red and blue flashes brightened the dining room walls. *The cops? An ambulance? Problem at a neighbors'?*

Heart thudding low in her gut, she took a hesitant step toward the dining room at another door knock.

She froze in the kitchen doorway, her gaze riveted on the front door and windows beside it, just visible past the dining room. Someone was on the porch, two someones, if the shadows were accurate, dancing with the blue and red lights.

The two shadows stopped shifting and one pounded on the door. "Open up! Freeborn County Sheriff!"

She took a step backward, ready to turn and bolt out the back, but a small, soft voice in the recesses of her head said, *I haven't done anything wrong. There might be a problem. Chemical spill. Gas leak. Lost kid. I should at least see what's going on.*

She took a step toward the door, her hands clenching while she fought the urge to flee. *Out here, cops are the good guys. Right?* She paused, trembling. *But what if they're here to arrest me?*

She forced herself to take a few more steps toward the door. *They can't be. I haven't done anything wrong. Not here or anywhere else. I've never done anything but run away.*

Morgan opened the door and peered around the edge. The faint breeze felt incredibly hot and humid, despite being well after dark. "Is there a problem, officer?"

The young men wore short-sleeved uniforms, sweat shimmering on their bare arms and faces. Both had neutral expressions. One said, "Apparently there is, ma'am. We understand the owner of this house passed away a few weeks back."

She nodded, unsure what they expected her to say.

"We've received reports of a ponytailed young woman in a pink t-shirt and blue shorts wandering the neighborhood. Someone called, worried you're a burglar."

Morgan forced herself to remain still as the two young men watched her. "I can explain."

"We're happy to listen, ma'am."

She tried to meet their gaze and sound confident, but found it impossible. *Sheriff deputies. Two of them. Oh shit, oh hell. What do I do?* "I'm supposed to be here," she said, sounding whiney and lying, even to her own ears.

I sound like Gramma the first time they took us away, Morgan thought, flinching. *Just like Gramma.*

"Are you Darcy Harris?" the one to the left asked.

"No. I..." Far behind the deputies, across the street, a woman stood on her porch, openly gawking. "I'm Morgan. Morgan Miller. Darcy left me the house in her will. Honest."

The other deputy turned aside and muttered something into his radio while the first merely stared at her, the same patient expression on his face.

His partner returned and said, "We don't have any record of a probate transfer, ma'am. It's not in the system."

"I do!" Morgan said, flinching at the nervous tremor in her voice. "Have the records, I mean. I just got here today. Was sorting through the papers she gave me when you rang the bell."

The first deputy's head tilted. "She? She who?"

"Some financial planner named Bennet. Kathy? Karla? Kimberly? I dunno, but she's a finance manager something."

"Can we take a look at these records, ma'am?"

"Sure," Morgan said. "Of course. Everything's in the kitchen. On the table. I can go get them."

A quick nod from the deputy and Morgan hurried to the kitchen. She scooped up the unsorted pile and rushed back. "I have her business card. It's in here with the papers," she said. "Somewhere." Documents and envelopes slipped from her hands and fluttered to her feet, but she found the card and thrust it toward the deputies. "Here. You can call her. She'll tell you. I'm supposed to be here."

The second deputy accepted the card and reached for his radio. "Morgan Miller, you said?"

"Yessir."

The deputy nodded and walked a few steps away to talk on his radio.

Morgan said to the deputy watching her, "Sir, really, I just got here today and I like to run. For exercise, you know? I went out to blow off some boredom, not to seek places to vandalize. I didn't mean to cause any trouble."

"It's no trouble, ma'am. We're just checking on a complaint."

While one deputy watched her and the other listened to his radio, Morgan gathered up the dropped papers and tried to appear utterly non-threatening. She knew no one in Minnesota besides an investment planner who already thought she was trouble. Who would bail her out if they arrested her? Who would come to her aid? Would she just rot away in jail?

"There's a will, too," she said as she pulled it from the clump and stood. "Right here."

"It's all right, ma'am," the deputy said. "You just hang onto it for now, and try to relax, okay? We're just here to protect people.

Make sure everything's all right."

Morgan clamped her mouth shut but thought, *Right. Just like all the cops who have forced me out of bus stations and park benches. Who've told me homeless vagabonds can't sit in Starbucks and steal WiFi. Protect people. Sure you do.*

The other deputy returned a few moments later. "The firm confirms her story. Property transfer was filed today, but the records haven't been updated yet."

Morgan's knees softened, but she managed to stay upright. "Thank you."

The deputy returned Bennet's card. "Maybe make a point to meet your neighbors, ma'am, so this doesn't happen again. You have a nice night, now."

They turned to leave and Morgan stumbled behind them, knees quaking, to close and lock the door. Every house in sight had folks on porches or peering through windows, curious over the ruckus. Darcy's neighbors. All cementing their first impressions.

THREE

BAP, BAP!

Morgan jolted upright from a dead sleep and felt a hard slam of disoriented panic—Horses, horses everywhere staring, wanting to gallop over me!—then she let out a breath as she recognized Darcy's house. Someone was banging on the front door. Grimacing, she untangled her legs from a ragged old afghan and managed to roll off the couch without falling on her face. Please, not the cops again, she silently prayed as she got her feet beneath her.

Bap, bap! "Hello? Anyone home?" a man's voice called out.

She stumbled toward the door, pausing at the window to sneak back a curtain. An old but well-maintained pickup with an NH decal on the door sat in the driveway while its tallish driver stood on her porch, a line of sweat running down his unshaven cheek. Nerdy, wire-framed glasses seemed at odds with the buttoned chambray work shirt, jeans, and scuffed electrician's belt around his hips. Morgan nearly squealed. The internet guy? Oh hallelujah!

He stepped back, startled, as she ripped the door open and ushered him in, but instead of complying he asked, "You wanted a WiFi hookup this morning?" his voice a warm rumble and his eyes lost behind a shock of sandy-brown hair and the glasses.

"Yes. Definitely," Morgan said, squinting against the brilliant morning. The air lumbered heavy and slow with humidity, each breath sliding down her throat like soup. "Please, come in. I really need internet access."

"I didn't mean to wake you, ma'am. If this is too early-"

"You're right on time. I just..." Morgan swallowed as she realized she was barefoot, wearing the same tee and shorts she'd run in the evening before. She also hadn't showered, combed away her couch-hair, or even put on her bra, which was lying in plain sight on the floor by the couch. She surely looked and smelled hideous, but her only hope for connectivity hesitated on the porch, staring at the welcome mat while she stood there half-dressed.

Shit.

"I didn't mean to oversleep. Can you wait? Just forty-eight seconds or so?" she asked as she snatched up the bra and her knapsack. "Please. Come on in. I can't work without WiFi." She tried to offer a cheerful smile, but her own deepening embarrassment had stiffened her cheeks.

She backed toward the hall with her knapsack clenched against her chest. "I'll be right back. Okay?"

He nodded without speaking and she fled, hurrying into the powder room. Tee off and bra snapped on—pointedly not acknowledging her bare reflection in the mirror—she yanked it into place with one hand as she pulled a clean shirt over her head with the other. Through the sleeves and straps, and, deciding her rumpled shorts would do, she released her ponytail and tugged her hair loose as she opened the bathroom door.

The internet guy waited just inside the door. "You're quick," he said.

She shrugged and muttered a vague comment about mornings and college, but speed had become a habit. After nearly a lifetime of bathing and sleeping in shelters and group homes, the quicker she showered or changed, the less anyone had a chance to stare. Or ask questions. She couldn't remember the last time she'd taken a leisurely shower or fussed over her appearance.

"Been there," he said. "I hated morning classes too." He smiled at her, his eyes glimmering behind smudged lenses, just a buttoned-down, tool-belted geek sweating in the heat. "So," he asked, "how long has your connection been down?"

"Honestly, I have no way to know. I just got here yesterday. This is actually my friend's house."

He started to say something, but closed his mouth and shook his head before trying again. "Where's the router?"

"Uh, I think it's in the office," she said, leading him across the living room. "All that techy stuff is Darcy's domain." Morgan's throat tightened. "Was her domain. She passed away. I'm kinda floundering with all this."

He'd barely entered the room before pausing to point at the shattered Mac. "That her domain, too?"

Morgan moistened her lips and shrugged, not sure how to respond. Had Darcy broken her own computer? Had the vandals? "I don't know," she said at last. "It was like that when I got here."

He gave her a sideways glance then continued on to the little black box on a shelf above the desk. He lifted and examined it, turning it in his hands. "DSL. There's power but no connection. Your phone working okay?"

Morgan reached for her pocket before realizing he surely meant the land-line. "The kitchen phone? No. I can't call out."

"Hopefully it's just a bad signal." He pulled out the desk and knelt behind, handing her some fallen papers, a carved wooden foal, and a picture of a big dog wearing a Santa costume in the snow. He stretched to plug a sensor into the wall outlet. He eased out and, frowning, asked to see the kitchen phone. He disconnected and tested it and, still frowning, said, "It's not a bad signal, there's no signal."

No signal? Didn't Bennet say the bill had been paid?

"I'll check the box," the internet guy said, his tone reassuring, "and if there's no signal there either, I'll call the co-op and get them out here to fix your line."

"That'd be great," she said. "Thank you."

Self-consciously smoothing her hair and wondering how many neighbors peered at her from behind their curtains and blinds, Morgan followed him to the yard and a gray box bolted to the side of the house. Dogs chained in both next-door neighbors' yards barked. She wasn't sure if they were barking at each other or at her, but the wad of fuzz to the north was very upset, while the black and tan monster to the south paced back and forth on his tether, his woofs more frustrated than angry. Were the two dogs Ranger's canine friends? Morgan watched the dogs and wondered if she'd ever find Ranger, or if he was even still alive.

The internet guy opened the phone-box and fiddled within for a few moments before declaring her connection dead, then he punched a number into his cell phone. "Hey, May?" he said, smiling at Morgan, "Nick Hawkins. I have a lady in Hackberry with no signal. Can you send a crew out?" He nodded and gave her address. "Yeah, she needs her DSL ay-sap." Another nod then he asked Morgan, "Darcy Harris?"

Morgan stumbled as the grief clenched her heart again. Darcy. Ranger. God, what a mess. "No. She... She passed away."

His brow furrowed and he covered the mouthpiece on the phone. "Can you pay the back-bill? It's a hundred eighty six dollars and change."

There had been some banking papers in Bennet's envelope, and a couple of sizeable checks she'd set aside before the police had disrupted her sorting, more than enough to pay the phone company. "Yes," she said. "I'll just have to go to the bank first."

He relayed her agreement and set up the appointment for the following morning. As he knelt to close up the connection box, he said, "No charge for today. But if you ever need system upgrades or the house wired for Ethernet, I'd appreciate it if you'd keep me in mind."

"Sure thing," she said and accepted his proffered card.

* * *

Morgan showered and ate a cold breakfast of leftover pizza and orange juice before sitting down to the mess Bennet had left her— including bank statements and utility bills and a receipt promising to return the abstract for the house. She sorted every document or envelope into its appropriate pile before tackling them one at a time. She read over the forms she'd been instructed to sign, a stack of papers from a life insurance company, and a deed to a couple of shares of an oil well in Oklahoma. She added up the checks and noted one was drawn on Harvest State Bank. She'd seen a little building with their logo during her run the day before and wondered if they could cash it for her. Twenty-two hundred dollars was a lot of money, more than enough to pay the upcoming utility bills and get the internet turned on.

Deciding it was worth a try, she pulled on her shoes and readied for a run. Instead of jogging up and down all of the neighborhoods, she ran directly to the one-block stretch of old buildings and businesses serving as Hackberry's town center.

The air conditioning in the bank was a welcome respite from the sticky swelter outside. A grim, middle-aged woman hunched behind a desk near the door, banging on a keyboard. Across from her, a young couple in jeans squeezed each other's hands and struggled to appear hopeful.

Morgan gave the couple an encouraging smile and continued on to the only teller. The transaction was simple enough; a few glances at her Wisconsin Non-Driving ID, three explanations of why she was there, and a trip to the house to get a copy of the will was all she needed to cash the check. Once the cash lay piled on the counter, the teller cheerfully mentioned that for a mere $25 she could open an account and deposit all those other pesky checks, even get a checking account of her own!

Morgan pocketed the cash and told the teller she'd think about it.

When she turned to go, the young couple had already left and the woman behind the desk didn't seem grim at all, more like a worried and exhausted mother. She had a crystal bowl of chocolate candies beside her monitor and sighed as she reached for a handful.

Morgan felt a sharp tang of pity as she wondered how often bank policy insisted the woman had to tell people 'no' when her heart wanted to say 'yes'.

Outside, an elderly woman struggled up the single step with her walker. Morgan opened the door for her and offered to help, but the woman's eyes narrowed and she muttered, "Go away. Just because I'm old doesn't mean I'm helpless."

"Good morning, Mrs. Parson!" the lady behind the desk chirruped with strained cheer.

Mrs. Parson clomped on toward the teller and muttered, "It's cold as a witch's left tit in here. You trying to give me pneumonia?"

The banker-mom's expression froze into a grimace and she reached for a fresh handful of chocolate.

Morgan scooted out the door.

A crusty boat of a Buick idled just past the step with a fluff-ball yapping at the window. Its black-bead eyes glimmered at her, pink tongue behind white-needle teeth, bitsy paws scraping at the glass. It might have been the little neighbor dog which had barked while the internet guy checked the phone line, but all long-haired pooches looked alike to her.

Morgan left the dog to its barking and started a leisurely lap around the town to burn off her creeping boredom. Almost everyone had a dog, it seemed. If not rushing and woofing around their yards as she passed, they leapt at the windows, some standing on furniture, others bouncing against curtains. Did Darcy get Ranger because everyone else had a dog? Was she lonely? Need protection? Was he something to take care of?

But she took care of me. Morgan kept running and told herself her throat clenched from the heat.

When she returned to the block-long business center, Morgan paused to squint up at the sky. She saw no clouds and felt no breeze, nothing but the weight of the sun baking her. How could a place so far north get so hot?

The old woman with the walker struggled to get into her car without letting the yap-monster loose. Morgan took a step to help her, but halted as the woman glared.

"You're that thief who was skulking around yesterday," she snapped, shoving the dog further into the car.

"Ma'am," Morgan started, "I'm not—"

"So you're a liar too? Stay away from me or I'll have you arrested."

Morgan stood slack jawed and stammering as Mrs. Parson slammed herself into her car and sped off.

* * *

Morgan returned to the house only to decide to leave again. She needed groceries, especially fresh vegetables, and other supplies to help her sort through Darcy's clutter.

And she needed to try to find Ranger.

The cab driver was reluctant to wait while she ran her errands, but a promise of a large tip, along with a running meter, seemed to reassure him. Hawkins' Grocery wasn't much larger than an urban market, but its brightly-lit shelves and bins had a good selection of staples and produce. Bags of groceries stashed in the cab's trunk, Morgan directed the cabbie to the humane society.

They sat in the parking lot while Morgan watched people come and go, a few bringing animals, fewer still taking them away. A little girl beamed as she carried out a creamy-yellow kitten, but the cat looked terrified. How did the shelter decide who would give the pets a good home? Would she qualify, even with the will?

"Meter's running, ma'am," the cabbie said.

Morgan grabbed her backpack and exited the cab.

The folks in the shelter, while helpful, seemed dubious of her explanation, but they led her through the stray room, then a room of large, adoptable dogs. Only one resembled the photographs of Ranger: an angry, snarling stray picked up across the county from Hackberry. The staff had named her Berta.

Morgan filled out missing dog forms and let the shelter folks photocopy the picture of Ranger in the Santa hat, but there was nothing more she could do.

The cab ride to Hackberry seemed longer than yesterday's trip with the accountant; more fields, more ponds, more empty countryside passing outside the window. The world appeared picture-postcard pretty, lush, green, and wholesome, but Morgan barely noticed. Another evening of utter boredom waited. She wished she was again surrounded by concrete, steel, and the rush of urban clatter, leaving her invisible in a crowd of people rushing to their next task.

FOUR

THE OPPRESSIVE HEAT BROKE as Morgan carried her purchases from the cab. Once on the porch, she stretched and managed to smile at the afternoon. Cooling gusts felt comforting yet energizing, a welcome change from swelter and grief. Reluctant to face countless horses staring at her in every room, she considered staying outside a while to enjoy the breeze, but clenched her teeth and lugged her groceries into the house to put them away. That task finished, she walked through the main floor with the kitchen garbage can and tossed in every horse figurine and picture within reach. The wallpaper border would have to wait until she had a stepladder, and the saddle still sat in the office corner, but the house felt cleaner, lighter, and far less oppressive.

Relieved, she returned to the porch to sit on the swing and watch Darcy's neighborhood. Laughing and squealing kids jumped on a trampoline just visible behind the house across the street, and, at the house on the corner, an exhausted-looking woman in scrubs wrestled a car seat out of her battered minivan. Somewhere, well behind Darcy's house, a lawn mower struggled to catch.

Darcy's house. Darcy's neighbors. And I think that old lady called the cops on me.

There were no faceless crowds in Hackberry, no place to blend into, to become one speck among many. There were only separate individuals. People with names. Folks others recognized on sight. These were Darcy's people, not hers. She was a thorn in the town's collective thumb. An outsider. The hated 'other'.

Oh, Darcy. Why'd you have to die and make me come here? Morgan watched a plump, middle-aged woman stumble past, propelled forward by two eagerly-sniffing hounds. The dogs stopped at the bank of mailboxes to sniff and pee. The woman wiped sweat from her brow and her gaze met Morgan's. When Morgan nodded hello, the woman smiled, waving a quick and friendly 'Hi!' before being abruptly dragged forward again.

The woman disappeared around the corner and Morgan's feet twitched, restless. Sighing, she left the porch and stretched for an evening run.

Her mind wandered, drifting along with the pounding of her feet on pavement and path. During a casual run, she'd often mull over her current batch of articles and reviews for the website, or what city she'd visit next. Today her grief and loneliness led her thoughts to Darcy.

She blinked away tears forming at the corners of her eyes, tears she blamed on the wind in her face, but as she turned to the highway and not the neighborhoods—don't want anyone calling the cops again—she thought of the last time she'd seen Darcy, had hugged her, had wished neither had to go.

They'd been roommates in college for two semesters, their dorm room awash with piles of Darcy's clothes. Since she had generous parents, Darcy also owned the microwave, the coffee pot, decent linens, too many horse posters, and a mini-fridge full of food. Morgan had very little to pack but two changes of clothes and a few dearly loved CDs.

P!nk complained from the radio, her low, lyrical scream rising to warbling wail as Morgan stuffed her meager pile of crap into a pillowcase. Despite endless tutors and help-centers and late study sessions fueled by coffee, her grades sucked and she'd been shown the door. *So much for Wisconsin's Foster Kids to the Future program. So much for busting my ass just to get accepted to Maginaw State in the first place.*

"Where are you gonna go?" Darcy asked, shivering. Beside her, snow sputtered outside of the window.

Morgan managed to cram three more CDs between her only other pair of jeans and a ratty sweatshirt. "I don't know. Somewhere warm, I guess. Get away from all this damned snow." The room, once pleasantly cool, had turned chilly.

Darcy shifted, arms crossed over her chest. "But how are you gonna do that? You don't have any mon—"

"I'll figure out something. Always do." Morgan shrugged. "Besides, my state check'll come the first of the month."

Shaking her head, Darcy pushed off from the wall. "That's nearly three weeks away. It's almost Christmas, for Christ's sake. At least come home with me for the holidays. My folks... they'll be happy to have you. You know they will."

Morgan closed her eyes and suppressed a shudder. *Home? Parents? More busted bones and cigarette burns? No fucking way.* "You know I can't." She leaned into her pillowcase, cramming down the clothes. *Maybe I can squeeze my blanket in. It'd be better than nothing if I have to sleep on a bench.*

A chilly drip hit her forehead and she frowned at the ceiling as another splattered her cheek. *It's my last day here. Of course there's another leak upstairs.*

Darcy's voice hitched. "Just until your check comes. Pony, please. You can't leave me."

Morgan turned, clothing, blanket, and her hatred of the nickname momentarily forgotten. "Hey," she said, rushing to Darcy. She grasped Darcy's forearm and stared her in the eye. "It's all gonna be okay. I'll be fine. I've moved from place to place my whole life, and I know all about being broke." She wiped a tear from Darcy's cheek. It felt cold, and, down the hall, some band kid beat a bass drum.

Morgan managed to give Darcy a sad smile. "It'll be an adventure, the whole world for me to explore. I'll be fine. I promise."

"But I won't." Darcy sniffled and dragged her fingertips beneath her nose. Cool drips landed on Morgan's arm, her shoulders. "What am I gonna do without you here? How will I manage going to class? How can—"

"Oh, Darcy." Morgan held her friend's face in her hands despite the leaky ceiling splattering her fingertips, her arms, her legs, and her face. "Don't sell yourself short. I know it's scary, but you'll be fine."

"No, I won't. Not without you." Darcy wiped trickling drips from her nose again. Her voice gurgled through the flood, "I've spent my whole life searching for you. I love you. You're my family. You can't just *go*."

Cold dribbled from Morgan's lashes, making her blink, and, beneath her hands, Darcy's face burst into a gush of water, blown apart by wind. Then the drippy ceiling ripped open with a rocket slam of thunder.

Morgan flinched, scrunching her eyes from the blinding burst erasing the liquid remains of Darcy's face. Morgan's legs quivered beneath her, exhausted and stumbling over rough terrain. No longer breezy afternoon, it had become full-blown night, the sky a greenish riot of lightning and thunder, pummeling her with wind and rain from all directions at once.

One arm rose to shield her face as she scrambled forward. Another peal of thunder brightened the world, lightning crackling down to illuminate a dirt road between two cornfields, no houses within sight. Somewhere, far away, a siren screeched a long, urgent wail, an alarm Morgan hadn't heard since she'd left Wisconsin.

I'm lost in the middle of nowhere during a tornado warning? Her instinct screamed for shelter, but she saw none, nothing but corn and a road caught with her in the storm. Already well past exhaustion, she ran.

The cornfield on her left gave way to pasture, overgrown and clotted with weeds. Just beyond, before the next field began, a crumbling concrete driveway cut through the tangle. Morgan scrambled to it. A little sign stood at the end proclaiming 14753 in pale, rusty numbers on a dark background. Morgan's hip grazed the sign as she leaned into the abrupt turn, nearly buckling her quaking legs.

Lightning arched across the sky and down, brilliant pillars supporting a ceiling of electric fire that dumped peanut-sized balls of hail. Hip throbbing from its ricochet off the sign, Morgan fought for balance, and to maintain momentum, as she barreled down the lane toward a shadow of a house. The hail stung her drenched skin, pelted her head, and turned already slippery footing treacherous. She winced as a heavy hunk hit her forearm, sending pins and needles to her hand.

The yard was as overgrown and tangled as the pasture, the lone tree dead and twisted against the roiling sky. Tattered remnants of a child's swing hung from a cracked and sagging branch, the wind whipping rope and rubber into the air only to snap them back again. Morgan scrambled up crumbling steps to the porch, her left foot catching on a rotted bit of board. She fell, sprawling hard to her belly.

She gasped, hail pelting her legs, then she shoved herself up and forward again. The windows and door were empty wounds and Morgan scrambled in.

She tottered, arms wheeling for balance at her abrupt skid. The floor was gone, leaving only the darkened streaks of joists crumbling into the cellar, the remnants barely illuminated by diffuse flashes from the grumbling sky above. Much of the roof had collapsed, giving her little protection from wind and hail and, as a fresh crackle of lightning brightened the house's shattered interior, she saw ancient char and dark streaks reaching up the walls as if in supplication.

Morgan kept to the bit of burned and twisted flooring just inside the door and tried to catch her breath. Of all of the places in the world to seek shelter, she had to get stuck with a burned out husk of a house. She turned, sagging, and lowered herself down, spine against the porch-side of the doorframe. Rain and hail pounding on the house left her thankful for the bit of wall and porch roof.

Lightning struck nearby, out of sight yet turning the yard and field a brilliant purple-white. The simultaneous bark of thunder shook the floorboards beneath her. Morgan remained sitting, watching the storm, and struggled not to let panic overtake her as she realized she had no idea where she might be.

She took a welcome drink of rainwater as she searched through the disoriented file of her brain, seeking the memory of a long-burned house along the route into town. Construction and repairs, yes. Abandoned, certainly. Burned out? Not a single dwelling came to mind. And the numbers at the end of the drive? All of the country-road houses she'd seen had four digits, not five.

She stared at the sagging ceiling as she tried to decide what to do. She'd seen no lights from any other houses, and certainly nothing resembling civilization, even far in the distance. Wind whipped around the house, goose-pimpling her chilled skin, so she rubbed her arms to warm them. While she had little fear of freezing to death—it was July in the Midwest, after all—the thought of spending the entire stormy night cold, wet, and barely sheltered did worry her a great deal. What if lightning struck the house? What if the storm blew it down around her? What if she caught pneumonia or a branch fell on her head or... or anything?

The wind quieted as if assuaging her fears, and thunder grumbled dully from the distance, but the rain fell, undaunted. Wind and lightning soon returned, every bit as eager and vicious as before, only instead of coming from behind the house, the gusts whipped around the side, sometimes slamming fresh rain into Morgan's face. She shifted toward the questionable shelter of the burned out interior and rubbed her shivering arms and legs.

She'd left her pack at the house, but, after checking her pockets, found a crumbled wad of cash, some loose change, keys, and the bare-basics flip phone Darcy had bought her years before, miraculously not drenched.

She flicked it open and flinched at the familiar pink-and-purple fractal screen. 9:48PM. She'd started her run around five-thirty. Six, maybe. About four hours of running, God only knew how much through a storm.

Morgan sighed and closed her eyes and the phone. *How far can I run in four hours? An easy lope is about six miles an hour so that's—*

Her eyes flew open and she groaned, banging the back of her head against the doorframe a couple of times. *Twenty four miles. I might be more than twenty miles from Darcy's house, and I don't even know what direction it is!*

She felt panic edge into her psyche, but she bit her lip and flicked on her phone. *A ride. There's more money at the house. Surely plenty. Just need a cab.* She let out a relieved sigh when the call finally connected. Despite her pleas, they could do nothing to help her without an address. There'd been no street listed on the sign at the end of the drive, only five digits she couldn't quite remember. Something with a one, and a seven. Maybe. And the lady at the cab company insisted even if she had the whole number, it was useless without a street to find it on.

Frustrated, Morgan released the call. She wanted to cry, but she was too cold. *I don't know anyone here, just that greedy Bennet woman, and, even if she could find me, her card's in my pack. The cops could surely find me, but I think I'd rather freeze than deal with them two nights in a row.* She clicked through her call log to review everyone she'd talked to since her arrival in Hackberry.

Three calls, all outgoing. The cab—no help—the shelter—surely closed *and* unable to help—and the internet guy.

Wind whistling all about her, she stared at his number as her thumb hovered over the connect button. Would he answer this late? Could he find her in this storm? There were a ton of computer and smart-phone apps to locate people and places and create maps by GPS signals—any of which would have made this catastrophe easier and none of which worked on the crappy flip-phone Darcy'd bought for her—but he was a computer guy. He might have a GPS something-or-another search app. He seemed nice.

And at least he wasn't the cops.

Still she hesitated. She didn't know him, had only talked with him a few moments. He was a man, a stranger, far bigger and stronger, and not only was she considering asking him a massive and likely inappropriate favor, she'd be alone with him in his vehicle. At his mercy.

NH Network Services. Button-down computer geek. With a tool belt. Who seemed nice. Her thumb moved toward the connect button, shivering.

Cracka BOOM, as lighting struck a tree across the road, brightening the world and turning one massive branch into shards. The tornado siren continued, bleating in the distance, and a fresh pelting of hail slammed against the porch roof. Some rolled off, balls the size of walnuts and grapes. A strip of siding peeled way and crashed against the tree.

What choice do I have? Saying a silent prayer, Morgan closed her eyes and pushed connect.

The phone rang twice in her ear before he answered, mumbling, "It's Nick," and, like before, electronic beeps and warbles filled the background. He grunted, maybe lifting something, and other men groaned in exasperation.

"Um. This is Morgan. Morgan Miller?"

"Just a sec. Hang on."

Morgan sighed and pushed wet hair off her face. The wind was changing direction again.

Beebly-bap, clung, clung, clung, SCHREE-WAHHHH, followed by a quiet, "Shit." Louder, but off the receiver, "Chuckie, can you *get that?* I'm on the phone here."

Over the rumbling thunder, she barely heard, "Fuck you, Hawkins."

Music played, vaguely classical and commanding, like Wagner with an electronic bent. "There. See?" Nick sighed. "Morgan who?" he asked, and the electronic noise started up again.

Someone in the background yelled for Chuckie to hurry the fuck up and equip the right sword this time.

Morgan sighed and rubbed her eyes. *A video game. Goddammit.* "Morgan *Miller.* You came to the house this morning. I needed WiFi?"

He grunted, "Hang on," and the warbles changed to squeals and clangs.

"Look," she said, "you're obviously in the middle of raiding a demon stronghold or some other instance of grave importance, but I really, *really* need some help here."

"The house in Hackberry, right?" he said. "I thought the co-op was coming in the morning. I can't really do anything until you have DSL service."

"They are, and I know. That's not—" Another slam of lightning and thunder shook the house and she curled, mewing silently, to cover her head with her arms as grit fell from the ceiling.

"What the hell was that?" Nick asked as the game noise faded. "What happened? Are you okay?"

Morgan's lower lip quivered, but she managed to not blubber. "I'm stranded out in this storm. Some burned up farmhouse. I don't know where I am or—"

"What? Did your car break down?" The volume of his voice changed again, as if the phone shifted against his cheek. "Where'd you say you are?"

"I don't *have* a car," she said, peering out from beneath her arm. "And I have no idea where I am. Some abandoned farm. I got caught out in this and I don't know what to do." Despite her attempts to crush it, a sob escaped her throat. "I didn't have anyone else to call."

"Okay, okay," he said. "Hold on. You're on a cell, right?"

"Yeah. Just a crappy flip phone, though." She drew her knees up and pressed her face to them, both hands clenched at her ears. Out there, on the other side of his phone, she heard the familiar sound of Windows coming to life.

"Lemme find you," he muttered, keyboard keys clacking. Time dragged until he said, "Gotcha. Quarter mile off county Road S22, just north of... Elk Creek Marsh? You're in *Iowa?*"

Morgan swallowed. Iowa? "Is it too far? Do you know someone I can call to come get me? An address I can give the cab—"

"I'll be there in about fifteen, twenty minutes. Tops. Heading to the truck now."

"Thank you," she said, relief quaking her voice.

"No problem. I was tired of the game anyway."

She smiled and let out a hopeful sigh. "Still, thank you."

She heard a couple of doors slam and a vehicle start up. He stayed on the phone with her, giving her occasional updates as he crossed roads or passed landmarks.

"I should be getting close," he said. "Let me know when you see my headlights."

Morgan stood, squinting into the storm. No lights were visible in the direction she'd run from, but someone approached from the other way. A truck, maybe. Higher up, not low like a car.

"I think I see you," she said. "Just past the field on your right. If that's you."

"It's me," he said, as the truck turned in the drive. The call clicked off.

He drove up to the house and turned so the passenger door faced her. "You picked a hell of a place to hole up," he called out as he exited the cab. No longer buttoned down, he wore a faded radio-station t-shirt over jeans and tennis shoes which sunk into the mud.

She nodded, rubbing her arms and trying not to let her teeth chatter any more than was absolutely necessary as she picked her way down the ruined steps.

"I can't believe you found me."

Despite her insistence she could manage, he reached out for her, grasped her by the waist, and lowered her safely to the mud as if the action was as effortless as fetching a glass from a cupboard. "You've got to be freezing. C'mon, I've got a blanket behind the seat."

He flung the door open and, true to his word, pulled out a blanket, wrapping her in it before helping her into the truck.

Once he settled in behind the steering wheel, she tried to explain what had happened without sounding like a lunatic, but found it impossible. In the end, she settled for "I just took a long run, got lost, and the next thing I knew, I was caught in the storm."

He glanced at her out of the corner of his eye. "Okay," he said, then offered a smile as warm as his voice. "Are you still cold?"

She drew the blanket tighter around her. "It's better now. Thank you."

He chuckled. "You don't have to keep thanking me. You like coffee? There's a gas station in Lake Mills, just a couple of miles from here. They always have a decent pot."

"Coffee sounds fabulous!"

"Thought so," he said, turning right at the end of the drive.

The coffee was indeed decent, and it warmed Morgan nicely as they turned onto a highway. She started to apologize again, but he stopped her. "This is nothing," he said, waving off her concern. "Once, my sister's best friend's cousin called me at three AM, drunk."

Morgan glanced at him, her eyes narrowing. "Sister's best friend's cousin?"

"Yeah, sounds like a bad joke about hillbilly inbreeding, I know. She was just some high school kid who'd gone to a college party with her friends, and didn't want to get in Dutch with her folks. So she called her cousin who called Beth who said to call me. So she did. I drove more than an hour to pick her and her two girlfriends up at some frat party, then hauled their drunken butts back home to Albert Lea." He shrugged and pulled up at a stop sign, waiting for a semi to turn before continuing on. "They were damn lucky they just got drunk. Coulda been a lot worse."

Morgan nodded to hide her shudder. *Definitely worse.*

He glanced at her again. "You're not going to puke all over my tools, are you?"

She glanced at her muddy feet propped on a toolbox. "No. Just mud."

He grinned. "Then all is well. Be home before you know it."

Morgan gazed out the window, frowning, her face a ghost illuminated by dashboard lights. "It's not my home. Just a house Darcy left me in her will. I don't even want it."

"Why not? It seems like a decent place. Well built. Solid. Big back yard. And Hackberry's a nice town. I think it's a perfect place for a home."

Morgan shrugged. Hackberry hadn't been particularly nice to her.

They rode in silence a while, wipers whooshing across the windshield. Nick said, "I honestly didn't mean to offend you, it's just the house has a lot of potential. Sure it's cluttered and needs some TLC, but I bet if you cleared out the junk, you'd be surprised how great it is."

"Our site hasn't been updated since..." she swallowed the lump low in her throat, "since Darcy died. I just want to get it functioning again, figure out how the ads work, then I'm moving on." Finally warming, she laid her head on the seat back and yawned. *I need sleep. And a hot shower.*

"You have a website?" he asked.

"Yeah, Darcy and I run Frugally Urban dot com, a division of Pony And Mule Web Development. That's our company. Well, Darcy's company." Morgan shrugged and yawned again, eyes drifting closed. "Mostly I travel around, reviewing cheap stuff. Food. Entertainment. Whatever. She does all the real work."

Whoosh-whoosh from the wipers, rhythmic and comforting. Familiar. Darcy'd had an ancient boat of a Chevy in college and they used to go to the town library, to movies, to the mall. It drank gas and backfired once in a while, but it was big, safe, and dependable. Students with newer cars struggled in subzero weather, but the Blue Beast always started right up. It ignored little collision mishaps—like the time Darcy accidentally backed into a post at a gas station and barely dented the chrome fender—and never hesitated at speed-bumps or ruts in the road.

Morgan's head rolled to the side, her forehead against cool glass. So many rides in Darcy's car. Trips to watch meteor showers. Concerts. Shopping. Long, rambling talks as they barreled down dirt roads. Darcy steering with her knees while she wrestled her hair into a ponytail. Morgan searching for bubble-gum pop on the radio. Laughter and junk food and calling 'hey baby!' to dangerous boys on street corners as they sped past.

Good times, Morgan thought, drifting along with the whoosh-whoosh. *God, I miss you, Mule.*

"We're here," a man said in the dream, maybe one of the dangerous boys they'd just passed, but she and Darcy had moved on, sitting at a stoplight, about ready to turn into the mall. They were going to look at earrings, pick some for Darcy's big date.

"Ms. Miller? We're here. Do you need help getting to the house?"

Morgan lifted her head. "Eh, whaa?" Her mouth felt gummy and tasted like stale coffee. She blinked, bleary, and saw Darcy's house illuminated by headlights.

She blinked again, disoriented, before realizing where she was. *The internet guy. He picked me up at the farmhouse.* "Oh. Sorry," she said, stretching and rooting in her pocket for her damp wad of cash. "How much do I owe you for gas?"

He waved aside her offer. "Don't worry about it. I'm glad to help."

Morgan winced at her pitiful fistful of money. *Seven ones and a five. Twelve measly bucks. To drive all the way to Iowa and back and rescue me from a storm.* "No. Really. You came so far to help me. I need to give you something for your time and trouble." She held the money out for him and said, "If this isn't enough, I have more in the house."

"I'm not taking your money," he said, shaking his head and gently pushing her hand toward her. "Not for picking you up in a storm. Anyone would've come to help you."

She pursed her lips and grumbled to herself. Darcy had always been the same way and there was no arguing with some people, especially principled Midwesterners. But he was an internet guy, and she still needed help getting online. "Can you at least get my WiFi working again?"

"That I can do." He smiled and winked at her. "I am a network services professional, after all."

She put the money away and reached for the door. *Good. I can definitely pay you for that, then.* "So you're not too busy tomorrow?"

"No. Not too busy."

Her hand paused on the door handle. His voice had turned flat, almost annoyed. "If you have other jobs—"

He sighed and managed to smile at her. "Ms. Miller, I guarantee you I have *plenty of time* to get your WiFi up and running tomorrow."

"It's Morgan. So, tomorrow then?"

"I'll call May at the co-op and find out when the crew will be here for your DSL. I'll set up your WiFi right after."

Morgan opened the door and hopped out. "Awesome. And thank you."

She started to unwrap the blanket, but he said, "I'll just get the blanket tomorrow... or whenever. And you really don't have to keep thanking me, okay?"

She nodded and closed the door. He waited in the drive, headlights chasing away the night, until she was safely inside.

FIVE

MORGAN WOKE EARLY enough to cook eggs and toast while berating herself for not buying clothes when she was in Albert Lea. Yesterday's t-shirt and shorts had been clean before the storm but were now a muddy mess, and her other set—which she'd slept in—reeked of sweat, old couch, and too many long, sticky runs. And the morning was already far too hot to wear jeans and a long-sleeved shirt.

Habit demanded she start her morning with a nice, relaxing run. *Can't*, she told herself. *My shoes are still drenched, I have to wait for the phone people, and I need to find something clean to wear so I don't stink.*

Sighing, she climbed the stairs to shower and root though Darcy's wardrobe. They'd often shared clothes in college. Sure, Darcy was shorter, but she used to be only a size or so bigger around. Maybe, with luck, there'd be a shirt or khakis or *something* which might fit.

The bedroom at the top of the stairs was nearly empty, just a narrow bed and dresser with a stack of totes in the closet. The middle bedroom was packed floor-to-ceiling with boxes and framed horse art, leaving very little space to move around. The largest bedroom, apparently Darcy's room, was a mess of discarded clothes and clutter surrounding a rumpled bed. Morgan tried the closet first, finding dark blouses and skirts, a few dressy trousers—all three sizes too big—and fitted business attire better suited to Darcy's mother. Piles of shoes littered the floor: dressy shoes, sandals, and wintry boots, not a tennis shoe in sight. Morgan eyed the skirts and blouses doubtfully. Maybe they'd work. With a belt.

She hadn't worn a skirt since she'd first entered the foster care system, and only then because dresses were all they'd given her. Sighing, she closed the closet and climbed over a pile of dirty laundry to the dresser.

The pickings there seemed to be better. Pullover shirts and jeans, a few pairs of capris and Bermuda shorts, still too big, but possibly useful. In the bottom drawer, beneath two pairs of jeans with the tags still on them, she found a faded pair of cutoffs in the size she currently wore, covered in signatures from girls on their dorm floor.

Morgan held the shorts, fingers tracing some signatures— Karen, Rhianne, Melissa Jaye—as her eyes stung. They'd been Darcy's favorite shorts that spring, and everyone had signed them, encouraging Darcy to hurry up and get well. Even though Darcy had few friends, the girls on their floor—maybe even their whole dorm—had banded together after the mess with Ryder. Darcy wore them a few times afterward but, well before summer break, she'd outgrown them and tucked them away.

Morgan traced her own name, scrawled in sharpie above the right-side rear pocket. Memories again assaulted her, good ones, of sipping malted shakes with Darcy at the sandwich shop and studying algebra in the commons. Of lunches in the dorm cafeteria, movie night, watching Karen play volleyball and Melissa Jaye trying to convince them to join the student caucus.

Morgan stripped to put on Darcy's shorts and a not-too-awful-huge t-shirt, no belt required. Her own dirty laundry in hand, she returned downstairs.

Every bit of clothing she owned fit in the washer with room to spare, so, seeing no reason to waste water on a partial load, she returned upstairs to grab an armful of Darcy's discarded dirties. Laundry churning away, she looked about the kitchen and wondered what she was going to do with herself.

She washed her breakfast dishes and put away the teacups Darcy had left in the strainer. She scowled at the sprawl of papers she was supposed to read or sign, then shuddered and turned away. Instead, she folded the afghan and, after contemplating the internet guy's mud-smeared blanket, decided it too needed washed before she returned it. But a blanket alone wouldn't make a load of laundry, so she returned to Darcy's room for more clothes, mostly jeans and towels, and piled them in front of the washer.

But the first load hadn't finished. It had barely been ten minutes.

Groaning, she paced the kitchen and dining room. *All of this solitude and inactivity is going to drive me insane,* she thought. *If I can't run, I need work to do, deadlines, goals. Something!*

She paused, a slight smile forming. *Once I have WiFi, I'll need to get to the site and update things, get the business running again, so I'll need Darcy's username and password. Surely, she's left them somewhere.*

Hopeful, she sat at Darcy's desk to systematically search for any URLs or passwords. She'd emptied two drawers and had flipped through every book on one shelf—having found nothing more interesting than a photocopied recipe for crispy onion chicken—when someone knocked on the door.

The phone people!

Cheered, Morgan hopped up and hurried to the door, but, past the curtain, she saw the shape of a woman and a large dog.

She cracked open the door and peered out at a graying woman struggling to keep her dog still. Morgan made herself smile, but didn't open the door any further. "Can I help you?"

"Oh, thank goodness there's someone here," the woman said,

smiling. Barking and wagging his tail, the dog lunged forward and leapt at the screen door.

Morgan lurched back automatically and stammered, her gaze darting from the dog's huge paws on the screen to the woman's relieved face.

"I'm Jannis Knudsen? From the tan house next door? Frank and I've been watching the dog for a while now, and I wasn't sure..." The woman trailed off, peering through the crack. "Can I come in?"

Ranger! Morgan felt a surge of relief as she recognized the slobbering, friendly retriever from Darcy's avatar. The neighbor, not the shelter, had obviously taken him in. Pushing aside her natural hesitation, Morgan opened the door.

"Oh!" Instead of coming inside, the woman squinted at Morgan, almost releasing the dog in her obvious surprise. "Darcy!? I heard... but..."

"No," Morgan said, struggling to hold her ground and control her rising panic. "I'm not Darcy."

"Oh," the neighbor said again, her face coloring. "I'm so sorry. After she came home from college a couple-three years ago she'd had her nose done, her cheeks, chin... Just for a second, I thought—" She gave Morgan an embarrassed shrug and said, "You're about the same age, same dark hair, so similar, and the dog is obviously excited to see you." She shook her head. "I'm sorry," she repeated.

Darcy didn't have dark hair, Morgan thought, but she said, "It's all right. I'm her friend. Morgan. Darcy... She... She died." The words sounded harsh and cold and Morgan felt another clench of grief.

The woman sighed sympathetically. "Ahh! You must be her college friend? Darcy's mother and I were close, and Anne had mentioned that Darcy made one good friend at college."

Morgan forced another smile. "This is Darcy's dog, Ranger?"

The dog panted at her, nearly grinning, tongue hanging out and dribbling onto the welcome mat. He woofed, low and deep and friendly at the mention of his name. Morgan hesitated then let him sniff her hand through the screen. He tried to lick her despite the thin barrier.

"He is," the woman said, ruffling the massive beast's ears. "Poor thing was stuck in the yard for days with no food or water. I hope it's all right that we took care of him." She smiled. "Can we come in?"

Morgan opened the screen wider and stepped aside as Ranger barreled in, his tail spinning like a gleeful propeller, and raced through the house. The woman entered, still smiling, and held out her hand.

Morgan ducked around her to close the screen, pretending she didn't see the offered hand. "I'm sorry. Your name was?"

"Jannis. I live next door. The tan house."

Morgan felt a sliver of her panic subside. The woman was just Darcy's neighbor, the one her mother had liked. "You're a teacher, right?"

She beamed. "Home Ec, yes. Middle schoolers."

Ah yes, seventh grade cooking, *a hell I never want to repeat.* "All those thirteen year olds and their hormones? You must be very brave."

Jannis grinned, shaking her head. "Not really. I'm just a seasoned veteran of the puberty wars."

An unexpected chuckle burbled from Morgan's belly, and it felt nice. Comforting. "C'mon in, and, please, forgive me. I'm not used to..." She shrugged, uncertain what else to say.

"You're fine, hon. I'm sure this has been awful for you."

Morgan nodded and managed to meet her neighbor's gaze despite her stinging eyes. "Thank you for taking care of him."

"We're happy to. He's a sweet dog." Jannis said, looking past Morgan to Ranger sniffing down the hall. "We did hear about Darcy," she continued, "but when I saw you there at the door, I thought it might've been a mistake, and she was only hurt in the accident."

Morgan frowned. "The accident—what did you hear? No one's told me anything." She took a shuddering breath and clenched her hands together. "Do you know anything at all?"

"Only that there was a car accident. Least that's what I heard from a deputy who came by while I was here mowing and watering the plants."

Morgan flinched and took a step back. *Car accident? But Darcy rarely drove!*

"I don't mean to upset you, honey," Jannis said. "I know it's terrible news. I just couldn't bear to leave the place unattended. Neighbors watch out for each other. I hope that was all right. I didn't mean to intrude."

Ranger had reached the kitchen and was apparently banging around beneath the table, if the crashes and clunks were to be trusted. Jannis chewed on her lower lip. "I'm so sorry to dump the dog on you like this, when you're obviously still grieving. I can take him back home until you're ready for him, if you want."

"The dog's fine," Morgan said, flinching as one of the kitchen chairs flipped and crashed onto the floor. "And you're not intruding, I'm just..." she shrugged, the words clogging in her throat. She sucked in a deep breath and managed to meet Jannis's concerned gaze. "I looked and looked all over the internet and didn't find any news about Darcy's death, not even an obituary. Just a death notice the day I came here."

Jannis nodded. "There wasn't anything. The deputies only told us she was in a car accident and they were holding information pending notification of her relatives."

Tears sprang to Morgan's eyes and she stumbled away from Jannis to sit on the sofa. "She didn't have any relatives, not with her folks gone. Only me. So there was no news because I didn't answer my phone? No *obituary*? How was I supposed to know something happened to Darcy? All I got was a couple of phone calls from some stupid 800 number. I Googled them, I did, but I thought they were trying to sell me something and just ignored them when I should have picked up!"

"Morgan. Hon. Please." Jannis sat beside Morgan and tried to rub her between the shoulder blades, but Morgan jerked out of reach. Jannis sucked in a startled breath then said, "None of this is your fault. I gave the deputy your email and phone number a couple of weeks ago. Someone should have contacted you right away."

How'd she find my number at all? How does she know so much about me? Morgan shifted to hide the preparatory twitch in her legs even as her gaze darted to the unlatched screen door. *Three steps and I'm gone,* she thought, willing her breath to stay steady despite the frantic hammer of her heart. She was amazed at the calm curiosity in her voice. "How'd you get my email and phone number?"

Jannis nodded toward Darcy's office. "The deputy asked us if we had any idea how to contact relatives, and I figured Darcy kept those things the same place her parents did: right there on her Mac. Sure enough, you were in the Address Book."

"The computer's broken. Smashed."

"What?" Jannis stood and hurried toward the office. "It was fine last week when I came over for some of the dog's toys." She stopped in the open doorway, hands clenching. "Those rotten little snots," she muttered, stomping in.

Morgan followed. "You know who did this?"

Jannis sighed, shoulders slumping as she stared at the mess of circuit boards and wires. "Two boys from down the road. They're always getting into trouble, throwing rocks at people's pets, breaking windows, that kind of thing." Her cheek twitched and she turned her head to look at Morgan. "I chased them out of here twice, a couple of weeks ago. But that computer was just fine."

* * *

Jannis brewed a pot of tea while Morgan babbled through disjointed memories and struggled to control her grief.

"Once," she said, daubing a kitchen towel at her leaky nose, "Darcy and I'd gone to a movie, some animated thing, I think, and we saw this kid, he must've been eight or so—"

But it wasn't a kid. Was it? she thought, pushing at the memory. Her left hand shook and she rubbed it on her thigh. It felt frozen. *Was it? I'm not sure.*

"A kid?" Jannis asked as she brought the pot to the table.

Morgan rubbed harder. "Yeah. He'd fallen. Something with his knee. Darcy helped him."

Morgan felt her brow furrow. *No. That's not right.* He didn't fall. He was hit. Hit by a car. Gah, I hate when my memories get all jumbled like this.

She took a breath and gripped her knee to keep her hand from grinding into her thigh. Darcy hadn't helped the boy—nearly everyone leaving the theater saw the accident and rushed to him—instead she'd chased after the driver, finally stopping them by throwing a pot of geraniums at the rear windshield. Shy, quiet Darcy. Who never spoke up about *anything*. Then she'd pulled an old woman from the car and kicked her. And kicked her. By the time the cops got there, the old woman was every bit as bloody as the boy, and far less conscious.

Morgan raised her head, her eyes narrowing. *No, that wasn't right, either. Yes, Darcy had thrown geraniums at the car, but it was a kid driving. A teenage boy without a license who was so scared he'd pissed his pants.*

Not an old woman.

Morgan's feet twitched, pushing her chair back. *Yes, an old woman was kicked unconscious. But not then, not with the kid driving the car. Not then.*

Morgan fought against the need to bolt and tried to remember. *That kid, Darcy'd stared down and kept still until the cops came. She never kicked him, never hurt him at all. Just took his keys and—*

Morgan shook her head, focusing past the excited bark of a nearby dog. *No! Someone else had kicked an old woman. Gramma. Kicked her bloody. Nearly killed her. Not in the road. No. Blood. On linoleum. Wasn't there blood on yellow linoleum?*

The barks became louder, more frantic. Morgan heard a low, heavy thud, yet she kept nibbling at the memory, barely formed. *Was it Gramma? Someone else? It's important. Isn't it? Why can't I remember? Gramma died while I was in foster care. I was eleven, maybe twelve. She'd been sick a long time by then, too sick to watch us since right after Cas was born.*

She shook her head, struggling to focus on the wisp of memory. *So it wasn't Darcy who kicked her bloody. Libbey? No, Darcy kicked her bloody. But, that's not possible. Darcy never met Gram. It had to be—*

"Morgan?" Jannis asked, gripping Morgan's shoulder and shaking her. "Are you all right? There's someone at the door. Do you want me to get it? Morgan?"

"It was Darcy!" Morgan knocked Jannis aside as she scrambled to her feet.

Jannis staggered a step, blocking clear access to the back door, so Morgan turned to escape through the dining room and hurdled a fallen dining chair. She reached the front door, barely registering Ranger's excited, wriggling bark. A shift of her hip knocked the big dog aside, and she yanked the inner door open with one hand while the other reached to shove the screen out of her way. She took a single step straight through, hurtling herself blindly against a man on the porch.

"Ho! Hey! Are you all right?" the internet guy said, catching her. Before she could kick, scream, or pull away, he shifted, holding her behind him and blocking Ranger as the dog barreled through the unlatched door.

The dog bounded around them, joyous barks and flailing tail, and, after a confused frown, the internet guy let Morgan go. "The dog scare you?" he asked, glancing at Morgan as Ranger sat at his feet, tail still wagging, tongue lolling out. He let Ranger sniff his hand then ruffled his ears.

Morgan flushed and she shifted away. "No, I—"

Jannis rushed to the porch. "Morgan, are you all ri—" She stopped, eyes widening. "Nicholas Hawkins? I haven't seen you since that semester you splattered frosting all over yourself and your team. Or was that your brother?"

The internet guy grinned and stepped toward her. "Missus Knudsen! It was definitely me. My mom still complains how the food coloring made my shirt look like it had the measles. On picture day, no less. And there was some pink frosting left in my hair, too. I haven't lived that down either."

Jannis laughed and gave the internet guy a quick hug. "The Great Frosting Explosion was on picture day! I completely forgot about that." She beamed up at him. "How've you been? Your brothers and sisters? I haven't talked to your folks in ages!"

He shrugged, still grinning. "Eh, we're all good. Working,

mostly. Mom's cut her hours at the hospital to spend more time with the grandkids, and Dad's running the station now. Kait's husband got a job in Dubuque, so we rarely see them, but otherwise we're all just pretty much keeping on keeping on. How about you? Still teaching?"

Jannis winked. "Five days a week, from August to June, just like always. Frank keeps pestering me, but I'm not ready to retire."

Panic fading, Morgan leaned against the porch rail and listened to the soothing rhythm of their conversation without really paying attention to the words.

She ran her fingers over Ranger's head, stroking him, and he basked in her distracted attention. She was present but invisible, not the object of attention or suspicion, and she breathed easier. As the pair talked, Morgan's thoughts returned to Darcy.

So it was a car accident. Oh, Darcy! She wiped a tear away with her free hand. *Where did that old memory of you and the kid with the car come from?*

A vehicle stopped in front of the house, doors opening and closing as the internet guy—Nicholas, Jannis had said—laughed over a recollection of a school play. Footsteps approached. Still petting the dog, Morgan glanced over her shoulder. She'd expected to see the phone people, but a man and a woman walked up in khakis and blazers. Neither looked pleased.

Ranger pulled away from Morgan's hand and jumped up, his front feet on the rail. Despite a wagging tail, he let out a low bark as if to say, *I don't know you. Why are you approaching my house?*

The stocky, slightly-graying woman walked in front, the man, perhaps a decade younger and well muscled, behind. He carried a file folder in one hand and, as he shifted it, Morgan saw a dark and ominous smudge in the shadow of his jacket, strapped down below his left arm. A gun.

Heart slamming, Morgan turned to face the pair and creaked out, "Can I help you?" Her right hand sought the comforting heft of Ranger's head. Behind her, Jannis and Nick fell silent.

Ranger's warm presence, his bulk, seemed to grant Morgan strength. *He's still wagging. Maybe they're not a threat.*

"Morgan Miller?" the woman asked, her gaze darting to the others on the porch before returning to rest on Morgan.

Morgan wanted to bolt, but tightened her spine and held herself still. "Yes." Ranger stopped wagging as he looked up at her. He let out a low, worried whine.

The woman pulled a badge from inside of her blazer. She wore a holstered gun at her hip. "May we speak with you a moment?"

A tremor ran through Morgan's arm to her hand on Ranger's head, but she clenched her fingers into his fur. *Steady. Steady.* "Is there a problem?"

"Just need to have a word, ma'am," the woman said, a false smile on her face.

A blue panel truck with *Rural Frontier Cooperative* emblazoned across the side parked behind the cops' car. Morgan swallowed. *The phone people.*

"I'm kind of busy today," she managed to say as she gestured out to the work truck. "Can we do this another time?"

"It'll just take a moment, ma'am," the woman replied, stiff smile never wavering.

Morgan moistened her lips and nodded. "Okay. Just a sec, all right?"

She turned away from the cops without fleeing or falling, and managed to meet Nick's concerned gaze. "Can you supervise the phone hookups while I deal with this?"

"Sure." He reached out to touch her arm. "Sure."

She drew away from his touch and smiled her thanks despite

her quaking fear. "I've got the money. It's in the house."

"It's okay. Go talk to them. I'll handle the crew."

Morgan intended to approach the police, but they'd already climbed onto the porch. Tail wagging, Ranger rammed his nose in the woman's crotch for a good long snort before moving on to her partner's polished loafers.

"Sorry about that. I'll take the dog." Jannis grasped Ranger's collar and dragged him back.

"It's all right, ma'am," the woman said. "Part of the job."

Despite a near constant demand to run pinging in her brain, Morgan managed to meet the woman's stony gaze. "Are you taking me in?"

"Should we?"

Morgan shrugged. "No. I just thought..."

"Miss Miller, regardless of what you might see on TV, we tend to prefer to talk to people before 'taking them in'." She frowned at the gaping work crew, and Jannis and Nick's concerned stares. "Can we speak inside?"

"Um, okay." Morgan grimaced at Jannis, Ranger clenched and wriggling against her legs, then staggered to the screen door and opened it. The dining room waited ahead and to her left. She stumbled in, pausing to right the chair Ranger had knocked over. "Is here okay?" she asked, fumbling her grip on the chair as she remembered her manners. "Can I get you something to drink?"

"We're fine," the woman said. "Please. Sit." She sat, smiling expectantly at Morgan while her partner handed her the folder.

Morgan sat, nearly falling into her chair. "What's this about?" she managed to ask. "I told the cops the other night that Darcy'd left me this house in her—"

"I'm Detective Jill Hildebrandt," the woman said as she opened the folder, "and this is my partner, Detective Lee Kramer. We just have a few questions concerning your friend's death."

"Okay. Sure. I don't know how much help I can be." Morgan clasped her hands together on her lap and managed not to stare at them. Detective Kramer opened a note-pad, but said nothing.

"When's the last time you spoke to Miss Harris?" Hildebrandt asked.

"June seventeenth," Morgan said without hesitation. "But we didn't really speak. We'd texted." She took a breath and raised her gaze from the edge of the table. "It's still on my phone, if you'd like to see."

The detectives agreed so Morgan opened her text listings and handed over her phone.

Kramer examined it for scant few moments then said, "There are no other texts or calls during the month of June on here except from Miss Harris." He pushed a couple of buttons and added, "A few outgoing, but no other incoming calls. None. And no voicemails."

Hildebrandt's eyes narrowed. "How do you explain that, Miss Miller?"

"I don't know anyone else," Morgan said, her voice cracking. "No one who'd call or text me, at least."

"Did you clear your call or voicemail log?" Hildebrandt asked. "We can check."

"It's a really cheap phone and my voicemail's never worked. Check anything you want. I haven't cleared my call log for weeks. I make business calls from time to time, but no one ever calls me but Darcy."

Hildebrandt pulled out a pen and tapped it on the top paper within the folder. "Why did she go to Wisconsin?"

Morgan lurched back as if slapped, her heart slamming as she struggled not to babble, or bolt. "Wisconsin? What was she doing in *Wisconsin?*"

"We just asked you the same question."

Morgan ran a shaking hand over her face and into her hair. "Wisconsin? God. Is that where she..."

"Yes, Miss Miller. Why would she go there?"

Morgan struggled to come up with a reason, any reason, why Darcy would return to Wisconsin. "A college alumni thing? I don't know. She never said anything."

"What did you discuss in your last conversation?"

Stay still, stay steady. Morgan shifted, one foot curling around the chair leg. "She wanted me to visit. Offered a plane ticket and everything." Her other foot crept around to clamp her to the chair. "I told her no. Maybe I should have said yes, maybe I—"

"Where were you on June seventeenth?"

"New York. I was there until the twentieth, I think, then I went to Hartford."

Detective Kramer wrote while Detective Hildebrandt said, "New York? Why were you in New York?"

Morgan clasped her hands together again. "I move from city to city to research and write articles for our website, FrugallyUrban dot com. Darcy runs it..." Morgan swallowed and met the detective's gaze. "Ran it. I just write the articles."

"How long have you worked together on this site?"

"About four years. She had this idea and needed a writer, so she asked me." Morgan lowered her gaze, knowing the statement was only partly true. Darcy had, in fact, worried about Morgan surviving alone and traveling, so she'd created the site to give Morgan an income. And to keep track of her.

Both detectives made note of her statement. Hildebrandt plucked a piece of paper from the pile. "Miss Miller, it appears you didn't exist at all until you registered for classes at Maginaw State College. You have no driver's license, no voting records, no bills, no other records beyond a pay-as-you-go cell phone, a pre-pay MasterCard, and a debit card through an online bank account. Can you explain that, Miss Miller?"

"I was in the foster system as a kid. All that stuff is sealed, and I haven't done much since college."

"Except move from city to city?"

Morgan swallowed and nodded. "Yes."

"And where did you meet Miss Harris?"

"College. We were roommates."

"I see. Miss Miller, did you know that Maginaw State's records indicate that you and Miss Harris' attendance overlapped by barely more than one calendar year?"

"Yes. I..." She swallowed. "My grades weren't all that great and I just couldn't stay anymore, so I..." Morgan blinked and managed to meet Detective Hildebrandt's gaze. "I dropped out, middle of my second year."

"But Miss Harris graduated? Correct?"

Morgan rubbed her upper arms. "Yeah, she did."

"With a communications degree? The same major you'd had?"

"Yes."

"So. Miss Miller, why did Miss Harris start sending money to your online account *four years* after you left school?"

"I told you. We started a website. Darcy managed it, I wrote the articles. She paid me for my writing."

"And that site was SkippityCheap?"

Morgan managed to control her disgust. "No! FrugallyUrban. I told you."

"FrugallyUrban. Right. Which was why you were where again, on June seventeenth?"

"New York. Then Hartford."

"Let me get this straight. You and Miss Harris operated a

website and she stayed here, rarely leaving the house, while you moved around from city to city, right?"

"Right," Morgan sighed, wondering why these questions kept going in the same darn circles.

"And, for four years, you were paid for writing articles for this site?" When Morgan nodded, Hildebrandt asked, "Was your salary based on profits, or the length of your articles?"

"Word counts. Three cents a word for six articles a week plus occasional special features."

"Ah. So you were, in effect, Miss Harris's employee?"

Morgan flinched. She'd had the same thought many times but Darcy had always insisted they were partners. *Partners? I never knew any official information about site traffic or how to moderate comments or even fix a typo once a story was posted. Sure, I could travel wherever I wanted—or could afford—but I had to write about what Darcy said to. When Darcy said. And not once did my preferences on color or graphics or anything matter. Hell, she had to know where I was every single day, but I didn't even have an access password. I was more like an employee.*

"Miss Miller? Were you actually Miss Harris's employee?"

Morgan wove her fingers together. *Darcy liked to be in control, and I always just let her. It was easier that way.* "Sort of. She said we were partners, but, yeah. She was the boss. I just wrote the articles."

"I see. Why, then, did she leave nearly everything she owned to you in the event of her death, including a rather substantial life insurance policy?"

Life insur– Morgan leaned forward, her voice rising as her feet unhooked from the chair. "Are you accusing me of... of extortion?"

"Miss Miller, we never mentioned any such thing."

"But you implied it!" Morgan snapped, standing. "Let me tell you why she left me this cluttered mess of a house and her dog and all this other *crap* and left me stranded here in po-dunk

Minnesota. We were friends, okay, *friends*. She was the only friend
I ever had, and after I left school we kept in touch, email, phone
calls, whatever. When she started her website she asked me to work
with her. That's right. *Work*. Check my goddamn tax records if you
want. I claimed every damn penny as income, every last one. Even
from odd jobs that paid cash."

Hildebrandt's stiff smile never wavered. "There's no reason to
get upset, Miss Miller. We've already subpoenaed your tax records."

Morgan flumped into her chair. "Then why are you asking me
these stupid questions?"

"Because she died unexpectedly, Miss Miller, and left you
a great deal of property and assets. Asking questions about such
matters is what we do."

"I know she died," Morgan said, swallowing past the constriction
in her throat. "I was told just a few days ago. But I didn't know what
happened or why she left me so much. She was just my friend.
After her folks died, we talked all of the time, and when she started
FrugallyUrban she brought me in to write articles. Just articles. I
haven't seen her since I left school."

Hildebrandt's smile shifted, widening slightly, and Morgan felt
herself press against her chair. "What about the other sites, Miss
Miller?"

"Other sites?" Morgan asked, brow furrowing. "What other
sites? We did FrugallyUrban."

"Ah, but Miss Harris also transferred you money from
HiggenPop, GlimmerGals, The Short Basket, and SkippityCheap."

Morgan shook her head. "No. We didn't do those, just
FrugallyUrban. I told you, Darcy handled the tech stuff and
I wrote the articles." She stammered then added, "HiggenPop
and SkippityCheap are competitors. I never wrote for them.
Just for Darcy."

Hildebrandt slid a piece of paper to Morgan. "Can you explain, Miss Miller, how the same reviews often appeared on all those sites, with various bylines and a few slight changes in content?"

"No. It's not possible. I never, ever wrote for them. Just Darcy."

"Apparently all income from those sites and three others were paid directly to Miss Harris. She then deposited a portion of the money to *your* online account. Can you explain that, Miss Miller?"

"No. We only talked about FrugallyUrban. Never anything like this." Morgan stared at a page of financials listed under Darcy's name and social security number and felt her stomach clench. *Eight sites? And FrugallyUrban only made twenty six thousand last year. That barely covered what she paid me!*

"There are other income sources that Miss Harris utilized, but at this point we and the Wisconsin DCI are mostly interested in your involvement with these websites, Miss Miller. And how you, a rather minor employee, became full owner of, essentially, her entire estate."

Morgan shook her head and felt her hands tremble. *Minor employee? Other people wrote for her?*

"I... I told you. We were friends. I wrote articles and reviews. She paid me. This..." She pushed the paper away. "I didn't know anything about all this."

"And you haven't seen her since college? Roughly six years ago?"

Six and a half. Morgan nodded. "Right. Just talked on the phone, G-Plus hangouts, Skype... That kind of thing."

"Yes, well, that leaves us with another ripple, Miss Miller. Miss Harris died in an accident."

"Yeah. Car accident in Wisconsin. You just told me."

"Her car ran off the road, into a gully."

"A *gully?* Oh my God."

"When was the last time you saw Miss Harris?"

Oh, Darcy! What were you doing? Morgan's upper arms shivered so she crossed her arms over her chest to rub them. "I told you. When I left school."

"How is it, then, that we found your fingerprints in her car?"

"That's not possible," Morgan snapped, hands balling into fists near her armpits. "I haven't seen her in almost seven years and her dad bought her the car for graduation. I've never, ever, been in her car." She glared at the detectives. "Ever. And even if I was—which I *wasn't*—there's no way you'd have my fingerprints to check against. Why are you lying to me?"

"Because she wasn't alone in the car, Miss Miller. DCI found blood and hairs on the passenger side that didn't match Miss Harris. Who else could it be, if not you?"

Morgan stood, shaking. Darcy avoided being alone with anyone, and she certainly never let anyone she didn't know in her house *or* her car. She'd become a recluse and had nearly quit driving entirely. "Someone else? Someone *else* was in her car? Who? Was it a carjacker? Did they hurt her, did they—"

Hildebrandt's voice was dead calm. "We need to know where you were on June seventeenth, Miss Miller."

Morgan glared at both detectives. "I told you. New York. I stayed at High Town, a hostel in Manhattan. Registered and everything, but I paid cash. For four days in a row. Call them. I paid every morning and was at bed check every night. Whoever was in Darcy's car, it wasn't me."

SIX

MORGAN SAT ON THE PORCH SWING and watched the detectives return to their car. She knew that Jannis puttered inside, making some sort of snack while a load of shorts, t-shirts and undies finished up a spin cycle right there in the kitchen. The phone people were rattling around the basement with Nick-the-internet-guy supervising. Oh, and the dog had been put out back, corralled by the fenced-in yard, to go potty and burn off some energy.

There was still a mess of papers on the kitchen table to deal with, to sign or deposit or file someplace. A different stack of papers lurked in the dining room with worrisome lists of websites and clients and other people Darcy had on the payroll, people who surely wanted to be paid for work they'd completed weeks ago. The house was a filthy mess of junk, stacked boxes, and accumulated, disorganized crap. There were a couple of days' worth of groceries in the fridge, two unmade beds upstairs, a lawn that needed mowing, neighbors who called the cops over jogging in broad daylight, and God only knew what other surprises were about to land on her head.

As the detectives drove away, Morgan decided that she really didn't give a rat's ass about any of it. Darcy had stuck her in po-dunk Minnesota but she wanted to go home to the city. *Any* city.

She sat there a long time, staring at the street as some monstrosity of a farming implement rattled by. Was it an irrigator? A cultivator? A fold-spin-and-mutilator? She had no idea. Only that it was huge, loud, and totally alien to her. The kids on their bikes, laughing and squealing and generally being kids, were just as alien as the machinery. The pickup trucks. The lack of sidewalks. One and two-story houses with big yards and big trees and cheery flowers in the front. The only concrete lay on the road, a highway that had less traffic than any side street she'd traveled in nearly seven years. The only steel clanked past in farm machinery and family cars. No crowds, no cabs or newsstands or coffee shops. Nothing that made any sense at all.

She was lost, trapped in the middle of fucking nowhere. And it was all Darcy's fault.

How could you do this to me? Dammit, Darcy! How could you? I thought you were my friend.

Morgan sniffled and wiped her hand beneath her nose. She couldn't decide if she was more upset over Darcy's lies, being stuck with Darcy's mess, or being told she wasn't the only one working with Darcy, talking to Darcy. Living for Darcy.

I thought I was your friend. That we were partners. But no. You lied to me, lied these past four years.

You were all I had! her mind screamed as her gaze turned toward the brilliant sky, its blue impossible and unseen from city streets. *All I had since just about the day we met. My only friend, my confidant, my rock. But I was just a tool, wasn't I? A writer to exploit. A little, worthless cog in your big business plan. I trusted you, Darcy Harris, and what do you do? You lie to me then you stick me with your shit and your sites and your—*

"Ms. Miller?" Nick said from the doorway. "Phone line's clear and we're just about ready to turn on your DSL. Once we get you connected, it'll take a few more minutes to get the WiFi running."

Morgan stood, sniffling the worst of her tears, and she managed to nod. "Okay. Good."

"I hate to interrupt," he said, "but it needs a login and password. I can make random ones, if you want."

She managed a shaky smile and opened the screen door. "It's okay. I'll write one down."

Behind her, some mammoth beast of agricultural machinery rattled by as she squared her shoulders and entered the house.

Morgan found a scrap of paper easily enough. She even had a password in mind. She took a deep breath and scribbled *m7B6C3N11mo* despite her fingers cramping around the pen.

Her hand shook as she handed the scrap to Nick. "Lowercase on the m and m-o, uppercase on the rest, okay?"

"You betcha," he said, shifting his glasses slightly before entering her code. "What do you want to name your network?"

"How about 'this is mine'?" she asked. *Mine. I'm paying for it. And no one can just up and take it away or change the rules without telling me. It's my life, my memory, one I haven't been able to lose no matter how much I run.*

He chuckled a little. "Sure thing. Let me finish this setup, then we'll boot up your laptop and see if we can get you logged on."

Morgan nodded and tried not to look at Darcy's horsey mess everywhere. Her stomach twisted and her vision wavered. *I never should have answered that call from Bennet. Never should have—*

"Morgan? Morgan, honey? You okay?"

Morgan sniffled and nodded at Jannis, even managed a shaky smile. "Yeah, I'm okay." *My only friend spent the past four years lying to me, I'm stuck in her house, with her mess, and the cops think I killed her. But, yeah, I'm okay. I'm freaking fantastic, in fact!*

Jannis offered a consoling smile before glancing toward the dining room. The two phone guys stood past the doorway, fidgeting and pointedly not-looking at the folder with a Freeborn County Sheriff seal on the front.

Aw, hell, they need paid. "Just a sec," Morgan said, and she knelt to reach behind the couch for her backpack.

The phone guys accepted their cash and left quickly, but Jannis remained, watching her. "C'mon and sit down. Have a cookie."

Morgan's throat tightened and she shook her head. *I don't want to sit down, I want to run, run away from all of this!*

But Nick still worked on her connection in the office—he, too, would need paid. Out in the back yard, Ranger let loose a volley of cheerful barks.

Morgan covered her face with her hands and wept.

She barely resisted Jannis leading her to the kitchen and soon found herself sitting at the table with a glass of iced tea and a plate of crispy rice treats. With chocolate chips.

"How... how did you make these? There wasn't anything in the cupboards."

Jannis smiled and sat across from her. "I teach Home Ec, hon. I always have basic baking ingredients handy because you never know when someone might need a little cheering up. Besides, these are a lot quicker than my killer brownies." She pushed the plate closer to Morgan. "Try one. They're good."

Morgan had first tasted crispy rice treats while at her second foster home. Her foster mom had made them for her to take to school on her birthday, one of the few points in her childhood that had felt normal. They'd been plain and not as pretty as Jannis's, but magical nevertheless. For that day at least, everyone in class was her friend. "Okay." Morgan picked up a cookie. It felt soft, slightly sticky, and smelled so, so good.

"Don't let those detectives bother you," Jannis said as Morgan took a bite and closed her eyes to the simple bliss of rice and marshmallow. "They don't know what happened any more than we do."

"I know they're just doing their jobs," Morgan said. "And it's not just that. It's..."

Jannis said nothing as she sipped her tea and nibbled on a corner of a rice treat.

Morgan too, took another bite. "I... It's just I trusted Darcy, you know? I thought we were a team. But she had all these things, *did* all these things without telling me."

"We all have our own lives, Morgan," Jannis whispered. "You surely couldn't expect her to inform you of every little decision she made."

Morgan felt another sob struggle to break free. "But she lied! She said I was her partner! We were in this together! But she had other sites, other writers—"

"Morgan, listen to me. Darcy obviously loved you very, very much. And yes, she probably should have discussed more of the business particulars with you. That's true. But would it have mattered? Would you have cared?"

"She should've told me anyway," Morgan said, raising her gaze to Jannis. "I don't know why she went to Wisconsin, don't know who she met or why, and now she's dead."

"That's not your fault either. It was an accident."

Morgan flinched and returned her attention to her cookie. *Was it an accident? Someone else was in the car, someone Darcy was alone with. But she'd told me that she didn't trust anyone but me. So she lied about that, about the sites, maybe about everything. And now she's dead. Maybe killed by that other person.*

Morgan shook her head and pushed the cookie away. *It had to be an accident, Darcy was too quiet and timid to get herself murdered. Besides, that other blood might've been years old, from the dog or her mother or any of a million reasons. It was just an accident.* Morgan swallowed and raised her head again to look at the cluttered froth of a kitchen. *I miss you, Mule, I just wish you wouldn't have left me all this mess.*

"I'm sure she loved you, and she did the best she could."

"I know," Morgan said at last. "I'll be okay once this all sinks in. It's just been so much, so fast."

"Ms. Miller?" Nick called from the living room.

"We're in the kitchen," Jannis said.

"I'm getting a good signal," Nick said as he entered the kitchen. "You ready to try your WiFi?"

"Yeah. Thanks. My laptop's in my backpack." Morgan stood and took a quick sip of tea as Jannis held up the plate of treats for Nick, who shook his head.

He followed Morgan to the living room, then to the office. "Some of the basement wiring was old and really disrupted the signal, but we put in new line all the way to the modem. The signal's rock-solid now."

Morgan nodded. "Cool."

She listened to him explain the modem and WiFi router, and how to reboot the system if need be. At his instruction, Morgan started up her laptop and grinned when, like magic, *ThisIsMine* appeared in her available networks. Login went through without hesitation and *FrugallyUrban's* familiar site filled her screen, still full of stale information awaiting updates. All of its vital data lay smashed and scrambled in the desk's cubby, along with other sites, other writers' work, all languishing, stalled, and losing readers—and revenue—by the day.

While Nick, the internet guy, was right there. He'd done a great job so far. Hadn't he?

Morgan felt her smile tighten. *You dumped this mess on me, Darcy? Fine. It's mine now and I can do whatever I want. Like get it up and running then sell the bastard. Get clear the hell away from it, you, and all of this.*

"Well? Can you log on?" Nick asked.

"WiFi's working great. Thank you."

While Nick picked up his tools and filled out paperwork, Morgan closed her laptop and stood.

"I have a computer question," she said.

Nick continued to fill out a receipt. "Sure. Ask away."

"How much will you charge me to fix that computer?"

He paused and raised his head to look at her, eyes glittering from behind his glasses. "That one? The Mac?"

She nodded. "That one. How much?"

He squinted at it, shaking his head. "I don't know if it's possible. The case is smashed to hell, the motherboard's in at least six pieces and the hard-drive..." He frowned and looked at her. "You're better off just buying a new one."

"All I really need is the hard drive," Morgan said. "At least the data on it. All the important stuff has to be on there, 'cause it sure isn't written anywhere I can find. I can't update her sites without access codes, and I don't even know where the servers are or anything."

"Server locations aren't a problem—they're trackable online—but since you're not the original owner it might take months to get the hosts to cough up the access information. So, yeah, you'd need at least login cookies or a password."

He mumbled and knelt to pick through the electronic remains. "I can't guarantee anything, okay? But I can hook it up to a diagnostic and see what we have." He lifted a dented box from the mess and turned it over in his hands. "It's not looking promising."

"But there's a chance, right? It's the only way I can get the sites updated and making revenue again."

He looked at her, gaze questioning, but said, "There's a chance. Might get complicated and expensive if I have to re-compile data by hand. My materials cost shouldn't be too bad, but *time* could really add up."

"What's your bill rate?"

"Fifty an hour. And you already owe about a hundred seventy dollars just from today, between new cabling, WiFi router, and time."

She nodded, relieved. He worked cheap! She had a pile of checks from the financial planners in her pack. If he kept repair costs under a few grand, she'd surely still have enough money to survive a while on her own. But if he fixed the computer, in two or three weeks she'd have a business, a real, profit-generating business that wouldn't be dependent on location, bosses, or a regular schedule. She could even hire someone to do the marketing or sell off some of the other sites.

Might not be able to take my run this morning, but I can make some forward progress, at least. And once FrugallyUrban's fixed, I'm selling this damned house and all the crap in it.

Morgan smiled. "I'll pay cash, weekly, if you're willing to try."

* * *

Nick returned an hour or so later with a case of equipment, mumbling something about how limited workspace at the shop made it difficult to relocate and repair something as fragile, and important, as her data, but Morgan really didn't listen. After Jannis left, she'd washed and sorted more laundry, tidied the kitchen and otherwise puttered around the house until she desperately wanted a run.

She offered Nick full use of the dining room table, the kitchen table, Darcy's desk, anything he wanted, and, while he set up his workspace, she made a quick retreat upstairs.

He had cleared off the dining room table and was arranging broken computer parts on a rubber mat when she returned in fresh running clothes.

"Do you need anything from me?" she asked as she tucked her

hair into a ponytail.

He shook his head and unfastened a layer of broken circuit board dangling from the hard drive. "Nope. I'm good."

"I'm going to take Ranger for a run, but I'll be back in a bit. Fifteen, twenty minutes, maybe."

She watched him work for a moment, then went to the kitchen to grab Ranger's leash.

The dog flipped out at the sight of it, barking and twirling and jumping around, but one stern 'sit' from Morgan sent him still, if squirmy, on his haunches. Once the leash was clipped on, he leapt about again, gleefully barking, but he seemed well-accustomed to being walked, not pulling even as he hurried to pee on the bush just past the gate.

Are all big dogs like this? she wondered, smiling, as Ranger sniffed around then peed again. The two dogs she'd known before, pets of foster parents, had been large and friendly too, always ready to play, and gentle despite their gruffness. And once, when a foster-sister's drunken father had come in the middle of the night to steal her away, the snarling dog had protected the children, not letting the man into their bedroom.

A good dog is a good thing to have, her foster mother had said later that night as the police dragged the man away. She'd hugged the panicked girls, stroked their hair and assured them that no matter what, Samson would watch over them. Always. He'd give his life for them, if need be, so go on back to sleep. You're safe.

Ranger sat at her feet, wagging his tail and staring up at her with blind adoration, much like Samson had done all those years ago.

She ruffled his ears. "Let's see how you like running, boy," she said and his goofy dog grin seemed to promise that he'd like it a great deal.

He wanted to wander back and forth at first, to sniff this and
that and pee on another dog's fence, and it took a block or so of
Morgan's relentless jog to keep him on track. Once he seemed to
understand her intent, she sped up, the leash a loose tether as he
fell in beside her.

She checked her heart rate and relaxed into her run, Ranger's
steady breathing a comforting pentameter to complement her
stride. She repeatedly crossed the town as she worked from the
eastern edge to the west, then from the south to the north, but no
one glared at her, and a few people actually waved.

She waved back but kept running, avoiding the roads leading
out of town for fear she'd lose herself again and end up as lost as
the night before. Once she and Ranger had run down every street,
she returned to the house, unclipping his leash in the back yard and
using the fence as support to stretch.

She felt hot and sweaty, but in a good, refreshing way.

Ranger gulped down almost all of the water in his dish and she
stretched as she refilled it with a hose attached to a spigot near the
back door. Once his bowl had been refilled, she took a quick drink
before bending and running a refreshing jolt of cool water over the
back of her head.

Ranger dropped a grimy ball between her feet. She laughed and
flung it across the yard, grinning as he chased it down and brought
it right back to her.

If nothing else, she had a good dog and a plan. For the first
time in a long time, it felt good to be alive.

SEVEN

NICK FROWNED AT THE MESS on the diningroom table. "The diagnostic says your control board is shot and your file system will need rebuilt, too."

Morgan leaned in the kitchen doorway and sipped her iced tea as she waited for the oven to heat up. "That's bad, right?"

"Pretty bad. I can order a new control board and recode your file system, but it's looking like about fifteen percent of your data is just gone."

Fifteen percent? Not great, no, but it doesn't sound so awful. "So eighty five percent of the files are all right?"

"No. You're missing twelve to eighteen percent of your *data*, which is scattered randomly throughout the files. A piece here, a hunk of code there..." He leaned back in his chair and stretched. "So. If I can get your file system working again, it'll connect up the bits and pieces of the files and give us a better idea of where the holes are."

Morgan sat, staring at the mess on the table, and she swallowed back a tight, acrid taste in her throat. "That does sound bad."

"But it's not impossible. I'll know more once I get the new control board, and I have a Unix drive I can pillage for other parts." He gave her an encouraging smile. "I'll put a rush on the 'board and should be able to get this drive physically running again by mid-day Monday. Then I'll build a new file system. After that, it'll be like putting together a jigsaw puzzle with a few pieces missing. As I find complete files, I'll put them on a fresh drive and you'll be good to go."

Just have to get past the weekend, Morgan thought, nodding. The oven dinged, and she stood. "What are the chances we'll get FrugallyUrban's access codes?"

He smiled. "About eighty, eighty five percent that the cookies are intact."

She smiled back. "Hey, that's lots better odds than Vegas."

"I've done a lot of coding and data repair. There's a good chance I can replace some of what's gone, as long as it's not unique content, like one of your review articles. If it's programming data, I should be able to find it, and fix it."

Morgan sighed. "Passwords are unique data."

"Hey, don't look so worried. The real problem will be incomplete or missing cookies. The sites are likely WordPress, so a good cookie will let you in to admin. It's a standard hack. Once there, you can create your own username and password and be working without a hitch."

Hope remains. Morgan looked past Nick as Ranger trotted in from the living room with a day-glo green tennis ball in his jaws. He dropped it square in Nick's lap.

"Ah, jeesh, sorry about that," Morgan said, rushing to them. "He seems to really like playing fetch."

Nick waved off her concern and plucked the sloppy wet ball from his lap. "Most retrievers do. It's their nature." Grinning, he held the ball and moved it back-and-forth above Ranger's head, taunting the dog. "You want it? You want it?" he said. Just as Ranger quivered as if he was about ready to burst apart, Nick tossed the ball into the living room where it bounced off a chair and disappeared. Ranger scrambled after it.

He seemed like a nice guy. Friendly. Regular and normal and helpful. And Ranger liked him.

Their eyes met for a moment and Morgan swallowed as she

took a slight step backward. His work was done for the day, but she didn't want him to go. Not yet. Not when she'd be all alone for nearly three full days.

"Hey, um," Morgan said, her hands fidgeting as a thread of panic sliced through her at the thought of Darcy and Ryder and how a nice, quiet guy hadn't been so nice.

It's not the same, not the same at all, she thought, shaking her head. *I've already been in his truck and nothing happened. Jannis knows him and likes him a lot. Ranger likes him. He's just smart and kind and my age. A nice man. A really nice man. Can't I be friends with a nice man?*

Nick pushed up his glasses and turned to face her. Morgan felt her cheeks get hot. *I can't believe I'm doing this.* She took a breath and tried again. "You hungry?"

Ranger returned with the ball and dropped it at Nick's feet. He stood to toss it. "I know it's coming on to afternoon, but there's no need to feel obligated to feed me. Just let me get my stuff cleaned up and I'll be out of your hair until that part comes on Monday."

"That's not what I meant," Morgan blurted, blushing again as Nick turned to look at her. "You've been so nice to me, with the storm and coffee and these repairs and all, and, well, I was gonna toss in a pizza and, um, can't eat the whole thing by myself. So, I thought..." She shrugged, unsure what else to say without sounding like a desperate idiot, so she fled to the kitchen.

Hands shaking, she ripped open the pizza box. *What was I thinking? That just because he took pity on me last night, rescued me, that he has all day to sit around and keep a flake like me company? Hell, Morgan, you have no idea if he has a wife or a girlfriend or—*

"Ms. Miller?" Nick said from the doorway. Ranger dropped the ball at his feet and he plucked it from the floor and flung it backwards without really looking at it. "You okay?"

Morgan managed to get the plastic off the pizza without

dropping the whole thing on the floor, so she snatched open the oven door and slid the pie in. "I'm sorry. I don't really know you and I shouldn't have even thought that you might—"

"I have nowhere I have to be," he said. "And pizza sounds fine."

* * *

Pizza cooked and a bag of salad added to the menu, Morgan settled across the kitchen table from Nick and chuckled as he unscrewed the top off a fresh bottle of Mountain Dew he'd fetched from his truck.

"You do know that stuff'll kill you?" she said as she dragged a slice of pizza onto her paper plate. "Ruin your kidneys and all."

"Eh, it tastes good." He shrugged, grinning as he raised and tilted his plastic bottle toward her in a toast. "To lunch on a lovely summer day?"

She smiled and raised her own glass of iced tea. "To lunch."

They clunked their respective beverages together. "Look out kidneys, here it comes!" he said before taking a drink.

Morgan laughed. And it felt nice.

"So. Where ya from, Ms. Miller?" Nick asked as he dumped a pile of salad onto his plate. Ranger returned with the ball but decided to flump beneath the table and pant.

Morgan rubbed the dog's belly with her foot and wondered how much to mention. "All over," she said at last, then decided, *what the hell.* "And it's Morgan. Please. Ms. Miller reminds me of my mother and we do not want to go there."

"You were named after Morgan le Fay, from the King Arthur legends?"

I wish. Morgan tried not to wince as she remembered the time Libbey had dragged her to see a Morgan horse. She was maybe six and they'd stood in a muddy ditch beside a pasture of shiny dark horses, Libbey shaking a fistful of freshly-picked weeds to entice them. One massive beast had finally accepted her offer and delicately plucked a few weeds from Libbey's hand.

"Hey, pretty baby," her mother had cooed, a soft, contented smile on her face, a smile Morgan had never seen before or ever again. She'd touched the horse's wide forehead and giggled as its fine, bristly muzzle worked against her fingers to get the last of the leaves.

"Isn't she pretty, Morgan?" Libbey had said, glancing at her, still smiling like the twenty-year-old-girl she was, before returning her affection to the horse. "I named you after them because you're so pretty. Like they are. With dark brown hair and eyes. Did you know Morgan's are my favorite? There was a Morgan harness racer at a stable I worked at one summer, before I got knocked up with you. Such a sweet boy. I even got to brush him out and feed him a few times."

Libbey had stroked the beast's head again, whispering soothing murmurs, then bent to grab more weeds. As she'd held out the fresh offering, the horse snorted and fled. The rest of the horses had turned too, somehow spooked.

"No! Don't go! Please!" Libbey had called, but the horses had trotted away to the far side of the pasture, their tails up like flags. "I don't know when I can come back! Please!"

But the horses had resumed grazing, none paying any attention to the two people in the ditch.

Libbey'd sagged for a moment, weeds crushed in her fist, her head down, and she'd taken a shuddering, sobbing breath. "I just wanted to pet the horses," she'd whispered. "Why can't I ever pet the horses?"

Morgan had quickly pulled a few grasses and weeds from

the mud, hoping to help, but her mother's gentle smile faded as she watched the horses, soon replaced by the familiar sneer. Still clutching the grasses, Morgan lurched a step back, away from the coming explosion.

"What did you do?" Libbey'd snarled as she turned, her handful of weeds crushed in her fist, more of a weapon than an offering. "What the fucking hell did you DO you *little bitch?!?*"

"Nothing, Libbey. Nothing! I promise! I'm sorry!" It hadn't mattered.

It had never mattered.

Of course Morgan had made some noise to scare it away and earned the vicious beating. Of course it was all Morgan's fault for ruining it, and of course she'd deserved the bruises on her back and belly. Again.

At least it hadn't been another broken arm that time. A few lashes from the leaves, but no busted bones. Morgan tried not to wince as she shoved the memory aside. "No, I'm actually named after a breed of horse. My mom was crazy over them, I guess."

He chuckled and grabbed a slice of pizza. "Seems your friend was, too."

Horses, horses, always plagued by horses. Morgan shrugged. "Weird, huh?"

"Nah. One of my sisters was horse crazy when she was a kid. It happens." Nick's smile was warm and genuine, brightening his steadfast face. "It's a nice name. Unique yet user-friendly." He handed her the salad bag and added, "It suits you."

She shrugged again, unable to remember a time when she actually *liked* her name. As she poured a portion of salad on her plate, she asked, "And you're Nick, right?"

"Nick Hawkins. Lived here my whole life. Well, this county, anyway."

"Hawkins? As in Hawkins Grocery?"

He laughed and nodded, the cheer bringing golden lights to his blue-gray eyes. "Yep! That's my Uncle Pat's store. Spent most of my teenage years bagging groceries and stacking apples. I do all of their computer programming and hardware installations now, so I'm there keying in price adjustments most weekends."

His grin widened as he poured a dollop of dressing on his salad. "Pat seems to think he deserves a cut rate for putting up with my crap all through high school."

Morgan ate, happy to listen to him talk about the goofy things he did in the store when his uncle wasn't around. Nick's voice had a cozy lilt in its friendly Midwestern twang. For the first time in a long time, she didn't feel so utterly alone.

"Listen to me ramble," he said, catching her gaze. "What about you, Miss Morgan? What's your story?"

Her feet twitched against Ranger's belly and he grunted. She started to push away from the table, to fling her legs around and bolt, but Nick's concerned gaze kept her there, kept her still.

"If that question was inappropriate, I apologize," he said, watching her. "I didn't mean to offend or overstep—"

"My family was killed when I was little," she blurted, wincing at his shocked gasp. "I spent most of my life in the foster system."

"That must've been awful."

"It wasn't great," she admitted, unable to stop a nervous chuckle as the years of pent up loneliness and regret fell out of her. "The state sent me to my Uncle Paulie and Aunt Mary for a while. That was okay, I guess. They were old and mostly ignored me, but she got sick, some kind of cancer, I think. And after she died, Uncle Paulie, well, he just faded away. Quit caring about himself and didn't bother to feed me or take me to school. I was eight when the state took me away again."

He nodded for her to continue, but didn't say a word.

"So I bounced from hell hole to shit heap. Some folks were nice enough, some hollered all the time, or just wanted a slave." She shrugged then, unable to explain feeling worthless, like an empty bottle cast aside for recycling over and over again. "But the state had incentive programs for us fosters to go to school. It took me a year and a couple of crap tests, but I finally passed and went to college. And that's where I met Darcy."

She choked back the tightening in her throat. *Why am I telling him all this,* she thought, *this man I barely know?* but the words kept coming, a long backed-up flood she couldn't stop or control. "She was the only friend I ever had. We were roommates, closer than sisters."

He smiled and grasped her hand. For once, she didn't yank away. His grip was strong and comforting. Solid. "I'm glad you found her."

"Me, too." She managed a smile. "We'd shared everything. Clothes. Laundry soap. Secrets. Everything. Darcy's birth family had died in a car accident right after she was born, but she'd gotten adopted by a really nice couple that couldn't have their own kids. They loved her, took care of her. She had a house and pets and vacations to Mount Rushmore. So she was lucky there. I never had any of that."

Morgan took a deep breath and glanced away, shrugging, as she removed her hand from his. "You surely don't want to hear all this."

"I don't mind listening."

She sighed. *Maybe I need to tell it, at least Darcy's part of it anyway.* Morgan looked back at him, at his warm, caring face, and finally nodded. It felt good to talk, to remember, to let Darcy's memory free without all the mess of the house and cops. "We had so much in common, but we were opposites too. Like I'm shy, but Darcy was almost unable to go to class, she was so afraid of people. She'd sit in the back corner, as far away from everyone else as possible. If anyone approached her she'd lock up, unable to move or speak or anything. You know how if you come across an animal in a road, sometimes they'll freeze?"

"Yeah, either that or run back and forth in terror."

"Exactly," Morgan said, nodding. "Darcy would freeze. I'd run. She was methodical, I was creative, but we both majored in communications. The same but opposite." She smiled again, remembering how Darcy called her 'Pony', first because of her equine name, but later because she was so prone to bolting away. And she'd called Darcy 'Mule'. If Darcy made up her mind, nothing could change it. Ever. They'd even drawn little two-headed horses on their notebooks and tennis shoes. Pony and Mule. Friends forever.

At least until Darcy died. And lied to her.

Nick's brow furrowed. "I understand your skittishness. Hell, if I'd spent most of my life being passed around like a hot potato I'd be jumpy too, but why did your friend freeze like that? What was she afraid of?"

Morgan was on her feet and scrambling away before she knew she was moving at all. She barely heard Nick call her name or the sound of her shoes rapping out the door and down the back steps. She ran, south toward the far end of town and the fields beyond. The wind teased her hair and dried her cheeks as the tears streamed down, scalding like her memories. Her childhood had been horrid, a random mishmash of abuse, neglect, and servitude as lawyers and social workers decided what was best for her. The same bureaucracy had, however, granted Darcy a childhood filled with people who loved her. So much the same, yet so vastly different. But she and

Darcy both knew that Morgan had really been the lucky one.

She had never been raped.

* * *

Morgan heard little more than the rhythmic crunch of gravel beneath her shoes and a low flutter of wind through the corn as she ran. From the day they'd met, Darcy had been stiflingly shy, but when Ryder had recognized the anime character on Darcy's t-shirt and asked her if she wanted to maybe play Mario some time, she'd blushed then almost folded into herself and disappeared. In a way, Darcy's trembling nervousness was cute. She'd been home-schooled and had experienced only limited contact with kids her age, especially boys. Boys were alien, fascinating, intriguing. But to actually talk to a boy, perhaps date a boy, well, to Darcy, the concept was both highly desirable yet utterly inconceivable.

Morgan flinched and took the next left to barrel down a field road. Morgan had spent most of her life in homes with brothers, and had even gone on a few dates. She barely understood Darcy's fascination. Boys were boys. What was the big deal?

With the best of intentions, she'd ultimately been the one to convince Darcy to go out with Ryder. They'd shared a class and she'd found the Chemistry major to be quiet, bookish, and totally ignored by the other students. He might not have been as bright as Darcy, but he was... soft. Inoffensive. Invisible.

Safe.

Who better for super-shy Darcy, she'd reasoned, than a guy like Ryder? They could geek out over science fiction movies together. And it wouldn't hurt her to get away from the books and have a little fun.

Darcy had finally succumbed to temptation, and Morgan heard

all the giggly details of an evening of video games and microwaved burritos until the wee hours of the morning. Darcy and Ryder's second 'date' had been another quiet pairing of *Doctor Who* and pizza in the dorm lounge. They ate lunch together twice, then, on a Friday, Ryder had shyly offered to skip gaming and pay for a movie, take Darcy on a real date.

Darcy had spent the afternoon fretting over her clothes and hair, and had wistfully wondered if pasty-bland Ryder would try to kiss her. It had been so great to see her smile.

Morgan had waited up to hear all about the date, but Darcy didn't come home, didn't call or answer her phone, and, when curfew came and went, Morgan notified campus security.

Ryder's roommate hadn't seen him either, and the police soon arrived. No one at the movie theater remembered them, or the pizza joint, or anywhere else they were supposed to go. Morgan sat a tense vigil with Darcy's parents, Ed and Anne, waiting for even the tiniest slip of news. Had there been an accident? Had they run off to get married? Two quiet, nerdy college kids didn't just fall off the planet. Where *were* they?

Ryder staggered back to his dorm in the wee hours of the morning and his roommate turned him in. After a brief interrogation by campus security and the local cops, Darcy was found naked and semi conscious in a storage room behind the gymnasium, still suffering the effects of a date rape drug Ryder had made in Chem Lab.

Morgan continued her vigil with Darcy's parents through reports from doctors, through meetings with the police, lawyers, and school officials. In the end, Ryder had gone to prison and Darcy had gone to therapy—it and the remainder of her tuition, books, room and board fully paid by the college. Morgan's grades that semester and the next had been abysmal, but she did everything she could to help Darcy heal, at least until the academic office banished her from classes.

After Ryder, Darcy trusted no one, nor allowed herself to be alone with anyone but Morgan or her parents. Always. They'd even talked about it back in May, how she'd never spoken to the UPS guy, how she preferred video-conference meetings with vendors, or how she bought nearly everything online so she wouldn't have to step into a crowded store.

Seven years after Ryder, Darcy was still terrified of strangers and, unexplained trip to Wisconsin or not, there was no way, no possible way, that she'd allow someone else in her car.

Morgan reached the end of the field road and stopped, bent at the waist and hands on her knees, to catch her breath. She tried again to reassure herself that the blood in Darcy's car was old, but the sick twist in her gut wouldn't let her worry die. "Darcy's parents are dead," she said aloud, "and I was in New York. Who would Darcy let into her car?"

The corn offered no answers, only rustling whispers in the wind.

Morgan caught her breath and stood, looking out over the fields. The corn was mid-chest tall and, in the distance, she saw Hackberry's grain elevator and water tower. She smiled at the landmarks and stretched. *Finally learning my way around and I'm not getting lost this time.*

Quads loosened nicely, she stood straight again, gaze riveted on the water tower as a realization pinged in her head. Darcy, a healthy, twenty-five-year-old hermit had died. In Wisconsin. Where they'd gone to school.

Where Ryder was imprisoned.

And blood was in Darcy's car.

Morgan sprinted for home.

EIGHT

MORGAN'S CLOTHES WERE ONCE AGAIN FILTHY with road dust and mud. Her legs hurt, her feet throbbed, but, with the grain tower in sight, she managed to make it back to town without getting lost. She walked up the back alley toward home while Ranger barked and raced back-and-forth just inside of the fence as if demanding to know what she was doing taking a run without him.

"Hey buddy," she said, a guilty tremor in the pit of her stomach as she entered her back yard. "Sorry you got stuck out here alone. I just..." She sighed and knelt to pick up his ball while he covered her face in doggy kisses. "I got hurt really bad once," she confessed, her voice soft. "*Really* bad. PTSD bad." She tossed the ball and Ranger charged after it. Watching him sprint across the yard, she mumbled, "I couldn't run then, so whenever I get scared now I run away. I don't mean to, but... I can't help myself. I'm too broken, I guess."

Ranger bounded back with the ball.

"Sometimes I think I need someone, something... I don't know. Maybe to be steady when I can't. It was Darcy, but now I have you, right?"

He looked up at her, tail wagging as if to assure her that he totally understood. She threw the ball again and sat on the back steps as her mind shifted to Darcy's death.

A short search online would tell her if Ryder was still in prison, but... but what if he wasn't?

An electric-green dragonfly flitted around her head, apparently curious as to what grimy creature had entered its realm. It sped

away when Ranger approached, then came back, hovering just past
Morgan's nose before continuing on with its afternoon hunting.

Ranger dropped the ball in her lap. "What if he's loose? Will
the police believe he hurt her again?" she asked, but Ranger's focus
was on the ball and his only comment was to *throw it, throw it please!*

Morgan tossed the ball one last time, then stood, waiting for
Ranger to return and follow her into the house.

Her laptop lay where she'd left it on the office floor, a scrap of
paper on top.

Handwritten, in an efficient mish-mash of print and script was:

I didn't mean to upset you. Please call me and let me know
you're okay.

Nick

Aw, shit. Morgan felt a tight clench in her lower belly. She'd
run away in yet another Morgan Panic, during the middle of lunch,
leaving the poor guy not only confused but un-paid.

Crap.

Cursing herself for running away—*Again!*—she sat on the floor
and opened her laptop. A few clicks on Google indicated Ryder had
been released from prison nearly a year before and transferred to a
psychiatric hospital in Oshkosh.

Shaking, Morgan closed her laptop and stood. *Ryder's out of*
prison, now Darcy's dead, she thought, pacing while Ranger watched.
Do I call the cops? Lock the doors? What do I do? Paper crackled in her
fist and Morgan opened it to see the wadded note from Nick.

Call me and let me know you're okay, written in an odd yet
efficient hand.

He's worried about me, Morgan thought, shame tainting the back
of her mouth. *He's rescued me, bent over backwards to help me, and all*
I've done is run away. And it's late Friday afternoon. Heading into the
weekend. And he hasn't been paid. So much for making a friend.

She found his receipt on the dining room table beside the cloth-covered remnants of the broken hard drive. Not only was the total due more than reasonable, she had ample cash in her pack.

I should've paid him at lunch, before lunch, she thought as she dug out her cell phone. *Damn you, Morgan, can't you keep your feet still long enough to pay your bills, at least? Get him taken care of, then call the cops and tell them about Ryder.*

The phone rang twice before he picked up. "It's Nick," he said, sounding distracted, but Morgan heard no electronic beeps or boops, only keyboardy clicks.

"Hey," she said, shifting on her feet, her free hand clenched against her pounding forehead. "It's Morgan. Sorry I ran off like I did. I—"

The clicky sounds stopped. "Morgan? Thank God. Are you all right? Where are you?"

"I'm home. Well, at Darcy's house."

"But you're okay?"

"Yeah. Just had to run," she said, stifling down a nervous laugh. "I do it all the time."

"As long as you're okay," he said, clicks resuming and his voice sounding distracted again.

"I'm fine," she said, gaze rolling to the ceiling. "Totally normal for me, but, well, I *need* to pay you."

"Eh, you can get me on Monday. I ordered your part and it should be in that morning sometime."

"No. You don't understand. I have to do things like this right away, because I'm a ditz and it doesn't take much for me to totally space stuff off, and then it becomes a problem."

"Uh huh," he mumbled. "You can just pay me Monday when I bring your control board."

Morgan rubbed her eyes. She was not going to leave him short of cash for the weekend, especially not after all he'd done for her. Uh uh, no way. "Can't you just come get the money? Because I *will* forget, then I'll feel guilty."

"Can't," he said over the clicks. "Working at the store updating pricing and sales for this next week, and they're a mess."

"After you're done, then?"

"It'll be too late. I have to go. Glad to know you're all right."

And the call clicked off.

Morgan closed her phone and frowned at Ranger. "I think he's mad at me," she sighed. *Not that I blame him. But I have to make that other call.*

The envelope the detectives had left sat on the sideboard. Morgan opened it and rooted through to find the older detective's card.

Detective Hildebrandt answered on the third ring.

Morgan paced across the dining room and tried to keep her voice level. "Darcy was raped, in college. He's out of jail. Have you—"

"Miss Miller," the detective said, "we are well aware of Miss Harris's past trauma, and I assure you that we've met with her prior assailant and do not, at this time, consider him a suspect."

Morgan stopped pacing and gestured at the ceiling. "But Ryder's in *Wisconsin*. He's hurt her before. How can he not be a suspect?"

"We have already looked into his potential involvement, Miss Miller, and, based upon evidence, will no longer pursue that possibility."

"But..." Morgan wanted to scream, but managed to clench back her fury. "But *why*? He raped her and left her for dead!"

"I'm not at liberty to say, Miss Miller. I have to go now."

Morgan stood there, staring at her silent phone, mouth working but no sounds coming out, other than confused gibberish. *How can they not consider him after all that's happened? It makes no sense!*

She paced, Ranger watching, and felt panic gather in her muscles. She'd already taken two runs and, despite the need to bolt pinging in her brain, she remained rational enough to realize that a third sprint, especially one fueled by fear and worry, would likely injure her exhausted legs and, once again, leave her stranded and lost in the middle of rural nowhere.

I have to do something! she thought as she paced from the living room to the kitchen and back again. *I'll go mad if I have to stay still. Stark raving insane. Gotta run, gotta go, gotta—*

"I'm sick of all this mess," she muttered and pulled a stack of papers off the dining room sideboard. Then a pile of books. More papers.

They fluttered to the floor in a low, rustling thwump, a bigger mess and sprawl than they were before.

Morgan sat on the floor and sorted, muttering, "Garbage, garbage, garbage," as she worked. Newspapers from a year and a half ago. Old magazines. Time Life books. Years-old horse calendars. Recipes and movie reviews printed off the internet. Filthy, musty piles of crap.

She found garbage bags under the sink, and an empty packing box flattened and stuffed beside the fridge. Papers went into the bag, books in the box. She emptied the top of the sideboard and opened the first drawer, nearly everything going right into the trash as she worked her frustration against the mess.

Halfway through the drawer she found tourist-trap saucers, matchbooks, and spoons, so she located another box and a black marker to label the boxes. *Papers for recycling. Books. Junk.*

Kelly Clarkson blaring from her laptop, Morgan continued to sort. By the time her grumbling belly suggested that she might want to think about supper, she'd filled five trash bags with paper for recycling, two boxes of assorted trinkets and junk for Goodwill, and four boxes of old books for the library.

And the dining room was, if not clean, at least presentable. Morgan rewarded herself with a glass of iced tea and a five-minute stretch before a closet-by-closet search for the vacuum cleaner.

She had removed dusty-musty curtains from one window and had just climbed onto a chair to remove the second set when someone rapped on the front door. Ranger was excited to see them.

Jannis smiled from beyond the screen. "Hey, hon," she said as Morgan opened the door and invited her in. "I was just heading to town and wondered if you needed anything from the store or wanted to tag along." She glanced into the dining room and grinned. "Cleaning?"

"Trying to clear out excess junk, anyway," Morgan said as she stretched and popped her back. After years of living out of a backpack, clutter and excess confounded her. "I'd love to go to the store. Can you give me a minute to change clothes?"

Jannis assured her she had plenty of time, so Morgan changed and fetched her pack.

The evening ride to Albert Lea was nice enough, still unfamiliar but no longer alien, and Morgan found Jannis to be decent, if talkative, company. After a few stops to pick up odds and ends, Jannis pulled into Hawkins Grocery's parking lot and fished a store ad from her purse. "I usually shop at HyVee, but Hawkins is having a great sale on top sirloin," she said, showing Morgan the flyer as they walked toward the door. "Would you like to come over for supper tomorrow? Frank grills an amazing steak."

Morgan shifted her pack higher on her shoulder and wondered if Nick was still keying in price changes. "Sure. What can I bring?"

Jannis laughed and patted Morgan's arm even as Morgan flinched away. "Just bring yourself, hon."

Before Morgan began to protest, Jannis grabbed a cart and

hurried toward the produce.

A teenage clerk stocked a shelf with butter crackers—On Sale! 1.99!—a few steps ahead and Morgan asked him if Nick Hawkins was around. The boy grunted an affirmative and gestured toward a set of steps leading up to a windowed office.

Morgan paused at the closed door at the top, not sure if she should bother him or not, but the door opened and a beefy, middle-aged man in an apron caught himself before running headlong into her. His nametag said *Pat—Manager* and laugh lines smiled beside his eyes.

"Sorry, miss, this area isn't for customers," Pat said, the lines deepening into a comfortable grin, much like Nick's. "Is there something I can help you with?"

"I... I just need to talk to Nick."

"Go on in, then," Pat said, giving her a friendly nod before hurrying down the steps and calling out for Clark to grab a mop.

Nick sat at the far side of the room facing a computer monitor but his gaze focused on a pad of paper beside the keyboard. He typed steadily, not looking up as one screen changed to another. He paused only when she approached.

"Dammit, Rob, I just told Pat I won't be done for another half hour or so," he muttered, as he glanced at the screen and resumed typing. "It's not my fault you'd fucked up the numbers. Again." He typed three numbers on that screen and said, turning toward her, "You mighta convinced him to make you assistant manager, but I'm not taking the blame for—"

He stammered and burst to his feet. "Morgan? What are you doing here?"

"Jannis needed groceries," she said, shrugging, "and, well, I thought, since I was here, that I could pay you?"

He sighed, shaking his head and smiling. "You didn't have to do that. I told you I could wait 'til Monday."

"I know." Morgan shrugged off her pack. "But I need to take care of this." She glanced up at him before rooting in her pack. *How can I explain that if I don't pay you right away, I might forget all about it during a run, or think that I had because I intended to, or any of a hundred things?* Her hand closed around the envelope of cash and she nodded to herself. *At worst, I'll pay you twice. That's far better than not paying you at all.*

She held the envelope out for him, and her smile faltered as he hesitated.

"I don't want to leave you strapped for cash," he said.

"You won't. Just take it."

"Thank you," he said at last, putting the envelope in his pocket without opening it. "I didn't mean to upset you earlier. It really wasn't—"

The door behind them banged open and a college-aged guy in a store apron stomped in. "Dammit, Nick, you *know* I need those fucking prices," he snapped, gaze raking over Morgan. "You're supposed to be keying in updates, not playing footsie."

Morgan flinched away even as Nick strode forward to insert himself between her and the young man. "She's a client, so watch your mouth, Rob. And you know damn well I would've finished more than an hour ago if you hadn't listed the wrong SKUs to start with. So shut your yap, take responsibility for your own fuck ups, and get your ass back to work."

The boy sneered and took a step closer to Nick. "You're just pissed because Uncle Pat made me assistant manager and I'm your boss."

"And I used to babysit you." Nick sighed and turned away. "Just do your job and let me do mine, so neither of us will spend another weekend listening to your folks making excuses for you."

Rob muttered an expletive and left, slamming the door behind him while Morgan looked from Nick to the door then back to Nick again.

"Sorry about that," he said. "He's my cousin, an only child, and, somehow, he got the idea that he's the end all authority on the universe and the world owes him its adoration." He gave Morgan an embarrassed smile. "His bark's a lot worse than his bite."

"It's okay," Morgan said, dragging her pack over her shoulder. "I've met a lot worse." She nodded goodbye and turned to go. "Have a good weekend."

"You too," he said, a perplexed frown on his face. He still stood in the middle of the office when she closed the door.

NINE

ON THE RIDE HOME FROM THE STORE, Morgan pressed against her door, knees up and arms curled around them, leaving Jannis unable to touch her without stretching. Dark fields sped past under a chattering cloud of endless conversation and friendliness. Everything outside the window seemed so big, so vast and empty, the fields illuminated by lightning from a far away thunderhead.

Flinching away from yet another touch-attempt, Morgan shivered and rubbed her arms. *My only friend in this rural wasteland is a touchy-feely chatterbox. Yay for me.*

Jannis fell silent, perhaps for a quarter mile of road, then she asked, "Morgan, I know it's none of my business, but are you all right? Did Nicholas say something, do something?"

Morgan turned her head to gape at Jannis. "Nick?" she asked, confused. He'd been consistently gallant and kind. Sweet. "Why would you think—"

Jannis stared straight ahead, her features briefly brightened by the headlights of an oncoming car. "You haven't said more than a couple of words since you left him, and you're curled up against that door like a frightened kitten."

Unwilling to let anyone think Nick was the reason for her nervousness, Morgan forced her legs to relax, made her feet press against the floor beside her pack, but her arms remained wrapped around her belly and her shoulder crushed tight against the door. How could she tell this woman, her neighbor who had already helped so much, that her constant attention was stressful and intimidating? "I just get... overwhelmed sometimes, that's all. He was fine. Busy. I just needed to pay him."

"Of course," Jannis said, obviously not agreeing.

Morgan pursed her lips. "You don't believe me?"

"Morgan, honey, I've taught middle school for thirty-seven years. I know infatuation when I see it."

Morgan resumed gazing out the window. The Hackberry sign approached then passed. "I am not infatuated."

"Of course you're not."

They continued in silence the few short blocks to the house and Jannis pulled in her own drive. "I could invite him to the barbeque tomorrow night," she offered.

Morgan's cheeks grew hot as she fumbled for the latch. "No." She popped the door open and snatched her pack from the floor. Before Jannis could argue, Morgan said, "My friend just died, leaving me a mess to take care of, and I'm a city girl trapped in a sea of cornfields. Everything's just a bit too much too fast, okay? I'm stressed, not infatuated. So please, please do not invite him. He's just the guy who's fixing the computer, and to make it into anything more is not only embarrassing, it's unwarranted." She climbed out of the car and managed to smile back at Jannis. "Thank you for the ride. I'll see you tomorrow."

Before Jannis could respond, Morgan ran to the house, her thoughts churning. *Infatuated? Me? No way.*

But later that night, as she tried to fall asleep, she wondered.

* * *

After a long day of cleaning, laundry, and lugging papers to the recycle center, Morgan almost looked forward to Jannis's cookout. While still quite cluttered, the house was too big, too quiet and lonely, and her ears perked up at every rumble of traffic or wisp of conversation from folks walking down the road.

For the first time since arriving in Hackberry, she hesitated before entering most rooms, heart thudding, hands growing clammy, as she listened to the lonely echo of her own breath. She didn't long for conversation or togetherness, just the shine of someone else's face, the momentary gleam in their eyes that said *I see you, you're here, so am I, and we're both okay.* The weight of solitude wore on her, reminding her of the horrid memory of the hours she'd spent sick, bleeding, and alone. Of Breton, of Caspian, of Noriker. Of Libbey, gone to buy her dope. Of Darcy, disoriented and terrified in the hospital.

Morgan shivered and turned her thoughts away before she ran screaming out the door.

I need people, she thought as she set macaroni on to boil. *Safety in numbers, feeling like part of the hive. Alone, I'm a target, or at least I feel like one.*

She played fetch with Ranger as the pasta cooked, then, after she'd rinsed it and mixed in the mayo and chopped vegetables, decided she should shower before the party.

No one hid behind the bathroom door, in the closet, or anywhere else, and Ranger plunked down on the rug to gnaw on a hunk of mangled rawhide. Assuring herself that no one would enter without Ranger warning her, she turned on the shower and stripped, brushing her teeth while the water warmed.

She'd avoided looking at herself in a mirror for as far back as she could remember, but when Ranger stood and left the bathroom her gaze met her reflection's. She looked tired. Drained. And light filtering through the thin curtains accented the crisscrossing snarl of scars beside her left armpit. She turned, losing the scars once again to shadow, and kept her gaze rooted on the sink.

Far away, in the clotted recesses of her memory, a child,—Caspian? Bret?—pleaded, nearly screaming, *No! Please! I'll be good! I promise!*

Her memory looked up from a book, the pages ghostly and pale, lost to time, while her childhood self lay on her bunk, frozen, as the pleas continued. Then they stopped. Silence, much like the trembling quiet in her mind before the footsteps and the low creak of her bedroom door.

Without looking at her reflection, Morgan rinsed her toothbrush. She turned, dropping it in the sink, when Ranger bounded into the bathroom with a different chew toy.

"Hey, Buddy," she said, hand shaking as she rubbed him behind the ears. "Mind if I lock you in here with me?"

Ranger thumped his tail and assured her that he did, in fact, not mind one bit, so she closed the door.

A good dog is a damn fine thing. Oh yes.

They keep you from being alone.

* * *

Morgan put Ranger in the back yard and walked over to Jannis's precisely five minutes before six, but nearly a dozen people were already there. She was the youngest by more than a decade and recognized no one but Jannis, but she plastered on a smile and tightened her grip on the bowl of macaroni salad.

Jannis led her to a picnic table under an awning, introducing her to everyone they passed. They all seemed quite nice, but an aging woman named Betty was already giggling-drunk, and a doddering old coot flirted shamelessly with any female within earshot. Since the old fellow gripped his walker with one hand and cupped his hearing aid with the other, Morgan cautiously flirted back, always keeping both hands on her bowl as a ready excuse to avoid shaking hands.

Once she'd survived a circuit of introductions she'd barely remember, Morgan released her macaroni salad to the table and wondered if she could retreat back home. Or maybe stay if Jannis had invited Nick after all. She looked around, half expecting to see him approach with a bag of chips and an aw-shucks grin, but saw only older people talking.

A blondish middle-aged woman, Midwestern plump and on the tall side, stood across the table and squirted brown mustard on a bratwurst. "Jannis says you're from Madison?" she asked, glancing up and smiling into Morgan's eyes before returning her attention to a bowl of potato salad.

"When I was a kid," Morgan admitted, shrugging. "Been moving around a lot since college, though."

"Wanderlust lands in youngsters' feet sometimes," the woman said, nodding, as she moved around an elderly man eyeing a cherry trifle. "Our youngest daughter is a wanderer. In fact, she insisted on backpacking her way across Europe a couple of years ago, when she was sixteen. Her father, of course, had a conniption. His baby was not going to be alone and on foot in a foreign country, by God."

Two women to Morgan's left snorted and looked at the far end of the table at a stocky man scooping watermelon onto his plate. "*I* had a conniption?" he said. "I seem to recall *you* were the one frantic over rapists, thieves, and terrorists."

"Only because of the news," the woman said, flicking her hand to shoo a fly. She glanced at Morgan and winked. "They make it sound like the whole world is dangerous, but it's really not."

The man nudged aside a big guy in a cowboy shirt to stand beside his wife. "She says that now, but you should've seen her pacing and fretting at the airport. Beth's excited and ready to start her journey, while Donna here's a nervous wreck. You'd think she was going off to face a firing squad."

"You let your daughter go to Europe?" Morgan asked. "At sixteen?"

The man laughed and Donna said, "Backpacking? Oh hell no. But she did get to tour Italy and Greece with a school youth group." She popped a chip into her mouth and added, "I chaperoned."

The man winked at Morgan. "I think it was just an excuse to crawl through art museums in Florence. She had more fun than the kids did."

"I love to travel, but Mark never wants to go anywhere." Donna nudged her husband, "I have to take what I can get. Where all have you been?"

Morgan fetched a paper plate and felt all eyes turn to her. Her hands shook. At least Nick wouldn't be a stranger. At least he wouldn't stare. A quick glance assured her that he still hadn't come, so she put on a brave smile and said, "East coast, mostly. Boston, Philly, Charleston. Wherever whim takes me. It's not so much about traveling and sightseeing and all. I'm just not good at staying in one place very long."

Mark said, "Well, I hope you decide to stay in Hackberry a while. It's a nice town."

"And your house is just darling," Donna added. "It's just the cutest thing."

"Oh yes, it is!" one of the other ladies murmured.

"It's really not my house," Morgan said, shrugging. "My friend died, and, well, I dunno…"

"Aw, hell," Mark mumbled, glancing past Morgan. "She's coming."

The man in the cowboy shirt muttered, "Fuck," and turned away to retreat toward the back fence. The two ladies at Morgan's left also made a hasty exit toward the rose bushes, leaving their beverages sitting on the table.

"She? She who?" Morgan glanced over her shoulder but just saw a milling group of middle-aged and elderly Midwesterners in jeans, comfy shirts, and ten-dollar haircuts.

"Midge Parson. And she brought that damn dog." Donna scurried around the table and scooped a few more things onto Morgan's plate before nudging her to the right. "Gotta move, honey. I think there are some chairs over here."

Mark followed close behind Morgan's left elbow. "I cannot deal with her today. Not after the mess in Evanstown."

Morgan let them herd her away, but, as she looked back, she saw the old woman from the bank hobble to the food table, the yappy little dog tugging at the end of its leash. "You know her?" Morgan asked.

"*Everyone* knows her," Donna whispered. "She used to run the patient accounting department at the hospital, and she expected every service to be paid in full, not in thirty days or ten days, or even day after tomorrow. Immediately. Always right this moment. And if you didn't have insurance she'd make your life a living hell and be garnishing your wages before you'd even got home from the emergency room."

"Lots of folks around here are out of work and can't afford insurance," Mark said, "but she didn't care, didn't believe in payment plans or assistance or scheduling cheaper outpatient procedures. The bill was the bill. Period. And it was due right then, preferably before treatment, spare no expense, accept no excuse." He paused before adding, "She thought everyone, insured or not, was trying to swindle, steal, and cheat the hospital. There's not one glimmer of compassion or patience in that woman. Thank God she finally retired."

They found an empty bench and a chair between the lilac bushes and the back porch. Donna motioned for Morgan to sit on the bench. Morgan sat, and Donna plunked down beside her.

Mark handed Donna his plate and pulled the chair close enough for Donna to put a foot on the seat. "What can I get you ladies to drink?" he said.

"Just tea," Donna said, craning her neck to see past the other attendees. "Please don't come over here. Please don't come over here," she mumbled.

Morgan scrunched into her corner of the bench as she glimpsed the yappy dog in the midst of denim-covered legs. "Iced tea's fine," she said. "Thank you."

Mark nodded and turned toward the food table. He squared his shoulders and said, "Cover me, Danno, I'm going in."

Morgan heard Donna chuckle, then Mark strode into the retreating crowd.

Morgan glanced toward the driveway as a middle-aged couple walked up to join the party. Still no sign of Nick or his truck. Maybe Jannis had decided not to invite him after all.

"Looking for something?" Donna asked.

"No. No one."

Mrs. Parson tottered past, led by her little dog and glaring at anyone who drew too near. Her gaze landed on Morgan and Donna. Her lip curled back in a sneer. "Should have known you'd hunker down with thieves," she snarled at Donna then continued on.

Donna released a relieved breath. "Thank goodness that's over."

"I don't know why she thinks I'm a thief," Morgan muttered, picking at her supper. "All I did was jog around town."

"Don't let it bother you," Donna said, shrugging. "She labels *everybody*."

"Some people are just like that," Mark said, handing Morgan a plastic cup of tea. "You can't let it get to you."

Donna removed her foot from the chair and, nodding, met her

husband's gaze as he sat. "I keep trying to remind myself there's good in everyone," she sighed. "But it's a struggle."

Awkward silence stretched between them and Morgan asked, "Are we still talking about Mrs. Parson?"

Mark attacked his melon. "No. Our youngest son married a woman who..." he shrugged. "He's a good boy, so there must be good in her. Somewhere."

"Not that I've found," Donna muttered before taking a sip of her tea and starting on her supper. "But, enough of that mess. Tell us a little about yourself, Morgan."

"Not much to tell, really," she said. "I'm pretty boring. When I'm not wandering about, I mostly write reviews for an urban living site, but it's a mess right now." She shrugged. "I've been trying to get the website updated since my friend died... then I guess I'll be running it, too."

Mark grinned. "Ah, a writer and an entrepreneur!"

Morgan laughed. "Not really."

"Do you write anything besides the reviews?" Donna asked.

Morgan shrugged and looked away. "Kind of. I've published a couple of little stories on e-zines, but they don't pay anything, so they don't really count."

"Of course they count," Donna said. "Writing is writing, and published is published."

Morgan smiled and chewed. It really wasn't quite that simple. It's not like she'd ever had anything in print. "What do you folks do for a living?" she asked.

Mark said, "I work at the fire station over in Glenville. Assistant Chief, supposedly, but I mostly make sure the county lives up to its promises for our guys." He frowned at his plate. "Thirty years on calls only to spend the rest of my days filling out paperwork or arguing on the phone with bureaucrats."

"I bet you have a lot of stories to tell," Morgan said.

"I can tell you to keep your smoke alarms working and a fire extinguisher in your kitchen. We've lost too many people over the years because they didn't buy a simple little battery."

"Oh, don't start preaching about fire safety again," Donna said. "Morgan's a bright girl, not a grade-schooler."

"Maybe so," Mark said, glaring at her with a good-natured frown. "But if you're ever caught in a house fire, you don't try to stop it yourself, or save *anything*. You just get out. You hear?"

Morgan had seen a couple of apartment fires and was ever thankful she'd been across the street and not inside. "Yessir. I'll smash through a window and jump if I have to."

Mark chuckled. "Atta girl. I knew I'd like you."

Morgan glanced at Donna. "What do you do, ma'am?"

"I'm on the pulmonary ward at the hospital," she said. "Pneumonia, emphysema. Lots of breathing treatments. It's always a barrel of fun, but I've cut back on my hours. It's just too tiring. Rather play with my grandkids."

Morgan asked about their grandchildren and both produced pictures, Mark's in his wallet, Donna's on her phone. Four of them, and another on the way. Morgan *ooohed* and *aaahed* appropriately, and found herself fidgeting when Donna asked if she had any children.

"No, not me," Morgan said. "Until a couple of days ago, I'd never even had a dog before, let alone kids."

"So, does that mean 'not yet', or 'not ever'?" Donna asked.

Morgan stammered and Mark said, "Don! You're embarrassing the poor girl!"

"It means the opportunity hasn't arisen," Morgan blurted before Donna could respond. "So, I guess I haven't really thought about it."

Mark picked at the last remnants of his supper while Donna watched Morgan with tight curiosity. "You're a pretty girl, Morgan. I'm sure you've had at least some opportunity to consider children."

"I don't really stay one place very long. And... I never knew my dad, and my mom..." she shrugged. "I grew up in the foster system and, well, when I have kids, *if* I have kids, I want something better than that for them. Two parents. Stability. Little league and piano lessons and all that stuff I never had." She managed to meet Donna's gentle gaze. "It just hasn't happened and I won't even think about having kids until I know it will."

* * *

Morgan felt a flash of surprise as night fell. Three hours had sped by while she chatted with Donna and Mark, and a few others who had joined their conversation. Despite Morgan's initial apprehension, everyone had been wonderfully friendly, and she'd even been invited to join the Hackberry Lions by the big man in the cowboy shirt. She'd seen more pictures than she could count, of babies, teenagers, hot rods, remodeling projects, and one grand-puppy proudly passed around by a woman whose daughter had decided that, for this week at least, she was a lesbian. But she'd surely come to her senses soon.

Morgan and Donna helped Jannis clean up while Mark and Jannis's husband, Frank, bought beer at the gas station. Once the mess had been cleared, Morgan tried to wish everyone a good night, but Jannis insisted she stay and play cards. Without her, they'd be one person short of a full table.

Morgan found herself in the kitchen while Frank located the cards and Mark handed out beverages. Donna settled in beside her and opened a beer. "Ever play ten point pitch?"

"No," Morgan admitted. "Just rummy. A little solitaire." Across from her, Betty tittered and hollered for another beer.

"It's a trump game," Frank said, and explained the values of the cards. Morgan understood high, low, and jack, even the jokers and the three, but 'game' didn't make much sense at all.

"It'll make plenty of sense after a couple of hands," Donna assured her. "And I'll help."

"Help? Heh. Cheat, you mean," Jannis said as she poured a bag of pretzels into a bowl.

Donna innocently sipped her beer and winked at Morgan. "It's only cheating if you get caught."

Frank coughed a laugh as he shuffled. "Don't listen to them, Morgan. Jannis's still miffed because Donna won nearly every hand last time we played."

"She just got lucky." Jannis settled into her seat and reached for a beer.

"It's skill, baby," Donna said as Frank dealt the cards.

Morgan relaxed. The ladies were just teasing each other, like ball players talking smack.

Donna quickly sorted her cards then leaned over to help Morgan, explaining in whispers and the touch of her finger the various potential bids in Morgan's hand.

Mark won the bid and, as the hand played out, Morgan found herself relaxing. Jannis's little party had, intentionally or not, surrounded her with people who treated her like a member of their hive. A new member, certainly, but a member nonetheless.

Hours later, as Morgan walked home, yawning, she smiled. Not once after politely admitting her reluctance to shake hands had Jannis, or anyone else, touched her beyond the most casual of contact when passing a drink or a card. Mark or Donna always seemed to be in the way. As if they knew or understood. As if they were protecting her.

Morgan barely had time to consider why they would do such a thing before Ranger rushed to her, barking excitedly and chasing all such thoughts from her mind.

* * *

Morgan dreamed of sorting computer parts and musty old playing cards in Jannis's kitchen, which would have been a simple enough task if Ranger wasn't always trying to steal her trump. "I need that jack of clubs," she said, ruffling his ears, "but you can have this seven of hearts."

Ranger wriggled and took the card but immediately let it fall, his teeth baring in a low growl. His hackles rose, and his legs, usually bouncy and energetic, turned stiff, poised to lunge. He stared at her, through her, past her, his eyes no longer familiar and warm, but dangerous.

He said in an aw-shucks country voice, *I'm a good dog, oh yes, but I have teeth and I'm not afraid to rip you open with them.*

"Ranger? Buddy?" Morgan eased back, slowly, gaze riveted on Ranger's face, his hateful eyes, his teeth. Computer cables had tangled around Morgan's legs, holding her, and Ranger took a stiff step forward, the endless sear of his growl growing louder. A dribble of spit fell from his jaws and hissed on the floor.

I smell you, your hate, your filth, he snarled in that same aw-shucks country voice. He took another step, gaze focused somewhere in the back of Morgan's head, and his haunches settled downward, ready to spring. *I'm warning you, bitch. It's your last chance. Stay away from my people or I'll hurt you. Kill you if I have to.*

"It's just me." Morgan raised her hands to stop him, knowing full well she was powerless against eighty pounds of furious canine.

"Settle down, boy, sett—"

Ranger leapt, snarling, teeth snapping, and Morgan covered her head, lurching aside in the vain hope that he might not tear her to shreds, and she fell, startled, to the floor and darkness and the nearby snarls of her dog.

Panting and disoriented, she pushed herself up from the floor of Darcy's living room to see Ranger lunging at the front door in a wild, furious frenzy.

It wasn't her he'd wanted to attack, but whoever moved around on the porch. He clawed at the door, barking and growling, spittle reflecting glints from light that shone through onto his face.

A small flashlight.

Morgan pressed her spine against the lower frame of the couch, hands splayed on the rug and her heart slamming while Ranger snarled at the door.

Despite Ranger's snarls, the front door latch turned a quarter turn, then rattled, and Morgan thought a quick, thankful prayer that she'd locked it. She drew her feet beneath her. *There's escape out the back. Get to the gas station. Jannis's. Somewhere I'm not trapped.* Ranger, still illuminated by the light, took a step back and crouched, haunches settling, before he leapt at the door again in a snarling, snapping fury.

"You're lucky I don't kill you, you fuckin' dog," the person on the porch said, their raspy voice barely heard over Ranger's snarls. Not tall and heavy like a man, but shorter, softer. Morgan squinted. *One of the kids that had busted Darcy's computer?*

The light clicked off and Morgan heard footsteps move away then descend the steps. Ranger's furious lunges turned to threatening barks, then low growls as he paced at the door like a lion trapped in a cage.

Morgan stood, heart slamming, hands balled at her sides, for what seemed like a long time as cars drove down the highway. Somewhere nearby, a woman hollered for Cody to *shut the fuck up and get his ass to bed.*

Morgan took a breath and forced her hands to unclench. *Cody. One of the troublemaking kids Jannis had mentioned.* "It's okay," she said aloud. "Just a kid wanting to cause a little trouble. He's gone now."

Ranger paced, head low, tail straight, then he paused, offering one more dismissive snort before turning toward her.

He approached, cowering as if he was ashamed, but Morgan hugged him and informed him that he was indeed a very good dog.

TEN

MORGAN PUT THE JUVENILE INTRUDER out of her mind and focused on her work. By mid-morning Monday, she'd cleared most of the mess from the kitchen, living room, and dining room, other than several stacked boxes marked for delivery to Goodwill. Clutter was one thing—it could fit in the garbage bin if nothing else—but she didn't know what to do with ruined furniture.

She stood in the living room, frowning at a loveseat with a broken frame she'd just dragged from the back room, along with a sprung file cabinet and a highchair with a missing leg.

Who would keep a highchair without a rear leg? she wondered, shaking her head. *Will the garbage man take busted furniture?*

Ranger whooshed through the house to the front door and started barking and spinning about as Nick's familiar truck pulled into the driveway.

Smiling, Morgan went to the porch to meet him, Ranger barreling ahead as her furry, exuberant greeting committee. A woman from Jannis's party drove by in a minivan and honked. Morgan couldn't remember her name but she shyly waved. Although being noticed made her nervous, it was nice to be a member of the hive again.

"What's got you so cheerful?" Nick asked as he climbed out of the truck, a smallish cardboard box in hand.

"Nothing," Morgan said as she descended the porch steps. "Just waving to a neighbor."

He reached back into the truck for his toolbox. "Ah, good, you're settling in." Ranger sniffed the seat and seemed to contemplate jumping in, but Nick shooed him and closed the door.

"I'm not settling in."

Nick raised an eyebrow. "Oh? So the sun tea on the porch, opened curtains, and waving to neighbors doesn't mean a thing?"

She grinned and walked with him to the house. "Nope. That my new hard drive?"

"That and the master controller to get your old one spinning again." They climbed the steps and he opened the door for her, but Ranger rushed past them both and bolted in.

Morgan felt secretly pleased when he commented on how much better the house looked. "I need to get rid of some junk, though," she said. "How's garbage service out here?"

"It'll be curbside," he told her. "I'm not sure what pick-up day Hackberry has. Wednesday, maybe. It's part of your water bill, and the City Clerk can get you all set up."

"Do they take furniture?"

Nick continued on to the dining room. "Yeah, but they're not going to take that loveseat for free. You'll probably be better off making a trip to the landfill." He removed the cloth covering the old drive and folded it. "All county residents get two free trips a year, with a certificate from your city clerk. So the landfill itself won't cost you a thing."

"Cool. Do they have a hauling service out here?"

Nick sat and shook his head. "In Albert Lea. But I have a pickup and I'd be happy to help for free."

She started to protest, but he said, "Look. One of the joys of having a truck is that people call wanting help moving or hauling or pulling someone out of a ditch. It's *normal*, okay? I've driven appliances down from Minneapolis and dragged deer carcasses from muddy fields, and moved I don't know how many people from one crappy apartment to another. It would be my pleasure to help you get rid of some junk."

Morgan sat and scowled at him. "I'd have to pay you, for your time at least. For gas."

"Eh," he said as he pulled a plastic-wrapped part from the box, "it's what friends are for. Just feed me and we'll call it even."

* * *

While Nick worked on the hard drive, Morgan gathered up Darcy's will and walked with Ranger to the city clerk's office. The clerk was a chatty woman who explained everything Morgan might ever want to know about living in Hackberry, including contact information for local businesses and a listing of the summer's upcoming events— like the fireman's auction, county fair, Lions fundraiser picnic, and city wide yard sale.

Once Morgan accepted the handouts, the woman settled in behind her computer. "Which house did you move into so I can change your billing?"

"Darcy Harris's. 326 Fieldmore Dr—"

"You mean the Millers," the city clerk chirruped, typing away.

"No. *Harris*. Darcy Harris. She passed away last month."

"No, no, honey," the clerk said, frowning at her. "That was Miss Miller. She'd been in that house since I started working here year before last. She's the only one who died last month. Car accident. Very sad."

The clerk pursed her lips and looked at Morgan, her head tilting. "Come to think of it, I don't think I ever talked to her. She'd just stick her payment in the mail slot and hurry off." The clerk stood and pointed out the window at Ranger scratching himself beside the bike rack. "But that is *definitely* her dog."

Morgan rubbed her forehead and tried not to get annoyed. Darcy was achingly shy, yes, but—

"So. What name do you want on the account?"

"Mine. Morgan Miller. I'll be paying it until I sell the place."

"Okaaaay," the clerk said, shaking her head. "It's already listed under M. Miller. Did you need me to change the M to Morgan?"

Weird. Morgan gathered up her papers. "No. That's okay, just leave it M. When's it due again?"

"The twenty eighth. I sent the bills out last Thursday." The clerk frowned at her as if contemplating a two-headed bird. "Didn't you get it? It should have been in your mail Friday."

Morgan kicked herself for not even *thinking* about checking the mailbox, right there in front of the house. "No, but I'll go check. Sorry to bother you."

She hurried from the city clerk's office before being asked any more odd questions, then gathered Ranger and jogged back to the house. The mailbox, marked *326–Harris*, was utterly empty except for a deserted spider web sagging just inside of the door.

Deciding that Bennet must have turned off Darcy's mail, Morgan sighed and jogged back to the post office on Main Street. The mail clerk expressed his condolences and examined Morgan's Wisconsin ID and the signatures on Darcy's will before handing Morgan two rubber-banded stacks of mail. A quick look showed magazines, grocery flyers and assorted junk mail for the Harris's, but no water bill.

"One more place I can look," he said as he sat down at the computer.

"Morgan Miller, and you've taken over the estate of the Harris's at 326 Fieldmore, right?"

Morgan nodded as the clerk keyed in her information. "That's odd," he said, squinting up at Morgan before tapping the screen.

"You already have a box billed to the Harris's address."

"*Me?*" Morgan asked. "I've never been here before. How can I have a P.O. box?"

The clerk squinted at the screen. "Box 72, Pony And Mule Web Development, under the name of Morgan Miller. You opened it years ago. You don't remember?"

Morgan swallowed the bitter taste from her mouth. *The water bill now the post office?* "No. I've never been here before," she said, wondering if it was a lie, if she'd somehow forgotten.

"It's definitely you. Same soc, same out of state ID, same signature, all marked for a small business account," the clerk said as he stood. "The box has two keys, but the computer says you only took one. I'll get the other for you, and your mail. There's quite a lot."

He soon returned with a key and four more bundles of mail, plus five bins of packages. All of the packages and most of the envelopes were sent to FrugallyUrban and other sites, but a staggering amount of mail was addressed directly to her. Including the water bill.

Morgan gathered up what she could and promised to come right back for the rest. Confused, she managed to lug the first bin to the house while Ranger snuffled about looking for places to pee.

When she dropped the heavy thing on the kitchen floor, Nick came from the dining room. "Everything okay?"

"I don't know," Morgan said, looking from him to the bin and back again. "There's all this mail." She swallowed and wondered if she was losing her mind along with her memory. "I really was not expecting this much mail."

He, too, frowned wide-eyed at the bin of packages and the bundles perched on top. "That is a *lot*, even though your friend died a month ago."

"There's more. A lot more," Morgan said, then turned to head back to the post office.

Nick followed. "How *much* more?"

"About four times more," she said, shrugging.

"I'll drive you."

The mail clerk had found a few larger packages to add to Morgan's stack, and Nick helped her load the whole pile into the back of his truck. Nothing she saw had a postmark date before June 15th. Nothing.

Once they'd carried the mail into the house, Nick returned to repairs and Morgan sat on the living room floor, sorting. When she finished, she counted eleven piles for websites, three of which the cops hadn't listed.

A good portion went right into the recycling bag. Morgan stared at the remaining piles for a few moments before grabbing the closest stack of envelopes, most addressed to her care of GlimmerGals. com, Acquisitions Editor.

Many asked permission to submit freelance articles about makeup, shoes, hair accessories, and cosmetic surgery, all things Morgan knew nothing about. A few included neatly-typed reviews and articles. Two were short romantic stories. Five were rather sizable checks, and almost all commented on how the links were down so they sent snail mail and they hoped that was all right.

Morgan read each query, her stomach tightening. They sounded so much like her own letters to sites and publishers, asking to please, *please* have her work considered for acceptance and a pittance of cash.

She set the letters on the floor again and ran her hand through her hair, tugging on it. She knew virtually nothing about makeup, yet found herself an acquisitions editor for a beauty and cosmetics site she'd barely heard of.

Morgan let out a tired sigh. *What the hell have you gotten me into, Darcy?*

She rummaged through Darcy's office to find a pad of paper then sat down again near the sorted stacks of mail to make a list of office supplies to help her properly sort and manage GlimmerGal's queries, samples, and advertising payments. Darcy's filing method had been, apparently, stuffing anything and everything into a clothes-basket in the closet. Or a plastic bin, cardboard box, or shopping bag.

Morgan had just started sub-sorting her third set of envelopes when Nick said, "I have the control board attached and am running a preliminary diagnostic on the file system. It'll take a while, probably about an hour and a half. Think I'm going to go get some lunch."

Morgan stretched before finishing the letter in her hand, a cheerful, rambling gush about how advice on The Short Basket had changed her life. Morgan had no idea what kind of site The Short Basket was. She set the letter aside as if it had grown hot. "Okay. Sounds fine."

Nick paused, shifting in the doorway. When she looked up at him, he said, "I know you're kind of stranded here, so you're welcome to come along if you want. If you need groceries or whatever."

She sighed, glowering at the mess of papers and boxes as she realized her day had turned surreal. "Thank you. I think I'm all right on groceries, but I can use some office supplies," she said at last, standing. "Something to keep this madness from taking over the house. Do you mind taking me somewhere they sell file cabinets?"

He flipped his keys in his hand. "There's a Staples in Austin."

* * *

By the time they left Staples, Morgan was quite thankful Nick drove a truck. She'd purchased nearly a whole office worth of supplies to get things organized. As Nick lifted a filing cabinet into the back, they discussed lunch and settled on a barbeque joint.

They'd just received pulled-pork sandwiches when Nick's phone rang. Looking at the phone, he muttered, "Goddammit," then sighed and looked at Morgan. "Just a sec, okay?"

She nodded an affirmative and began eating as Nick answered his phone. "I'm with a client," he said, obviously annoyed. "I reminded you this morn—"

He listened, scowling. "No. I can't. I have her hard drive to process, then a whole computer to put—"

He sagged and picked up his sandwich with his free hand. "Bacon. Stop. I told you I can't help you today. I have—" He took a bite. "Uh huh. Right. Not 'til tonight. Well that's not my problem, is it? I was home all day yesterday and you could have—"

He rubbed his forehead and muttered at the table. "Fine. Fine! Just shut up a minute and I'll ask her, okay? Yes, she's right here. We're having lunch. Arrgh. Dammit, Bacon, just give me a sec. I'll call you back."

He clicked off his phone and gave Morgan an apologetic and embarrassed frown before picking at his lunch.

"Bacon?" she asked, curious and slightly amused.

"Yeah," Nick sighed. "One of my roommates."

Morgan grinned. "How did you end up with a roommate named after cured pork?"

"We've been friends since we were kids, we'd lived in the same neighborhood and hung out together since we were little. He's always been heavy, and always loved junk food and fatty meat. He got the nickname in fourth grade. The guys devised this bacon eating contest, and he ate more than a pound of the stuff, so the name just stuck. Heck, his mom even calls him Bacon." Nick chuckled and splurted ketchup beside his fries. "He's a good guy but, some days, I swear he has the same number of brain cells as a doorknob."

Morgan chewed and swallowed, noting that Nick ignored his phone as it rang right there on the table. "So what's up with Bacon?"

"He bought a couch more than a week ago," Nick said between bites. "And the folks he bought it from need it gone today or they're busting it up and taking it to the dump. I knew it, heck, we all knew it, but did he ask for help hauling it home last week? This past weekend? Nope."

Morgan chuckled and shook her head. She'd known plenty of people who couldn't plan past their nose.

"So," Nick said, gesturing with a fry as his phone rang again, "he expects me to drop everything I'm doing to pick up a smelly old couch right this minute because he didn't remember yesterday when we all were home." He attacked his sandwich. "It's not my problem," he muttered. "It's not."

"But it's bugging you," she said, trying not to grin.

"Only because I'd promised him weeks ago I'd haul it if he found something. I mean, heck, he's been sleeping on the floor at our place since his girlfriend kicked him out a couple of months ago." Nick raised his head and frowned into her eyes. "Frankly, I was hoping he'd save up a little and buy a cheap mattress somewhere and they'd deliver, but no. Smelly, hide-a-bed couch. In a basement."

Morgan covered her mouth with her hand before she started laughing. The expression on Nick's face—a combination of pity, revulsion, exasperation, and love—was both funny and adorable.

"You understand my frustration," he said, chuckling.

Morgan nodded. "Oh, I think everyone knows someone like Bacon. For me, the worst was a girl on my dorm floor. I swear, Stacy couldn't find her brain if it jumped up and bit her on the nose and held on. And planning?" Morgan smiled and sipped her tea. "She'd remember she had a test the morning *of* the test. Everything was a crisis. Mad dashes, lots of screaming and throwing things. And I don't think she wore a clean shirt all semester because she always forgot to do laundry."

"Heh. Must be Bacon's sister."

Morgan winked. "Let's hope so. The world's safer if they don't breed."

Nick laughed, deep and hearty, then his phone rang again. He sighed and reached for it. "You sure this is okay? I can drop you off at the house."

"Of course it's okay," she said, waving off his concern. "I can be an extra set of hands if you need them. Get stuff out of your way, if nothing else."

He closed his gaping mouth then said, "You don't have to help."

"Really? Let's see," she said, holding up her fingers to count them. "You've rescued me from a storm, played fetch with my dog, got my internet working, driven me to get a filing cabinet and folders, and taken me out to lunch. I think I can manage to help move one little couch."

He chuckled and shook his head. "Hide-A-Bed. They're heavy."

"Yeah, well," Morgan said, "surely it'll be better than all that mail."

They smiled at each other, then Nick answered his phone.

* * *

They had no more than pulled into the driveway of a faded ranch house when a bearded ball of a man burst out the door and barreled toward them. He ran to the truck and ripped the door open just as Morgan managed to buckle herself into the center seatbelt. "Thanks, Nick. I know I'm a pain in the ass—"

Then he stopped, slack-jawed and babbling, as he stared at Morgan. "Holy shit. You didn't say *she* was coming."

Morgan swallowed, glancing at Nick as she struggled to keep her feet still. One hand fell to the seatbelt buckle, ready to release the catch and escape, even if she had to kick her way past Bacon to do it. *Don't stare. Please, don't stare.*

"Get in the truck," Nick said. "And put your eyes back in your head before you drop 'em in the driveway."

"Okay, okay," Bacon said, climbing into the cab. He huffed next to Morgan, knocking her against Nick before settling into his spot. He smelled faintly of cinnamon rolls and barbeque. "Um. Hi," he blurted, offering his hand. "I'm Bailey. Bailey Conner. And you are oh-my-God-amazing."

Morgan hoped the dried red streak alongside his thumb was barbeque sauce. She whimpered and leaned closer to Nick.

"Bacon, she's not interested in being your bestest friend, okay? She's a client. Put your hand away, and leave her alone."

Bacon nodded eagerly as he scrubbed his palm on his thigh. "No prob. I... I just wasn't expecting her to be so, so..." He swallowed and glanced quickly at Morgan's face before looking away again. "You didn't say she was *pretty*."

"Shut up, Bacon," Nick said as they backed out of the driveway.

"Shutting up. Totally." Grinning, he put both hands on his knees and stared straight ahead. They'd barely turned down the next block when he mumbled, "Wait'll I tell Scott that your client is—"

Nick slammed on the brakes.

Morgan yelped, startled, but Bacon slammed hard against the dashboard. He leaned back, gasping. "What the hell?"

"One time warning only," Nick growled. "We're doing you a favor, okay, a big goddamn favor, and she agreed to help. You so much as breathe one word to Scott or Chuckie about her, I'll not only beat the living shit out of you, I'll kick your ass out."

Bacon babbled, mouth working as he looked from Nick to Morgan to Nick again, then he managed to say, "You wouldn't. Couldn't. How can you manage to make rent if-"

"My name's on the lease, yours isn't. She's a nice lady who doesn't need to be ogled by you, and she's a client, okay? I *work for her* and Scott isn't gonna screw that up, especially over some flea-infested shit of a couch. You get me? If you can't shut the hell up, you can pack your crap and move out right now."

Bacon nodded, swallowing, his gaze on his grubby shoes. "Gotcha. Sorry, Nick. Shutting up now."

Morgan sat between them, stiff and nervous, but Nick sighed and drove. As houses once again turned to fields and ponds, Morgan tried to relax.

"Chuckie's mostly okay, but Scott's kind of trouble," Nick said, his voice lowering. "He…"

Nick sighed and shook his head, then Bacon mumbled, "He's a slut."

"Oh, gee, thanks," Nick said. "I was trying to be nice here."

Bacon stared out his window at a passing field of cows. "You're always nice. Chuckie's a spaz, I'm a slob, and Scott thinks with his dick. We've been that way since we were kids and everyone knows it. I make the messes, Chuckie freaks out, you figure out a way to fix it before we get in trouble, and Scott's too busy flirting to even notice."

Nick sighed and kept driving.

"I won't tell Scott, okay?" Bacon said, glancing over. "Chuckie will find out, he always does, but you're right. Scott doesn't need to know."

"Thank you."

Morgan looked back and forth between the two friends and wondered if she should have let Nick drop her off at Darcy's.

* * *

The couch was indeed smelly and in a basement, but the stairs to the back yard were wide and straight. Morgan assigned herself the job of carrying cushions and holding doors. It didn't take long for the two men to wrestle it outside and into the truck.

She found Bacon to be incredibly polite and gallant in his own nervous and awkward way, always shuffling ahead to open doors for her. Once they'd finished loading the couch, he held the truck door open and waited for her to get buckled in before entering. He babbled all the way home about how great it was going to be to sleep on a couch again.

Morgan smiled at his excitement. Having slept on a few benches, cots, and floors herself, she had to agree that a couch was a definite improvement.

A Pontiac with a missing fender sat in the drive as they pulled up. Nick's hands tightened on the steering wheel. "Did you call him?"

"I... I, uh..." Bacon mumbled, glancing at Morgan before looking at his shoes. "Well, I..."

Nick grumbled and turned off the truck. "Dammit."

"I was running out of time," Bacon mumbled as he climbed out of the truck. "You wouldn't answer your phone. What was I supposed to do?"

"Believe that I'd call you right back like I promised, and have enough sense to realize you can't cram a couch into his *car*." Nick opened the door and gave Morgan a bright and totally false smile. "You can wait out here if you want."

"Scott?" she asked.

"Yeah. Just to warn you, he hits on any female with a pulse."

"Or tits," Bacon blurted, then he turned bright red and bolted for the house.

Morgan shrugged. Even among the homeless and vagabonds, there were plenty of men like Scott. "I'll be okay."

"All right," Nick sighed. "Let's get going, then."

He and Morgan had the couch halfway out of the truck bed when Bacon and two others emerged from the house. One was average height, slender, and scurrying, the other taller with a confident stride.

Bacon trailed behind, a huge grin shining from behind his fluff of a beard.

"Well. What do we have here?" the taller one asked, gaze raking over Morgan. The other guy merely nodded hello.

"Miss Miller, this is Chuckie and Scott, friends of mine. Guys, this is Miss Miller. She's a client."

"Just a client. Cool," Scott said, easing closer to run a finger across the outer bone of her wrist. "So, Beautiful. You like coffee?"

Nick let go of the couch and Morgan half expected an urge to flee as Scott's glancing touch moved to the side of her palm, her pinkie, and he gave her a slow, seductive smile.

Morgan blinked. *Coffee and a caress? Dude, I'm not interested in playing your game.* As Nick came to stand beside her, she smiled into Scott's big brown eyes. As he reached to grasp her hand, she curled her fist away from his touch and said, "Not gonna happen. Let's get that straight right now. 'Kay?" She finished with a bright warning grin, which only made Scott lick his lips.

Bacon and Chuckie glanced at one another and backed away as Scott said, "Ooh. A challenge." He grinned and reached for her waist. "I like a chall—"

Before Nick could step between them, Morgan swung her right hand up, bapping the heel of her hand against Scott's throat as she thrust her left fist straight against his solar plexus. He staggered back, coughing and gasping. She hadn't hit him hard, just a firm, quick tap to make his throat and diaphragm clench and momentarily cut off his air. St. Mary's Women's Shelter gave free rape prevention classes every Wednesday night, teaching how to knock 'em back, then run. If he'd been a real attacker, he'd be on the ground and she'd already be a block away.

"Pretty sure I just told you no, but you *obviously* weren't listening. I'll try to be clearer. I'm *not interested* in having coffee, and I *did not give you permission* to touch me," she said, almost feeling sorry for the poor guy. "Try that crap again, I might have to really hurt you."

Scott grumbled and took a step toward her, but his scowl collapsed when he glanced at his friends. Chuckie smirked and Bacon doubled over laughing.

Nick merely shook his head before reaching past her for the couch. "Let's get this thing in the house."

"Yeah," Scott said around a last weak cough. "Let's get this over with."

Morgan stepped aside to give the men room to work. Once they'd wrestled the couch out of the truck, she hurried ahead to the steps.

She pushed the entry door in and stood aside to hold the screen wide. Nick met her gaze for a brief moment, just long enough to smile and nod into her eyes before the couch slid through.

* * *

After fetching the cushions, Morgan stood on the steps, wondering if she should enter or not. Chuckie answered the question for her when he opened the screen and told her to come on in.

The others were somewhere deeper in the house; Scott yelled at Bacon for having too much mess in the way.

Chuckie grabbed two cushions and said, "C'mon. It's this way."

Morgan followed. The place smelled of microwave burritos, sweat, and stale beer, with all the seating facing a big screen TV. A panicked, wild-eyed, black-and-white cat burst out of an open door halfway down the hall. It zipped between her feet and disappeared somewhere behind her.

Chuckie stomped forward. "What was Igor doing in your room? I've told you and *told you* not to lock him in here."

"He likes me," Bacon said as he pushed armloads of clothes and pizza boxes out of a corner.

"He likes all your *food*," Chuckie said as he dropped his pair of cushions on the floor. "And you *know* it makes him sick. He shits all over everything again, *you're* cleaning it up."

Bacon glanced at Morgan and winked as if to say 'See what I have to put up with?' then he helped Scott and Nick maneuver the couch into its chosen corner.

Chuckie pressed past her and back down the hall, presumably to find the cat, as Nick said, "You guys want to watch the language? There's a lady present."

"Yeah, a lady who kicked Scott's ass," Bacon sniggered.

Scott slammed his end of the couch against the wall. "Shut up, pork rind."

"Guys, c'mon," Nick said. "Knock it off."

Morgan leaned the cushions against the wall. "I'll just go wait in the other room."

Chuckie sat on the couch with the cat in his arms, stroking its head and back even as it squirmed to get loose. He glanced up at her then back to the cat. "Scott's not all bad."

"I'm sure he's not," Morgan said, shrugging. "I just don't like being touched."

"I figured." Chuckie glanced up at her again. "They're good guys, all of 'em. Even Scott. He just don't know it." His hands clenched and he stood, meeting her gaze long enough to say, "Don't you hurt him, okay? We'll be good 'long as you don't hurt him."

"I think he learned his lesson," Morgan said, smiling. "I don't think I'll need to hit him again."

"I ain't talkin' 'bout Scott." He nodded once, as if to drive his point home, then hurried off to chase his cat.

ELEVEN

NICK SAID LITTLE ON THE RETURN TO DARCY'S HOUSE, and Morgan found his silence baffling. Had she said something wrong? Should she have bantered with Scott instead of punching him in the gut? She could think of nothing else that might have been suspect and her heart sank. She scrunched her eyes closed and thought a silent curse. *He's one of the nicest people I've met, and I just had to beat up his friend for flirting with me. Way to go, Morgan. Should have run away like I always do.*

When they turned onto the highway leading to Hackberry, she said, "I didn't mean to upset you. I'm sorry. I shouldn't have hit him."

"What?" He gaped at her before returning his attention to the road. "That? God, no, you were perfect. He needed his ego brought down a notch." Nick glanced at her again and managed to smile. "Do not feel guilty about Scott, okay? You were fine."

"Then why are you mad at me?"

"I'm not mad at you. Honest."

"Okay." Morgan looked out the window at the fields passing by. It was a pretty day, bright blue sky with a few cotton-fluff clouds, the land brilliant and green. And maybe Nick wasn't her friend anymore because she'd done something wrong.

"I should have just dropped you off at the house instead of dragging you along," Nick said. "You didn't need to deal with Scott, or that filthy couch." He frowned and glanced at her. "I'm sorry."

She turned to contemplate him. "I was happy to help, and,

jeesh, it's just a couch. It obviously made Bailey really happy."

"Yeah, well..." he started then turned his head to stare at her. "You remembered his name?"

"Sure. Bailey Connor."

Nick smiled and shook his head as he returned his attention to the road. "No one ever remembers his name. He's just Bacon. It's even embroidered on his work shirts."

"Should I call him Bacon instead of Bailey?"

Nick laughed then, sweet and warm and himself again. "You call him whatever you like."

Will do. Whatever tension had existed seemed lighter, less threatening, and Morgan smiled. Her feet once again sat propped on Nick's toolbox, but her shoes were clean, not muddy. *Oh, crap! The blanket!* She reminded herself to give it back to him as soon as they got to the house.

"You're a *client*," Nick said, tugging Morgan from her thoughts. "And it was grossly improper of me to drag you out to my crappy house, let alone have you help carry an even crappier couch. I apologize."

"Your house is fine," she said. "And at least you have a home." She shrugged and tried not to sound as insignificant as she felt. "I mostly move from hostel to homeless shelter."

"Morgan," he said, frowning at the road, "you have a house."

"No. It's Darcy's. I'm just stranded there."

His hands clenched the wheel. "She's gone, Morgan. The house is yours. Maybe you need to accept that."

She winced. On one level, he was right, but on another... Everything was still Darcy's regardless of whose name was on the water bill.

"Nothing there is mine," she said at last, hating the whine in her voice. "It's her colors, her furniture, her history, her mess, her

everything. She's dumped it all on me, left it for me to clean up."
She shrugged. "I'm just a homeless vagabond and I don't deserve—"

"Stop right there," he said as they drove into Hackberry. "I've
only known you a few days but you're obviously a lot more than
a vagabond, and who says you don't deserve to have a house or
manage a handful of websites or any of it?" He glanced at her, his
gaze stern. "Is there someone who's not allowing you to better
yourself or do whatever you want? Someone who says you can't do
this or can't be that?"

No one but me, she thought, flinching as the realization struck
her. "No," she managed to say, her voice small.

She swallowed, hand grasping the door latch. She was in a
moving vehicle, a pickup, high off the ground. The houses and
neighborhood had become familiar, some of the faces, the kids, the
cars. *Oh, God, what do I do?*

Darcy's house stood less than a block ahead and Morgan stared
at it, her tongue flicking out to moisten her lower lip. *He'll stop soon.
Hang on. Just a few seconds more.*

"Look, I know it's really not any of my business, and I know you
had a tough time growing up, but why can't you run FrugallyUrban
or any of the other sites? Why can't you have a house and a dog and
a home business? Lots of people do it, why can't you?"

He pulled in the driveway and turned to look at her as if
readying his next question, but, before he could speak, Morgan
opened the truck door and murmured, "Because I run. It's safer
that way." Without looking at him, she bolted, ignoring the tears
stinging her face.

* * *

By the time she'd exhausted herself enough to return to the house, Nick had unloaded all of her purchases, leaving them stacked tidily in Darcy's office, and had poured himself a glass of water to sip while he sat at the dining room table and examined data on the diagnostic screen.

Ranger barreled through the house, barking and happy, to present her with a sloppy-wet ball.

"I let him in," Nick muttered without glancing at her. "Hope it's okay."

Morgan grimaced at the goopy-ball slime and flung it toward the back room. "It's fine," she said, guilt tightening her belly. She'd left him here, alone, for nearly an hour, to deal with her mess. "Thank you."

"Yeah. Well. I have good news and bad news about your hard drive."

Great, she thought, not feeling great at all about any of it. "What's the bad news?"

"Your drive wasn't just smashed, it was hacked by someone who had no idea what they're doing. They totally fried your file system. It's completely trashed and'll have to be rebuilt from scratch." He shrugged. "I'm running a preliminary sort now, but the re-coding could take a few days, maybe a week. Depends on how many complete files there are, how many bad ones, and how long it's been since your friend cleaned up her drive."

He shrugged and took a sip of water, still not looking at her. "From what I'm seeing here, she probably never did any routine maintenance on her files. Fragments everywhere."

Morgan sat around the corner from him and resisted the urge to reach out and grasp his hand. She clasped hers in her lap instead. "Okay. What's the good news?"

"I'd over-estimated the data damage. Less than ten percent has been corrupted, and a good hunk of that is the file system and OS. Re-connecting the damaged data sectors ought to go a lot quicker than I first thought, just another few days, tops." He finished his water and set the glass aside. "You should be rid of me by sometime next week."

Morgan swallowed. "Don't be mad at me. Please."

"Why would I be mad at you? You're gonna be leaving as soon as you get the site cookies and, besides, you're just a client. Right? And I'm just here to provide a service."

"That's not fair," she said, bursting to her feet. She wanted to flee but her legs were tired, quaking. "I can't stay."

"Why not?" he asked, standing as well, and his gaze bored into her. "What's so God-awful about Hackberry that you're itching to run away from it?"

Darcy's kitchen phone rang, and Morgan clenched her hands. "Nothing. Nothing's wrong with Hackberry. It's me, okay? I can't stay anywhere for very long."

He glanced toward the kitchen and its ringing phone then back to her. "Why not? What are you running from, Morgan? It's obviously not anything legal, not warrants or subpoenas or tax evasion, because the cops would've arrested you. Is there some abusive ex out there looking for you? You running from a drug lord or pimp or something?"

She fell into her chair and buried her face in her hands. "No. Nothing like any of that. I'm not in any trouble."

"Then why the hell are you running?" He paced, scowling, and asked, "And why don't you answer your damned phone?"

"It's not my phone," she threw back. "It's Darcy's."

"No," he said, staring her in the eye. "It's *yours*. Why can't you accept that?"

The phone quit ringing and the answering machine clicked, picking up.

She stood again. "It's not mine, it can't be mine, I can't—"

"I thought we came to an understanding, but you go and got a goddamn *dog*? You think a goddamn dog will stop me from getting what I want, bitch, you're fuckin' mistaken," the answering machine growled and both Morgan and Nick turned to stare into the kitchen. The voice was low, raspy, and furious. Dangerous.

Morgan took a quick step back. *The same voice as the other night, when Ranger attacked the door. Oh, no!*

"What the hell?" Nick stomped toward the kitchen, but Morgan grabbed his arm and shook her head, a low, terrified squeal escaping her throat.

"We need to go!" she whispered, fighting against her rising panic.

"Fuckin' bitch. I shoulda just killed you, maybe slit your fuckin' throat instead of just leaving you in that goddamn gully."

Her brain screamed to run, but Nick's arm around her held her still. Trapped and unable to bolt, she curled into him, desperate to get away from the awful voice.

"Where's Morgan, you fuckin' bitch? You know where she is, I saw it in your fuckin' eyes, and I'll come back, goddamn dog or not, and we *will* finish our conversation."

"Shh, shh," Nick said, holding her, stroking her hair and leading her toward the living room as she clenched against his chest. "I'm here, it's okay. You're safe."

The horrid voice followed them, screeching and vile. "You fuckin' know how to reach me. Tell me where she is or next time I *will* kill you."

The message clicked off and the machine chirruped while Morgan shuddered in Nick's embrace. He shifted, reaching into his pocket, and she buried her face against him when he said into

his phone, "I need a deputy at 326 Fieldmore in Hackberry, and I
need one now."

* * *

Morgan sat on the couch, shaking under the afghan, as the
deputy and Nick listened to all of Darcy's new messages. She
blocked her ears with her fists and rocked, silently wailing at the
first muted sounds of that hateful voice.

There had been a lot of messages on the phone, so many she'd
lost count as the deputy and Nick clicked through. She had assumed
many messages were trivial calls from Darcy's friends, neighbors,
maybe contributors to the other sites—and Morgan herself had
checked in at least five or six times after Darcy went offline—but
now she wondered what else had been left there. Did the person
from the porch call before? Were there other threats?

When she braved another listen, she heard the voice ranting
about "fuckin' truth, Morgan," so she covered her ears under a
pillow and curled into a ball.

Ranger jumped on the couch and laid beside her, his head a
heavy comfort on her hip. He'd saved her from the intruder on the
porch, the same one who'd just threatened to cut Darcy's throat,
and Morgan managed to reach out and touch his fuzzy face. "Thank
you, boy," she whispered.

Ranger thumped his tail and licked her fingers in reply.

After what seemed like a long while, Morgan felt footsteps
approach. She opened her eyes and lifted the pillow from her ears.

Nick knelt before her and managed a shaky smile. "There are
thirty-seven messages altogether."

Morgan nodded, her stomach twisting.

"Eight of them are pretty bad. They've called for some detectives to come, okay?"

"Okay," she said, wondering if 'No' was even an option at all.

The deputy walked past and onto the porch, listening to someone squawking on his radio the whole while, but Morgan couldn't understand what they were saying. Someone who'd killed Darcy wanted to find her. Hurt her. But why?

As she took a breath she realized Nick continued to watch her, the worry in his eyes overwhelmed by a solid resolve that brought her an unexpected measure of comfort. No one had ever looked at her that way before, had quietly waited for her before.

Nick touched Morgan's shoulder, and she didn't flinch away. "Do you want me to stay? Do you want me to go?"

"Stay," she said, managing to push herself upright as Ranger jumped off the couch. "Definitely stay. If you can."

He sat beside her a long while then asked, "Is that why you run? That voice on the phone?"

Morgan shuddered and drew her knees up to her chest. "No," she said at last. "I run... I run because of the blood."

* * *

School that day had sucked. Starting with getting in trouble for homework she hadn't begun, let alone finished, to the utter embarrassment—and biting ridicule—of a bug in her shirt during lunch, she could barely imagine a more awful day. Then she fell asleep in math and got detention.

She knew Libbey would be furious, but at least it gave her a chance to do homework for a change.

Bret had taken the bus home, so Morgan had to wait for Libbey alone. She vaguely remembered a teacher—Music or Art—had sat beside her. The teacher had asked if she was all right, as if having vermin scuttle out of your clothes and onto your lunch tray in front of the whole class would make anyone all right, but Morgan had assured her that she was. Which was true. Even if Libbey spent another whole night dragging them to every gas station and 24-hour store in Madison looking for enough booze to knock back her nightly headbanger headache, Morgan, for once, had her homework done.

Then the teacher, a gentle-faced woman with a few gray hairs at her temples, had asked if Morgan, and her brother, felt safe at home.

Morgan told all of this to Nick in a rambling, desperate flood; her shame, confusion, then terror over what the teacher might do if she knew the truth.

But Libbey had arrived then, honking and angry and glaring behind the wheel of a crappy car she'd borrowed from a friend—or, more likely, a guy she'd just blown for a couple of bucks—so Morgan had run to the car, to her mother, and had left the teacher behind.

"I'm done with this shit," Libbey had said, mashed and bent cigarette hanging from the corner of her mouth. "Done. Fuckin' goddammit it, Morgan, I have better shit to do than pick your lazy, troublemaking ass up at school. Doesn't matter what you did this time. Vandalism. Mouthing off. *Does not fucking matter.* So I don't want to hear your fucking excuses. You're damn fuckin' lucky they found me at all, you know that? I was working at Benny's—"

Turning tricks at Benny's. Just admit it, it's not like I don't know what you do. I've seen it, Morgan thought, rolling her eyes.

She hadn't made any sound and her face was turned toward the window, but somehow Libbey knew she'd back-talked, even if only in a thought. The slam against the back of Morgan's head knocked her against the dashboard and bloodied her nose.

It wasn't the first time, so she just wiped it away and kept watching the buildings whoosh past.

"Don't you fuckin' sass me. You're no better than me and we both know it."

"I don't suck dick," Morgan muttered, then squealed as Libbey wrenched the car aside, scraping it down a row of parked cars, the sparks flying inches from Morgan's face.

"Those dicks keep you fed, fuckin' ungrateful bitch," Libbey snapped as she slammed Morgan with her fist. In the back seat, Bret, Caspian, and baby Nori screamed, terrified. Libbey either didn't care, or didn't notice. "You'll see. Someday you'll shove out a brat and know what love is."

By the time the car screeched into the parking lot of their crappy apartment, Morgan knew Libbey'd call her in sick the next few days at school to give the bruises and abrasions time to heal.

Morgan dragged her ratty book bag up the stairs and waited, staring at moldy, cracked linoleum as her mother unlocked the door. Even the boys were silent, both wiping at their bloodied noses or bruised cheeks, but as soon as they entered and the door was closed, Libbey tore the book bag from Morgan's hands and beat her with it, again and again and again, while screaming at her for her mouth and ruining her workday and how she was goddamn fuckin' lucky she didn't just kill her and be done with her shit.

The boys cowered in the corner, Bret protecting their barely-toddling baby sister, but Morgan took her beating silently, as always, her head covered by her arms as her back absorbed most of the blows.

Libbey kicked Morgan in the gut, her usual parting shot, and sent Morgan to bed without supper and to think about what she'd done and how she should be grateful for such a loving home.

Morgan went. Limping. It felt like something in her back had been knocked loose, but she climbed onto the upper bunk she shared with Bret and tried to ignore the pain.

Nick had said nothing by this point, he just sat beside her, listening, then Morgan said, "As I lay there, tasting blood, the pain in my back so bad I could barely move, I decided I should run away. But where could I go? I was seven. But all I could think about was how I should run, right then, run and never come back." She took a breath and looked into his kind, worried eyes. "Just run and run and run. Sometimes I still need to run, especially when I'm scared."

"I'm so sorry," he said, quickly touching her hand before pulling away again.

"Yeah, me too. But, see, not only did she have one of her headbanger headaches—which were awful for us to endure—she was mad, really pissed, and without me there to beat on, she started on Bret and Cas and Nori. Nori wasn't even a year old. I heard them crying, screaming, Bret begging her to stop, and I just lay there with my sore back, trying to read and stay silent while my brain kept telling me to run."

"What happened then?" he asked, glancing up as the two detectives came in and followed the deputy to the kitchen.

"The screaming stopped," Morgan said, her voice soft and far away. A child's voice. "So Libbey came for me."

She reached for Nick's hand and clenched it tight. "She... beat me again and dragged me to the kitchen. My brothers, my baby sister, they were duct-taped to their chairs. Their mouths were foamy. She'd made them eat spaghettios with roach poison dumped over it. Baby Nori was dead, I think, and Cas unconscious, but Bret was still alive, looking at me. He tried to talk, to tell me to run, but I couldn't. I just couldn't. She had me, held me, by the arm and the hair, and the linoleum was slippery. I couldn't get away. She taped me too, right there at the table, and there was nothing I could do. I tried, but she *had* me.

"There wasn't much more spaghettios, not enough, so she yelled at me, then stabbed me seven, maybe eight times. Then she left to buy dope."

She pulled her hand away. "So I sat there for forever, crying and bleeding and alone. I sat there and watched my brothers die right in front of me. No one came, even with all the crying, even when kids were obviously being hurt, still no one came, not until the neighbor couldn't hear their TV show over my screams. *Then* they called the cops. That's the American way, isn't it," she muttered, barking out a harsh laugh. "Turn a blind eye to blatant abuse until a dying kid keeps you from enjoying *Wheel of Fortune.*"

"How'd you survive that?" Nick asked, sorrow in his voice.

"Stomach pumping. Lots of surgeries. Too much therapy." She shrugged and raised her chin. "I lost a kidney from the beating, and can't raise my left arm very far behind me, but otherwise I healed. I just don't let people touch me anymore. If no one touches me, they can't grab me or hurt me or tape me to a chair like that ever again."

"Not everyone wants to hurt you," Nick whispered.

"I can't take that chance. I run before they can." She took a shaky breath. "I lost every decent foster home I ever had because I'd freak out for no reason or suddenly run away. I failed most of my classes. I've never done anything or hurt anyone. Ever. All I do is *run.*"

The two detectives walked from the dining room and frowned at Morgan. Detective Hildebrandt said, "Miss Miller, I think this time we might need to take a trip to the station."

Morgan stood and glanced at Nick before staring at the detectives. "Okay. Am I under arrest?"

"Just for questioning, Miss Miller. We'll drive you."

"I'll call my lawyer," Nick said. "Don't say anything until she gets there."

"Get me a male lawyer," Morgan said, glancing back to Nick as the detectives escorted her to the porch. "Please. I haven't had much luck trusting women."

TWELVE

DON'T TOUCH ANYTHING, DRINK ANYTHING, Morgan reminded herself as she paced in the interrogation room. *Cops on TV shows are always looking to trick suspects into giving DNA and fingerprints. Not gonna let them trick me.*

There was a mirror on the wall, just like on TV, the door was locked—she'd wiped the knob clean with the hem of her t-shirt after touching it—and her table and chairs were bolted to the floor. She'd begun to wonder why they'd left her alone for so long when the door opened.

"Sorry to keep you waiting," Detective Kramer said, entering. "Would you like a pop or something?"

Despite being thirsty, Morgan curled her fingertips against her palms. "No thank you. Who made that awful phone call?"

"We're not sure yet," Kramer said, sitting. "Still waiting on the transcripts. Why don't you take a seat?" He leaned forward and asked, "Since we'll likely be here a while, is it okay if we call you Morgan instead of Miss Miller? Less cumbersome and all that."

Morgan sat. *Good cop, bad cop, and the good one's trying to be friendly.* "Sure, I guess."

Detective Kramer reviewed the contents of his folder and silence stretched until Morgan said, "Nick said he'd call for a lawyer."

"Yep, and he's here filling out... Ah, here we go," Kramer said, nodding slightly as Detective Hildebrandt opened the door. She clutched a stapled bundle of papers and ushered in a tallish, slender man in jeans and a softball jersey for the West County Ravens. He looked to be somewhere in his forties and carried an expanding file folder, but no briefcase.

"Hey, Ed," Detective Kramer said, standing and offering his hand to the man. "You really didn't need to miss the last couple of innings for this."

"Part of the deal, Lee. You know that. Besides, we were losing anyway." He shook Kramer's and Hildebrandt's hands then sat beside Morgan and introduced himself as Ed Biddermahn. "So," he said to the detectives. "Other than my client receiving threats, what brings us all here tonight?"

Kramer said, "I'd just mentioned to Morgan that we'd been transcribing all forty-two phone calls."

"Forty two?" Morgan asked. "Nick said there were thirty-seven."

Hildebrandt said, "Thirty-seven new messages, but forty two total in the queue. We believe that your friend, Miss Harris, listened to the first five, but didn't delete them. At this point, we're assuming they came before her death, the other thirty-seven after, but we can't determine the specific dates or callers until we cross-reference against the phone records." She glanced at the stack of papers before handing them to Morgan's lawyer.

Kramer said, "We can give you both a few minutes to read the transcripts, but, Morgan, before we discuss the calls, would you be willing to—"

Biddermahn said, "No, first, you are going to forfeit every comment she made while you previously interrogated her without benefit of Miranda or counsel."

"She's not a suspect," Kramer replied. "We will, however, video tape today's conversation and send copies to our BCA, the Wisconsin DCI, and the Waupaca County Sheriff."

You're bringing in the Wisconsin DCI? For a phone call? Morgan kept her voice steady. "What if I say I don't want to be taped?"

"Then you're free to go. You're not a suspect, but you may have information that'll help us determine what happened to your friend."

Morgan turned toward her lawyer, who nodded and assured her videotaping was common practice.

"Okay," Morgan said at last. "But I honestly don't know anything."

"You let us worry about that," Kramer said. "We've gathered copies of your friend's phone records. Over the past several months, she received a great deal of calls from a series of disposable cell phones. The calls have been traced to several locations within Oshkosh and its suburbs."

Morgan clamped her hands together to keep them from shaking. "Is that where she died? In the gully?" *The gully, just like the call said. Oh, Darcy!*

"Not exactly," Kramer admitted. "Darcy Harris's Kia went off the road alongside a bridge about forty miles northwest of Oshkosh, in a rural area near the town of Waupaca." He paused, watching Morgan as if expecting her to gasp or blink or flinch, but she just stared back, perplexed.

"Okaaay," she said, confused. "What's in Waupaca?"

"A foundry, some Indian historical sites..." Kramer muttered, returning his attention to his notes. "The car wasn't visible from the road and was finally discovered by two boys playing in the woods."

Morgan swallowed the awful taste from her mouth. "*Discovered?* How long was she down there?"

"Approximately a week," Kramer said. "The windows were down, and, well, between storms and the local fauna, positive identification of the remains proved tricky."

Oh, Darcy! Morgan's stomach lurched. "*Animals* got to her?"

"Yes," Kramer said, his glittering gaze boring into Morgan.

"And we don't believe it was an accident."

Unable to remain still, Morgan stood, gaze darting to the locked door. "Just like the phone call said?" she asked, lower jaw shaking so hard she could barely talk. "Are you saying that person drove her off the road *on purpose* and left her there for the animals to *eat*?"

Biddermahn said, "You need to sit, Morgan."

As Morgan stood there, babbling, with Biddermahn tugging on her arm, Kramer clasped his hands on his folder. "I know this must be very difficult for you, Morgan, but her seatbelt was fastened—"

"What? No. Darcy *never* wore a seatbelt."

Kramer leaned back, blinking. "She never—"

Morgan sat in her chair and brushed off Biddermahn's touch. "Never. I don't know if she kept them in the Kia, but she cut the seatbelts out of her old car and couldn't bear to wear tight clothes or even sleep under tucked-in sheets. Not since Ryder. Is he in your tidy little packet of papers? How he tied her up and raped her?" she asked, despite stinging tears. "He's the only one who ever tried to hurt Darcy. Maybe he did this. Why aren't you badgering him instead of me?"

"We're just trying to find out what happened to—"

"I don't know what happened in Wisconsin," Morgan said, her voice shaking, "but I do know there's no way Darcy would use a seatbelt nor would she let *anyone* else into her car. Anyone."

"Why would your friend try to visit your mother in prison?" Kramer asked so softly Morgan barely heard over her hammering heart.

"She wouldn't," Morgan said. "She knew I hated her."

"She signed in, Morgan. We have copies of her driver's license, even a tape of her in the waiting room." Hildebrandt pulled a paper from the stack and slid it toward Morgan. It was a sign-in sheet for Taycheedah Women's Correctional Institution. Near the bottom, dated weeks before their first days at college, nearly two full months before she and Morgan had met, Darcy L. Harris had signed into the prison visitor log, requesting to see Liberty Miller. A notation in the margin stated that the inmate refused the visit.

Morgan shook her head and tried to lurch away from the insane assertion, but her bolted chair refused to budge. "It's not possible. I didn't even know her back then. This is just a sick trick!"

"Morgan," Biddermahn soothed, but Morgan barely heard.

She took a few harsh breaths, her hands clenching as she struggled to control her panic. "Someone called Darcy's phone looking for me, threatening me, and you're sitting here telling me lies about Darcy? What's wrong with you people? I'm telling you it's Ryder! Why won't you listen to me?"

"We'll track down who made the calls, but to do that, we need to know why your friend was in Wisconsin," Kramer said.

Morgan burst to her feet again and paced alongside the wall. "I've told you I don't know!"

"But you *do*," Hildebrandt said. "Almost every call on the answering machine was for you, not your friend. Eight threatening calls came from the same person you heard today. Whatever happened in Wisconsin, it's about *you*, not Darcy."

Kramer pulled another folder from beneath the one he'd been using. "We have copies of your official records, Morgan. You were born in Madison, and were in foster care all over the—"

"And after I was kicked out of college, I got the hell out of Wisconsin!"

Biddermahn said, "Morgan, you need to calm down, and you need to sit. Now."

Morgan blew out a frantic huff of air and plopped onto her chair, hands clenching and unclenching against her thighs. "My family's dead. I don't know *anyone* in Wisconsin anymore, other than some kids I went to college with, and I haven't had contact with *any* of them, besides Darcy, since I left school nearly seven years ago."

Morgan took a breath and glanced at the mirror behind the detectives. *Damn Wisconsin cops. Did nothing to help when I was a kid, just kept taking us away, then sending us back once Libbey pissed clean. Look how great that turned out.* "I have *no* connection to Wisconsin," she said to the glass. "Not anymore. I left and never looked back."

"Why, then, would you receive threats on your friend's phone?"

"I don't know. A crazed stalker fan of the site?" Morgan offered, rolling her eyes. "It happened to a novelist whose blog I read. Some dude kept calling her, and finally showed up at a book-signing. She tasered him."

"This is a serious matter, Morgan," Kramer said. "Almost every call was for you. Why is that?"

Morgan stared at the table. "Darcy used my name for the contact person on the sites. I don't know why, okay? But there's all this mail, boxes and boxes of it. The calls were actually for her, they had to be. She was just using my name." She shrugged and unclenched her hands. "She was so shy, maybe it made her feel safer, pretending to be me. Maybe she didn't want anyone showing up on her doorstep. I swear I don't know."

"Morgan..." Kramer said, frowning. "You really expect us to believe the calls asking for *you* were really for your friend?"

Morgan swallowed back the lump in her throat. "Look, I don't know *anyone*. I don't have *anyone*. All I had was Darcy and now she's dead." She stole a glance at the door and shifted in her chair. "I have no friends, no family, nothing but the mess Darcy left me when she died, and I absolutely have not spoken to anyone from Wisconsin, not since I left school. I've spent the last few years running from city to city, writing articles for Darcy's site and scraping by.

"It's all I do," she added, managing to meet Kramer's gaze despite her shaking jaw. "I run. I just run. No one is going to call me, let alone threaten me. It's just not possible."

"How did the caller know about your dog?"

Ranger? "Maybe they saw him in the yard. Maybe because someone tried to break in through the front door a few nights ago and he barked at them. But... I thought that was just the kids who busted Darcy's computer before I even got here. I dunno why whoever hurt Darcy in Wisconsin would know about my dog."

Kramer stared at Morgan for a moment. "A busted computer? What was on it? How was it broken?"

"Website logins and files, mostly," Morgan said, shrugging. "I think. I don't really know. Nick's trying to repair the data fragments or something to let me login to our website. That's the only part I know about. And it was smashed into lots of pieces. Really busted up."

"Do you still have the computer?"

"No, I don't think so. Nick kept some parts of the hard drive but threw them away once he pulled the data bits off. I think that's what he said, anyway. There aren't any pieces anymore, just digital gibberish."

"All right, so the physical evidence has been destroyed," Kramer grumbled, writing in his notebook again. "Since you don't know why your friend was in southern Wisconsin, and you insist you were not there with her, then you'll be willing to give us your fingerprints, plus a hair and DNA sample—"

"Not without a court order," Biddermahn said, gathering up Morgan's papers. "She's already testified that she was in New York at the time of death, and you've confirmed it. We're done here."

* * *

An hour or so after arriving, Morgan fled the interrogation room with her lawyer following behind her. She wanted to adjust her laces and run and run and run until she fell exhausted at the side of the road. But she had papers to sign, for both the sheriff and her lawyer, personal effects to pick up, and a final quick conversation with Biddermahn.

"You need to calm down," he said as they walked toward the exit. "When you have a comment, whisper it to me, and I can phrase it appropriately."

"I... I'm not good at remaining calm when I feel threatened."

He stopped to frown at her. "Then be fully aware that neither of those detectives are as country-stupid as you might want to think they are, and you *will* find yourself locked up if you say the wrong thing at the wrong time and they believe that you had even the slightest bit of involvement in your friend's death." He opened his expanding file and, after stuffing in his copies of Morgan's papers, pulled out a card. "Call me before you say anything else to either of them, all right? Let me at least try to do my job."

She took his card and nodded past the guilty twist in her gut. "Sorry. I don't mean to be a pain, but if I feel trapped and can't get away, I... I have to do *something*."

"We'll work on that," he said, then turned to go.

Morgan pocketed his card and flipped on her phone, only to find her call-list on screen. *Bastards checked my phone again!* she thought, grumbling her way out the front door. Attention focused on her phone, she'd finally located the number for the cab company when a man called her name.

She looked up, startled, to see Nick standing on the sidewalk, his hands stuffed in his pockets, while, behind him, Biddermahn talked with Donna and Mark, the couple from Jannis' barbeque. "You okay?" Nick asked, approaching Morgan.

"Yeah, just aggravated," she said, relieved to see him. "You didn't have to come get me."

He shrugged and gave her an embarrassed grin. "I couldn't leave you stranded."

"What are they doing here?" Morgan asked, gesturing to the three talking nearby.

"They kinda insisted," Nick started, voice trailing off as Donna hurried up to them.

"Morgan!" she said, "Oh, thank goodness you're all right. When Nick called asking for a law—"

Nick's eyes widened and he turned to snarl, "You *know* her?"

"Well, I, uh, we..." Donna babbled, face reddening.

"We met at a barbeque. Over the weekend," Morgan said, taking a step away as Donna grasped Nick's arm and he jerked it loose.

"Goddammit, Mom, I told you to stay out of this."

"Your mo... Your *mother?*" Morgan stumbled a step backward, and another, then tripped over stone edging, gasping as she fell on her butt in a planting bed.

"You two just can't leave it alone, can you?" Nick snapped as he reached out to help Morgan to her feet again. "I told you, she's a *client*. Stay out of it."

"You finally find a girl who interests you and you expect us to just ignore it?" Donna asked.

Nick steered Morgan toward his truck. "Yes, I do."

"Nick, wait," Mark said, approaching as Nick opened the truck door for Morgan. "You called asking for help. That's what we're doing—trying to help."

"No," Nick said as Morgan climbed in, "I called asking who's a good defense attorney because mine only does contract law and wouldn't give a referral. Showing up here and poking your nose into things is not helping." He closed Morgan's door and stomped around to the driver's side.

Frowning, Mark mumbled and gestured toward the sheriff's office. "What if she'd needed bail money? What then?" He shot a pointed look at his son.

Nick snatched open the driver's side door and climbed in. "Stay out of this, Dad. All right? Just stay out of it."

"But we're here to help you!" Donna called out.

Nick started the truck and glared at his parents. "It's *help* when you ask for assistance, or there's a problem you can't cope with. This, *this* is interference." He put the truck in reverse and muttered, "Stay out of it," before bolting away.

They drove a couple of blocks with Nick glaring out the windshield and his hands clenched white on the steering wheel before Morgan said, "Sorry to cause you so much trouble. I... I was gonna call a cab."

"You are no trouble," he said, right hand opening as if it had cramped, then the left, and his voice softened. "It's my parents who are trouble."

Evening breeze on her face, Morgan shrugged, listening to the sounds of neighborhood bars and shops as they drove through Albert Lea's downtown. "They seem to care about you a great deal and they just want to make sure you're all right." She glanced over at him. "Trust me, parents who love you maybe too much are a lot better than the alternative."

"Pfhh." He braked at a stoplight and took a deep breath. "Maybe. But it doesn't make them any less of a pain. They're always trying to give me money and fix me up with women." His hands opened, fingers splaying out, and he tapped his fingers hard on the steering wheel, *bap bap bap!* "Just because I haven't settled down or got some girl pregnant doesn't make me gay."

Morgan squirmed, not sure what to say. She'd never really considered what pressures parents might put on their single sons.

The light turned green and Nick clamped the wheel again. "Dad actually asked me that, when Dougie got married a couple of years ago. Dougie's my younger brother. Twenty-one. One kid and another on the way. He married a crazy bitch because of a one-night stand, but I'm the one they fuss over. Me. The guy who thinks that maybe, just maybe, commitment and a little affection ought to be prerequisites before falling into the sack with someone."

Another light turned red. Nick sat there, fuming. "Last I knew, looking for the right girl doesn't make a guy gay. Sleeping with other guys makes a guy gay. But can my father see that? My mother? Oh hell no. They just see that I'm nearing thirty and they don't have any grandkids on the horizon and there's only one possible explanation."

Morgan watched him, uncertain what she should say.

"I'm sorry," he sighed, turning left at the light. "You didn't need to hear all that. And you didn't need to get dragged into my parents' skewed quest to get me married off."

"It's all right," she said. "Really. It's, well, *normal*. I think I need more normal."

"Morgan, I can honestly say, you're just about the nicest, most normal person I've met in a long time, even if your life is nuts." He chuckled then, shaking his head, and they drove in companionable silence until the next red light.

"You hungry?" he asked. "Wanna get a cup of coffee or something?" He glanced over at her. "And I haven't even asked about what happened with the sheriff. You were in there a long time."

"I could eat," she agreed. "And there's not a whole lot to tell, I don't think. They just wanted to know about the phone calls and why Darcy was in Wisconsin. I don't know anything about any of it, so there wasn't much to talk about."

She frowned at the passing houses as downtown turned to residential. "I don't think they believed me. They kept asking me the same questions in different ways."

"They surely can't believe you're involved."

"Yeah, they kinda do." She shrugged. "Maybe. I don't know. I guess they're looking into things, so that's good. Right?"

"Are they looking into why you're getting threats on your friend's phone?"

"The calls weren't for me. Just like the sites, Darcy was using my name, maybe because it made her feel safer. I dunno, it's just a big mix-up." Morgan shrugged and watched Albert Lea slide past her window, mostly to ignore Nick's frown.

"Sorry my folks got stuck in the middle of it," he said. "I just didn't know who else to call after-hours. My lawyer's answering service wouldn't even pass on a message to call me back, because nothing in a contract couldn't wait until morning." He turned the corner onto a wide street flanked by strip malls and chain restaurants. "But Dad said to call Ed. And I did. Glad he worked out."

"Thank you," she said. "He was great. Especially since he saved me from myself."

They quickly discussed restaurant options and settled on a little coffee shop at the end of a strip mall.

Morgan's sandwich was passable, but the coffee was great, and she found herself cozied into the corner of their booth with a steaming mug as Nick talked about his family. Two brothers and two sisters, four nieces and nephews—two more on the way—and more aunts, uncles, and cousins than Morgan could keep straight in her head. Only his youngest sister, Beth, was also unmarried, but she was just eighteen and about to start college.

Morgan found such a vast and complicated family fascinating. She'd known little of her own family, and wanted to forget most of what she had experienced. Nick's memories, in contrast, were full of detail, humor, and fondness.

Despite his current aggravation with his parents, he smiled easily as he spoke of most everyone other than Dougie's wife, especially the children.

"I want kids someday," he said, picking at the last of his supper, "but it has to be with the right girl." Then he shrugged. "I dunno. Either it'll happen, or it won't."

Morgan shifted under his polite scrutiny and admitted, "I don't know if I'll ever have kids. Part of it's because I don't stay anywhere for long, and that's not really conducive to child rearing, but mostly, it's because I don't want to end up like my mother."

"I don't think that's going to happen," he said. "You're too nice a person."

"Yeah, well, my template for good parenting is pretty messed up," she said. "I'm actually a little afraid of kids. I don't want to take the chance that I might hurt them."

"Hey. First of all, you are not your mother. Second, you're aware of how messed up things were with you, and you *can* consciously do things different, especially with your own kids."

"But... abuse runs in families. Generation after generation after—"

"Third," he interrupted, grasping her hand as her gaze blurred. "Ken's wife, Trish, grew up in hell. Yeah, it wasn't quite as bad as yours, but she loves their kids and is a fantastic mother. She's mentioned several times how proud of her kids she is, and how they won't ever know how bad it can be. She says the shit stopped with her. There's no reason it can't stop with you, too."

He squeezed Morgan's hand. "You're your own person and can make your own choices."

She drew her hand away. "You're just saying that because you've spent most of this past week rescuing me."

"Nah, I'm saying it 'cause it's true. Don't let someone from your past dictate how you're allowed to spend your future."

She stared at her supper a moment, her thoughts churning. Maybe he's right. *Maybe I can shove the shit of my past behind me. Move forward on my own terms.*

She took a sip of her coffee. *I just have to figure out how.*

THIRTEEN

MORGAN HAD CHECKED every lock and every window before curling on the couch to sleep with a broom clenched in her hands, Ranger snoring on the floor beside her. Ready to fight instead of run, she lay there a long time, listening to the thud of her heart and awaiting a creak from the porch or rap at the window. None came. She didn't realize her eyes had drifted closed, but sat up, startled and scrambling for the dropped broom, when Nick knocked on the door the next morning.

Once he'd settled in to work, she buckled Ranger into his leash and set off for her morning run around town. As she rounded the corner to head back home, Ranger let out a low, threatening growl that jolted Morgan to a stop, heart slamming. Her hand tightened on the leash and she scrambled a step back, then another, scanning the bushes and porches and parked cars, but saw no one other than an elderly man mowing his dinky front yard with a lawn tractor and two little kids running through a sprinkler.

Still Ranger growled, attention focused on a bed of azaleas, his hackles up and his head low. Mrs. Parson's little fluff-ball dog burst out of the bushes moments later, yipping and snarling. It lunged at Ranger, trying to bite his privates, but Ranger plucked it up by the scruff of the neck, shook it twice, and tossed it aside. Again and again the little dog attacked, while Morgan tried to get between it and Ranger without success.

"Hey! C'mon!" she said as the dog zipped between her feet for the umpteenth time. "Quit that!" She dragged Ranger toward

Darcy's house only a block or so away, but the little dog constantly flanked them, making their progress achingly slow.

Desperate, she tied Ranger to a fire hydrant and snatched up Mrs. Parson's dog. He squirmed, yelping, but she held on, keeping herself between Ranger and the troublemaker.

"Stay here," she said to Ranger then jogged to Mrs. Parson's while Ranger barked and tugged at his lead.

Mrs. Parson's car stood in her driveway, driver's-side door open. The dog in Morgan's arms squirmed, whining, as Morgan stood in the drive, unsure what to do.

"Hello?" she called out.

From behind, she heard, "How dare you try to steal my Chauncy!"

"He was running loose. I just wanted to bring him home," Morgan said, turning to see Mrs. Parson stagger around the corner of the house. Perplexed, she added, "I haven't stolen anything, ma'am. Honest."

"I caught you taking my dog to sell him to a dog fighting ring!"

A *dog fighting... WHAT?* Perplexed, Morgan shook her head and approached, dog held out like an offering. "Look, ma'am, I found him running loose. I'm trying to return—"

"Give me my Chauncy and leave us alone!" Mrs. Parson barked. She snatched the dog from Morgan's grasp then slapped her across the face. "Rotten thief!"

Morgan took a step back, eyes widening and her hand covering her stinging cheek. Too shocked to run, she said, "What's wrong with you? Your dog was loose and I brought him home, so you *hit me?*"

"Yes I did," the old woman snarled, staggering a step closer to Morgan. "You come here, poking around, looking for stuff to steal. I'm not gonna let you take my Chauncy."

"I'm not... I didn't..." Morgan said, taking a step away from the furious old woman as she fought the urge to run. "I was just trying to *help*."

Mrs. Parson lurched closer to poke Morgan in the chest as she enunciated each word. "So help, by getting—"

"Is there a problem?" Nick asked as he hurried across the yard to them. "Ranger's tied up, bark—"

Mrs. Parson turned, still glaring as she cradled her rotten little dog. "Why, it's Nicky John Hawkins. I haven't seen you since you were what, fifteen? Sixteen?" She looked him over, top to bottom. "You're damn lucky your lazy-ass father had the fire station's insurance and not the crap the hospital tried to sell your mother. Chemo *and* a bone marrow transplant? Lot of money to waste on a sniveling brat."

Nick stood beside Morgan, mouth agape and staring. "Excuse me?"

"You heard me," Mrs. Parson snapped. "I know what happened. Filed all your paperwork myself. After conning the insurance into wasting good money on treatments and surgeries, you finally had to steal marrow from your bigger, stronger brother because you were too weak to survive on your own."

Morgan grasped Nick's arm and tried to tug him back toward the house. "Let's just go."

Nick held fast, still glaring. "I had cancer," he said, voice low and angry. "I was a kid."

"Aw, poor widdle Nicky Hawkins. Too sick to play outside. Too weak for anything but books and computers and beepity-boopity video games. How'd it feel watching your brother play football and hit home runs and get all the awards, Nicky? Even your baby brother could out-run you when he was still in diapers. Bet he still can."

Nick glowered, his cheek twitching, and Morgan readied for his verbal explosion, but instead he merely flicked her the finger and said, "Cram it, you old bat." Still glowering, he turned to stomp toward Darcy's house.

"Could you *be* any nastier?" Morgan took a step toward Mrs. Parson. "Just... Just stay away from us and keep your meanness to yourself."

Then she trotted to the house.

* * *

"Cancer?" Morgan asked once she'd followed Nick inside. Her belly felt twisty. Sick. "Chemo and bone marrow transplant? Are... Are you all right?"

"I'm fine," he muttered, barely glancing at her before stomping into the kitchen. "Was a long time ago, when I was a kid. Ancient history." He pulled a Mountain Dew from the fridge and slammed the door. "Damn bitch," he muttered as he ripped off the cap. He took a long drink and swallowed, wincing as if it tasted bitter.

Morgan swallowed, watching him. "You sure?"

He sighed and met her worried gaze. "It's really not a big deal. I had bone cancer in my shoulder. My mom, she's a nurse, and well, she knew something was wrong and we caught it *really* early. Took a lot of surgeries, grafts, and a rebuilt joint, but I got to keep my arm."

"Oh, Nick," she whispered, reaching out to touch his hand. "You must have been terrified."

"Yeah, well," he said, shrugging, then took another sip of pop. "The chemo and radiation pretty much sucked, but thanks to Ken I'm okay now. Really."

"You're sure?"

He nodded and managed a smile. "Positive. Other than a

sluggish thyroid, I'm cancer free and everything's working fine. Has been for years. Honest."

"Okay," Morgan said, searching his eyes. *Bone cancer? Oh, Nick, you could have died! What would I have done if you'd died?*

He sighed and lowered his gaze. "It was a long time ago and I don't hardly think about it anymore." He brushed past Morgan. "Let's just forget the whole thing, okay? She isn't worth our time."

He settled in to glower at the computers, and Morgan let him be, excusing herself to rescue Ranger from the hydrant and console him with a game of fetch. Nick was right. Mrs. Parson wasn't worth the aggravation.

Reassuring herself that Nick was all right, Morgan spent the remainder of the morning sorting the mountain of mail into boxes, folders, files, and the packages—mostly small appliances, beauty products, money-management CDs, and scrapbooking supplies—by their intended website.

Eleven sites, she thought, shaking her head at the overwhelming mess. *How did Darcy manage eleven sites without ever mentioning it to me?*

She bookmarked each site on her laptop and explored them to get a feel for their services and regular users, mind boggling at the alien concepts of facial wraps and multi-layered hole punchers.

Most of the new sites had forums, and many posters had expressed concern and aggravation over the lack of updates from their beloved Morgan. Morgan posted on each board that she was a personal friend of the site owner and there had been a family crisis and computer problems, but, soon, things should get smoothed out. She signed each posting as "M", growing increasingly concerned over why Darcy had used her name so frequently.

She visited FrugallyUrban last. She added a comment to the latest article that explained, briefly, that Mule had unexpectedly passed away and that she, Pony, was at Mule's house trying to sort through the business end of things and it might take another week or so. After a request for folks to be patient, she added her email address in case anyone had a concern she needed to respond to directly.

I don't want to run an internet business, Morgan thought as she backed out of the site, *but it doesn't look like I have much choice.*

FOURTEEN

AFTER DAYS OF MULLING OVER WHAT TO DO about the sites, Morgan came to a decision midway through Thursday morning's run. Since she knew nothing about site maintenance or running an online business—and frankly had little desire to learn—she would offer to sell the sites to their top users. That way, the sites could continue, their regulars would be happy, but someone else could collect the headaches and pressure. And revenue.

The thought of not having to worry about makeup, stock portfolios, or scrapbooks cheered her, but losing FrugallyUrban twisted her gut. *What else can I do?* she thought as she turned down Fieldmore and gave Mrs. Parson's house a cheerful good-morning wave, her own passive-aggressive "gonna kill you with kindness, bee-yutch" she'd utilized since their argument.

Morgan's running autopilot apparently remembered the jab, but her mind remained on business, and Darcy's sites. *Nick's tried several times to explain coding to me, but it might as well be Greek translated to Swahili. I'm just not getting it. There's no reason to keep a headache I simply don't understand.*

Morgan checked her heart rate and stretched before climbing Darcy's steps. *But if I don't have FrugallyUrban, I don't have any income,* she reasoned. *And if I don't have income, sooner or later the insurance money'll run out and I will need to get a regular job. Somehow.*

She unclipped Ranger at the door and he barreled through the house to his water dish.

"Good run?" Nick asked from the dining room.

"It was okay." Morgan flumped into a chair across from him. After a long while of toying with Ranger's leash, she said, "I think I'm gonna sell the sites."

He shrugged and tapped a few keys. "I thought you would."

"You don't need to sound so enthused."

"I'm not going to pretend I'm thrilled that a good friend is leaving a perfectly lucrative business behind because she doesn't want to do site maintenance." He glanced at her. "It's not brain surgery, Morgan, just a little PHP."

"It's more than the maintenance stuff," Morgan sighed as she stood again and walked toward the kitchen. "It's accounting and policing the forums and questions and comments and fans and people who just want to gripe." She paused in the doorway to look him in the eye. "It's the bullshit, Nick. Yeah, I could maybe muddle through with the maintenance, but I absolutely am not good with bullshit."

He grumbled something under his breath and resumed examining code. "So, Ms. Anti-Bullshit, what's on your schedule for today?"

"Lawn work. I haven't mowed since I got here and it's looking pretty ratty. I need to get that done, I guess, then it's back to emptying closets."

"The house *is* looking pretty good," Nick said, smiling at her and Morgan felt herself blush.

"I still have to start on the basement and garage," she said, grimacing. "Not looking forward to either of those."

He leaned back in his chair and frowned. "The basement's pretty bad. It's like a maze of furniture and boxes down there. Some of it's moldy."

"I know. I saw," she sighed. "And it's gotta go. Maybe I should just get a big dumpster and get it over with."

"That'd go a lot quicker," he agreed. "I could probably convince the guys to help haul stuff out some weekend if you're willing to feed them. Maybe even get the rest of your upstairs emptied out, too."

Morgan closed her mouth before she started babbling her astonishment. "Really?" she managed to say. "Wow. Working for *food?* That'd be awesome. I'll even supply surf and turf if they want."

Nick laughed. "Pizza and beer will be just fine. Just order lots. Bacon has quite an appetite."

"Will do!" Morgan said, and mood lifting, scrounged up the phone book. A couple of calls later, she had a huge dumpster scheduled to be delivered the next afternoon, and she could keep it up to two weeks before paying additional rent.

She returned to the dining room to find Nick scowling and finishing up a phone call. "Chuckie and Bacon are in, but Scott's being a pain," he said as he pocketed his phone. "Says he's only available *this* weekend." He frowned at Morgan and said, "Sorry about that. He's only saying that because he knows it's too short notice for the garbage company and that you'll never get a dumpster by then."

Morgan grinned. "Actually," she said, her voice teasing, "The guy told me the same thing, that normally there's a week or so wait for the big ones, *but* they had a big client pull out this morning and they have a couple of extra units just sitting in the lot. So..."

Nick grinned back. "Seriously?"

"Seriously. They're delivering it tomorrow."

Nick sniggered and pulled out his phone again. "Scott is so gonna shit over this," he said, almost laughing. After starting the call with a 'You're *sure* you can't help out next weekend?' Nick told Scott that this coming Saturday was a go. And wouldn't let him back out.

Nick was still grinning when he closed the call.

"So we're all set for this weekend?" Morgan asked.

"Yep," he said. "It's a date!" Nick cringed, one hand briefly covering his mouth, but his gaze had locked on hers.

A date? He called it a date! Morgan smiled back, feeling blood rush to her face.

Then she retreated to the kitchen to wash her breakfast dishes.

* * *

Like every other part of the house, the garage was packed with boxes, junk, and garbage bags full of site mail, but a snow shovel, hose, and lawn mower were in a relatively clear spot near the door. Morgan wrestled the rattly beast out to the driveway. After scowling at the rust-obscured instructions and cussing the pull-cord, she managed to get it started.

She hadn't mowed since she was a kid, one teenager among many doing regular chores in a group home outside of Milwaukee, but the steady rumble beneath her hands calmed her. She let her mind wander and relished the labor in her back and legs, so different from a run. *Good, clean work,* she thought, smiling as she hugged the mower around a tree.

I've never been afraid of work, she thought, pushing the mower ahead again. *So why am I so afraid of managing the sites?* She let the concern flutter about her mind and settle where it would.

She paused to wipe sweat from her brow. *I don't want to do it because then I really will be stuck. Responsibilities. Schedules.* She sighed and tightened her ponytail. *Stability. Can't run if I have those things. And we all know I must run. It's what I do.*

Ranger playfully barked at the mower then circled the yard in a wild burst of speed. Morgan smiled at his energy but kept mowing.

She'd almost finished, just two more passes to go, when Nick came out the back door.

Morgan couldn't hear what he was saying, so she cut the engine and, as her ears cleared, heard him holler, "I found a cookie."

* * *

Morgan finished the back yard and hurried into the house. "It's not on your list of sites," Nick said, glancing at her, "but it's a WordPress login cookie, plain as day. Let's see if you can bring it up."

Morgan fetched her laptop and sat across from him, fingers poised over the keyboard. "Ready."

He read off the data, Morgan confirming each piece before she hit enter. Her screen cleared as the site loaded, browser icon spinning, and Nick stood beside her as they watched the page open.

The screen said MORGAN AUGUSTINE MILLER—02171991 with a list of links below.

"Me?" Morgan asked, glancing up at Nick before returning her attention to the site.

During the moment she'd looked away, other graphics had filled in, including the flag and seal for the state of Wisconsin and the logo for Wisconsin Social Services.

Heart slamming, she clicked on a link and her birth certificate popped up to float over the main screen. "I don't understand," she said, hand shaking as she closed that window and clicked another link—her foster placement order from the state. The URL said 1426storagethings.com, not anything close to Wisconsin Social Services.

Morgan swallowed bitter dryness from her mouth and looked up at Nick. "How could Darcy have access to this stuff?" she asked, voice cracking. "I was a minor. It's supposed to be sealed. And this isn't even a state site."

"I don't know," he replied, glancing away.

Morgan closed her laptop and turned to face him. "But you have an idea."

"She's been using your name," he said. "Maybe it's like identity theft. If she was paying you, she already had your social security number. With that and your birth certificate, she could do a lot of damage. She's just storing the documents on a secured proxy server."

"But for what gain?" Morgan asked, watching him round the table and return to his monitor. "I'm barely squeaking by, living on the street and in shelters. I don't have anything *worth* taking."

"I dunno," he said as he sat. "But I can't see how it's for something good."

Morgan stared at her laptop and realized that she couldn't think of anything good either.

FIFTEEN

THE NEXT AFTERNOON, with a tummy full of lunch and a fresh glass of iced tea beside her hip, Morgan settled in to sort through two more boxes. The first held fancy glassware padded by old, embroidered linen. She marveled over the stitching on a pair of pillowcases, her fingertips caressing the pink and green threads that illustrated a bouquet of flowers. A little paper tag was pinned to one corner and it said, in Darcy's tight script, *Great Gramma Isabell Reen. 1940 something.*

Morgan smiled and carefully folded the pillowcase. Darcy's adoptive family had welcomed her and given her such nice things. She put the pillowcase and a few other items in the maybe-keep pile, but set the box with most of the glassware beside the eBay pile. She could not imagine using cut, fluted, crystal stemware. They were pretty, though.

The next box was stuffed with ragged cookbooks and yellowed papers. Receipts, magazine recipes, old coupons. Junk, mostly, that she sorted right into the trash, but a thick cloth-bound book lay on the bottom, its calico cover stained and ragged.

She opened the home-made photo album and looked at sepia-toned faces she didn't know, many with names written below. Children and old people and skinny women in housedresses, most surnamed Thursby and Reen. Morgan flipped slowly through pages of pictures, careful not to crack the brittle paper. Sepia turned to shiny black and white, and soon those pictures became colorized as the fashions changed. Women wore pants and short, perky dresses.

The men's overalls became suits and shirts with ties; some folks wore jeans.

Harrises arrived, their dark hair and eyes so different from the blonde Thursbys. There were several pages of Anne Thursby and Edgar Harris's wedding, their understated silken finery almost alien to Morgan's eyes.

Darcy's adoptive parents. This must be Anne's album. Ed and Anne slowly aged as Morgan turned pages. They bought a house. A car. A new stove. But the only children were in massive family portraits, or at Christmas, maybe Thanksgiving. Sadness clung to the couple's eyes, dark within otherwise happy faces as time flipped by, page by lonely page. There were to be no children for Ed and Anne, until a scrawny mutt of a girl—

Morgan turned the page, expecting to see Darcy at any moment, but all the breath fell out of her at the next photograph: a bruised waif who couldn't muster a smile, cowering in a rancid-green dress meant for a kid twice her size. A label across the bottom was stamped *Morgan, age 9. Wisconsin Social Services.* "No!" she said, her hands shaking. It was her own foster image, the rotted thing they'd put on her folders and records and 'available for placement' pamphlets.

Out there in the dim, fading space around her, far away from the battered, cowering child swimming in the ugly borrowed dress, Nick came, asking what was wrong. Someone else was screaming, terrified and panicked.

But Morgan barely heard. *How'd Anne get that? Keep that? They adopted Darcy, not me!* slammed in her mind over and over again, as if it were a hammer intent on pounding a spike through her psyche. Her wail choked off as she scrambled to her feet. She didn't notice the glass of tea she'd knocked aside, splashing against the wall, didn't hear Nick rush in, calling her name. She just tripped over the piles of books and mementos between her and the front door. Nothing mattered but escape.

Lungs heaving deep, desperate breaths, she yanked the door open and burst through to the porch. The open air welcomed her, whispering her name.

She obliged, down the steps and to the road, feet pounding on pavement, her ponytail swishing across her back.

* * *

Morgan ran, the steady rhythm of her stride propelling her forward. She sprinted off the highway and turned, gaining speed as she blew right by the co-op to pass the gas pumps, city clerk, and machine shop. Three more houses and she hit gravel. Sweat poured down her face, drenching her in the sweltering July afternoon.

"Morgan!"

Up a slight hill then down the other side, soybeans on her left, corn on the right. There was a sheep pasture a mile or so up ahead, she knew, with a pond. She'd run past it before.

"Morgan! Please!"

A flock of quail burst from the ditch to her right, wings beating around her, but she ran through them, oblivious to their fright. She thought only of running, the purge and release, floating in the blankness of her mind.

"Morgan! For God's sake! STOP!"

She lurched into a tight yet tottering skid, the toes of her Nikes kicking up a poof of road dust and her arms flailing for balance. Momentum made her take another step, then two, or slam face-first into the gravel. She blinked, panting slightly, her eyes widening at the empty fields and un-paved road.

Where am I? she thought as panic gripped her. She flung sweat from her brow and tried to still the terror quivering her jaw as she looked to the fields beside her. *How'd I get here? And where the hell IS here?*

Somewhere, nowhere, just another empty gravel road like last time.

"Not again," she choked out. "I can't keep doing this!" She bent at the waist and gripped her knees as she sucked in one deep breath after another, far more afraid than winded.

Someone approached from behind, their footsteps heavy and plodding, and she spun on her toe to see what chased her, ready to sprint from—

"*Nick?*"

He half stumbled, half jogged into view over the hill, one hand gripping his side, the other arm pumping to keep his momentum going.

Exasperated with herself, she sighed and trotted up to him. "Nick! What... Why..."

He took a few heaving breaths and grasped her shoulder. "Are you okay?"

Confused, she shook her head and babbled. "I... Uh... *What?*" But he watched her, genuinely worried, maybe even scared. She swallowed down her guilt and nodded. "I'm fine. Not sure how I got all the way out here, but I'm fine."

"You scared the crap out of me, that's how you got out here," he said, still gasping for breath. He stood straight and turned away from her to pace alongside the road and rub his side. "God-damn you're fast." He looked up to the sky and pushed up his glasses as he huffed out a lungful of air. "Shit, I'm outta shape. You're gonna kill me if you keep doing this."

"Do what?" she hedged, feeling her cheeks warm even under a flood of evaporating sweat. "Go for a run?"

He stopped his pacing to stare at her, his mouth falling open before slamming it shut. A low growl escaped his throat and he barked, "Go for a *run*? Have you lost your goddamn mind?"

Morgan took a startled step back. She searched for a retort but found none, no way to explain how she'd again found herself alone and uncertain on a lonely gravel road. Her mouth worked, silently stammering alongside her thoughts. *How DID I get out here?*

A rusty pickup wheezed by with a load of chickens in the back and left a cloud of dust in its wake. Morgan coughed.

Nick, however, didn't seem to notice. "So now you're quiet?" He ran a hand through his sweat-dripping hair and turned away from her to stomp alongside the ditch. "Jesus goddamned Christ!"

"I don't know why you're mad at me."

He turned back to her. "I'm not *mad*. I'm scared and confused and I don't know what the hell happened or why we're clear the piss out here."

"I don't either." She wanted to flee, to fall again into the blank nothing of her mind, but she swallowed the urge away and thought of roots growing from her feet to keep her planted at the side of the road. She had to know what sent her into a mindless run. *Had* to. Before she lost her nerve and ran again.

She watched the thundering anger and frustration in him depart like a cloud's shadow leaving a field as he came to her, searching her eyes. "You don't know what happened?"

"No," she said, shaking her head. "I never know." Her vision darkened and she pulled her head back, twisting, and started to turn.

She bit her lip and barely heard the small cry escaping her throat. *No. Not now. I need to know why I black out sometimes. Please!*

"Morgan," he said from the dark, his hands on her shoulders gently shaking her. "Morgan!"

She blinked and a glimmer of light entered her vision. Still the need to flee called, wanting, needing her to escape with it into the sweet, painless dark.

"Look at me, Morgan. C'mon now. Look at me."

She shook her head and mewled, but a trembling shaft of brightness found its way in, stinging her eyes. She scrunched them shut and jerked her head aside, but Nick gently grasped her chin and made her face him again.

"Morgan. Not past me. *At* me. Come on, Morgan. I need you to look at me."

More light as her vision fluttered, much like the quail wings she hadn't noticed breaking around her. Then Nick was there, staring at her. "Look at me. Morgan. Right here," he said, motioning for her to look at his eyes. His hand moved toward her face then back to his, directing her vision like an airline ground crew. "Right here, that's a girl." He smiled, still holding her shoulder with one hand. "You back?"

She rolled her head to loosen a weird cramp in her neck. "Yeah. I think so. What happened?"

"Same thing as before, but a lot quieter."

"I... I don't understand. Why are we out here in the fields?"

He released her shoulder and hunched to look her straight in the eye. "You don't remember standing up screaming then running out the door?"

What? "No. I..." She glanced away to think, her brow furrowing. "I don't remember anything like that."

"What do you remember? What's the last thing?"

"Iced tea. Just poured us both a glass. Gotta dig through those new box... es..."

"Look at me, Morgan. Come on now. You can do it."

No, no no! Gotta run, gotta flee, don't wanna get hurt again!

"Morgan?"

She cowered and tried to pull away, blind in her fear. *Have to run, before he hits me hurts me tries to kill me. It happens, it always happens. Gotta go, go, go! Gotta RUN!*

"Morgan!"

She blinked then and groaned, jerking her shoulders from his grasp. "No. It's not the same. It's not!" she muttered, staggering away as her vision cleared. *He's not. Nick won't hurt me. He's never hurt me.*

He followed. She could feel his presence, hear him moving close behind. "What's not the same? Where do you go? Tell me. Talk to me."

"I don't go anywhere," she snarled despite the fierce trembling of her jaw, her hands. "It's dark. Just dark. Always dark. And I *hate* it." She took a breath and turned to face him. Made herself grimace a smile to show some expression, *any* expression other than blank fear. "How'd you do that? Drag me out of the dark?"

He smiled back, embarrassed. "My nephew. My brother's boy. He has epilepsy and every now and then his neurons will suddenly short circuit and he flails and screams and has no idea who he is or where he's at. All we can do is hold him, talk to him, try to get him to focus. Maybe it distracts him from whatever's happening in his head, I dunno, but usually it helps."

"How old is he?"

"Six. Almost seven. Been like that since birth."

Poor kid. "That's a hard way to live." She looked down, confused, at the gravel and dust on her shoes. She'd seen lots of things there over the years after a long, dark run. Mud. Wood shavings. Blood. All in all, road dust wasn't so bad.

"Do I flail?" she asked, barely hearing her own voice. "Do I scream?" A carload of teenagers zipped by, churning up more dust, but she was too scared to breathe much of it.

"No flailing. You just turn to run. But you screamed the first time, like someone stabbed you. The rest have been pretty silent."

Shaking, she raised her head. "The *rest*? You mean I've done it more than once?"

"Yeah. Five or six times just since I caught you. You ran out of the house, oh," he glanced at his watch, "almost forty five minutes ago. We've been out here in the road a good half hour at least." He gave her a quiet wink. "Forgot to grab my sunblock and I think I'm starting to burn."

She wanted to smile at his teasing, but she was too astounded and shocked from what he'd just told her. She'd always assumed that she'd have a single dark fugue and wake up, not fall into a series of them. *Is that what happened in the storm? What if they just keep coming and never stop? What then? Would I run myself to death?*

A sick glurgle twisted her stomach and she rushed to the ditch to toss up what remained of her lunch. Egg salad on wheat with a pickle on the side. It stank.

"Maybe you need to see a doctor," he said.

"No shrinks," she snapped, turning to face him as she wiped her mouth with the back of her arm. "No fucking shrinks."

He smiled, nodding slightly. "Actually I meant a medical doctor. Maybe you'd been hit in the head, a concussion or something, and they—

"No doctors." She winced and turned away, shaking her head as she walked in the direction the car had headed. Surely civilization was that way, maybe hidden by the trees on the hill.

Nick trotted to catch her. "Okay. No doctors. But there's something wrong."

"I'm not crazy," she snapped, marching up the hill.

"I never said you were crazy," he sighed, "I think you're scared and hurt, still, over what happened to you as a kid. And it's not going to get better unless you—"

She turned, glaring at him. "Unless I confront it? Weed it out? Medicate it into oblivion? What do I need to do with my past, eh? Maybe seal it up in a baggie and toss it in a freezer like a cheap cut of meat?"

"I don't know, but it's not right that you're living like this, always on the run from something you can't even remember." He frowned at her. "How often does this happen, Morgan? These runs where you don't even know where you are?"

How could she explain that until she came to Hackberry, she rarely let her pack leave her shoulder because a dark run could happen any time and she'd find herself in another city, or a bus or train or a warehouse somewhere? That the best she could do was manage to survive day by day?

Her eyes stung and the fields blurred, but she kept walking, soon cresting the hill. Well ahead, she saw Hackberry's familiar water tower and felt a flush of relief. *Not so far, then, this time. Only a half mile or so.*

"Morgan, please," he said, touching her arm. "Do they happen a lot?"

"When it's bad, they come every couple of days," she whispered. "I might go a month without one. Maybe, if I'm lucky."

"Is it because of what happened with your siblings?"

"Yes." She shrugged. "Maybe." At last, she met his gaze. "I don't know, okay? They just do. It just gets dark, and I..."

Angry at herself for crying, she stopped walking and scrubbed the tears away with the back of her wrist. "I run, all right? I *run*. I know you want me to stay, and I know you want me to do the sites, but I cannot stay in one place. As much as I like it here, as much as I like *you*, I just can't. I don't know if tomorrow I'll wake up in St. Louis or Orlando or the coast of Maine. That's no way to run a business, especially one as complicated as Darcy left."

He watched her, gaze aching and sad. "Screw the websites. It's no way to run a life, Morgan." He searched her eyes. "What if you run into traffic or off a bridge or something? What then?"

Muttering, "Then I guess I'll die," she ducked aside, but he grabbed her arm and turned her to him again.

"What'd you just say?" he asked, gaze boring into her.

She swallowed. "That I'll just die."

"I won't let that happen," he said.

She tried to turn away, but he wouldn't let her. "I don't see how—"

"Something is causing this. Whether it's a bump on your brain or forgotten trauma or whatever, *something* is making you run. If we find out what it is, and fix it or face it or build it a pedestal to sit upon, maybe, just maybe it won't plague you anymore."

"I don't know if I want to know," she admitted. "What if it's worse than the dark?"

"Nothing is scarier than in the dark," he said. "It's like a creepy lump in the corner when you're trying to sleep. In the dark, it's a monster, but with the lights on, it's just a pair of jeans over the chair."

Spoken like someone whose worst childhood fear was a boogeyman in the closet, Morgan thought, *not a drug-crazed mother using you as an ashtray. Or a punching bag.*

"I run. I. Just. *Run.*" She searched his eyes, hoping, wishing he'd understand. "Something in me's broken, okay? It's just the way it is."

"No," he said, shaking his head as if the motion could throw the thought across the field beside him. "You might be dented, but you're not broken. Morgan, I..." He paused, shifting nervously on his feet as he sighed and looked away.

"Oh, just say it," she said, half expecting either a verbal flogging or the insistence that she could fix her own dang computer, he was so tired of her running at the drop of a hat—because, after all, that's what everyone else in her life had ultimately told her.

But instead he looked into her eyes and reached out to take her hand. "There's a birthday party tonight for my niece. I'd like you to come."

She blinked, startled, and, despite the clanging demand to yank her hand free and run away, managed to hold her ground. "A... A birthday party?"

"Yeah. At Ken and Trish's. I've thought about inviting you for a couple of days now, but, well..." He stared at the ground and took a deep breath before meeting her gaze again. "You're not broken, Morgan. You're a lot stronger than you think. And I hope you'll come."

She searched his sweet, kind eyes and squeezed his fingers, but didn't let go. "Okay," she said at last. "I'll come."

SIXTEEN

Back at the house and nervous, Morgan managed to climb into Nick's truck without shaking out of her skin. *What was I thinking?* her mind raged as she looked out at the fields and ponds as they sped past. *A party? With his family? Oh, God, I've lost my mind.*

Nick fidgeted in his seat, his lips pursed together. "I have to stop by the house," he said as they turned onto a different highway. "Shower quick. Change clothes." He glanced her way and gave her a nervous smile. "I'll hurry."

"Do I look okay?" She plucked at her blouse, thankful that she'd picked up a few decent clothes the last time Jannis took her into Albert Lea. Surely khaki capris and sandals were better party attire than cutoffs and tennies. She'd even put a pretty barrette in her hair instead of tucking it all in a ponytail. No makeup though. Whether she owned a fashion website or not, she had no intention of putting colored goop on her face.

"You look amazing," he said and she blushed, wishing he didn't need his right hand to shift gears. She liked holding it.

* * *

Chuckie and Scott sat on the couch playing a first-person-shooter on an X-Box when she and Nick walked in. Both glanced up at them, but Scott quickly turned away, taking the moment to shoot Chuckie's character in the back of the head. Nick excused himself and hurried down the hall, leaving her standing in the living room.

Scott reloaded his weapon. "Big date tonight?"

Morgan blushed. "Not exactly. Just a kid's birthday party."

"Pff. A party's a helluva~"

"So your house tomorrow?" Chuckie interrupted as his character returned to the game. "And we're emptying a basement?"

Morgan tried to settle her nervousness. "Yep. Maybe a garage."

As soon as Chuckie appeared on screen, Scott went looking for him. "You better be feeding us," Scott muttered as he hid behind a post. "And not some crap store-brand chips and pop."

"I have popcorn and grape koolaid ready to go," Morgan said, managing to keep a straight face. "And lots of it." Down the hall, a shower started.

Scott turned, gaping. "What the hell? I'm not clearing out your crap for fucking day-old popcorn!"

"She's pulling your leg, asshole," Chuckie said as he scoped in on Scott's character. The first shot ricocheted off of the concrete post, but the next hit Scott's character in the shoulder and sent him staggering back.

Scott cussed, scrambling to get a bead on Chuckie as Chuckie asked, "What *are* you feeding us?"

"I was thinking pizza and beer, but I'm open to suggestions," Morgan said.

Chuckie chased Scott down a ruined alley, "Sounds good to me. Tamper Downs has the best thin crust in the county, and great hot wings, too."

Morgan grinned. "I can do hot wings, sure."

"If he gets hot wings, I want cheese bread!" Scott said, still trying to out-run Chuckie's shot.

Morgan pulled dirty socks from a chair and sat. *Hot wings, cheese bread, and pizza.* Got it. "No problem. Any preferences on beer?"

"Cold," Scott said. "And not that froo-froo lite crap you ladies drink."

"Actually, I'd prefer Pepsi," Chuckie said. He leaned back, whooping and cheering as his shot hit home and Scott's character slumped to the ground. He glanced back at Morgan and said, "But don't make a special purchase for me, okay? Beer's fine."

Morgan smiled and nodded, adding Pepsi to her mental list.

* * *

Nick drove through a tidy middle class neighborhood in Albert Lea to a ranch house with balloons tied to the front deck. The driveway was full of cars, so Nick parked alongside the street. He'd barely turned off the engine when a little boy bolted out the front door and ran to them yelling, "Uncle Nicky! You came!"

Nick chuckled, tooting the horn a couple of times before he got out. "'Course I came," he said as he scooped the kid up and flung him over his shoulder, carrying the boy to the sidewalk beside Morgan's door. "I told you I would."

He set the boy on his feet and grinned at Morgan as he reached for her hand. "And I even brought a friend. Morgan, this is Brandon, my nephew I told you about. Bran, this is Morgan."

"A girl?" the boy said, face scrunching up. "You. Brought. A. Girl?" He looked at Morgan then back to Nick. "That's gross, and you know it."

Nick laughed and ruffled Bran's hair. "Is not. And, besides, it's your sister's party, so it's only fair there's another girl."

Brandon fell in beside them as they walked across the yard.

"Okay, but can't you do Legos with me anyway?"

"Course I can," Nick said. "Moonbase Zeta Max or Attack of the Car Crashers?"

Brandon rolled his eyes. "Car Crashers is kindergarten stuff. Remember? It's either Moonbase Zeta Max or Pirate Mayhem Treasure Explosion for big kids like me."

Nick gave Morgan a wink. "Oop. Sorry, I forgot. But I know your mom doesn't like the pirate Lego game. We both got in trouble last time."

They reached the front deck. "Yeah," Brandon sighed as he trotted up. "It makes too much mess so she put it up. I'll get out Moonbase Zeta Max." He opened the door and zipped inside calling out, "Thanks Uncle Nicky!"

Morgan struggled not to laugh. "Moonbase Zeta Max?"

"Yeah. Space ships and ray guns and drilling for moon-oil. It's fun, especially when the robots attack." He opened the door for her. "You like Legos? I'm sure we can get you a space ship and a couple of gun-wielding oil drillers. Maybe between the three of us we can defeat the robots."

"Never played," she admitted as she walked in, then stopped, taking a startled step back against Nick.

A towering brick of a man stood just inside, holding a grimy, wriggling toddler in the crook of his arm. Behind him, a plump woman hefted herself out of a chair where she'd been stacking fresh-folded kids' clothes into a laundry basket.

"You're early!" the man said, his gaze quickly assessing the pair. He offered his free hand. "And you must be Morgan."

"I am," she admitted, hesitating before braving a quick shake of his massive paw.

The woman was nearly as tall, and she shouldered him aside as if he were no bigger than a kitten. "Oh quit being all nosy, Ken," she said, shooing him away from the door. "Give her some space. Nick said she was shy, remember? And guests or not, you're still not getting out of bath time."

"Well, dammit. Can't say I didn't try." Ken kissed his wife's neck then wandered off. The toddler wriggled and tried to escape, waving bye-bye all the while.

The woman smiled into Morgan's eyes. "I'm Trish, and we're glad you came. Don't let big ol' Ken intimidate you. He usually only scares fires." She winked then turned her attention to Nick. "Almost an hour early? Who are you and what have you done to my favorite brother-in-law?"

"Sold him to the gypsies," he said, accepting a quick hug. When Trish gave him a perplexed frown, he shrugged and said, "Actually, I was kinda hoping to make an appearance early and get out of here before JoAnn and I got into it again."

Trish walked toward the kitchen. "Pfft. Quit worrying about that. She always picks a fight with someone. Oh! Nick, can you take that basket of clothes to our bedroom, please? Just put it on the bed. And, Morgan?" she asked, glancing over her shoulder and waving Morgan toward her, "You have any experience with cheese?"

"Um. A little?" Morgan replied, following Trish's encouraging wave.

The sunny kitchen was painted white with royal blue accents, and nearly every bit of counter was claimed by groceries or pink-frosted cupcakes. "A little's more than enough," Trish said as she rummaged through a drawer and produced a knife. "It's just Colby-Jack and Ritz crackers. You can cut vegetables, if that suits you better."

Morgan accepted the knife as she felt a rapid fwump-fwump noise beneath her feet. "Cheese is fine."

"You can't imagine how much of a help this is. My neighbor's in the hospital, the washing machine was busted for a week, and the tranny went out on my car. It seems like I've fallen behind on *everything*." Trish pulled a massive block of cheese from the fridge and handed it and a cutting board to Morgan. "Just move stuff out of the way," she sighed, brushing a limp shock of hair aside with the back of her hand. "Stack it if you have—"

Her head tilted and, frowning, she hurried from the kitchen and hollered, "Ken! The washer's making that noise again! I thought you said it was fixed!"

Left alone in the kitchen, Morgan stacked two packs of buns on top of the coffee maker and had just slit open the cheese when Ken ran past, bubbly pink suds splotted over his shirt. "Shit, shit, shit," he muttered as he flung open a door and charged down the stairs. "Nick!" he yelled right after he reached the bottom. "I could use some help down here!"

Morgan sliced cheese, giving Nick an *I have no idea what's going on* shrug as he, too, hurried to the basement. The guys cussed and muttered and made wet, clangy sounds downstairs, and Trish didn't return. Once the cutting board became too crowded, Morgan found a plate in one of the cupboards and arranged cheese slices on it.

The front door opened and banged closed. Morgan leaned over to see Nick's mother and a teenage girl drop a pile of presents on the couch.

"Morgan!" Donna said, grinning. "I hoped you'd come." She hurried to the kitchen, teenager following, and asked, "Where is everyone?"

The girl wore a baby-blue *I Want My MTV* off-the-shoulder t-shirt under strings of bright white beads. Morgan tried to hide her flinch. Libbey had worn a similar shirt when working, only it was shorter and showed her belly.

Morgan pushed the memory away. "Trish went to bathe the baby, I think. Brandon's fighting robots with his Legos, and the guys are—" A loud creak-clank rang from the open basement door, and Morgan shrugged. "Something with the washing machine."

Donna scowled. "Not again. They just got that damn thing fixed. Beth, tell your father to quit gossiping on the radio and get in here." The girl hurried out, screen banging behind her, and Donna gave Morgan a consoling frown. "So they left you here alone to slice cheese amongst the chaos?"

"It's okay. I like to stay busy."

The toddler ran in then, giggling and naked. Donna laughed and said, "Oh no! There's a bare in here!" in mock horror.

The toddler squealed in reply and ran to the far side of the kitchen table where she crouched, partially hidden by a highchair. She laughed and peered around it, giggling and sweet. Morgan couldn't help but smile.

"Amanda Justine Hawkins! Get back here!" Trish said, huffing in with a diaper and a pink dress. "You have to get dressed for your party so Mommy can maybe squeeze in a shower."

Amanda squealed and bolted, laughing, just out of her tired mother's reach. She tried hiding behind Morgan's leg, one cool little hand gripping her bare calf, and Morgan teased, "Oh no! I'm *scared* of bares!"

She lifted a piece of cheese and met Donna's amused gaze. The older woman nodded, so Morgan slipped the treat to the fugitive. Amanda escaped to the living room, stuffing cheese in her mouth and laughing with a glee only happy toddlers knew.

* * *

Morgan could not remember ever being in such a cheerfully crowded house. More than a dozen adults had crammed into the living room and kitchen, more spilling out to the back yard, all talking or playing with the horde of children.

Morgan had spent most of her time in the kitchen quietly washing dishes and helping with food prep. By the time Nick, Ken, and their father climbed drenched and sudsy from the basement, nearly every family member in attendance had come in to meet—or at least view—'that girl what Nick brought'. If the random murmurs were accurate, she'd become quite the topic of conversation.

"You doing all right?" Nick asked as he gratefully accepted her offered glass of iced tea. "I didn't mean to leave you stranded in here."

"I'm fine," Morgan assured him. She glanced past to wave a greeting at a skinny woman whose name she couldn't recall. "Everyone's really nice. Curious, but nice." Morgan smiled at her cooking companion and said, "Beth here's been running interference."

The college-bound girl grunted as she scooped potato salad into a serving bowl. "Just from the touchy-feely types. Mom's ushered most of them out to join the game, anyway. Be right back." She carried the serving bowl out the back door.

Morgan resumed filling deviled eggs and arranging them on a plastic *Happy Birthday!* tray. "You have a really nice family."

Nick snagged an egg from her tray. "Thanks. They can get brutal when it's time for the cake and ice cream, though," he said before munching.

"Hey, don't be hogging those," Ken said, reaching around Morgan for a couple of egg halves. "Volleyball start yet?"

Morgan nodded toward the back door. "'Bout ten minutes ago." Ken hurried off.

Nick watched Morgan as he finished his egg. "You're handling this a lot better than I thought you would. All these people."

"Crowds don't bother me," Morgan said as she filled another egg. "I actually relax in crowds. Safety in numbers and all that jazz."

"No wonder we had to park clear the hell in Timbuktu," a woman said from the living room, loud enough to be heard over the ballgame on TV. "You didn't tell me this was a family reunion."

"Hold that safety in numbers thought." Nick sipped his tea and turned to stand between Morgan and the living room door.

A glittering pixie of a woman strode in, wearing denim short-shorts and red platform heels. She clenched a frothy day-glo pink package in one hand and sighed loudly as she surveyed the kitchen. "Patricia, Patricia, Patricia," she muttered, shaking her head. "All the counter space full. Again."

But there are more than twenty people here, not counting the kids. Where should she have all the food prep? The garage? Morgan swallowed and stole a glance at Nick, whose jaw had tightened. He set his glass on the counter and waited.

Apparently oblivious to Nick and Morgan, the new arrival tossed her head and pushed aside a tray of birthday cupcakes so that they nearly tottered into the sink. Then she put the present in the empty swath where it sat, lonely and sparkling.

Beth returned from the back yard and muttered, "Hello, Jo-Ann," before saving the cupcakes from ruin. "So glad you could come."

"Why thank you!" JoAnn surveyed the fixings. "Burgers and chips? Again? Doesn't Patricia believe in fiber?"

"My kids poop enough already," Trish muttered as she came from the back yard with a preschooler who obviously needed to pee.

JoAnn smoothed her sequined top and watched Trish herd the kid toward the bathroom. "Be a doll, Douglas, and make me a margarita, will ya?"

"No booze," Beth said as she made room for the cupcakes near the stove. "We're in Trish's house, remember? And, besides, you're still pregnant, aren't you?"

"Smart, Bethany," JoAnn said before rooting in her oversized sprawl of a purse. "And such style sense. It's no surprise you got accepted to a state school."

Nick's hand flung out and he grasped Beth's arm. He shook his head but Beth snatched her arm free. "If y'all will excuse me," Beth said, plucking a bag of cheese puffs from the counter, "I have work to do."

Doug's gaze landed upon Nick and Morgan. He nodded a tired hello while his wife smeared on fresh lipstick. Nick nodded hello back. Obviously brothers, they had similar features and coloring, but Doug was taller than Nick and almost as thick as Ken.

JoAnn clicked the lid back on her lipstick "So. Nicholas. Didn't expect to see you here today."

"My niece just turned two," Nick said, as if that explained everything in the world.

Doug reached for his wife's arm. "The guys are watching baseball in the other room. Why don't we go see who's playing?"

"No, let's not. Just look at him," JoAnn said, gesturing the lipstick toward Nick. "There's a pentagram on his shirt! At a child's party!"

Nick shrugged and managed an easy smile despite the tight twitch in his cheek. "Sorry, Jo. It was clean and I happen to like Godsmack."

"Jo-Ann!" she snapped. "Just look at him, Douglas! His hands are covered in grease, he needs a haircut, and surely hasn't shaved in at least a week. For goodness sake, it's a wonder he's not drinking out of the milk jug or urinating in a corner. He has no manners.

I've done my best to add some refinement to your family, but *he* still refuses to listen." She tossed the lipstick into her purse. "Why are we even here? All of my friends are at the fair."

"Because it's Mandy's birthday party?" Doug offered.

"Rather be at the fair," she sighed, disdainful gaze returning to Nick. "And who's he hiding back there? I don't recognize her."

Morgan eased further behind Nick and wished she could escape.

Doug shrugged and JoAnn muttered, "Why did I even think I could marry into this family? No one knows anything."

"I know that you love pushing people around and acting like you're better than us." Nick shifted on his feet and added, "Where's Jake? Isn't he a suitable fashion accessory?"

Doug flinched, but JoAnn took a step toward them. "At least we look decent when we go out in public." She smirked and said, "My home business is doing quite well. How's yours, Nicholas? Any clients other than your Uncle Patrick yet?"

"Actually, yes," he said. "Been working solid for a while now. Maybe the economy's finally picking up." He paused and Morgan saw a wisp of a smile. "So, selling cosmetics door-to-door is lucrative?"

Doug rolled his eyes as he eased toward the living room and the other men cheering the baseball game.

"Yes! In fact, I brought Patricia and your mother their orders tonight." JoAnn smiled sweetly and rooted in her purse again, "So who's your companion, Nicholas? Did some poor girl finally ignore your wretched manners, and wouldn't she *adore* a catalog?"

Nick glanced at Morgan, who took a breath before mumbling, "No thank you. I don't have any use for makeup."

"Nonsense!" JoAnn offered a glossy catalog despite Morgan obviously holding half a hardboiled egg in one hand and a goopy spoon in the other. "Why, I just read on GlimmerGals that every woman should make time every single day for self-appreciation and indulgence."

GlimmerGals? Aw, hell, that's one of Darcy's sites. Morgan clenched herself still and glanced at Nick.

JoAnn didn't seem to notice Morgan's dismay, instead she flipped though the catalog to show a page of bath oils. "All of our Luxur-Oils are on sale this month, thirty percent off! Just think," she said, smiling as if imagining clouds of cherubs, "after a few relaxing minutes soaking in a hot bath, your soft, silken skin could smell like gardenias or, *mmm*, bayberry!"

"Um," Morgan said, glancing at Nick again, "I'm pretty sure Bayberry is for Christmas, and isn't July kind of hot for a long, soaking bath?"

Nick covered a chuckle with his fist. JoAnn flinched as if struck. Her assured facade fell for a moment, revealing a desperate anxiousness in her eyes. She snapped her catalog closed before stuffing it into her purse. "Nicholas has obviously been a bad influence," she muttered. "If you're going to be snotty about it, you don't even *get* a catalog."

Morgan was about to apologize—she hadn't meant to be snotty—but Trish came through again, dragging a different kid. She glanced their way and said, "Oh, JoAnn. Before I forget, there's a check for you on the entertainment center for that zit cream I ordered."

JoAnn's assured, plastic smile returned. "See? *Someone* appreciates my advice. Now if I can just get her to do something about that horrid weight of hers." With a toss of her head, she strode back to the living room.

"Ain't she a joy?" Nick muttered as he reached for his tea.

"She seems really insecure," Morgan said.

A shriek erupted from the living room and JoAnn returned, waving a check. "You ass!" she muttered, rushing to Nick while

Doug helplessly trailed behind. "I've told you and told you and *told you* that it's capital-jay, little oh, capital aye, and little *en-en!*" She shook the check in his face and Morgan could plainly see a red capital E scribbled after the *JoAnn* that Trish had written in black ink.

Looked like it was written in sharpie. It had bled through the paper.

"There is no E in my name!"

Nick sipped his tea. "Wasn't me."

"I know it was," she grumbled, still shaking the check. "What do you expect me to do with this?"

"Cash it?" he said, shrugging. "It is made out to you."

She lowered her voice to a growly whisper. "My name does not have an E and you have no business putting one on it!"

"I didn't do it," Nick said, calm in the face of a woman who smelled like gingerbread cookies soaked in tequila. "Why would I?"

"Because you live to piss me off," she muttered.

"No, I actually do everything I can to *avoid you*. Trust me on this, I do not want you making yet another scene all because of me." He took a sip of tea and added, "You do it often enough on your own."

"Douglas," she muttered low and threatening, "make him admit what he did."

Doug flinched and swallowed, his cheeks pinking. "I think he's telling the truth, sweetie."

Trish chose that moment to peek in the back door. "Morgan, Nick, bring the last of those eggs, willya?" She then took a deep breath and hollered, "Supper's ready! C'mon, everyone! Let's eat!"

SEVENTEEN

"So, WHERE YA' FROM, MORGAN?" Trish asked later that evening while she ran a coffee cup through rinse water. "And how in the world did you meet Nick?"

Morgan accepted the cup and dried it as she explained her odd traveling lifestyle. "As for Nick," she added, "I actually found him in the phone book."

Trish laughed and started scrubbing a serving tray. "Wow. He was lucky, then. I don't think he's gotten much business from the ad."

"So it's been slow?" Morgan asked, not really sure if his work was any of her business.

"Yeah. He got laid off almost three years ago after the place he worked closed, so he decided to try doing his own thing for a while. But no one has any money for that stuff. They just muddle through themselves, I think." Trish rinsed the tray and handed it to Morgan. "It's too bad. Nick's a sweet guy, and really good at what he does."

"Yeah, he is," Morgan agreed.

Beth came in from the back yard with a fistful of plastic forks. "Found these in the wading pool," she sighed. She stretched to look over Trish's shoulder to the back yard. "Gawd, that woman! I can't believe she's still trying to sell Aunt Karen makeup."

Morgan leaned toward Trish to see as well. "Karen's the blind lady, right?"

Beth slumped against the counter to pick through a relish tray. "Yeah, and she's eighty seven." She gave Trish a sideways glance.

"Think Karen'll hit 'er with her cane?"

"We can only hope," Trish muttered as she finished washing another tray. "Maybe it'd shut her up, at least." She glanced at Morgan and offered an apologetic frown. "Forgive me for that comment. That wasn't very kind of me. I should be more compassionate."

Beth popped a black olive in her mouth. "No you shouldn't," she said, grinning, then rooted in a cupboard.

When Beth bent over, Morgan suppressed a smile. A red sharpie peeked out from the back pocket of her Chic cutoffs.

Once Beth had wandered off to collect cans, Trish and Morgan resumed tackling the mountain of dishes. "I hope we haven't scared you off," Trish said. "The Hawkins clan can get pretty rowdy sometimes."

"Everyone's been fine," Morgan said. "Nice." She glanced at Trish and added, "Curious. I gather Nick hasn't brought many girls around."

"Not one in the fifteen years I've known him, and it's a damn shame. They just can't see past the geek, I guess." She shifted to look Morgan in the eye. "You two serious?"

"I... I don't think so," Morgan admitted. "He's just fixing my computer, then I'm moving on." She fidgeted under Trish's calm stare. "Mostly we're just friends."

"Uh huh," Trish said. "If you say so." She returned to the dishes and said, "He's trying to rescue you, you know. Just like Ken rescued me." She chuckled, her smile wistful and happy. "And those Hawkins boys can be so charming that way, damn them."

"You don't look like you've ever needed rescuing."

Trish handed Morgan the next tray. "Oh, honey, you have no idea. My mom ran off when I was in diapers and my dad raised me, mostly by yelling to get him another beer. When we moved up here,

I was thirteen going on thirty. I was a wild one, that's for sure. Boys, drugs, fights, you name it, I was doing it."

She dropped bowls into the sink and resumed scrubbing. "I was actually in Nick's grade, since he'd been held back a year. Ken, though..." Her voice faded to a soft sigh, "He was a starter on the high school football team, even as a freshman, and was just the cutest thing, all big and cuddly and innocent, in an 'I will run over you and turn you into hamburger' kind of way. And I thought, I can take him."

Morgan tried not to gape. "You asked him out?"

"Oh, heck yeah," Trish said. "First day I saw him, but it was more than that. I wanted to show the other middle school bitches I wasn't afraid to ball the biggest, brawniest guy around. That was Ken Hawkins."

She glanced at Morgan and said, "Oh, close your mouth, hon, it wasn't as bad as all that. Ken, being Ken, said he had to date me a while first. He soon found out my dad was an abusive drunk, and, well, next thing I knew, Mark and Donna were at my house, talking to my dad and loading up my stuff. I lived in their basement until I graduated high school. Ken was almost done with his fireman's training then, so we just got married."

Trish smiled and released a happy little sigh. "I finally got to ball him. And it's been a great time ever since."

"Glad you found him," Morgan said, astounded that a life that started so much like Libbey's could turn out so differently. "Where's your dad?" she asked. "I don't remember seeing him tonight."

She shrugged. "He lit the stove while sloshed about four years ago, and the whole trailer burnt up. Ken and Mark were on that fire, but there wasn't anything they could do."

"I'm so sorry," Morgan said.

"Eh, no great loss. He was an abusive shit, even when sober.

Besides, it's better this way. My kids don't ever need to know how bad it can be."

* * *

Nick asked, "You sure it's okay?" as he pulled away from the house well after dark. "I can take you home first."

"We're like a mile from the store," Morgan said. "And there's no reason for you to waste the time, or the gas, coming all the way back here after taking me to the house."

"Maybe so," he said, turning the corner, "but you've already endured my family. I hate to have you sitting around while I key in prices."

Morgan chuckled. "Your family was great. Especially Trish. And I don't mind waiting."

"She is awesome. Ken's a lucky guy."

Trish is pretty lucky herself, Morgan thought.

Nick pulled up to a yellow light and eased to a stop as it turned red. "Sorry, though, about JoAnn. She can be a pain."

"Why does she hate you so much?"

"It's stupid," he said, glancing at her before watching the intersection again. "You sure you want to know?"

"Everyone else seems to," Morgan said. "I heard whispers, but everyone clammed up if I came near."

"Yeah, there is that," he sighed. "See..." he sighed again and looked at her. "Dougie's high school sweetheart dumped him to go with some other guy to the prom."

"That stinks."

The light turned green and Nick pulled ahead. "No kidding. Anyway, he was depressed, and convinced me he needed to get drunk. So I took him out drinking."

"A high school kid? You *didn't!*"

"Sure did. I think I had one beer the whole night. Doug, he finished off the pail. Anyway, we were at some sports bar and there were these college girls, three of them, and they were all flirting with me."

"With you?"

"Yep. But I don't pick up girls in bars. It's a policy of mine."

"Good thing," Morgan said, chuckling. She found it impossible to imagine Nick hitting on a drunken floozy.

"Yep. It's just asking for trouble. Some stuff out there an antibiotic won't cure. Dougie, though, he hadn't formed any such policy and he was getting mighty upset that these ladies weren't giving him the time of day."

"But he was a drunk high school kid!"

"Exactly!" Nick said, glancing at her as he stopped at another light. "Two of the girls were just having fun, being silly and flirty. One though, was dead serious."

"JoAnn."

"Right again! She was coming on strong, but I wasn't interested. It was awful. Anyway, she got ticked when I turned her down flat then she threatened to just go do my drunk buddy, more out of spite than anything."

He sighed and turned toward the store, a block or so ahead. "Anyway, I was about to send her on her way when Dougie chimed in that he'd love to take her to the car, and so they left. I tried to stop him, but he told me to fuck off. He could barely walk, so I figured he was safe. At worst, she'd take his eight or nine bucks. Anyway, she came back barely five minutes later and flipped me the bird. I found Doug passed out in the backseat with his pants unzipped."

"Oh, no."

"Oh, yes. About a month later she called saying she's pregnant with Dougie's baby and her folks have kicked her out of the house. Dougie refused to believe he was too drunk to get the job done that night at the bar, so he manned up and married her right away. At the reception, we all learned she'd been dating some rich college kid, but he dumped her when she got knocked up. That's why she called Dougie."

Nick turned into the lot and found a space to park beneath a sunny banner that proclaimed *County Fair Daze!* "So there she was," he said, "no rich parents, no rich boyfriend, only my hapless brother to fall back on. And he fell for it."

"That's awful."

"That ain't the worst of it. The kid isn't Doug's. He loves Jake like he is, we all do, but he's not Doug's."

"He might be, though. Right? There's a slim chance?"

"Nope," Nick said as he put the truck in park and turned off the ignition. "Jacob was born full-term just six-months after she'd picked Dougie up in that bar. There's no way he's Dougie's kid. Or even that rich prick's kid. Jake's still one of us though, one of ours, but JoAnn hates me because I tried to talk Doug out of marrying her, and because she'd tried to trap me instead and failed. Jake's almost two now and any of us would take him in a minute. JoAnn, though, doesn't fit in. All she cares about are appearances. None of us are like that."

It's all that insecurity, Morgan thought as she climbed out of the truck and walked with Nick across the parking lot. "Why didn't they bring him today? There were certainly plenty of little kids."

"Because he's not white, so she's ashamed of him. That's why Beth hates her so much. Mom and Trish keep trying to help, but Beth just wants to kick her ass." He pushed the door open. "Of all of us, Beth's the last one I'd want to mess with."

"Beth? She seemed really sweet."

"She is. But she's also ruthless. She didn't just get accepted to Minnesota State, she got a full-ride scholarship for volleyball, and not because she bats it around. She has three older brothers and trust me, she hits *hard* and is not afraid of a little pain."

The store had a few late stragglers buying supplies for the weekend, but Nick didn't seem to notice as he hurried to the stairs. The office was deserted, all the computers dark, and it took a few moments for Nick to wake one up and settle in to work. While he clacked away, Morgan stretched in the empty corner near the door. Her legs wanted a run, but they'd have to wait until morning.

She thought of Nick's family, their interactions, some of the whispers she'd heard. "Am I your only other client?" she asked when he stood to get another packet of price changes.

"Currently, yeah," he admitted, nudging up his glasses. "Sometimes I get a call for a corporate wiring job or a virus removal, but they're few and far between. Pat's my only steady work."

He found what he was searching for and returned to his chair. He set the papers down and turned his head to smile at Morgan. "You've really saved my ass, financially speaking. I don't think I've thanked you for that. What you paid me today will last me at least a month."

"You're welcome," she said as she stretched a quad. "I wish I could do more."

"You keep me busy, you pay cash, and you pay right away," he said, keying through a set of screens. "Can't ask for more from a client."

Morgan frowned. *Am I really just a client?* Worry gnawed at her until she asked, "You could handle the programming and maintenance stuff for the sites, couldn't you?"

His hand paused over the ten-key pad. "Yes. Technically speaking, they're not all that complicated. Once the coding's cleaned up and streamlined, it'd probably take me twenty hours or so a week to keep up with all of them, maybe less."

At fifty dollars an hour, that's a thousand bucks a week, she thought, belly clenching. *A lot of money.* Her voice quavered as she asked, "Is that why you want me to keep the sites? To stay? Because I'm a good, paying client?"

He turned his chair to meet her gaze. "No. I..." He frowned and stood, shaking his head. "It's not the sites, or the work," he said, watching her. "I don't want *you* to go. With or without the sites, I want you to stay."

Oh, Nick. I run. I always fucking run! She managed to take a breath, then said, "I don't know if I can."

Her voice sounded terrified. Broken. He came to her, reaching for her trembling hands. "I know. But can't you try? For yourself? For us? Just *try* to stay?"

Her feet twitched, and she shifted toward the door, but her gaze remained locked on his, so sweet and gentle. So warm. Full of promises and hope. Offering a life of light, like Trish had found. If only she could stay.

"Okay," she said, nodding. "I'll try."

EIGHTEEN

SATURDAY MORNING, Nick and his friends began hauling clothes, bedding, furniture, and countless boxes of junk out of the basement, while Morgan checked for important papers and mementos to keep.

About half had been excavated by mid-morning and Morgan felt yet another twinge of guilt for sending a box of perfectly useable blue mason jars to the landfill. As Bailey lugged it away, she shook her head and cursed herself for not calling an antiques dealer to take a look through the basement. While some stuff had water damage or mold speckles, most—like the mason jars—remained in decent shape.

She hated wasting things, yet she stood there, box after box, armload after armload, declaring Darcy's property as trash. She'd just sent a basket of decade-old dress shoes on their way when a woman squealed, "Oh my gawd! It's just like Hoarders!"

Morgan turned around to see Beth climbing into the dumpster with a wide, foolish grin on her face. Trish lugged a big plastic tote into the back yard while Ranger 'helped' by leaping about and barking.

"Hey!" Morgan said, rushing over to drag Ranger out of Trish's way. "I didn't expect to see you guys today."

"What? And miss out on a good decluttering?" Trish huffed the tote beside the table and set it down. It was full of cleaning supplies and garbage bags. She stretched, popping her back. "Beth and I *live* for estate sales, yard sales, rummage sales, you name it. There's no way we'd miss this."

From the dumpster, Beth cheered, "I found a Furby!" and she held the old toy up like a trophy. Morgan laughed. To her it was junk, but to Beth it was a treasure.

The girl climbed out of the dumpster and ran to them, findings clutched in her arms. "This is awesome!" she said, grinning. "It's cool if I keep this stuff, right?"

Nick trudged up with a box of books and asked, "Does Mom know you're here getting more junk?"

"Yeah," Beth said, still grinning. "She was gonna come too, but JoAnn asked her to babysit." She giggled and stuck her tongue out at her older brother. "So, nyah."

Morgan quickly deemed Nick's box of romance novels and decorating magazines to be discardable. "If it's okay with your folks, it's okay with me," she said, much to Beth's delight. The girl carefully placed her treasures near the corner of the fence and, giggling, danced around her brother and rooted through the books as he lugged them to the dumpster.

Trish bent to pull out a box of garbage bags. "You're sure this is cool? I actually thought Beth and I would help you clean instead of helping you make a bigger mess, but I should've known the bargain monster would appear." Beth let out another gleeful squeal, and Trish glanced over, shaking her head, as Beth ran past with a pair of moon boots. "That girl and her Etsy."

Morgan asked, "She's selling the stuff?"

"Oh yeah. She has an Etsy store and website. RetroBeth. She's totally into 80's and 90's kitsch and is a wiz at pricing late 20th century collectibles." Trish frowned at Morgan. "You sure this is okay?"

"It's wonderful," Morgan said, relieved some good would come from the junk. "She can take anything she wants."

* * *

By the time Morgan and Trish left to pick up lunch, the guys had each kept a few items, but Beth's pile was taller than the fence. Mostly kid's toys, decor items, and fashion accessories, it looked like junk to Morgan, but Beth danced about the yard and rooted through the discards, obviously delighted with the morning.

Morgan and Trish stopped at a convenience store for cold pop and beer before getting the pizza. And wings. And bread. And onion rings. If she was feeding the crew, might as well go all the way, Morgan reasoned.

As they drove back in a car that smelled wonderfully like sausage and cheese, Trish asked, "You sure you can afford all this, hon? Need me to chip in some?"

"I'm good," Morgan assured her, smiling at the fields they passed. The wide, green landscape no longer felt alien, but familiar. Safe. "I'm just relieved so many people came to help. It'd take me forever by myself."

Silence settled in the car for a few moments then Trish said, "Nick has a lot of people who love him. He says there's work to do, folks generally show up."

Morgan nodded. They were all there for Nick, not for her, which was perfectly understandable. She was a stranger, an outsider. A client with a messy house.

"You're good for him. And you're a sweet, sweet girl. So we're here." Trish glanced at Morgan before returning her attention to the road. "Look, I'm not good at talking about some things, I'm not eloquent or smart or anything like that, but..."

She sighed, pausing at an intersection before turning. "But most of the main family met you last night, and you passed muster with everyone except JoAnn." She chuckled and glanced at Morgan again. "Which, frankly, made everyone else like you that much more."

"Really?" Morgan asked, startled. "I can't remember hardly anyone's name, and I barely left the kitchen."

"Well, you got me when you played along and snuck that cheese to Mandy. Most people would have been annoyed to have a wet, screaming kid run around like that."

"Really?"

"Yeah," Trish muttered. "Really. I have horror stories of what some folks say and do when Bran has his seizures out in public. Most people are assholes, Morgan. You're not."

"Thank you, I—"

"Anyway," Trish interrupted, "I just wanted to let you know that Mark and Donna already think you're all that and a bag of chips, me, Ken, and the kids think you're pretty awesome, and Beth, well..." She laughed as she turned into Hackberry. "She heard you tell JoAnn that July wasn't hot bath season, so she's probably your biggest fan of all of us. Well, except for Nick of course."

Morgan blushed, not sure what to say.

"I know you said you don't stay in any one place very long, *but* I just wanted to make sure you knew that *if* you decided to stick around, you've already got the Hawkins clan covered."

Trish parked in the front yard and turned off the car. "And I for one hope you decide to stay."

Morgan grabbed the bags of wings, rings, and bread as she climbed out. "Nick and I talked about it last night," she admitted, opening the car's back door with the intent to snag a pack of pop. "I told him I'll try. No promises, but I thoug—"

"Hey, Morgan!" Beth called from the porch. "There's someone on the phone for you!"

Happy and bouncy, Beth returned to the house but Morgan stood there, slack jawed, her heart hammering. *She answered the phone? Oh no. Please. No.*

"Morgan, honey, you okay?" Trish said, hurrying around the car, but Morgan couldn't answer beyond a terrified blubber.

Nick sprinted from the dumpster, up the steps and across the porch, calling out, "Get away from that phone, Beth. I'll take it!" before the screen slammed closed behind him.

Nick! Don't! The bang of the screen knocked Morgan loose from her rigid fear and she rushed forward, bags clenched in her shaking hands.

She ran through the house in time to see him snatch the receiver from his startled sister's hand and bark, "Who is this?"

Morgan stood in the kitchen doorway, heart thudding and the scent of onion rings filling her senses. Beth took a step back, eyes wide as she stared at her brother. Beyond her, Chuckie stopped near the back door with an armload of Christmas wrapping paper. He too, gaped, his gaze darting from Nick to Morgan to Nick again.

No, God, no, Morgan thought. *Not another phone call.* She swallowed a bitter taste from the back of her mouth but remained where she stood.

"Morgan?" Trish asked from behind. "What's going on?"

Morgan felt Trish touch her arm and she cringed away, shaking her head as she watched Nick. "Uh huh," he said, glowering. "No, I don't think you under—"

He sighed and leaned against the wall by the phone. "No, I am obviously not Ms. Miller, and I have no idea—" He rolled his eyes and mouthed "It's okay," to Morgan before saying, "Look, lady, I understand what you're trying to tell me, I'm just not the person you should be telling it to, okay? I have nothing to do with advertising. I just—"

He closed his eyes and banged the back of his head against the wall, frustrated, and Morgan let out a relieved breath as her knees nearly buckled. *It's just a site advertiser. Thank you, God. Thank you.*

"She's right here, but she's gonna tell you the same thing," he muttered, pushing away from the wall. "We don't want—" Another eye roll and a heavy sigh. "Goddammit. Just hold on a sec." He held out the phone, palm over the mouthpiece, and said, "Want to buy an ad for GlimmerGals to run on some magazine's website from September 'til the end of the year?"

"Not really," Morgan said. She set the food on the counter and reached for the phone, her hands still shaking. "But I can tell her."

Nick let her take the phone and Morgan released a quaking sigh as she said, "This is Morgan Miller. How can I help you?"

While Morgan tried to explain that she didn't even know if the site would be operational in September, Nick turned to Beth and snarled, "Do not, under any circumstances, answer that phone."

Morgan barely heard the sales woman blabbering in her ear as she watched Beth's eyes grow wide and pained. "But... But..." the poor girl stammered, "I was just getting a drink. And it was making a soft chirpy sound, like, like the ringer had gone bad, and—"

"We turned off the ringer," Nick snapped. "So don't touch the damned phone!"

Trish came to stand near Morgan as Bailey sweated in the back doorway and asked why everyone was hanging out in the kitchen. Still the sales woman yammered in Morgan's ear about ad rates.

"Okay," Beth said, eyes welling with tears. "I won't touch it. Don't be mad at me, Nick. I was just trying to help."

"I know," he said, anger falling out of him in a huff of air and released tension. "I'm sorry I yelled at you. Just leave it alone, okay?"

"What's going on?" Trish asked, glancing at Morgan before glaring at Nick. "Morgan looked scared shitless out there and I don't think I've ever seen you yell at Beth."

Morgan and Nick shared a silent glance then Morgan turned away to tell the sales woman, "Thank you, but I'm just not interested." Then she hung up the phone and disconnected it from the wall, telling herself she should have done it days ago.

Maybe I should run, just go and never come back, she thought, but took a breath instead. Waves of shudders sent her teeth clacking and she dropped the phone at her feet. She felt cold, so cold, despite the sticky July day, and, shivering, she rubbed the goose pimples on her bare arms.

"Shh," Nick said, hurrying to her. "It's okay. Just a sales call." He wrapped a warm, comforting arm around her and tried to lead her from the kitchen.

Trish dropped her stack of pizza boxes on the counter and said, "What the fuck's going on here?"

"Don't, dude," Chuckie said, eyes narrowing at Trish. "Can't you see she's terrified of the phone?"

"Of a *phone?*" Trish asked, taking a step toward him. "That's bullshit. Mine rang at least six times last night and she didn't flinch. In fact, she once answered it just like Beth did. It's not the damned phone, idiot. It's who might be on it."

She glared at Morgan and Nick, lips pursed. "You said you run. A lot. Who's chasing you, Morgan? Some abusive ex?"

"Stay out of this, Trish," Nick said as he led Morgan to the dining room.

"No. I need to know whose ass we need to kick," Trish said, following. "Who's making her afraid to answer her own goddamn phone in her own goddamn house?" When Nick frowned at her, she said, "You know I can't stand it when some *man* decides to be an abusive fuck just so he can feel all big and bad and inform the world that he's packing a dick."

Trish stopped in the living room doorway and glowered. "Fucking asshole. Who is he? I'll bust his skull in myself. I'm a big girl. If I can take Ken, I can take down any man, especially with a ball bat."

Morgan rubbed her forehead. "It's okay," she sighed. "It's not like it's a secret."

Nick sighed and stared at his sister-in-law. "We don't know, okay? It's no ex causing trouble, just a nasty voice on the phone making threats. There's a mess with the computer, a bunch of websites with lost logins... Stuff that shouldn't be in Morgan's name, but is."

"The guy on the phone might have killed my friend, the one who died and left me this house." Morgan turned her head to look at Trish. "We don't know what's going on, or why, just that it's all twisted up and the guy on the phone keeps threatening to hurt me."

Trish's eyes narrowed. The others gathered behind her.

"You call the cops?" Chuckie asked.

"Yeah," Morgan said. "They're checking into it."

"Fucking cops," Scott muttered then stomped off to the kitchen. "I spend two weeks in jail for a little weed, but some shit who hurts little girls is still running loose?"

Everyone jumped when the backdoor slammed, taking some of the tightness in the air with it.

"What do you want us to do?" Trish asked.

"I don't know if there's much anyone can do," Morgan said, standing. "They called asking for me long before my friend died. Weeks, maybe months, now. And I have no idea who it could be or why they hate me so much."

"But something in this house might tell us who, or why," Nick said. "That's why we're checking *everything* before it's thrown away."

NINETEEN

AFTER FINDING NOTHING IMPORTANT in the basement, the guys ate lunch and turned their attention to the garage full of site mail. Beth had deemed the mail utterly boring and worthless but was, however, *delighted* to sort through the upstairs bedrooms and haul the excess to the dumpster.

"Sorry I blew my top earlier," Trish said, removing the smallest bedroom's ratty curtains, which looked like they'd once been old sheets. "I have issues, I guess."

Morgan ran a broom around the edge of the ceiling. Cobweb spiders had constructed quite a sprawling mess of webs and they needed to go. "It's okay. We all have them." She shrugged and swept the light fixture, just a glass bowl over a single bulb that would have to be taken down and scrubbed. "I certainly do."

"Yeah, well, an abusive ex shouldn't be my first thought," Trish said. "Just the expression on your face..." She shook her head and tugged the curtains from the rods.

"Like I said, we all have issues." Morgan ran the broom around the ceiling again, and down the corners to catch any straggling webs. *Maybe I should move up here instead of sleeping on the couch. Have a regular bed for a change.* She shook the tangle from her broom then swept it into a tidy pile.

"Who hurt you?" Trish asked, her voice soft.

It's impossible to keep a secret around this family. Feeling Trish's gaze following her, Morgan sighed and carried her broom to the closet. Her voice caught as she said, "My mother."

"I'm sorry."

"Me, too." Big, droopy webs stuck to the corners and down the entire back of the closet, so Morgan swatted the spiders with the broom before brushing the mess away.

Sighing again, she turned and ran right into Trish. "Oh, hey, I'm sorry," Morgan said as she tried to slip past, but the bigger woman grasped her and pulled her into a firm hug.

"I... I don't like being touched," Morgan said, her voice muffled in Trish's soft shoulder as she struggled.

"I know, sweetie," Trish said, still hugging despite Morgan's fading attempts to push away. "I know. It's 'cause your mama never loved you, but that's okay. We're here. And we won't let anything bad happen, ever again."

Morgan felt tears sting her eyes as Trish held her in the sunny room, gently rocking. Despite herself, Morgan relaxed against Trish and released a big heaving sob.

Never loved me, never wanted me. Never wanted any of us. All she did was hurt and hurt and hurt...

"Shh," Trish whispered, her embrace gentle and unflinching as she held Morgan close and stroked her hair. "It's okay. Shh. Let it out, honey, it's okay."

"She killed them. She killed all of them but me. Why them, but not me?" Morgan bawled, hands clenching desperately at whatever they found while Trish stood steady, letting Morgan's tears soak her shirt.

The astonishment in Trish's voice cut close. "Your mama killed her *own babies?*"

Morgan nodded, holding on as Trish's embrace tightened. *All of us. All of us but me. All of us because of me.*

"You poor thing," Trish whispered, cradling Morgan like her mother never had. Morgan sobbed, pouring her terror and loneliness onto a woman she barely knew. She stood there, crying and crying, until her legs felt weak. Watery.

But her heart felt so much lighter, like a miracle.

"Let me tell you something," Trish muttered as Morgan's sobs faded to deep, shaky breaths. "Your mama was a worthless bitch. No real woman hurts her own babies. Ever. You're a treasure, Morgan, and you never did anything to deserve a mother like that. So stop blaming yourself."

Her voice softened and she pulled back to hold Morgan's face in her thick hands. "You hear me?" she said as she wiped some of Morgan's tears away. "Don't you worry about her any more, or whoever's calling you on that damned phone. I'm here, Nick's here, and no one's gonna hurt you ever again. Not unless they get past us first."

Morgan nodded, sniffling and wiping at her nose. "Okay."

Trish held her gaze, stern but gentle. "And no one will get past Nick. *Ever.* Not if he can still breathe."

* * *

Beth had adorned herself with layers of scarves and costume jewelry. She was happily munching a cold piece of pizza and rooting through a box of trinkets by the time Morgan and Trish carried the remaining garbage and cleaning supplies downstairs.

"This stuff is so cool!" Beth said, grinning at Morgan and her sister-in-law. "Three Swatch watches, two mood rings..." She lifted a golden necklace and pendant from her sprawling pile of keepers. "Do you see this? Electroplated sand-dollar!"

"You share half of that money with Morgan," Trish said.

"Oh, that's okay," Morgan said. Thirsty, she hoped there was sun tea left in the fridge. "It's just junk to me."

"It's not junk, it's Retro-Beth!" Beth giggled as she found a pair of blue plastic earrings that looked like bottle caps.

"Share it anyway," Trish said. "Where are the guys?"

"Drooling over some car they found." Beth said. "It doesn't even run."

"Well, we've got to get going, hon," Trish said as she walked to the back door. "We're supposed to meet your mom at the fair around six and it's already after five."

"Yeah, yeah." Beth rooted through the box and let out another delighted squee. "A double-wrap belt! Sweet!"

Chuckling, Morgan filled a glass with cold tea and wandered outside to see the car. She stopped, taken aback at the sight of Darcy's old Malibu. It was a little rustier, and had an extra dent in the back fender, but she'd recognize the Blue Beast anywhere. The men had the hood open and all four leaned in, poking around while Trish craned her neck to see past them.

"That was in the garage under all that site mail?" Morgan asked, trotting up. She grinned as memories, all good, sang in her heart.

"Sure was," Scott said, his voice soft and adoring as he stroked the front fender. "1981 Chevy Malibu Classic, the last year before Chevy fucked with the lines so they'd look more like a Caprice." He sighed happily. "Navy blue metallic factory paint, all original inside and out." Another seductive stroke of the fender and he sighed, "Helluva car."

Beth wandered up as Morgan sighed as well. *So many memories.* "Yeah it is."

Nick raised his head and looked at her, perplexed.

Morgan shrugged. "Darcy drove it when we were in college. Was a great car."

"You can't hardly kill these things," Scott said as he returned to the engine. "Change the fluids, the gas, the wires, the hoses and belts... It might just run."

Morgan shook her head. "I doubt that'll do it. Darcy said the carb went out. Maybe it was the fuel pump. Something like that anyway, but it was *years* ago."

He frowned and stood straight again. "Something in the fuel line, eh? That's not so tough to fix. But it's all a moot point without the keys."

"Keys?" Beth said. "I found some old car keys upstairs in that little bedroom." She trotted to the dumpster and climbed in while the others watched.

"She ain't gonna find shit in there," Chuckie muttered. Everyone else nodded in agreement.

Nick closed the car hood and wiped his hands on his jeans before coming to stand with Morgan. "You okay?" he asked, his voice low. "You look like you've been crying."

"I'm fine," she whispered back, smiling. "Just had some girl talk." He beamed when she grasped his hand.

Time passed while Beth rooted around and Trish checked her phone. "We gotta get going, hon!" she called out. "Your mom's expecting us."

"I know it's here," Beth said as she tossed a box aside. "It was with the tennis shoes and fanny packs. Just another minute!"

Trish sighed. "You guys coming to the fair tonight?"

Scott didn't seem to hear, he was so enamored with the car, but Bailey said, "Yah. Got concert tickets last week."

Chuckie turned to gape at him. "Only you would pay good money to see the Beauties of Bluegrass!"

Bailey scuffed his feet against the driveway gravel. "So I like old time country music. Big deal. So sue me."

Chuckie grimaced and said to Trish, "I gotta work tonight. Besides, once you've whacked off to fluffy-footed chickens or bluegrass beauties, you've pretty much done it all."

"That's not fair," Bailey muttered, blushing. "I don't tease you about listening to Abba."

Chuckie flipped him the finger. "Don't be dissin' my Swedish hotties, asshole."

Trish laughed at the guys. "You joining the family invasion, Nick? Best fireworks of the season are tonight."

Nick grimaced. "I think I'll pass. Crowds and livestock and pricey fried-crap-on-a-stick all to a bluegrass soundtrack? Not my idea of a good time."

Trish turned her attention to Morgan. "How about you, Morgan? Wanna come with us to the fair?"

"I don't know." Morgan paused then said, "I've never been."

Trish scowled, and the guys, even Scott, turned to look at Morgan. "You've never been to a fair?" Trish said.

It never even made my list. Morgan took a step aside, nervous under everyone's stares. "Um. No?"

"That settles it, then," Trish said. "You have to come."

"I'm filthy," Morgan said. "I'll need a shower and maybe—"

"I found it!" Beth exclaimed as she jump-skidded out of the dumpster. "Two old-style car keys on a Garfield keychain." She flipped it in her hand, grinning. "Woulda just kept it—Garfield is *super hot* right now—but his tail has snapped off."

Morgan recognized the keychain and she swallowed a lump in her throat. Garfield had been on the keys when Darcy's dad had bought her the car, and they'd been an inside joke. Gar for the Car.

Nick had leaned over to have a nearly silent discussion with Trish, but Morgan barely glanced at them before watching Scott and Beth. "They're the right keys," she said as Beth tossed them to Scott. "But the tail hadn't been busted off last time I saw them."

"This is so great!" Scott grinned and opened the driver's side door to slide behind the wheel. He tried to start it, but nothing happened. "Worth a shot," he said, climbing back out again. He took a breath and met Morgan's gaze. "How much you want for the car?"

"You can just have it," Morgan said. "I don't even drive."

"I... I can't do that," Scott replied, glancing back and gliding his hand along the door. "A dinged up coffee table and pair of galoshes is one thing, but a Malibu Classic? Even like this, it's worth at least a grand. Fixed up, maybe eight to ten. That's a lot of money."

"Just take the damn car," Nick said. "It's already prettier than that wheezy piece of crap you drive."

"You sure?" Scott asked, his face as hopeful as a kid at Christmas.

Morgan smiled. "I'm sure. When you fix it up, you can take us all for a ride."

Nick drew Morgan aside while the guys gushed over Scott's new car and Trish and Beth made their escape.

"What's wrong?" Morgan asked, searching Nick's eyes.

"Nothing," he said, sighing. "Other than my pain-in-the-ass sister-in-law informing me that I had to take you to the fair or she'd be forced to disown me."

He took a breath and put on a chipper smile. "So, would you like to go to the fair?"

Morgan's lower back ached from the day's work, and she had cobwebs in her hair. "I don't know," she said, pausing to chew her lower lip. "I'd kinda hoped for a cool shower and a lazy night on the couch with a book."

"Hey, my original big plans revolved around the fun-filled excitement of laundry," Nick said. "While neither can hold a candle to a shower and a book, the fair definitely trumps sitting in a Laundromat watching my jeans spin around a dryer."

He grasped her hand. "Or we could just go get a burger or something. Trish would still kick my ass, but at least it isn't laundry." His grin returned. "And I'd get to spend an evening with you."

She grinned back. "So you're saying I'm more fun than laundry?"

"Definitely. Gobs more." His eyes had locked onto hers, making her tremble. "Gobs and gobs."

Gobs, she thought as time spun away. *He has the most amazing eyes. Blue-gray warmed with golden flecks.*

"Do we need to get the hose?" Chuckie said from close beside them.

Morgan took a quick step aside, her face flushing hot and, beside her, Nick released a harsh sigh. "What now?" he asked.

"Tried four times to tell you we're taking off," Chuckie said, walking toward the street. "Just thought you'd want to know."

Morgan released Nick's hand and hurried to the guys as they climbed into Scott's Pontiac. "I didn't get a chance to thank you all," she said. "So, thank you!"

"Anytime," Chuckie said, the other two nodding. All three waved and moments later they were gone, the Pontiac backfiring once as it pulled away from the stop sign.

Nick walked beside her and waved at Jannis, who'd come out to water her nasturtiums. Jannis waved back. "We don't have to do anything," he said, "but I don't think I'm ready to call it a day."

"Me either," she admitted. It was barely past 5:30, on a Saturday no less. Still early. "So," she said as she turned to face him. "What's a fair like, really? Roping cattle and all that stuff?"

Nick laughed. "You're thinking of a rodeo. And, no, it's more livestock judging and food vendors and amusement park rides.

And a lot of people. There's always a lot of people, especially on Saturday, because that's the big fireworks show."

She must have made a sound, or an expression she wasn't aware of, because he frowned and leaned close, searching her face. "You've really never been to one, have you?"

Morgan shook her head. She hadn't done a lot of things. No money, no one to show her, no one who cared.

Scowling, Nick stood straight again and crossed his arms over his chest, his scowl deepening as Morgan answered no to each of his questions. "Ever have cotton candy? A corn dog? Make spin-art? Feed a goat? Ride a tilt-a-whirl?"

"No. None of those things."

He let his breath out in an aggravated rush. "Then it's about damn time. Go get cleaned up. We're going to the fair."

TWENTY

MORGAN RAPIDLY DETERMINED that cotton candy was delightful if sticky, goats were kinda cute, and she'd never be a fan of corn dogs. But the fair! Bright flashing lights and tractor rides and a little spinning card to squirt paint on. Nick's nephew Brandon had helped her pick the colors, and Morgan found herself often grinning at her painted card, all red and yellow and blue. How could something so simple be so fun?

Folks with kids headed home after the fireworks, so Morgan and Nick strolled the midway through thinning crowds. They lost at a ring toss game, but won a whistle by picking a plastic ducky out of a swirling pool of water. They even rode the Tilt-A-Whirl, bumper cars, and some crazed spinning thing called The Scrambler.

"This is amazing," Morgan said, grinning and trying to take it all in. "And the fireworks! Wow. I didn't expect them to be so bright, or so loud. And they had a *smell*. Amazing!"

"You'd never seen fireworks?" Nick asked, surprised.

"Not close up. Only from way off in the distance."

"That's just messed up. Everyone should see fireworks." He squeezed her hand. "If you ever think of *anything* else you missed out on as a kid, you let me know and we'll get it done."

They walked farther, past a t-shirt vendor and a pock-marked guy selling pretzels from a cart, then Nick asked, "Ever been on a Ferris Wheel?"

"No." Morgan looked up and shook her head, jaw falling open. "It's so tall."

"Then let's take a ride," he said, leading her to the line. "You can see the whole fair from the top. It's kinda cool."

An attendant opened the gate to let a group of teenagers out, then Morgan and Nick stepped in, settling the safety bar across their laps as they sat. Moments later, they eased upward to just off the ground, the ride pausing to let more customers off and on. Morgan stiffened when their seat rocked.

"Sure you're okay with this?" Nick asked.

He seemed utterly calm so Morgan nodded. The Ferris Wheel moved again, groaning slightly, and they swung eight feet or so above matted grass. Morgan forced her hand to unclench from the safety bar and she pressed her spine tight against the seat. They chatted, about nothing in particular, and Morgan had the distinct impression that Nick kept her talking in an effort to keep her calm.

They were not quite at the top when the breeze picked up and she shivered. The people below looked small, like toys.

"Cold?"

She shrugged, not sure if she shivered from the breeze or the height. Her feet swung over open air, nothing below for a long, long way but metal bracing and wires.

Silence hung between them for a quaking moment, until Morgan glanced over at Nick. He met her confused gaze and said, "Can, I, uh..." and slowly raised his arm to shield her from the wind.

His forearm was warm against the back of her neck, firm, electric, and she swallowed and eased closer, still looking into his eyes. The wheel moved again, to the very top, as his arm curled around her and cradled her against him. He was warm, so wonderfully warm, smelling of Dial soap and Old Spice deodorant. A good smell. A *man* smell. His eyes had darkened in the ride's lights, becoming aqua green flecked with bronze. They looked both terrified and happy at the same time, and she wondered if he saw the same dichotomy in her.

Two more sets of riders climbed in as they contemplated each other, Morgan acutely aware of her heart slamming and the moist, tacky dampness in her palms. Now full, the Ferris Wheel began its rotation and their seat swayed but she barely noticed. His free hand touched hers, tracing her fingers, entwining with them, and she felt time slow. Her blink took an eternity as he lowered his head, and she turned toward him, stretching to meet his kiss halfway.

His lips were firm and sweet, gentle and cautious against hers. The kiss lasted a mere heartbeat or two before he raised his head and gazed into her eyes again. "Morgan, um..." he whispered, as they swung along the bottom of the wheel's spinning arc, his eyes searching hers, desperate for an answer he couldn't seem to find. "Are you okay?"

She squeezed his hand that held hers against her thigh. "I've never really done this before." She swallowed and managed to hold his gaze. "I... I just..." she shrugged, not sure how to put it into words.

"You've always run?" he offered, still watching her.

She nodded, heart thudding against her ribs like a beast demanding to be let free. "Yes."

He moistened his lips and his hand in hers flinched as he asked, "Are you wanting to run now?"

"No. I want to stay right here."

He smiled, beaming, and kissed her again.

* * *

Since the Blue Beast blocked the driveway, Nick parked in the alley. Well after midnight, they walked hand-in-hand to Morgan's back gate and paused for another kiss beneath the maple. Both repeatedly shushed Ranger's barking exuberance, but he'd been alone all evening and refused to settle down. Sighing, Nick eased away from her and opened the gate, letting the dog's excitement assault him first. Morgan laughed as Ranger left Nick and came to her, whole body waggling. She ruffled his ears and told him he was a good dog.

Nick threw Ranger's ball then reached for Morgan's hand as he escorted her to her back door and the light illuminating the patio. "I promised to help my cousin repair an old computer and re-configure some outlets with USB charge ports in the morning, but I'm free after that. You up for something tomorrow afternoon or evening?"

Grinning, Morgan glanced at him from the corner of her eye as Ranger returned with the ball in his jaws. "I might be."

"Cool." Nick accepted the ball and threw it again before drawing her to him. "Until tomorrow then?" he sighed as he lowered his head to kiss her.

He embraced her, and her arms circled around his neck. She felt his heart thudding so close to her own, his breath beckoning, his hands on her firm and encouraging. He smelled good, so damned good, he made her mouth water. The very last thing Morgan wanted was to run.

Ranger's ball lay ignored at their feet and he whined, bounding around them. The whines turned to an aggravated bark and Nick sighed as he raised his head, one hand resting on the small of Morgan's back as he bent to pluck up the ball. "Okay, you dang dog. One more toss, but that's it. You hear?"

Ranger leapt backwards, chest down, tail wagging, and he bolted after the ball as Nick flung it into the dark.

"I better get going," he said, ducking close for one last, quick kiss.

Morgan's brow furrowed. "You're not coming in?"

He cleared his throat, breaking into an embarrassed grin, and shook his head as he glanced away. "As promising as that sounds, I, uh, hadn't exactly planned on kissing you tonight, let alone anything else, and I haven't really, um, come *prepared* for—"

Morgan felt her cheeks burst hot and she lurched a step away from him, shaking her head. "No! That's not what I meant."

His grin collapsed and he started to reach for her but pulled his hand back. "Aw, shit, Morgan, I'm sorry. I just thought... assumed..." He let out an exasperated breath. "God, I'm an ass."

She paced a few steps away from him, her head down, her breath coming in short, quick puffs. *Stay put*, she told herself. *Talk this out. It's okay. We're both adults and it was a reasonable misunderstanding. Everything's fine. He's a guy, remember? It's right there in the front of their brains. No reason to run. Calm down.*

"Morgan?" he asked, taking a step toward her.

"I'm okay," she assured him despite the high-tension tone to her voice. "I just hadn't considered that you'd take it that way. I only meant that I was surprised that you didn't want to get your tools and things. To help your cousin tomorrow." She swallowed and braved a glance at him. "I just thought you'd want your stuff, not that you... We..."

He flinched, looking mortified. "I can get them, then I'll head on home, okay?"

"Okay," she said, still pacing as she fought the urge to bolt.

He turned away and opened the door. The familiar sound of its too-tight squeak stopped her. She stared at him, her eyes growing wide. *He'll leave. And maybe not come back. Because he thinks I don't want—*

Nick, wait," she said, hurrying to him.

Ranger rushed past them both and into the house as Nick met her gaze. "It's okay. Really. I'm the one that—"

She placed a finger on his lips to silence him. "Listen to me for just a second, okay? Just one."

"Okay," he said against her fingertip, and she drew away her hand.

"This is all new to me," she said, struggling to keep her voice steady. "I've never let my guard down, never let anyone get close to me before, except Darcy. You're the first guy, the first man that I've ever cared for this way or considered being with, and... and I don't want to mess this up. Whatever this is."

"Oh, Morgan," he sighed, smiling softly, and he touched her cheek. "I don't want to mess this up, either."

"Really?"

He smiled and kissed her forehead before drawing her into his arms. "Really."

She snuggled her cheek against his softly stubbled jaw and he drew a breath as if to speak, but held it before slowly letting it out. A breath later, he asked, "So we're okay?"

She nodded and leaned back in his arms to smile up him. "We're just fine. Well, as fine as we can be considering I'm part of the equation."

"Oh, I dunno," he chuckled. "I kinda like your kind of math."

"Yay me!" she giggled until he silenced her with a kiss.

Moments later they entered the house, hand in hand, then came to a shuddering stop a few steps in.

The air stank of vinegar and pine cleaner with an undertone of bad eggs. Nick released her hand and rushed into the vaguely flickering dark as Morgan fumbled for the light switch. She winced at the sudden burst of light and immediately grimaced.

Her previously clean kitchen was trashed. Dishes smashed, refrigerator contents strewn about, and all of the cans pulled from the shelves and dashed onto the floor. Ranger wagged his tail as he licked slices of shaved turkey from linoleum swirled with condiments.

"Oh, gak, don't eat that!" Morgan said, rushing toward the dog, but Nick grabbed her.

"Don't touch anything. We have to call the cops."

"What?" she said, coughing around the thick stench. "But he'll get sick. There's a pile of scouring powder—"

Nick grabbed Ranger by the collar and forcibly dragged him to Morgan. "Hold him here. I'll be right back."

Morgan clenched the collar as Nick stepped carefully around and across the mess without disturbing the crazed swirls and smears. "Where are you going?"

"Stay. There."

He made it to the dining room then disappeared around the corner. Morgan knelt, heart slamming as she watched the archway, and let out a sigh of relief when he returned, nearly running. His face was very, very pale.

"Where's your flashlight?" he asked.

She stood. "Top drawer. Left of the stove."

He used the hem of his t-shirt to cover his hand as he pulled the drawer open. After retrieving the light, he banged the drawer closed again with his hip.

"Nick? What's wrong? You're scaring me."

He flicked on the light and brushed past her, heading toward the basement. "Take Ranger outside. I'll be right there." Then he was gone, rushing down the stairs. "Don't argue with me, Morgan! Just go."

Morgan went. She had just reached the far side of the patio when the whole house, even the patio light, went black.

"Nick?" she called out, shaking. She stared at her back door while Ranger struggled to break loose from her grasp. *Where are you? What's happening?*

As if in response, the back door burst open and Nick staggered out, coughing. "Morgan?" he called out as his light sought her. "You okay?"

She rushed to him. "Right here. We're fine."

"Thank God." He grabbed her, kissed her hard, then pressed the flashlight into her hand. He released her to pull his cell phone from his pocket, and pushed a single button before wrapping his arm around her waist to lead her away from the house.

"Yeah, 911? This is Nick Hawkins. I'm at 326 Fieldmore Drive in Hackberry. My girlfriend's house was broken into. They trashed the place and cut the gas line, busted up some electrical. I flipped the main, but you might—"

Morgan swallowed, eyes wide as she stared at Nick.

He listened for a moment. "Yeah, we just got back from the fair a couple of minutes ago. Found the mess when we came in."

Morgan clenched her fists and watched him. *The gas line? Definitely not a kid. Has to be the shit on the phone!*

Nick listened, nodding. "We're fine. Just send someone. We'll be at the end of the alley in my truck, okay?"

He snapped his cell closed and held Morgan tight. "It's gonna be all right, but we need to get a little distance between us and the house."

Ranger was excited to ride in the back of the truck, and they drove to the end of the alley to wait. They sat, silent and staring into the night, hands clasped between them.

A fire truck and three county sheriff's cruisers arrived in minutes, and a utility truck pulled in right behind. It seemed like the whole neighborhood came out to watch the show. Again.

Nick and Morgan were immediately separated and questioned about what had happened, but apparently their explanations satisfied the deputies. A few short minutes later they were together again, sitting on Frank and Jannis's steps while four officers searched the house. Morgan shivered in the cool night air, even with Nick's arm around her. Despite the day's tragic turn, she smiled. It was definitely better than shivering alone.

Jannis brought them coffee. "I should have paid more attention," she said, pressing a mug into Nick's hand. "Ranger went crazy about seven thirty, but Midge was out in the yard with her Chauncy, and you know how he *hates* Chauncy."

"It's okay," Morgan said as Jannis handed her a steaming mug. "You had no way to know."

Jannis rubbed her arms. "I should have *looked*, that's all. Assumptions cause nothing but trouble."

Nick and Morgan shared a glance and Morgan felt her cheeks warm. She laid her head on his shoulder and he tilted his head to rest on hers. Next door, the deputies scurried about and another car pulled into the yard. The two detectives got out and entered the house. Flashlight beams bobbed against the windows, giving the place an eerie look.

"Oh, what am I doing standing out here prattling like an old bat? You kids must be freezing in those light shirts."

Jannis left and returned with a quilt that she draped around them. "Sure you kids don't want to just come on in?"

"We'd better stay here," Nick said. "Just in case they need us."

They watched the house in relative silence for a while, until Jannis became bored and wandered back inside.

"About what happened earlier..." Nick sighed, nuzzling her hair.

Morgan shrugged. "Don't worry about it. It's okay."

"Well. Still." He sighed again and raised his head to look at her. "I've thought about it. You. Us. Making love. All that. I can't deny it."

Morgan's heart took a heavy slam somewhere near her liver, and she swallowed as she met his worried gaze. She didn't know what to say.

"I'm not all that experienced," he admitted. "I mean, I've done it. Twice. Just meaningless crap in college. Once I was drunk, once I wasn't. But neither girl mattered to me, was just one of those things to get out of the way. Not that that sounds very appealing or whatever."

"I know what you mean," Morgan said, sighing.

"I also kind of had a girlfriend for a while, end of my junior year. Her friends pretty much hated me and she wanted me to become something I wasn't, so it didn't work out. Shit, we fought so much we never slept together, and I've already kissed you more than I ever did her." He shrugged. "I guess I haven't had a very good track record with women."

She sipped her coffee and stared out to the road. "When I was a kid, when everything was so, so messed up, I used to keep a list of all the things normal kids did. Ride a bike and learn to whistle and go to a sleepover. Stuff like that. And I tried, I *worked*, to cross items off the list. Even if I only did it once, even if I sucked at it, I could at least say I'd caught a fish or played pin the tail on the donkey or whatever."

She squeezed his hand. "In high school, three things on my list were to kiss a boy, go on a date, and lose my virginity, because, well, maybe doing that stuff would help me fit in and make me normal.

The kissing part was easy. I'd just pick a boy and kiss him. I was in control of it. Makes it all a lot less scary, you know?"

"Yeah, I kinda do."

"Anyway, kisses, dates... pretty simple, except when the kissee or date wanted more, because then I wasn't in control anymore, and I'd run." She chuckled, nervous, as she remembered how Jason Everly, popular basketball player *all* the girls wanted to kiss, had not only accepted a kiss, but had trapped her in a corner, pinned her against the wall, stuck his hand up her shirt, and started to unzip her jeans. Her hard, panicked kick to his knee had finally granted her a chance to flee, and put him on the injured list for three games.

She felt her cheeks grow hot. "The last item... There was this boy, George Pattukowsky. Shy, skinny, odd. An outcast, like me. Worse than me, maybe, I dunno. He seemed safe enough and would let me be in control. He wouldn't even look me in the eye when I asked to talk to him, but when I proposed we both get the virginity mess out of the way, no strings attached, just do it and get it over with, he agreed. Later, when we met—"

Nick nearly spluttered out a mouthful of coffee. "That's how it happened? Seriously?"

"Just let me finish. Later, when we met, and I took off my t-shirt, he..." She paused to take a cleansing breath. "He came in his pants, he was so nervous. And all I did, all we did, was I took off my t-shirt. Then boom, semen spreading on his pants."

"Oh my God. The poor kid."

"I didn't know what to do," Morgan said, glancing at him. "And I couldn't... I couldn't go through with it after that."

"I can understand that. Yeah. You were both probably too embarrassed."

"Anyway," she said, her voice growing soft, "Monday, at school, everyone was talking about how we did it. Including George. And all the twisty, perverted things I was into, especially involving his monolithic penis. I got called a slut and a whore and a deviant everywhere I went. Then the couple of boys I'd seen a movie with or kissed or whatever added to the rumors and it got really ugly and awful really, really fast. And nothing had even happened except one scared boy saw my bra."

"Oh, Morgan," Nick sighed, holding her close.

"So, anyway," she said before taking a cleansing breath, "that was the end of me checking items off my list. After I ran away and had a chance to really think about what I'd done, I realized I wasn't approaching it right. It wasn't fair to me, or the boys, and maybe it was worth more than just a couple of crossed out words on a piece of notebook paper. Maybe I ought to care. Maybe I ought to matter."

"Exactly," Nick said, watching her. "I came to pretty much the same conclusion. Having sex just to say I had wasn't worth it to me. Not when I had a chance to really think about it."

"After the mess at school, I went on a couple of dates, but never touched anyone, or let anyone touch me," Morgan said, her voice catching. "Nobody. I never trusted anyone enough. Until Darcy. Until you."

Nick lowered his head to take a long, slow breath before looking up at her again. "There's something special about you, Morgan. I want to take my time with you, not just get it done and over with. Ya know?"

"Yeah, I do. Absolutely," she admitted, searching his eyes. "You told the cops I was your girlfriend."

He leaned back, startled, a slight grin brightening his face. "I did?"

"When you called 911."

His grin widened. "I guess I did. Are you all right with that?"

She took a sip of coffee and smiled at the curious tightening in her belly. "Yeah. I think I am." She wiggled her feet, holding them up in the light streaming from Jannis's living room. "See. Not running."

"Sounds great to me," he said, tucking the quilt into a cozy cocoon around them. "So it's official then."

"Just to warn you, even my second-hand experience with relationships is... Well, it's a mess. No good examples at all." Her voice soft, she snuggled close and they watched neighbors return to their own homes as she laid out her fears before him. "Darcy was raped and my mother was a prostitute."

He sounded sad. Aching. "I figured it was something like that."

"But I'm still a virgin. At twenty seven. And I've never even *observed* a normal, healthy relationship."

"Morgan," he said, gently turning her face toward him, "I won't hurt you. I won't ever hurt you."

She managed to smile despite the stinging in her eyes. "I know."

"And there's no rush, no pressure, no anything. I promise. It'll happen when it happens, or it won't." He wiped dampness from her cheek with his thumb. "But I'd like to have a chance to fall in love with you, to see what comes of it. If we can."

"I'd like that, too. To fall in love with you. Yes." *Oh, Nick, I think I'm almost there*, she thought as she returned his hungry yet cautious kiss.

"Mr. Hawkins? Miss Miller?" Detective Kramer said, approaching them.

They stood, hands clasped together, as they walked with the detective. The utility company had turned off the gas and aired out the house, and the electricity was back on. Every light in the place shone, except the living room.

"We're still dusting, but it doesn't look like they left any prints," Kramer admitted. "They'd dragged their hand though various concoctions and fluids but left nothing but smooth smears."

"So they wore gloves?" Nick asked.

"Medical issue, most likely. We found traces of what might be talc on the front porch. We also found a couple of stray hairs in the basement near the gas line, stuck in what appears to be ketchup and mayonnaise. Longish light brown hairs, anyway. Similar to the ones in your friend's car."

Morgan's eyes narrowed. "Ryder had dark hair."

"I know, ma'am," Kramer said, frowning at her before returning his attention to Nick.

"But he could have dyed it. He could have hired someone—"

Kramer looked her in the eye. "I know you think your friend's rapist is involved, but that is simply not possible. Ryder Masterson is not a suspect, okay?"

"Why not?" Morgan demanded. "Even after what he did to Darcy? Even after the crazy things he said at his trial? The letters he sent? Damn it, I *know* he's not in jail anymore!"

She stomped her foot, furious, and tried to shrug off Nick's grip on her shoulders. "My friend's dead and now Ryder's after me. This is *my life* we're talking about here and all you can say is 'he's not a suspect'? Why can't you just lock him up or something?"

"Ma'am, I understand your frustration, but Mr. Masterson served his sentence as required by law and I, again, assure you, he is not involved in this."

"Bullshit," Morgan muttered, but she let Nick quiet her.

"What *can* you tell us?" Nick asked.

Relieved, Kramer returned his attention to Nick. "We've sent the hairs out for identification, and there were a few tracks in the mess. We'll catch them. You were damn lucky you didn't get blown to kingdom come."

Nick said, "Whether it's this Ryder guy or not, it's the same shit who threatened her on the phone and we all know it. When are you going to find the bastard?"

"Sir, I assure you we're doing everything we can."

Nick grumbled, "So what are we supposed to do in the meantime?"

"You folks might want to stay in a hotel tonight. We don't think they'll come back, but the house is—"

"It's my home," Morgan said through gritted teeth. "I'm not abandoning it because of a little mess."

"That's your decision, ma'am." The detective nodded goodbye. "You folks have a good night. What's left of it anyway."

"You know, maybe he's right," Nick said as they entered the house to see almost every surface smeared with some sort of fluid. Dish soap. Cooking oil. Hand lotion. The living room light had been yanked from the ceiling and thrown to the floor, its wires dangling down and gleaming.

Morgan stared at the vicious coppery sheen. "Is that what you went to look for?"

"I smelled gas and saw sparks," Nick said, nudging the busted fixtures with his toe. "Of course I went to check." He gestured to the switch in the corner. "The utility company has disabled it at the switch. It's an easy fix. We can run to the hardware store tomorrow and pick out a new light. Get some gas line, too."

The house was almost spotless a few short hours ago. "Okay," Morgan said, trying not to feel overwhelmed while taking in the extent of the mess. At least the computer and Nick's tools were safe in the closet, and her backpack crammed behind the couch where she'd left it. Other than the light, nothing appeared broken or out of place. Just sticky.

Nick grasped her hand. "I really ought to take you to a hotel. You need to get some rest."

She took a final assessment of the mess and sighed. "I'm fine. Survived a lot worse than this. I'll just start cleaning it up."

She released his hand and turned toward the kitchen to locate a bucket and some cleaning solution not already dumped onto the floor, but paused when he said, "Fine. No hotel. But I'm sleeping on the couch in case the bastard comes back."

TWENTY ONE

WITH MOST OF HER FOOD SUPPLIES DESTROYED, Morgan made an early run to the convenience store for a few essentials while Nick slept. She'd set the kitchen stereo to play her music and was happily humming along and frying eggs when Nick wandered in, yawning and rubbing his stubbly face.

"Hope you're hungry," Morgan said, sliding the two eggs onto a plate before cracking two more into the hot skillet. "I've also made bacon and toast."

"Didn't know you cooked," Nick said as she set the plate on the dining room table.

Morgan returned to the kitchen to check her eggs, which were almost done, and for the plates of bacon and toast. "A little. It was one of the many chores I had in the foster homes, and group homes, *and* my work-study job in college." She set the plates down and smiled as Nick dug in. "I'll never be a Food Network chef, but I can cook the basic stuff and follow a recipe."

She made a quick dash to the kitchen and back again with the other plate of eggs. She'd just finished eating her first egg when she heard a familiar repeating chirp.

My phone? she thought, standing. *Who's texting me, on a Sunday morning, no less? Nick's right here, and the investment company's surely closed.*

"What is it?" Nick asked, using a hunk of toast to sop up the last of his yolks.

"My phone. Someone just sent me a text." Stomach twisting, Morgan hurried to her pack, still crammed behind the couch. Nick followed and she glanced at him while she dug through a mess of receipts and papers to find it.

The phone chirped and vibrated in her hand. Morgan let out a sigh of relief. The screen said RetroBeth had left her one message. "I don't remember giving her my number," Morgan said as she opened the phone, "but it's your sister."

The message said: *sry 4got 2 tell u b4 ur tx papers frm bdrm in bot L kit drwr. <3 <3 RB*

"I didn't give it to her either," Nick grumbled as he reached into his pocket for his own phone. "Everything okay?"

"Yeah." Morgan gave him a perplexed frown as she walked past. "I think she put some tax papers in the kitchen."

"Yeah, Beth," he said, following her. "What did I tell you about stealing other people's stuff?" A pause, then, "Yes, I'm here, and imagine our surprise to find my sister texting—"

Bottom left. Morgan opened the drawer to find a stack of big manila envelopes, each with a year written on the front.

Nick let out a harsh sigh. "It's too early for this, Beth. And, no, that's none of your business." He flicked his phone off and stuffed it away. "Sorry. She saw your phone and helped herself to your contact list."

"It's okay." Morgan stood, envelopes in hand. They were dated back to 1968. "We finally have some financial records."

* * *

"You eat, I'll look," Nick said, grabbing last year's tax envelope before Morgan could open it.

She shrugged and returned to breakfast, munching while he pulled out a stack of papers and a smaller envelope of receipts.

He glowered at the front tax form then rifled through. "Looks like she sent out a *lot* of 1099's last year. Maybe forty or so. Yours was the largest," he said, glancing at her. "But all their contact information is right here, so it shouldn't be too tough to track them down and see who's still on the payroll."

"Okay," Morgan said, not really listening. All these years. All this history. She picked up the earliest envelope and opened it. Edgar Harris had made less than $400 in 1968.

"You don't need to look at all those," Nick said, standing. "Last years' has everything you might need to find the other writers and contributors, plus all her business expenses."

He walked around the table, but Morgan had moved on to another envelope, and another. Darcy's father had begun doing his own taxes while in high school, working a job at a gas station, and on through marrying Anne, adopting their daughter, and ultimately sending her off to college.

"Morgan, really, you don't need to dig through those," Nick said, but she barely heard. Her belly felt sick. Twisty. And she was too startled to move from the table, let alone run, as she moved from one year to the next.

Each tax form was carefully filled in pencil, each receipt noted and paper-clipped. State and federal taxes were all written in Ed's clear, tidy hand until he died.

Including EZ forms for a teenage girl named Morgan. Morgan Miller.

"This isn't possible," Morgan said, hands shaking. "These aren't my taxes. I never worked at—" She unfolded the W-2 then flung the whole wretched thing to the floor. It, too, had her name on it. "Friendly Foods Enterprises. *Darcy* worked some burger shack for her first job. Not me."

Every bit of her trembled and she had trouble breathing. "Why is my name on these? I don't understand. I've never had a regular job. I'm too flighty. I run, I always *run*."

Her hands shuddered so hard they fluttered against the table with rapid taps that hurt her fingers, yet she could not still them. "I'm on her mail, her utilities, her websites, and now her *taxes*?" She managed to roll her head back and ask Nick, "What's going on? How can this be happening? Why am I on Darcy's taxes?"

"Let me see it," Nick said, his face pale. He plucked the form from the floor while she sat there, shuddering.

"I'm not Darcy. I swear I'm not," Morgan babbled as Nick read over the form. "I don't care what these papers all say. The mail. The crazy city clerk. We were college *roommates*. Friends. I have memories of her. I'm taller than her. My eyes are greener. She drives. I run."

Morgan let her head droop back and she groaned at the ceiling, "Why didn't I just run?"

Nick set that tax form aside and opened the following year's envelope. "Hold on," he said as he rooted through the contents. "We'll figure this out."

"I am not Darcy!" Morgan said, her voice rising. "And she's not me! I've never been to this town before that stupid financial planner left me here!"

Nick set aside the second set of tax forms and stood. "I need to show you something," he said as he hurried around the table to the sideboard. He pulled out a ragged photo album.

Morgan shook her head. "No. Please," she begged, watching Nick bring the album to her. "Don't make me. Please." She couldn't remember ever seeing the awful thing before, but she glared at it, teeth bared.

Nick knelt beside her and took one trembling hand in his. "Look at me," he said. "I know why you're scared, but it's okay."

"I don't want to see it," Morgan whimpered. "I don't want to know what that thing is."

I'm not Darcy and Darcy's not me. What the hell is going on? I have to know, but I can't, I can't, I can't!

"Do you remember the other day when you'd run out to the road?" he said, eyes searching hers. "By the fields?"

She nodded, watching his face instead of the horrid photo album. "When you invited me to Mandy's party? Yes, I remember."

"I found this on the floor while you were getting ready. You were looking at it before you ran."

Morgan's gaze darted to it. *How can something I'd never seen be so terrifying?* "No."

"Yes. You just don't remember. I want to show you something in it, okay? Then we'll look at those tax forms again." He touched her face, looked into her eyes. "You can do this."

"No it won't. It'll never be okay again." She looked at him, silently pleading. "It'll show me I'm crazy."

"You're not crazy," he said. "Just scared." His expression softened and he asked, "Can you trust me? Just for a couple of minutes more?"

Her heart slammed. She wanted to run, to flee, to bolt screaming from the house and never come back, but her shudders slowed and at last she nodded, even though she could not speak. *I have to stop running. I have to face whatever I'm always fleeing from. Have to.*

"Okay," he said, opening the book. "This is the page you were on."

Morgan grimaced at the photo of her in that horrible green dress. She definitely recognized the picture. So much shame and fear, so many bad memories, all tucked into a grimy—

"It's computer printed," Nick said, lifting it and turning it over. "Photo paper, yeah, but it's a bubble jet print. Feel it. See the dots? And it was taken in, what? 1999? 2000? This paper was manufactured in 2008." He held it up, pointed to a copyright under the manufacturer logo. "Do you see that, Morgan? 2008? At the earliest."

Morgan's shudders slowed. "It's a... a copy?"

"A fairly *recent* copy," he repeated, smiling into her eyes. He flipped another couple of pages into the album, showing her places where faces of babies and toddlers who looked like Morgan had been cut up and glued onto the page, covering other babies faces. He flipped on to pretty, dark-haired girls carefully trimmed and pasted down. While she watched, he peeled one away. It tore to reveal a crying, blunt-faced child of a similar age.

"Does this little girl look like Darcy?"

Morgan nodded, relieved. "Yeah."

"*Now* look at the taxes," he said, reaching for the page Morgan had dropped on the floor. He held it up to the light. "There's a smear behind your name. It's faint, but it's there. I think she erased her own and put yours in. Same thing on the W-2, since it's hand-written." He reached for the next tax form. "It's easier to see here, especially a faint curve of the D behind the first M. But this W-2 was typed, maybe computer printed. What does it say, Morgan?"

"Darcy L. Harris," Morgan said as if witnessing a miracle. Machine typed letters beneath her own name hand-written in ink.

"You're not crazy," Nick said. He kissed her and brushed her hair from her face with his palm as he searched her eyes. "But I don't think your friend had been telling you the truth about anything. Maybe for a long time." He paused, jaw tightening, then he said, "Let's get these picked back up."

* * *

While Morgan tidied their breakfast mess, Nick set up the computers on the dining room table. "I haven't shown you everything I've found on that hard drive," he said, eyes searching hers for understanding. "You were so upset after you saw that picture and that one WordPress cookie, I just didn't want to make things worse."

She sat beside him and grasped his hand. "What did you find?"

"Another cookie," he said, clicking a few keys. "It's archives of old newspaper articles."

He pressed enter and watched her as the screen loaded. "Articles about you."

A page opened with a list of links, all with sensational titles like *One Girl Survived!* and *Mad-Mother Survivor In Critical Condition.*

Dozens of them, from newspapers all over Wisconsin. Indianapolis. Dayton. St. Louis. Chicago. Even a short article in the LA Times. Arranged chronologically, they covered the first flash of breaking news of children found dead in project housing, to detailed accounts of the damage Morgan and her siblings had received, to Liberty Miller's crazed, horsey rants at trial, to a fluff piece about Morgan when she'd first been deemed available for adoption, complete with the picture of her in that hated green dress.

Morgan wanted to vomit. "Why get and keep these awful links?"

"They're not really links," Nick said. "Look at them. They're *printed* articles that have been scanned in, maybe from microfiche. I don't know how she got them all, but she stored them on another hidden website."

He leaned back and looked at her. "I've even Googled a couple of the articles themselves, typed in a few phrases, all of the titles. Nothing here is available online, except for her personal use. They're all from before newspapers put everything on the net, Morgan, from paper archives. Some of the newspapers don't even exist anymore and other notices came from Wisconsin Social Services. She surely hacked those."

Morgan looked at the screen then back to Nick. "Why?" she asked again, hand over her gurgling throat.

"I don't know," he said. "But this page was made with an early version of PageMill. It was discontinued in 2000."

She leaned back, shaking her head. "Maybe she just used an old program. It happens. People create things with outdated software all the time."

"Morgan, the software came on floppies and won't even load on a modern computer. Mac stopped supporting that OS years ago."

Morgan swallowed. *Darcy? What have you done?*

"There's more," he said, voice gentle. "And it gets worse."

"How can it get worse?"

He grasped her hand. Held it. "There's a digital time stamp on all electronic files that shows when it was first created. Like a copyright. The oldest scan on this site was made in 2002. Whatever she was doing, it's been happening a long time."

Long before we met in college. Jesus, she would have been eight or nine years old. No. It's not possible. She was my only friend!

Morgan lurched to her feet and ran to the kitchen to lose her breakfast into the sink.

TWENTY TWO

NICK WANTED TO STAY, to work on his cousin's computer another day, but Morgan insisted that she'd be all right. Once he left, she set out a fresh jar of sun tea and made herself look through Darcy's links.

All of them.

She skimmed pages and pages of notes from her social workers that detailed her fears, lack of trust, and tendency to flee. Court records that moved her from house to house, foster parent to group home. Police affidavits from neighbors at the time of the attack, and others from long before Libbey poisoned them all and went out to get her dope. Teachers. Relatives she didn't remember. The shop owner who sold her penny gum.

She saw low-res bitmapped versions of her and Bret's school pictures, all just a little bit crooked or ragged on the screen. One had a crease across Bret's face.

Tears welled in Morgan's eyes, yet she kept looking, reading. Psychology assessments and medical records and a flagged notation that she'd had her first period in October the year she'd turned thirteen. Extreme physical abuse. Severe psychological trauma. PTSD. Drug exposure. Bonding disorder. Psychosis. Blackouts. Desperate need for affection, over-eager to please, yet screaming terror at being touched.

Morgan read them all.

And all were accurate. Or had been.

Her official records finished, she moved onto the news articles.

They were harder to endure. Her stomach clenched at a page focused on Libbey's incarceration at Taycheedah Correctional Institution. How to send letters. How to make calls. How to help her appeal.

Had Darcy really tried to visit her like the cops said? Oh, God, no.

About mid-page, Morgan found a link with no title, just a number, and she clicked on it.

Crime scene photos.

One glance at Cas laying there, eyes open but gone next to a photo of her own blood drying on yellow linoleum. Morgan closed Nick's laptop and walked to the kitchen to cry.

Then she went for a run.

* * *

She ran dirt roads until her legs ached, then she wandered into a clump of trees surrounding a small, overgrown pond. She sat there a long time in the shade of a wind-twisted willow, mostly watching bugs and little fishes in the water while she tried to think.

Darcy knew where I went to school. My major. Everything. Because the social workers had written it in my files. It was all right there, on her computer.

Darcy had lied to her, from the very moment they'd met. Those long talks late at night when Morgan had bared part of her soul, Darcy already knew it all. She wasn't listening because she'd cared. No. She'd listened, she'd asked questions, only to feed a lurid appetite. She'd anointed Morgan with backhanded compliments and conditional kindness. Left her dependent. Left her scared and helpless and trapped, unable to survive without Darcy's oh-so-generous assistance.

Morgan's head rolled back and she looked up at the sky, bits and flashes of blue flickering from behind the leaves. *She kept* buying SpaghettiOs, sometimes eating the nasty things cold from the can even though they made her sick. She'd find some excuse to drive through prostitute row to comment about the whores, and the horses! Gah! She knew I hated horses, but she had all those posters and nasty little figurines and she always wanted to stop and pet the dang things. And then she'd see some poor kid, grimy and bruised, and laugh that maybe he, too, could run away into a scholarship someday. She'd copy my homework, tell me I was so lucky to have state aid instead of parents footing the bill. Why? Because I was lucky. It all was just handed to me. Never mind my scars or fears or blinding panic, I was lucky.

Morgan stood, blinking away the tears of betrayal.

But I loved her anyway. My friend. My only friend. But she used me. Hid things from me from the very beginning. And I sat there, I took it, ignored it, hell, I swallowed it because I finally, for once in my life, had a friend. Or at least I thought I did.

Morgan's jaw trembled as she loosened her legs for the run home. Her death was one last tweak, one last way to make me squirm. One last chance to control me.

"You might have left me stranded with all your crap," Morgan said aloud, "but you're not going to hurt me anymore."

She left the pond and ran down the road, feet pounding steadily on gravel. As she turned toward Hackberry, she muttered, "And neither is anyone else."

* * *

Morgan came in the back door to Ranger's delighted bark and Nick standing in the kitchen, glaring at her.

"Where the hell have you been?" he asked. "I come back and you're gone?"

"I went for a run." Morgan shouldered past him to get a glass from the cupboard. She needed a drink.

"A *run?*" he said, voice rising. "Without your phone or money or—"

She turned, glass in hand. "What I do with my time is none of your business and I can run any time I damn well please."

"I've been here almost two hours and I was worried, Morgan. *Worried.* You were alone out there!"

She turned on the tap and filled her glass. "I'm always alone."

"I didn't know if you left or were kidnapped by the creep on the phone or if you fell into one of your blackouts and were on your way to Fargo." He paced. "What was I supposed to do? Go looking for you? Call the cops? The airport? Shit, Morgan, you didn't even take your bag or the dog."

Morgan drank while he ranted, emptying the glass, then she filled it again.

"I was worried, okay?" Nick said, his voice settling. "Can't you understand that? I was scared something had happened to you."

"Why? So you could come along and save me again?" she muttered, brushing past him. "Maybe I don't need saving."

"What?" he said, following. "I'm not—"

"Yes you are!" she said, turning to face him. "Poor little Morgan needs to be saved and protected and coddled and treated like she's some fragile piece of glass. Boo fucking hoo. That's bullshit, Nick. I can take care of myself. I'm a survivor. Or didn't you read the newspaper articles?"

He pursed his lips and crossed his arms over his chest. "Yeah. A survivor who can't even drive."

"Do you know why I can't drive?" she snapped, struggling to keep from screaming. Or crying. "Because no one fucking taught me, okay? No one ever gave a shit about me. No one wanted to spend the time or effort to teach me anything, other than how to cook and clean and be a good little slave. And when I was done scrubbing floors and scouring bathtubs, it was off to bed for Morgan. Go be quiet and leave us alone, or we'll give you a beating until you will."

She took a step toward him. "So I never played Legos or went to a fair or learned to drive. So what? I taught myself what I needed, and I survived. It's what I do." She took a breath, glaring into his eyes. "But I had hope, dammit, hope that somewhere, someone would actually care about me instead of... of abusing me. Lying to me. Tricking me."

She felt tears sting her eyes, but she swiped them away with the back of her wrist. "Darcy was just like the rest, only sneakier. I trusted her, and it was all a lie, an elaborate ruse to make me jump through her twisted hoops and make me think she actually cared."

"*I* care," Nick said, braving a single step toward her.

Morgan's lower lip quivered, and her hands quaked, sending a tremble through her arms. "How long did you have that site? The one with the news articles?"

He blanched. "Same day as the first one. You were so upset, I didn't want—"

"See?" she said as she turned and stomped to the living room. "I thought you were my friend, but you hid things from me, lied to me."

"Just until you'd calmed down!" he said, following. "I didn't want you to run off again, or—"

"It's how I survive! How do you think I managed to get through my childhood? By sitting in a corner and letting people hurt me?"

"I'm not trying to hurt you! I'm trying to sa—" he said, then he clamped his mouth shut.

"You're trying to save me."

"That's not what I meant!"

"Deny it all you want. I already heard it's what you Hawkins boys do." Her arms crossed over her belly. "I might run, but at least I don't try to change people. Or lie to them."

"I haven't lied to you. Or tried to change you."

"Oh?" she asked. "Did you read those files? My psych reports? Maybe that news article about how I testified against my own mother on camera so I wouldn't have to face her at trial?"

He took a few deep breaths, eyes locked on hers. "Yes."

She clenched her teeth and muttered, "All of it?"

His eyes were sad. Pained. Desperate. "Every word."

"And not only did you not mention that you found them, you *read* them?" Tears stung again. "Before you kissed me last night? You'd read all those awful things? *Private* things?"

He started to reach for her but drew back his hands. "Yes, but, Morgan, try to understand, I just wanted—"

"When were you going to tell me?" she asked, turning away. "Were you planning to take me to your bed and ask about my hallucinations? Or was dinner conversation about my mother making me smoke crack more your cup of tea?" He touched her shoulder, but she shrugged him away. "Don't touch me. You have no right to know those things. My past is mine. And it's private."

"You're right. I shouldn't have invaded your privacy like that. But I just wanted to understand. To *help*."

She turned, furious, and managed to meet his gaze. "Is that why your family and friends have flocked around me? Because you told them how messed up I am and they too want to *help*?"

"No," he said, shaking his head. "No! I haven't told them any—"

"Then how do they know?" she asked, voice rising again. "Trish and your folks and your friends? How do they know I'm messed up and abused?"

He gaped for a moment before muttering, "You're kidding, right?"

"I am not kidding! Trish asked me about it, like she already knew. And is that why you invited me to the party to meet your broken sister-in-law? To talk to Trish because she was abused too?"

"First," Nick said, his voice firm and even, "I've never told anyone a single thing about you or your past."

"Bullshit," Morgan said. "They ask me, Nick, every goddamn one, and they're so sweet and kind and—"

"They ask because you wear your pain and self-loathing on your shirt like a fucking achievement badge. It's obvious you're hurting, been abused. Bad. I didn't have to say a word about any of that."

Morgan's eyes narrowed as Nick moved closer.

"Second they're falling over themselves being kind and gracious because they're thrilled I might have found a girl, a nice girl they all like, and the only thing they know is that I'm working for her and I think she's gorgeous and amazing and I hope she decides to stay instead of moving on. Because that's the only damn thing I've ever said. To anyone." He took another step closer, staring, pleading into her eyes.

"That's all you've said?"

"Yeah. The rest is all you, Morgan. You and that damn abuse badge you wear. It's like a neon sign. I never told a soul."

"Then what about me meeting broken ol' Trish?"

"Trish isn't broken," he said. "Trish is one of the least broken people I know. She's happy with who she is and what shit she had to climb out of to get here. It's JoAnn who's broken, not Trish."

Morgan took a step back, eyes widening. "JoAnn?"

"Yeah. I don't know what happened to her to make her into such a wretched human being, but whatever it was, it took any hope of decency with it. You might be messed up, Morgan, but you're a hell of a lot closer to Trish than JoAnn. You're just too scared to see it."

He turned and grabbed an empty box off the dining room floor. "Maybe I should just finish this disk repair at home," he said as he dropped parts and cables into the box. "If you're so by God bound and determined to be all alone in your pain and wretchedness, who am I to argue?"

"What are you doing?"

Nick wrapped her broken hard drive in a clean cloth and tucked it in the box's corner, then perched his laptop on the pile. "I can just send you the bill when I'm done," he said, lifting the box. "Along with anything useful I find. Or will that be lying and withholding information, too?"

Morgan blinked, shaking her head. "What? Where are you going?"

"Leaving. Isn't it obvious?" he said as he gathered up the box and turned to go. "You don't want me here, and if I stay we'll get into a fight. I don't want to fight you and I don't want to make it worse" He let out a sigh and his voice softened. "You're so pissed, if I stay, I'll make it worse."

"Nick, wait," she said, following.

He paused at the door. "My childhood sucked too, especially chemotherapy. But nobody knows, Morgan, not unless I tell them. It didn't define who I am." He turned his head to look at her. "And, just so you know, I didn't kiss you because I felt sorry for you, or because I thought I could con you into sleeping with me. I kissed you because I thought you were amazing. I still do. But you can't see it, and I can't change your mind."

Then he left and she was helpless to stop him.

TWENTY THREE

Morgan sat, staring at the empty dining room table until Ranger's urgent whining forced her to her feet. He had to pee.

She let him out back and sighed at the kitchen. Breakfast dishes had dried in the strainer, so she put them away. Then she washed the counters and stove with hot water and a scrubby sponge. Twice.

She was waist deep beneath the sink, looking for a non-dumped bottle of all-purpose cleaner to take stains off the floors, when someone knocked on the door.

She backed out, kneeling on the floor, as they knocked again. No police lights reflected on the dining room walls this time, but she couldn't see the door, either.

Sighing, she stood and walked to the living room to learn who dared to disturb her cranky solitude.

Trish and Beth stood on the porch, both waving when they saw her. "Oh, good, you're home!" Trish said, grinning as Morgan opened the door. "I called Nick, but he said he wasn't here today." Trish's smile softened. "Everything okay?"

"It's fine," Morgan said. "Nothing new. What can I do for you?"

"We just came to get Beth's stuff, and to see if you needed any help finishing the upstairs," Trish said, searching Morgan's eyes. "You sure you're all right?"

"Yeah," Morgan said, motioning them in. "Your stuff's still out back where you left it."

Beth bounded on past, but Trish stood in the living room, staring. "Tell me that's a ketchup stain on the rug."

"Actually, I think it's Tabasco," Morgan sighed. "I just haven't scrubbed it yet."

Trish came to her. "Morgan, honey, what happened?" she asked, one hand touching Morgan's arm.

Morgan flinched away. "Please don't touch me."

"Okay, okay," Trish said. "I won't touch you." She paused, frowning, and said, "But something's going on. Where's Nick? I thought he was going to help you—"

"He's obviously not here," Morgan muttered. She turned and walked to the kitchen. Surely, somewhere, she could find cleaning solution. Scouring powder. Something.

Trish followed. "Morgan. Honey. What happened?"

Morgan stood, trembling, hands clenching the sink rim. She stared out at Mrs. Parson putting a dress on a stupid concrete goose while her rotten little dog dug a hole. "Nothing. He's just gone home."

Trish stopped, mouth working. "But you guys seemed so happy last night. Nick's always been so..." She shook her head and asked, "Did he do something? *Nick?*"

"No." Morgan looked away from the window. "It was me. I got mad, so he left. He left me. And I don't blame him."

Trish hurried to her, but Morgan raised a hand to stop her. "Don't. Please. Don't touch me. I don't want any comfort or hugs or a consoling cry. I just..." Morgan scrunched her face up, and her hands balled on the counter.

"You just what, sweetie?"

"I just want to say I'm sorry. I just want him back."

Trish stomped past her and out the back door. "Beth!" she hollered. "We gotta go. Get that load in the car and we're leaving!"

And that's everyone, Morgan thought, sighing. *Darcy. Nick. Even Trish. All gone.* She ran water in the sink, waiting for it to warm.

Guess I can use bar soap or shampoo to get the stains out of the—

Trish stomped back in while closing her cell phone, her mouth set tight. "Get your purse," she said as she blew past.

Morgan turned, staring. "I don't have a purse."

"Well, goddammit, get whatever you carry your phone and money and bits and pieces of your life in. Get it, and get your ass in the car. Now." She turned and stared Morgan in the eye. "And don't even try to argue with me. Trust me. You won't win."

* * *

Trish parked along the street in front of Nick's house. The three women sat there, Morgan staring at the dashboard while Beth hummed along with her 80's music in the back seat.

"Go talk to him," Trish said for the umpteenth time. "You're not doing anyone any good sitting here."

Morgan shook her head. "I can't. Just take me back home."

"Look," Trish said, sighing harshly. "We all have to apologize sometimes. It's life. If you're in the wrong, then suck it up, get in there, and fix it. If he's the one who fucked up, then make him do the suck-it-upping. Just do *something* instead of leaving the both of you wallowing in misery because a few stupid words were said."

Fine. "I should just run," Morgan muttered, reaching for the door. "Get back to the coast again."

Trish flicked the door lock. "No," she said as Morgan struggled with the door. "No running. Not today."

Morgan leaned back, frustrated, and snapped, "Let me out of this car."

"Not until you agree to go in there and talk to him."

"You do know that I could agree then just leave once you let me out."

"You could," Trish said. "But you won't. You might be a mess at times, but you're not a liar. Or a cheat."

Morgan grumbled and glared out the window, not sure whether to be pleased or aggravated.

Trish said, "I've seen how you look at him, how he looks at you. It's like sparkles and fairy dust. Sweet, but disgusting."

Morgan rolled her eyes.

"Gushy crap or not, you're good for each other," Trish continued, "that's pretty freaking obvious, and I, for one, am not willing to pass up on years of cheesy family pictures because neither of you wants to say you're sorry. So quit wallowing in being miserable but right, get your ass up to the house, and one of you apologize."

Morgan sighed. "Fine," she muttered, and Trish unlocked the doors.

She managed to walk to the steps with a bit of dignity, but Chuckie ripped the door open and glowered at her, tearing the last desperate shreds of her self-respect away.

"I told you not to hurt him," he said. "So get the fuck off my property."

"I didn't mean—"

"Didn't mean to fuck him then fuck him over? Oh really? So he does all this shit to help you, drags *us* so deeply into his little 'I'm so happy!' delusion that we cleared out your fucking basement, *then* after you reward him with an overnighter, you just kick him in the nuts and send him on his way? What kind of twisted bitch are you?"

"Dude, c'mon," Bailey said, laying a thick hand on Chuckie's scrawny shoulder. "It's none of our business."

"It is so my fucking business," Chuckie snapped. "I've known Nick my whole goddamn life."

Bailey pulled on Chuckie's shoulder, but Chuckie wrenched away and spat, "'Least Nick got laid. Hope your nasty piece of ass was worth it." Seething, he stomped away.

"I'm sorry, Bailey," Morgan said, managing to meet his gaze. She and Nick hadn't slept together, but otherwise Chuckie was right. She had taken Nick's friendship, his help, and threw it in his face. "I didn't mean—"

"It's Bacon," he muttered, arms crossing over his chest. "What the hell do you want?"

"I... I have to talk to Nick." She swallowed and glanced back at Trish in the car, who motioned for her to hurry up already. "Just let me talk to Nick."

"He's busy."

Morgan sagged. "Bailey, please. I screwed up, okay? I did. I admit it. It's my fault. I just want to apologize."

"Why'd you hurt him? After all he's done?"

"I said some things I didn't mean because I was scared and upset. And it wasn't his fault. It was mine. I know that now. Please. Just let me talk to him."

"He *loves* you," Bailey snarled. "I thought you were a nice person."

"I am," Morgan said, heart slamming. "At least I try to be. But I screwed up. I just want to tell him I'm sorry."

"Then you'll go?" he said, chin rising.

She nodded. "I'll go. And never come back, if he, if you guys, don't want me to."

Bailey turned and pointed to the hall. "Last door. By the bathroom."

Chuckie slammed his door as she walked past and Morgan flinched. When she reached the closed door at the end of the hall she paused, head down. Steeling herself, she took a deep breath and knocked.

"Buzz off, Bacon," Nick said from inside. "I'm not in the mood."

Morgan grasped the latch, her hand shaking, and turned it. Locked. "It's not Bacon."

Nick yanked the door open and said, "What do you want? Was there something else I didn't tell you quick enough so you need to jump on my ass?"

"No," Morgan said. She swallowed and raised her head. "I'm sorry. I was mad at Darcy, at myself. I shouldn't have taken it out on you."

"Little late for that, isn't it?" he said, walking away from the door. His room was tiny, barely big enough for a twin bed and a desk. The desk and floor were piled with computer parts and cables.

A duffle bag sat on the bed and Nick stuffed clothes into it. "Why are you really here, Morgan? Need a ride to the mall, or maybe your roof re-shingled?"

"That's not fair," she said. "I never asked for any of that. You always volunteered."

He tossed his laptop into the bag. "Yeah, I suppose I did. Nick the Sucker, always leaping forth to be of assistance, whether he should or not." He took a breath and turned his head to glower at her. "You did ask for my help. Once. When you were stuck in the rain."

Morgan nodded, her stomach twisting so bad it hurt. "Yeah. So you could maybe tell me where I was. So I could call a cab."

"So now that's my fault too? That I was willing to—"

Morgan sliced her hands in front of her "No. That wasn't your fault at all. You were just being sweet and gallant. Like you always are."

"That's very magnanimous of you, Ms. Miller," he said, zipping the bag closed.

"It's not magnanimous, it's honest," she said, holding his furious gaze. "And I wasn't mad at you, I wasn't. I was embarrassed and upset over the things you'd read." She chewed her lip and managed to clamp back the tears. "I just didn't want you to know all those awful things about me. And if I can't run, I lash out. I'm so, so sorry I took my fear out on you."

His gaze softened. "I didn't read any awful things. I mean, I did, I guess, but what I saw, what I've always seen, isn't the abuse, it's the smart, funny, beautiful woman you are. You can't see how amazing it is that you're here at all, and I hate it that you're still trapped back there, in your past."

He took a step toward her. "It's just... You could have been so damaged, permanently hurt and dysfunctional. But I read the notes, *all* of them. You never did drugs or got in bad trouble or hurt anyone. Ever. All of the notes commented on how bright you were, curious and friendly and helpful and kind. Terrified, yes. Beat to hell, most definitely. For goodness sake, Morgan, you went from nothing, worse than nothing, and managed to put yourself into college on a full-tuition state scholarship. Do you have any idea how impossible that is?"

She shook her head. "It wasn't me, it was that Fosters for the Future prog—"

"I looked them up online," he said. "Other than you, every recipient of that grant has had a permanent home placement, one school district they grew up in, and plenty of encouragement and help. You did it *alone*, bouncing from place to place, school to school. You. Without family or friends or even a single guidance counselor to nudge you forward, you managed to get to college on your own. And, dammit, Morgan, if I know you, you would have done it even without the program."

"But I flunked out," she said, looking up at him.

"No, your grades fell because you spent nearly a whole school year helping your friend who'd been raped. I saw your transcript. You didn't *flunk*, you dropped below a 2.5 and lost your funding. So stop kicking yourself for caring for a person more than acing a class or two."

She looked away, but he grasped her hand. "Listen to me," he said. "There was nothing in there that scared me away or disgusted me. Nothing. All I saw, all I still see, is someone who's braver, tougher, and kinder than I can possibly ever hope to be. A survivor."

"Nick, I..." she said.

He touched her cheek. "You're a *survivor*, Morgan, and you did it without hurting anyone else along the way. You lived through a hell I can't even imagine, but you're always gracious and sweet. You're beautiful. That's what I see. You tell me that you're worthless or broken, but I just think about how JoAnn had the world handed to her and all she can do is complain. But *you*, the one person who should be angry and bitter and cold, everyone you meet loves you just how you are, scars and all."

Morgan tried to speak, but nothing came out.

Nick grasped her hands. "I should have told you as soon as I found the site. I should have. And I'm sorry. But I'm not sorry I read it."

She tilted her head, perplexed. "*What?*"

"It just makes you that much more amazing," he said, gazing into her eyes. "I wish you'd see that."

"I didn't mean to yell at you," she said.

"I know. But it's hard for me, almost impossible for me, to stand by and let you hate yourself."

"That's why you left?" she asked, gaping. "Not because I got mad?"

"You can get mad all you want," he said. "You have every right and reason to get mad. Even at me. All that's fine. But don't wallow in your hatred of yourself, okay? I can't take it."

She searched his eyes. "Okay," she said at last. "But don't hide things from me. Especially things like that site."

"Deal," he said, smiling as he drew her close. "Can we kiss and make up now?"

She grinned as his arms came around her. "Seems like a good time, don't you think?"

His lips were wonderful and warm, hungry yet comforting, and she gasped, letting her head fall back as his kiss moved from her lips to her jaw, her throat. She clung to him, whispering his name, even as he shifted, dancing her the few steps to his bed.

He looked in her eyes then kissed her lips, drawing her down with him. Her hip tilted up on the duffle bag and he yanked it away to gently press her onto the rumpled blanket, his hand warm on her waist, her hip, the bare skin of her outer thigh.

"Why were you packing?" she asked, breathless. His weight was an unexpected delight and she hooked one of his legs with her own. His backside seemed the perfect place to put her hand.

"Doesn't matter." He nuzzled her neck. Kissed it. Nibbled below her jaw.

Each touch sent a jolt through her, making her gasp, but she swallowed and pushed his head up so she could see his eyes. "I thought we agreed," she said. "Secrets?"

He sighed and slumped to the bed beside her. "Morgan, not this. Okay?"

She sat and stared down at him. "Yes, this. Where were you going?"

He glanced away to mutter a curse, then he met her worried gaze. "Wisconsin. Find this Ryder and make sure he leaves you alone."

"*What?*"

Nick pushed off the bed and stood. "The shit's been calling you. Scaring you. Tearing things up. I tried to step back and let the cops handle it, but they're not getting the job done. If you were home alone last night, there's no telling what might have happened and I can't take the chance you'd get hurt. I'm putting a stop to it. Now."

Oh, Nick! Morgan covered her bemused smile with her hand, then, shaking her head, said, "So even though we'd broken up, you were going to drive three hundred miles to defend my honor?"

He grinned. "We didn't break up. We just had an argument. Least I hoped that's all it was. And I notice you're not trying to talk me out of going."

"Not a chance," she said, standing. "Because you're taking me with you."

TWENTY FOUR

AFTER FACING COUNTLESS ROAD CONSTRUCTION delays, they arrived in Oshkosh after ten the following morning and, thankful for Google Maps, Morgan managed Nick's phone while he drove. The phone led them to a large limestone building near the lake with a small parking lot tucked alongside.

Inside, a harried woman smiled at them while a scrawny man in a bathrobe and slippers tugged on her arm and begged for a popsicle.

"We're here to see Ryder Masterson," Nick said.

The woman beamed. "Ryder! He'll be so pleased." Pointing the other fellow toward a young man in jeans, the woman had them sign in, then led them through a barred door and deeper into the building. "Everyone loves to get visitors, especially our recovering inmates."

Nick and Morgan followed past wide, sunny rooms where people in orange scrubs played board games or watched TV. The woman led them to a bright room on the left side of the hall. "Ryder," she called out. "You have visitors!"

"Least this time it ain't the fucking cops," a bald patient muttered, sneering from behind a plastic cup of juice. A haggard woman beside him played solitaire. She flinched and abruptly lowered her head to peer at them through her scraggly hair. Other than an obese man turning his electric chair to face them, no one else looked up from their checkers.

Morgan glanced at Nick. Nobody here looked like Ryder.

"Morgan!" the lump in the wheelchair exclaimed blearily, drawing her attention. "It's so good to see you. Where's Darcy?"

Ryder had been a skinny kid last time Morgan saw him, and she stammered, trying to reconcile the memory with what sat before her. He'd lost one leg at the hip and three tubes oozed fluid from his belly into bags hanging beside his chair. One long scar ran from his missing left eye to the corner of his mouth, leaving him with a permanent scowl. His hands had been strapped to the chair's arms, granting him just enough movement to operate the controls, but he tugged at the binds, obviously delighted to see her.

"She... she died," Morgan said, glancing at Nick again.

Ryder's once delighted face fell. "Died?" he said, sagging, his voice dopey and slow. "Why'd she die? I love her. Love Darcy!" He struggled weakly against his binds.

"It, it was a car accident," Morgan said, moistening her lips. Other patients had turned to watch the show. Many stared, but the woman playing solitaire rubbed the heel of her hand over her right eye and let out a low whine. The orderlies, however, kept talking in the corner as if nothing had happened.

"I never meant to hurt her," Ryder said, lone eye damp and pleading. "Never, never. I just thought that was how I was supposed to do it. What guys in my hall talked about doing, what I read online. How the girls were supposed to like it." He blubbered, helpless to wipe up his own snotty mess. "Did she know that, Morgan? Did she know I never meant to hurt her? I didn't want to hurt her, just love her. Like I was supposed to. Did she know? Morgan? Did she?"

Yep, that's love. Drugging her and tying her up so she can't say no or stop you from raping her then panicking and leaving her in a storage room. That's what every girl dreams of. Morgan reached for a box of tissues and managed to keep her tone civil. "Yeah. She was at your trial, remember? You told us all."

He let her wipe up the mess of snot and tears. He stank of piss and sickness. "I remember. I offered to marry her, to make up for my mistake, but she didn't answer. I... I don't think that man let her talk."

"He was her lawyer," Morgan said. "And, no, they don't let people talk at trials."

"I don't see my lawyer any more," Ryder said, eye rolling back to glimmer at her. "And you're sure Darcy's dead? My Darcy?"

"I'm sure," Morgan whispered. Nick grasped her hand and she squeezed it.

"She never came to visit me," Ryder said. "Ever. And now she's dead." He whimpered and turned his chair away.

Not knowing what else to do, Morgan let Nick lead her away. They left Ryder sobbing and alone.

The woman who had escorted them waited in the hall, scowling. "This wasn't a friendly visit, was it?"

"No," Nick said. "What happened to him?"

"After he nearly died from an attack in jail, they sent him to us, poor kid. We keep him medicated and under observation, so he won't hurt himself."

"So he can't get out?" Nick asked.

"Ryder? Never. Not even to the yard, thanks to his medication. Everyone else gets exercise time outside, and some of our soon-to-be released patients get work furloughs to prepare them for the real world, but the most exciting thing that poor boy has in his life is free time in the common room." She sighed and looked at Nick. "It's the same thing I told those police from Minnesota. He doesn't get out and we dial his few phone calls."

Her gaze turned to Morgan. "You the one getting the calls?"

Morgan nodded. "Yeah. Threats and things."

"In case you hadn't noticed," the attendant said, "we've medicated all the threat out of him."

* * *

Nick and Morgan drove west without speaking much. Near Green Lake, Nick said, "Ryder's not calling you, is he?"

Morgan bit her lip and shook her head. Wisconsin rolled past outside the window, both hated and home. "No. He's not."

"Sorry to drag you all the way out here for nothing," he sighed. "Just a waste of time."

"It had to be done," she said. "We had to know."

A few more miles of silence, and Nick asked, "You're from Madison, right?"

Morgan looked back out the window. "Yeah."

"Do you want to make a side trip there for lunch? Any family you want to see?"

She shivered and rubbed her arms. "Just drive."

Nick drove, stopping only for gas and drive-through food. It was late when they reached Hackberry, and Morgan's legs begged for a run. Instead she greeted her lonely dog and tossed the ball for him while Nick pulled her bag from the truck bed.

"You okay?" he asked. "Do you want me to stay?"

"I'm fine. Tired, mostly." She searched his eyes and her voice caught. "Did you want to stay?"

He swallowed. "I don't know. Yes. Maybe." Ranger returned with the ball and Nick plucked it from the ground and flung it aside. "I'm not sure what to do," he said, sighing as he grasped her hand. "I don't want to leave you here alone. What if..." He took a heavy breath and shook his head. "Since it's not that Ryder guy, it could be anybody."

Morgan shuddered. *Anyone.* She'd had the same thoughts most of the way home. "So far, it's only happened on the weekend, so I think Ranger and I will be okay for a few more days, at least. But I'd appreciate it if you'd check the house."

"I'm happy to." Nick touched her cheek. "I can sleep on the couch, too, if you want."

Morgan closed her eyes to his caress tingling against her skin. "Oh, Nick," she sighed, mouth opening to help her breathe. She opened her eyes again and met his gaze.

How could she tell him that the night before, in the motel on the outskirts of Oshkosh, she'd lain awake a long, long time, wanting him? She'd fallen hard for his gentle, geeky charm, and she knew it in her heart, even if there hadn't been an empty, hungry ache low in her belly and a desperate need to feel his touch upon her skin. They were adults, she'd reasoned in that cold, lonely bed, and he'd already mentioned that he'd thought of her too. He was just a room away, the next door down the hall. Surely he wouldn't turn her away. Surely he'd welcome her, hold her.

Love her.

Twice that night she'd found herself standing before his door in her sleepy-puppy nightshirt, trembling and desperately wanting to grasp the latch but terrified to go through the door.

She'd told herself that Libbey would have marched right in, and that realization had sent Morgan back to her room.

Now, a full day later, he stood in her yard, hand on her face, his gaze and touch so seductive, so compelling, it made her heart clench. "I don't know if... if I'd let you sleep the whole night on the couch," she admitted.

He smiled and kissed her gently. "It's too soon. You're not ready. It's okay."

She couldn't agree, nor could she deny it, so in the end she simply kissed him and wished he'd stay anyway.

* * *

The following morning, Morgan had finished nearly half the pot of coffee before Nick arrived, and she'd located most of the folks who'd received 1099's from Darcy the previous year by searching the sites and forums. Seven had been on the phone-call transcript the police had provided. She'd sent emails briefly explaining the delays and other issues with the sites, and asked not only for their patience, but their help.

Since her computer is still in pieces and I have no idea what data can and cannot be recovered, would you please detail the service(s) you provide HiggenPop.com, if you're currently under contract, and if you're awaiting payment of any invoices? Any other documentation you have would be greatly appreciated. Thank you so much for your patience.

Pleased to have made some real progress, Morgan clicked *send* on the eleventh email as she stood to answer Nick's knock at the door. She instead found Jannis and invited her in.

"I know you've got to be bored, stuck here all the time, so I was thinking you might really like joining our local Lions. They meet Tuesday evenings," she said, "and they're just a fun bunch of folks."

"Me? A Lion?" Morgan asked.

"Oh, it's such fun! We do lots of things for the community, like the kids' Halloween Party every fall, plus we collect eye glasses for the less fortunate, sponsor surgeons to visit Central America..."

"I don't know." Morgan nodded back to the country-blue walls of the living room. "I think I need to paint the house before I tackle anything as big as all that."

Jannis beamed. "So you're going to stay?"

"I... I'm not sure yet," Morgan said, shrugging. "Maybe. I think I'm going to try."

"It's because of Nick, isn't it," Jannis said, winking. "He's such a nice boy."

"Yes he is," Morgan managed to say, then she heard footsteps on the porch and turned to see Nick, grinning, box of computer parts in his arms.

Morgan opened the door for him and he said, "I found four more site cookies."

* * *

Morgan sat beside Nick at the dining room table, boggling over FrugallyUrban's workings as Nick tried to explain WordPress settings and how they interconnected to make a seamless site. Morgan barely heard. She was too thrilled to have the site back.

But not just FrugallyUrban. HiggenPop, WantAGadget, and The Short Basket, too. Three sites she actually could understand—plus a crafting site she could barely comprehend—but all working, active, income-generating marvels.

"We can make adjustments so it all runs a little quicker," Nick said, clicking on a button, "and other settings and plugins can make it more user-friendly and accessible, but it's all here, it's working, and you can update anything you want."

Morgan kissed him. "You are amazing! Thank you!"

A long moment later he drew back and smiled into her eyes. "Don't thank me yet. There are *thousands* of comments in the queues to review, and a lot of unopened emails in Darcy's box, just for FrugallyUrban alone."

"That's just fine. You got my site back."

A shadow crossed over his eyes, and she leaned closer to ask what was wrong.

"I'm almost done," he said. "So now what? Do we date? Do you leave? Do I work for you maintaining the sites, and, if so, how can I charge my girlfriend?" He sighed and searched her eyes. "What do we do now?"

"I don't know," she replied. "But we've definitely agreed on a price and rate for the disk repair, right?"

"Yeah," he said, sounding frustrated.

She leaned back. "Are you wanting to change the deal *now?*"

"Morgan," he said, staring into her eyes, "I can't stop thinking about you. I damn near went to your motel room night before last to beg you to let me in, and it just seems wrong to charge you fifty bucks an hour for something I'd happily do for..." He swallowed. "For sharing a frozen pizza at lunch."

"Too bad," she said. "We agreed."

He frowned at her. "I'm serious. This is important."

"I know," she sighed. She pushed off her chair and onto his lap, draping her arms over his shoulders as his hands found her waist, her hips. She kissed him, lingering until they were both breathless, then she looked into his eyes. "I went to your room that night, too. Twice."

"You what?" he asked, eyes wide.

"Yeah. But I couldn't knock. I tried, but I couldn't." She licked her lips and managed to hold steady. "I'm nervous, I'm scared, and I can't stop thinking about you, either."

She swallowed and her voice cracked as she said, "I have to pay you for the work you do. I cannot trade affection. Not after what my mother did to make a living. I just can't."

His expression shifted from astonishment, to horror, to shame. "I never meant for you to think—"

She laid a finger on his lips. "I know. So how do we make this all work? How do we," she whispered as she kissed his lips, his cheek, his neck, "go upstairs and see what happens when... when..."

He lifted her chin and kissed her, silenced her, shifting her in his arms as they stood. "We just go."

* * *

After barely a moment of hesitation at his touch, she quivered as he carefully peeled her clothes from her, lips and tongue following his hands, her fingers clenching into his hair. He sweetly kissed every scar, every shadow of puckered flesh, whispering her name all the while.

She tried to undo the buttons of his work shirt, but they fought her. Frustrated her. She finally got the damn thing open and tore it from his shoulders.

"Shh, there's no rush," he whispered against her skin as he bore her down onto her narrow bed. "Relax." He kissed her breasts, her belly, sending shocks through her.

"I don't know if that's possible, I want you so much," she gasped, barely able to breathe as she writhed beneath his caress. "Need this so much. Oh, Nick."

"Try," he said, his lips and breath impossibly warm. "Just tell me if I go too far, too fast."

His tongue traced past her belly and lower, lingering, doing amazing, impossible things, until she was helpless to do more than cling to him and cry out his name again and again at the waves thudding through her.

She lay there after, quivering, her world hazy and warm. "How'd you do that?" she asked, breathless, as he drew away.

He returned to her side, nude, skin to glorious skin, his kisses and touch tingling everywhere they went. "What else would computer geeks do online if not research how to make our women happy?" he chuckled as he teased her breast with his tongue.

"I am *very* happy," she said, shifting to face him, hold him, explore his skin. Her fingers trailed over him, and he trembled at her touch. "Are you?"

"Hope to be." He pressed her back again, his weight a welcome burden, her legs coming around his waist as if they belonged there.

She felt him twitch against her, heavy and hot, ready to love her, and she had to bite her lip to keep from crying out.

"Are you sure you can do this?" he whispered. "We can still stop. I don't want to hurt you."

"Don't stop," she replied, reaching for him. "You can't hurt me. I think I love you."

"Me, too." He grinned, leaning down to kiss her, and his breath tasted sweet when he found his way home.

TWENTY FIVE

"I HAVE AN IDEA," Morgan said as she traced curlicues on Nick's chest.

"You want *more?*" he mumbled, kissing her shoulder, then sighed, "Okay. But can you give me a few minutes to recuperate? Three times in a row has about done me in."

Morgan giggled. "Four. For me at least. And, lovely as another round sounds, I was actually thinking of something else."

Nick opened an eye and looked at her. "Oh? What exotic contortion do you have planned for me and my poor spent body, my lady of boundless energy?"

"I told you," she said, pinching him, "it's something else."

"What?" he laughed, batting her hands away. "What's your idea?"

"You could be my business partner."

He lifted to his elbows and looked down at her. "What?"

"Darcy cleared more than a hundred thousand last year. I need about twenty, maybe twenty-five to survive. You can have the rest. After expenses and all."

"Morgan, no."

She sat. "Why not? You'd be doing most of the work."

"They belong to *you.*"

"No," she said, "they *belonged* to Darcy. I just ended up with them. I can't run them without you."

He rose from the bed and paced. "I can't do that."

Morgan watched, smiling around a contented sigh. She'd never considered the male form delightful before, but he was just yummy.

He stopped to face her. "Did you hear what I just said?"

"Eh, what?" Morgan asked, grinning. *Yep. It's waking up.*

"It's too much money for what you're asking me to do."

She dragged her gaze up to his face. "That translates to a helluva lot less than your billing rate."

"So I'll be your employee *and* your lover?"

Morgan grimaced and flumped onto the bed. "Not when you put it that way." She sighed and stared at the ceiling, mind churning. *Oh yeah, make him your whore. What a sucky idea.*

Nick returned to the bed and knelt beside it. "How about this?" he said as Morgan turned her head to look at him. "I know it's kinda fast, but we could move in together. Share everything. The business. Money. The dog. A bed. Housework. Everything. Shit, I'm here all the time anyway. Why not make it easier on both of us?"

"You really want to share everything?" she asked, searching his eyes.

"Everything."

She rolled to face him. "On one condition."

"Name it," he said, hand gliding over the slope of her hip.

"Can you teach me how to drive?" She paused to give him an impish grin as she reached for him. "It's still on my list."

"Absolutely," he said, then kissed her and slipped back into bed.

* * *

By mid-morning two days later, Nick had unscrambled the access information for all but one of Darcy's sites. Morgan couldn't be happier. Of the folks she'd emailed, all but three had responded with their thanks for contacting them about work and monies due, tempered by condolences for Morgan's loss. She'd spent part of the previous afternoon setting up a PayPal account to pay the folks who'd completed articles and graphics, and much to the contributor's surprise, she immediately paid them.

A few of the contacts had actually requested more work, and Morgan spent a delightful hour chatting online with a woman who couldn't afford to buy The Short Basket, but was excited at the opportunity to manage its content for a portion of the profits.

As she clicked off the chat, Morgan leaned back in her chair and grinned at Nick. "And with that, we no longer have to worry about hot glue, framing supplies, or beads."

"Oh thank God," he sighed, clacking away as he set up Morgan's shiny new computer on a sprawling corner desk. They'd decided to make the larger downstairs room into a joint office. "I was worried we'd be stuck with that other gal who could barely knit. Least I think it's knitting."

Morgan stood to stretch. Knitting or not, it was awful. "Courtney will do great, I think. She has some cool ideas about weekly and daily topics, project sharing—"

Morgan's new iPhone rang and she pulled it from her pocket. Between sample suppliers and graphic design firms, it had been ringing most of the morning. Morgan smiled and clicked to accept the call. "Hey Beth," she said, leaning over to kiss the back of Nick's neck. "What's up?"

She listened as she wandered toward the kitchen for some iced tea, tossing Ranger's ball along the way. "Yep. We put your stuff in the kitchen before it rained last night, it's all fine."

"Mind if I go through the rest of the clothes upstairs and get 'em out of your hair?" Beth asked, chipper as always. "I have a woman emailing me wanting embellished sweaters and I think I saw a big pile."

Morgan poured her tea, phone wedged on her shoulder. "That'd be great. Just bag up what you don't want and we'll drop it off at Goodwill. See you in a bit."

Nick came in for a refill as well. "Beth again?"

Morgan poured. "Yep. She's gonna finish clearing out those clothes in Darcy's room."

"Good," Nick said, reaching for her. "I'd like to get it painted before the bed gets delivered."

She stretched in his embrace, almost purring as he caressed her back and butt. "A nice, big, new mattress," she sighed. Despite the compressed coziness of both sleeping in her bed, Morgan had been resistant to use Darcy's old one. It just felt wrong. And Nick, bless him, had understood. In fact, he'd helped her carry it out to the dumpster before it had been hauled off that very morning.

"Think of the space. The things we could do." He kissed her, holding her tight against him. "Maybe we should get more practice first."

"Your sister's on her way over."

He backed away, taking her hands, his grin ornery and promising. "We can be quick. I have tricks, you know."

* * *

Morgan managed to get her shorts zipped and hair tucked back before she reached the front door. Trish and the kids stood on the front porch with Beth. The whole gang came on in.

Trish gave her a sly look then grinned up at Nick pulling a shirt on as he half-stumbled down the stairs. "Silly kids. We'd have taken a detour, if you'd just asked."

"Nah," Nick said, ducking to give Morgan's jaw a quick peck before shuffling on to the office. "We were 'bout done."

Morgan blushed, Trish laughed, and Beth made a disgusted face. "I do *not* want to know!" she said, squealing as her brother turned around to grab her. "Aaaah! Stop it!" she said, squirming free. "You're covered in oogy sex germs!"

Brandon looked up at his mother. "Oogy sex germs?"

She tousled his hair. "Go on to the back yard with the dog, sweetie," she said. "He really likes to play ball." Brandon went, while Mandy ran giggling to her Uncle Nick.

"Do not tell me you were *doing things* in that big room that's full of clothes," Beth said to Morgan, still grimacing as Nick lifted Mandy to swing her giggling in the air.

"We weren't," Morgan said. "Honest."

"I hope not," Beth said, trudging up the stairs. "Because that's just gross."

Trish looked at Morgan and laughed. "So," she said as they walked toward the kitchen, "you two disappear for a couple of days, and now you're shacking up?"

"Thanks for making it sound so romantic," Morgan teased.

"Honey, I just call 'em as I see 'em." She gave Morgan a sideways glance. "You do look happy, though."

"That's good, 'cause I am. It's pretty awesome." She ducked into the fridge. "I gotta feed Nick. You staying for lunch?"

"Look at me," Trish chuckled, poking her flab. "Do I look like I pass up many free meals?"

Morgan pulled out leftover chicken, a hunk of cheese, and an armload of salad vegetables. "Good. You can help chop."

They'd barely started slicing onions and green peppers when the front screen door banged open and closed. Thinking Mandy had gotten out, Morgan hurried to fetch her but skid to a halt as JoAnn stomped in, glaring.

"You!" she said as she shook a piece of paper and rushed toward Morgan.

Morgan lurched a step back and bumped into Trish. "Me?"

"How did you get here?" Trish asked.

"I drove," JoAnn snapped, still shaking the paper. "Found the address in Donna's address book." She glared at Morgan and snapped, "You're Morgan, right? Morgan *Miller?*"

"Um. Yes."

Another shake of the paper. "*The* Morgan Miller? From GlimmerGals?"

Morgan's mouth worked silently as Nick came out of the office carrying Mandy. Both wore hats folded from big sheets of paper and Mandy swung a cardboard sword cut from a castoff box.

"What's going on?" Nick asked, dodging the sword before it knocked his glasses off instead of just crooked.

"I heard you have a lot of websites," JoAnn said, still glaring at Morgan. "Do you or do you not own GlimmerGals?"

"Sort of," Morgan admitted.

JoAnn shook the paper again. "How can someone who doesn't even wear fucking mascara operate such a great resour—"

"Don't talk like that in front of Mandy," Trish snapped.

JoAnn gave her a warning glare then said, "I spent most of last night celebrating because the woman who runs my favorite place in the world emailed me, asking if I'd be interested in taking over the site. Then my husband informs me that my idiot brother-in-law's mouthy little fuck buddy—"

Trish pushed past Morgan. "I told you to not use that language in front of my baby."

"Shut up, Trish," JoAnn snapped, still glaring at Morgan. "You sent me this email, didn't you?"

Morgan took a breath and slowly let it out. "You're SweetNSexyJ?"

"I knew it." JoAnn crumpled the paper and threw it on the floor. "You can take your offer and cram it."

Nick stood, slack-jawed and gaping, while getting pummeled on the side of the head and face by a hunk of dented cardboard. "You're an idiot," he said, pushing his glasses back up his nose. "That site brings in more than twenty grand in annual revenue from shoe advertisers alone."

"Yeah, well, if a cheapskate like you is encouraging your little tramp to unload it, it's worthless, isn't it?"

Morgan took a step toward them. "Actually, it's really profitable. I'm trying to sell it because, like I said in the email, my friend who originally owned it died. I don't know anything about fashion. If I can't sell it, it'll close down when the domain registration runs out in November because, profits or not, I'm not going to maintain it."

JoAnn's eyes narrowed. "Don't you dare shut down *my* favorite site."

Her site? "This isn't personal," Morgan said, "I didn't know you were SweetNSexyJ. If you don't want to buy the site, that's fine. *I don't care.* Someone else will want it, or they won't. Either way, *I don't care* because I don't care about flipping fashion! You have nothing to do with my decision and, dammit, you are not the center of the freaking universe!"

JoAnn gasped and was about to retort, but Morgan took another step toward her and snatched the paper from the floor.

"You might be insecure on the inside, but on the outside you're a spoiled control-freak brat who thinks everyone should bend over and let you have your way. You've made them all a little afraid of you and your mouth," she said, "but you don't scare me. You have *no right* to barge into my home uninvited, without even bothering to knock, solely so you can scream at me for *offering*, just offering, to sell you a profitable business cheap. Shit, being family I would have just given it to you, but even that wouldn't have been good enough, would it? You're a bitch, and I'm done. So get the hell out of my house—sorry Mandy—and consider your chance to buy the site retracted."

Morgan ripped up the crumpled email and threw the bits at JoAnn before turning to walk away. "Don't let the door hit you on the way out."

"You can't do this to me!" JoAnn snapped, tears welling in her eyes. "You can't talk to me that way or take away my favorite site!"

Trish smirked, arms crossing over her chest as Morgan stomped back into the kitchen. "She just did."

Morgan reached the sink and gripped the rim, head lowered, as she tried to settle herself. "Sorry," she said as the other woman entered. "I shouldn't have gotten so upset."

"You did great, and she deserved it," Trish assured her. "Wish I'd filmed the whole thing. Would've been a hoot at Christmas."

Morgan shook her head, chuckling. "You're crazy."

Trish picked up a knife and resumed slicing onions. "Eh, it keeps things fun."

Footsteps approached and Morgan looked over to see Beth carry an armload of sweaters to the dining room table. "Great stuff up there, Morgan," she said as she let the wad fall before digging in. "And I found a couple of books you might want."

"Books?" Morgan asked, curious. They'd carted out so many romance novels and magazines the weekend before, she couldn't imagine Beth finding anything else up there.

"Journals," Beth said as she pulled them from the sweaters. "Three of them. Crammed in the back of the closet."

The over-sized journals were made of calico-covered board in a style popular in the late 80's and early 90's. Morgan shook her head. "They're not mine," she said. "Just throw them away."

"But you're in them," Beth said, flipping through a few pages to show Morgan. "I thought at least you'd want to see."

TWENTY SIX

NICK WAS OUTSIDE MOWING when Morgan gathered the courage to pick up one of the journals. Darcy's mother had written her thoughts and musings there, along with mundane details of her life, but as Morgan flipped through, she saw that most of the entries were about Darcy.

I should have hidden it better, Anne wrote in August of 1999. *After months of brushing aside questions about her birth family, Darcy found her birth certificate. How can we explain who she is? How can we, without hurting her? According to the certificate, she's the 3rd live birth and she's demanding to meet her brothers and sisters. Find her birth mother. But she can't. The woman's a narcissistic sociopath who murdered her own children. What do I do? How do I fix this? Maybe Darcy'll forget.*

Two pages ahead, near the bottom: *That damn school and its fieldtrips. Showing the kids how to research articles and use microfiche. I should sue.*

Darcy knows. She knows who her mother is and she's been running around the house, screaming, so thrilled to know at last. Liberty's daughter.

She's not Liberty's daughter, she's mine. MINE. And that murdering tramp can't have her.

Morgan swallowed, her hand shaking. *Liberty? Oh, God, no. Is that why you tried to visit her in jail?*

She turned the page.

But Ed took her back to the damn library, mostly to shut her up, I think. I don't know what they expect to find other than more articles about her birth mother being in jail for murdering her own kids.

A space, then:

They're back, and now instead of Liberty, it's Morgan, Morgan, Morgan. Pestering us to meet Morgan. The one who survived. The one Liberty loved. They even brought home a copy of the article. Darcy's convinced she still lives here in Madison. She wants us to adopt the poor thing, for God's sake.

How can we even find Morgan? And would we want to? Surely she's messed up after all that's happened. Even if she's Darcy's biological sibling, do we need to bring an abused, traumatized kid like that into our home?

"No," Morgan said, shaking her head. "It's not possible."

Nick came in, sweaty and flecked with grass bits. "What's wrong?"

Morgan looked down at the journal then back to Nick. "Darcy was my *sister.*"

"What?" He sat beside her to read the pertinent passages as Morgan slumped against him. "She never told you?" he asked.

"No. Never. And I don't remember Libbey having another baby when I was two or so. Bret was a year younger than me, and I definitely remember him as a toddler. I was almost in kindergarten before Cas came along." Morgan looked up at him. "How could I not have known I had a sister between them?"

"What if she gave Darcy up right away? If you were so little, you might not remember her being pregnant."

Morgan clenched her hands in her hair, tugging. "She was in and out of jail a lot. Maybe it happened then." She swallowed and looked over to him. "Why didn't Darcy tell me?"

Nick handed Morgan back the journal. "I don't know, but her mom might." He kissed her, sweet and lingering. "Go ahead and read. I think you need to know what happened."

* * *

Nick was still awake, reading a *Game Informer*, when Morgan came to bed. "Well?" he asked, setting aside his magazine and cradling her as she snuggled against him.

"Darcy became obsessed. With Libbey, and with me. Those sites we found... she started them in middle school. Her parents even left Wisconsin because she'd become so determined to find me and was constantly trying to contact Libbey. Or visit the graves."

Morgan swallowed and tried to explain the unexplainable. "She tracked me down as soon as she turned eighteen and her parents couldn't stop her anymore. She went to Maginaw State, found me, and made herself my friend on purpose. Anne hated me. All those years. Because Darcy was obsessed. Maybe crazy."

"No one could hate you," Nick said, stroking her hair.

"Anne did. Until she met me. After Darcy was hurt." Morgan reached up to turn off the light. "I never understood why Anne kept telling me she was so sorry she hadn't met me sooner. I guess now I know. She expected me to be a monster, like my mother. Like she worried Darcy was becoming. She even insisted her parents call her Morgan. It's just messed up."

They snuggled a while, quiet. "I wish she'd told me," Morgan sighed.

"Maybe she tried in her own way," Nick said against her skin. "Maybe she left you everything not because you were friends, but because you were family."

"Maybe," Morgan sighed as Nick's hand found her breast. "Or maybe she started to believe she really was me."

"Did you run today?" he asked, breath warm against her shoulder.

Morgan laughed. "No. I forgot." She rolled to face him, her leg coming over his hip. "How could I forget to run?"

"Maybe you don't need to anymore. Maybe you found what you'd been looking for. Maybe you're finally home."

She grinned, basking in his attention. "If I quit running, I might get fat," she teased.

"That's okay," he assured her. His caresses grew bolder, drawing hungry little gasps from her. "You could be bigger than Trish and I'd love you just the same."

They made love, slowly, savoring each touch, each caress. After they finished, when Morgan's muscles twitched and Nick had slumped beside her sweaty and spent, he kissed her shoulder and, falling asleep, whispered, "Welcome home, Morgan. I'm glad you're here."

She lay there a long time, staring at the ceiling and listening to Nick breathe as she thought of Darcy and the mess she'd left behind. The house, the clutter, the tangled lies and identities. *Maybe she'd just wanted Libbey to admit she was her daughter,* Morgan thought as her eyes drifted closed. *She was just a poor, lost girl looking for her mama.*

She sighed and burrowed against Nick's shoulder, mind fading, reaching for sleep.

Or maybe she wanted to take my place, actually BE me, she thought, eyes bolting open. *The cops said they were having trouble identifying the body in her car. What if she's not dead? What if it's Darcy trying to scare me, maybe kill me?*

Worry ringing in Morgan's head, sleep took a long time to find her.

*   *   *

Morgan felt herself tense as the weekend approached, and, new locks on both doors or not, she thankfully agreed to spend the weekend away. They backed up the computers onto portable drives, loaded Ranger in the truck, and left Friday morning to spend the weekend attending outdoor festivals in southern Minnesota.

When they returned home late Sunday, the house was still standing, the doors locked, nothing out of place. They settled into a comfortable routine and Morgan found herself so busy with life, the sites, and rearranging the house that week, she didn't have time to think about the threats.

Leaving Nick home to finish a set of web updates before they left for the weekend, Morgan leashed Ranger and took a quick run across town and back. Quick jaunt finished, she jogged Ranger home in a bright and sticky August evening.

"Maggie? It is Maggie, isn't it?" A woman called out, waving. She stood in her front yard, spraying a hose while three squealing kids ran through the mist.

Morgan recognized her from the convenience store and waved back before trotting over. "It's Morgan," she said. "And you are?"

"Addie. Addie Jenkins." She offered her damp hand and Morgan shook it without flinching. "Sorry. I'm not very good with names."

"Me either," Morgan admitted. "You work at the convenience store. Right?"

"Yep," she said, rolling her eyes. "Mornings. We open at five. Whee."

Morgan chuckled.

A grade-school-aged boy slid on his belly in the wet grass while a littler pair of twin girls skipped and jumped in the cooling spray. Morgan smiled at the kids and tightened her grip on Ranger's leash. He didn't need to get sloppy wet before they had to load him in the truck.

"Now that I've dragged you over here, can I ask a huge favor?" Addie asked, shifting nervously on her feet.

"Uh, sure," Morgan said, wrapping the leash around her hand before Ranger decided to bolt and play with the kids. "What's up?"

Still fidgeting, Addie blushed. "Can you just keep spraying them long enough for me to run to the bathroom? Our AC's busted and I'd promised them they could play in the water 'til their dad got home from work, but I really gotta..." She shivered and held out the hose. "I won't be but a minute, but if I give the hose to Kevin, he'll slaughter his sisters. Can you just keep them from running into the road or killing each other?"

Morgan smiled, nodding as she accepted the hose. "I can do that, sure."

Addie hurried for the house. "You're a real doll. Thank you!"

Morgan sprayed the kids, grinning at their giggles as they raced around the yard. Soon she and Ranger were both splattered, and Morgan was almost sad to see Addie come back from the house.

"Thank you so much!" Addie said, sliding across the yard to them. She accepted the hose and said, "I can't believe how nice you are. The woman who lived in your house before wouldn't even look at us. And that poor dog," she said, smiling down at Ranger. "He rarely left the yard when she had him. Rain, snow, whatever, he was left outside alone."

Morgan laid a protective hand on Ranger's head. "Really? She always said how much she loved him."

Addie nodded over her shoulder toward Mrs. Parson's house, their mutual neighbor. "Your dog might've been neglected, but at least he wasn't kicked. That old bat next door drives me nuts."

"Me, too," Morgan admitted, glancing past Addie to the Parson house. She hadn't seen Mrs. Parson for days. No puttering in the yard, no dressing her concrete goose, no screaming at the poor clerks at the bank. Even her azaleas were looking untended and tired. "Is she all right?" Morgan asked. "I don't think I've seen or heard her all week."

"Ya know," Addie said as she aimed the hose at her son's butt, "I don't think I have either. Not since a week or so ago when she griped at Joe because the smoke from our grill blew into her yard and we were ruining her 'good air'." She rolled her eyes and lifted the hose to send the water falling like rain. "Who in their right mir.d bitches about their neighbors grilling a few lousy burgers?"

Morgan glanced at the house again, sitting there silent and accusing, its windows closed, the shades drawn. "She has to be at least eighty. Maybe someone should check on her."

"What? And wake the wicked old bitch of the south? I ain't doing it," Addie said. "Had enough ass chewings in my life already, thanks anyway." Her expression brightened as a dented SUV pulled in the drive. "Oh thank God he's finally home. Hope he found a decent air conditioner. It's just been too dang hot to sleep."

A sweaty man hopped out of the SUV, and the kids ran toward him, excited. Despite them being drippy wet, he hugged them all and let the little boy help him pull a huge box from the back. Morgan met Addie's exhausted husband and quickly begged off, insisting she had to get home. As she turned to go, letting Ranger once again have full run of his leash, she frowned at Mrs. Parson's house.

A week. We haven't seen the old lady for a week. What if she's hurt or dead or something, lying there, and no one knows?

Dammit.

She took a breath and started up Mrs. Parson's walk. Ranger let out a low growl as they approached and, inside, Chauncy barked and barked.

I'm insane. Crazy. Lost my flipping mind to come here, Morgan thought as she reached out to knock on the storm door, her other hand gripping Ranger's collar. The huge old Buick sat in the drive, dusty and forlorn, a few dead leaves plastered to the windshield.

Chauncy kept barking, undaunted, and Ranger's growls deepened despite Morgan hushing him. *One more try,* she thought, *and if I don't get an answer, I'll call the fire department or something.*

The storm door was unlocked, so she opened it and pounded on the inner door. "Mrs. Parson?" she called out, banging with her palm. "It's Morgan. From next door. Just hadn't seen you in a while and wanted to make sure—"

The door opened abruptly, just wide enough to show a middle-aged woman's face, pale and haggard beneath a scraggly shock of unnaturally bright auburn hair. A bent cigarette dangled from the corner of her mouth. "What d'you want?" she snapped in her hoarse, ragged voice as she kicked Chauncy away from the door.

Ranger's growl sounded like ripping cloth, endless and snarling, so Morgan held him behind her before he could lunge for Chauncy. She managed to meet the other woman's furious gaze. "I, I just hadn't seen Mrs. Parson in a while and wanted to make sure she was all right."

"She... My mom's sick," the woman snarled, still glaring from behind the barely opened door. She booted Chauncy again.

"I'm sorry to hear that," Morgan said, brow furrowing. "Have we met? You seem familiar, somehow. Maybe at the store or the bank—"

The door slammed and latched.

"Like mother, like daughter," she muttered as she dragged Ranger, still growling, down the steps and back home.

TWENTY SEVEN

MORGAN AND NICK SPENT THE WEEKEND watching a bass fishing tournament at a lake two counties over. Again, their house appeared untouched. The following Tuesday morning, Morgan was elbow deep in dishwater when Nick answered a knock at the door.

Morgan heard a woman's voice and, soapy breakfast bowl in hand, she glanced over, scowling as Detective Hildebrandt followed Nick into the kitchen.

"Good morning, Miss Miller," the detective said. She looked around, smiling slightly. "The house is looking really good."

Morgan rinsed the bowl. "I'm not supposed to talk to you without my lawyer present."

"Then I'll do all the talking. You can listen," Hildebrandt said. "Mind if I sit?"

Morgan and Nick shared a long glance, then Morgan shrugged as Nick leaned against the counter, his hands crossed over his chest. "Whatever," Morgan said as she resumed washing dishes. "You want a cup of coffee or anything?"

"Thank you, but no. This shouldn't take long." Hildebrandt pulled out a kitchen chair and sat before opening her notebook. "The Wisconsin DCI just wanted you to know that the DNA results finally came back, confirming your friend's death."

Morgan rinsed another dish. "That's not too surprising."

"No, but the DNA results on the stray hairs they found caught in the headrest were unexpected. They belong to a close female relative—her mother. We under—"

Morgan dropped the glass she'd been rinsing and it shattered on the edge of the sink. She turned, gaping. "Her *what?!*" she choked out, voice rising as, beside her, Nick turned pale.

"Her mother," Hildebrandt said, consulting her notes. "But we were under the impression that your friend's parents both passed—"

Heart slamming and her knees threatening to buckle, Morgan reached for Nick. "They did. Darcy was adopted as an infa..." She shook, barely able to speak. "Oh, God. Libbey, what have you done?"

Hildebrandt turned, staring. "Libbey? Libbey who?"

Nick held Morgan close. "Morgan and Darcy had the same birth mother," he said. "Liberty Miller. They were sisters. We just found out a few—"

"Great," Hildebrandt said, standing. Barking the information into her radio, she brushed past them both and through the house to the front door.

Nick and Morgan followed and they stood on the porch, watching as Detective Hildebrandt paced beside her car, hand on her radio.

"What do we do now?" Morgan asked, still quaking. *Libbey surely killed Darcy. Again, she's killed all of them but me.*

Scowling, Hildebrandt crossed the yard to them. "Let's go back inside," she said. Morgan and Nick followed her in, but this time the detective stopped in the living room and asked them to sit.

"Once we realized the calls and threats were directed to you, Liberty Miller became a person of interest. But we had nothing to connect her to your friend other than the one failed visit seven years ago," she said. "I wish you would have told us you and Miss Harris were related. Maybe we could have caught her, or had her moved to a more secure facility."

"A more..." Nick said, shaking his head, but Morgan leaned back, fear gnawing at her belly.

"*Caught?*" Morgan asked. "What the hell do you mean *caught?* She got thirty-five to life for what she did. She's not supposed to be *loose* for at least another fifteen years!"

Hildebrandt stared Morgan in the eye. "She was moved to a psychiatric facility more than fifteen years ago and, after extensive treatment and review, was granted entrance into a supervised mainstreaming program that helps inmates adapt to life on the outside."

Libbey's loose? Morgan gaped, unable to believe what the detective just said.

"What exactly does that mean?" Nick asked, holding Morgan tighter.

"She's had periodic employment furloughs for the past three years, with supervision and weekly drug tests. Until recently, she'd done quite well and—"

"She's a Narcissistic Sociopath *and* child-killing crack whore!" Morgan said. "Why would you let her loose for *a job?* What's wrong with you people?" She looked at Nick then back to Hildebrandt. "I thought the police were supposed to keep monsters like her locked up."

"We have to follow the laws, and the courts, Miss Miller, and those laws and courts decided that Liberty Miller had shown progress—"

"Progress?" Morgan said, standing. "People like her do not have progress! They lie and manipulate! Your friends in Wisconsin bought my crazy mother's bullshit, let her loose to party, then she killed Darcy." Furious and shaking, she searched Hildebrandt's eyes. "Where is she now?"

"They don't know," Hildebrandt admitted. "She disappeared off the jobsite some time ago. She stole a car and just drove away."

Morgan's knees felt week, so she sat, her mind reeling.

"Have you seen anyone lurking around lately?" Hildebrandt asked. "Has anything strange happened the past couple of weeks?"

Morgan shook her head and chewed on her knuckles. *Libbey's loose? Oh, God. This can't be happening. Did she break in instead of the kids? Was it her at the door that night Ranger freaked out? Did she try to blow up our house?*

"No," Nick said. "It's been really quiet lately, but we'd had a couple of problems before. Someone busted a computer before Morgan first got here, then there was the night someone broke the gas line and ripped up electrical."

Morgan clenched her hands together. "Yeah. And right after I got here, someone tried to break in while I was sleeping on the couch. It upset Ranger, but I thought it was just a kid."

"I've read the notes in your file and I don't think any of those were a kid," Hildebrandt said, writing in her notepad. "Taking loose change from your car or raiding your fridge? Sure. Graffiti? Maybe. That kind of property damage, not likely, at least not here in Hackberry."

Hildebrandt closed her notebook. "They've put a multi-state bulletin out for Liberty Miller and the car she stole from her employer—a 2004 Black Chevy Cavalier with Wisconsin plates. You see one, or her, you call me right away, all right? It's possible she might have stolen different plates, so any black Cavaliers, you call."

Nick nodded. "We'll call."

"Try not to worry," Hildebrandt said. "The last phone call indicated she was still looking for you, and she didn't know you were here. That's very encouraging. She probably spooked over her involvement in your friend's death and is on the run, states away from here. Don't worry. We'll find her."

Morgan had her doubts and, after the detective left, she checked each door and window to ensure it was locked.

* * *

Morgan barely slept the remainder of that week, but felt herself relax as they spent the weekend in crowded Minneapolis, visiting the zoo and the mall while Ranger stayed in doggy daycare. Again, they returned home to find the house just as they'd left it. Morgan frequently peered out the windows, watching for strangers and slow-moving cars, but saw nothing but neighbors, kids, and farm machinery, just like always.

Four uneventful weeks went by and Morgan decided that disconnecting the house phone—and the ongoing sheriff investigation—had scared her mother off. After all, nothing even slightly worrisome had happened for more than a month and Libbey had not been known for her patience. In fact, the stolen car had been found in Portland, Oregon, of all places, a perfect city for Libbey to disappear.

Maybe it's finally over, Morgan thought when fall arrived. There was so much to do, three rooms still to paint and countless tasks to ready the house for winter, plus site work and dealing with advertisers, negotiating with writers, and the daily review of comments and spam. Morgan tried to push Libbey out of her mind.

School had started, kids trudging up each morning under their heavy backpacks, and Morgan had taken to sitting on the porch, sipping her coffee and watching them as they waited for the bus in front of her house. She'd wave to neighbors and moms and Mrs. Parson's homely daughter walking the horrid fluff of a dog, but she stared down any stranger who came too close to the kids. Nothing bad was gonna happen to any child in her yard, on her watch. Not if she could help it.

The sites weren't making them rich, but they generated enough money to buy groceries and pay bills, maybe even squirrel a little away while Darcy's estate slowly grew for their retirement at a friendly Credit Union. For that, and so much more, Morgan was thankful.

She ran almost every day, sometimes intentionally missing a session, but occasionally she'd forget. And then forget that she'd forgotten.

They bowled in a couples' league every Thursday. Morgan had even visited a writing group, all aspiring novelists who met once a month at the Albert Lea library. They seemed nice, if a little weird. Artsy. Morgan had never felt artsy in her life.

Her life was good. Happy. Sunday dinners with Nick's family, chats with neighbors, and Trish dragging her to sappy movies. Fetch with Ranger and walks with Nick in the cooling evenings. Her own car, a zippy little Honda, in the drive beside Nick's truck. Work during the day, laughter and lovemaking at night. As she stood at the window and watched leaves fall on a crisp October afternoon, she knew she'd found a grand, amazing life of happiness and home.

It's almost perfect, Morgan thought as her hand rubbed her aching belly.

It would have been perfect, but her period had come that very morning, heralded by waves of cramps. She'd been nearly two weeks late and she'd never been late in her life. Nick had been holding his breath those two weeks, and she had too. They'd been careful with the condoms, always, always using them, but things happened. Mistakes. Miracles. Blessings that were not yet to be.

Ranger dropped a chew toy at Morgan's feet and she smiled as she plucked it from the rug and tossed it toward the kitchen. Her kitchen. New cabinets and a dishwasher and *everything*, creamy and warm instead of cold, depressing blue.

Nick walked from the office with a report in hand. "Sites are looking fine. Those new spam filters seem to be helping on WantAGadget, and we're getting more traffic every day."

"That's good." Morgan accepted Ranger's toy and threw it again. "Your mom called to remind us Beth has a game this weekend. Thinks she's going to start."

Nick grinned. "You wanna go?"

Morgan grinned back. "Like I'd miss seeing Beth kick volleyball butt. I told your mom to save us seats."

Nick reached for her hand. "Good. How are you feeling?"

"Okay, I guess," she admitted, shrugging. "It's just a period, babe. Had them most of my life."

"Yeah, but, I... I was thinking..."

She smiled, shaking her head indulgently as he pulled her into his arms. "You're just gonna have to wait a few days, big boy. At least 'til these cramps are gone."

He feigned being shocked by her comment then kissed her and gazed into her eyes. "Actually, I was thinking we both kind of wanted this to be a baby. How do you feel about, well, not using condoms for a while?"

She searched his eyes. "You want to try to have a baby?"

"It's more like not trying to not have a baby."

She kissed her sweet Nick. "You're splitting hairs with semantics, babe."

"Maybe so," he said. "But I almost died when I was a kid, and you did too. I know it's probably too much too fast, but I love you. Life is short, so why not grab all the happy we can, while we can?" He paused, searching her eyes, and his voice softened as he said,

"You haven't answered my question. How do you feel about just letting nature take its course?"

She stood there a long time, barely daring to breathe. "A baby? Really?"

He grinned. "I hear they tend to occur in such instances, yes. Of course, we'd have to get married first. Don't want to upset my mother."

Morgan giggled. *Upset your mother. Who regularly deals with JoAnn without so much as a flinch. Oh, Nick.*

"Now, see, here I am trying to be all coy and charming, trick you into marrying me by dangling the promise of babies in front of your nose, and all you can do is giggle?" He nibbled at her neck and pinched her butt. "Who are you and what have you done with my always-serious Morgan?"

She squirmed, giggling louder as she tried to bat away his hands. But he was bigger, and stronger, and she loved him so. And he knew it.

"Yes!" she giggled, dancing away as he chased her across the room for another pinch and tickle. Ranger bounded around them, barking.

Nick caught her easily and twirled her into his arms. "Is that a yes to the baby, or a yes to the wedding?"

"Both," Morgan said, breathless and happy as his lips found hers. They fell groping to the couch and, desperate for his skin, she tugged open his belt.

"Thought we had to wait a few days," he said against her throat.

Morgan giggled and unfastened his jeans. "I do. You don't."

She'd just dragged his zipper down when her phone rang, chirruping in the pocket of her jeans.

"Arrgh," Morgan muttered, reaching for it. "This phone always has the worst timing."

Nick grinned and slid his hand up her t-shirt and into her bra. "It's okay. Gives me a chance to flirt with impunity."

"You're a tease," she muttered, closing her eyes and shifting to give him easier access as she clicked on the call. "Kinda busy here," she said, trying not to sigh.

"Morgan," the ageless, genderless voice on the line rasped. "It's finally you."

Morgan's eyes bolted open and she struggled to get out from beneath Nick. The phone fell from her hand and landed on the floor.

"What's wrong?" he asked, reaching for it.

She cowered away, trembling as he plucked it from the floor.

"Who is this?" Nick demanded. He winced, then said, "Go fuck yourself." And he ended the call.

"It's okay, it's okay," he said, reaching for her. "Shh. It's okay."

"I thought it was over," she said, clutching at him. "I thought she was done."

Her phone rang again and Morgan nearly scrambled over the back of the sofa in her desperation to get away. Nick scowled and pulled out his own phone, pushing a couple of buttons. "Detective Hildebrandt? It's Nick Hawkins. She's back. On Morgan's cell, an unknown caller," he said, his phone wedged on his shoulder and Morgan's ringing in his hand as he recited the number on the screen. The ringing stopped and the call went to voice mail, then it started ringing again.

"Hold on," Nick told the detective, waking Morgan's phone and putting it on speaker. He looked at her, a finger to his lips, and held the phones close together. "You stay the piss away from my Morgan."

"Ah," the voice said, raspy and slow. "My daughter's live-in boyfriend." A chuckle, then, "Do you like to yank on her ponytail when you fuck her, nerd boy, or just slap her on that tight runner's ass 'cause she's a naughty little filly?"

Morgan flinched, fist pressed against her mouth. *She's seen us? Oh, God.*

"What the hell do you want? Hasn't she suffered enough?"

The voice laughed. "Let me talk to Morgan."

"Fuck you," Nick said.

"No, fuck you, nerd boy. Tell her I'm coming. Tell her I'm ready to kill her. And I'll make you watch."

Then the call went dead.

Morgan rocked, her mind repeating *Oh Libbey, oh hell! She's not in Portland!* over and over while Nick tried to hold her and talk to the detective. "Did you trace it?" he asked. "Record it?"

He clenched Morgan's phone. "Yeah, come get the phone. I don't think she's going to want to touch it ever again."

Morgan burst to her feet and started pacing.

"We'll need some contact information from it, but I can download it before you get here."

He closed his phone and watched her pace.

"It's never gonna stop," she said.

"It'll stop," he said, standing. "We can sell the house, change phone numbers. Move to Arizona if we have to. It'll be okay."

"She's been watching us. We might need to run away. Far, far away."

"I know." Nick's voice was hard. "The cops are coming. We'll go to my folks' place tonight and figure out what to do after that. Don't worry. It's still broad daylight. We're safe for now, and we'll be out of here long before dark."

* * *

Nick was still downloading her phone's data when the detectives arrived. "He's in the office," Morgan said, reaching for the comfort of her dog.

They'd just nodded their thanks when Nick hurried to them, phone in hand. Morgan barely heard the detectives' questions or instructions as she wandered about, mind churning. So much to do, to pack. Clothes and Ranger's toys and computers and things.

She went upstairs and stuffed clothes into Nick's duffel, enough for both of them for a couple of days. Toothbrushes. His thyroid medicine. Her pads.

By the time she lugged the thing downstairs, the detectives had gone and Nick was in the office printing reports and moving the current site files onto the external drive.

"All packed," Morgan said. "How long 'til the transfer's done?"

"Ten minutes. Maybe." He kissed her and gazed into her eyes. "It's barely 4pm. Early. Nothing's gonna happen in broad daylight, not when we can see her coming."

"Okay." She paced, restless. Ranger looked up at her and whined. "Do you want me to pack any groceries? Ranger's dishes?"

"My folks have bowls and we can buy anything more we need," he said, glancing back at her. "Try to relax. Just a few more minutes."

"I'm trying," she said. Nick's phone rang, and she jumped.

"It's my dad," he said. "Hey, look, Jannis is fiddling in her back yard. Why don't you go tell her goodbye real quick, and I'll be ready by the time you get back."

"You promise?" she asked.

He kissed her. "Promise. Go ahead and take Ranger with you. It'll do you good to get a minute of fresh air, and it'll give him a chance to pee. I'll be watching from the window. Just come right back."

"Okay," Morgan said, managing a smile. At least it was something to go do. Better than waiting scared in the house.

* * *

"Oh, Morgan, not again!" Jannis said, wiping dirt off her hands as she stood. She'd been weeding her flowers while, out by the alley, Frank raked leaves. "Maybe it's her idea of some sick joke. We haven't seen anyone strange anywhere!"

"Me either," Morgan said, her gaze darting around. She saw no one unusual, nothing out of the ordinary. Kids on bikes, older folks puttering in their lawns, and farming monstrosities rumbling down the highway. A lovely autumn afternoon in her neighborhood, nothing scary at all.

Ranger lunged for a squirrel, and Morgan let him pull her while she and Jannis walked to Frank. Morgan again explained why they were leaving.

"We're staying at Donna and Mark's a few days," she said as Frank hugged her. "Can you call us there if something happens?"

"Of course we will, hon," Jannis said, touching her arm.

A car on the highway backfired, the high pop almost lost under the rattle of a giant tractor. Morgan jumped, looking over her shoulder, as Jannis pulled her in for another hug.

"It's all going to be okay," Jannis said.

"Hope so." *But I have my doubts.*

Morgan said her goodbyes and walked to her back gate, looking about the alley for Libbey skulking in the shadows. Except there were no shadows deep enough to hide a person. A rabbit, maybe, but nothing big enough to hurt her.

She kept Ranger on his leash as they crossed the back yard and Morgan wondered if she'd ever see it again. *Would we really move to*

Arizona? she thought as she opened the back door. Arizona seemed so far away.

Ranger immediately crouched, tugging on his leash. His low, ripping growl prickled goose bumps on Morgan's arms. The air in her kitchen smelled like the fireworks. Dangerous. Explosive.

"Nick?" she called out, frozen and shaking just inside the door while Ranger's growl grew louder and louder, his hackles rising. Someone was in the house. Someone had brought that awful smell into her home. "Nick!"

Nick's soft cry slammed her in the gut. "Run, Morgan! Run!"

God, no. Nick!

Ranger's growl turned to a vicious snarl, teeth bared. Morgan let go of his leash. He burst forward, low and fast.

She followed. Running.

TWENTY EIGHT

MORGAN RAN, but Ranger was faster and he zipped round the corner into the living room in a snarling fury.

"Fucking dog!" Morgan heard, then an earsplitting crack filled the air, freshening the awful cordite stench.

"NO!" Morgan, only a few steps behind, skidded into the living room to find Ranger writhing and whining on the rug while Nick, bloody from mid-torso down, lay propped against the couch, his legs splayed on the floor. He was breathing, thank God, but his gaze remained rooted on Mrs. Parson's homely, aging daughter.

"Run, Morgan," he begged. "Please."

The woman stood over him, turning the gun from Ranger to Nick's forehead as she stared at Morgan. "No, no, Morgan. No running or I'll blow his head apart, splatter his fucking dork brains over this nice, new sofa. You do exactly what I say and maybe, just maybe, he'll live to compute another day."

"You can get away. Please, Morgan," Nick mumbled, eyes scrunching shut and his head tilting back as the gun dented the skin above his left eyebrow. "Go!"

"I'm not going anywhere. Not yet." *I've seen her a dozen times or more without realizing,* Morgan thought, brain churning. *Only talked to her once, barely noticed her. Been living next door since...*

Morgan took a breath, eyes narrowing. *Since that first weekend Nick and I left. I should have known! You were familiar, I knew it the first time I saw you.* "What'd you do to Mrs. Parson?" she hissed.

"Nothing you need to worry about," Libbey said, voice raspy and coarse, damaged from booze or cigarettes or who knew what else. She pulled back, gun pointing at Nick but no longer against his eyebrow. She let out a low whine and rubbed the heel of her free hand against her forehead, muttering, "Shut up shut up shut up! Headbanger headache! Shut up!"

Instinct insisted Morgan take a step back, but she grit her teeth and pressed forward instead. *I'm not a terrified kid anymore, you crazy bitch. I WILL find a way to stop you.* "Get away from him, Libbey."

Libbey crammed the gun against Nick's left eye socket. "You never did call me Mommy." She sounded almost regretful.

"Is that all you wanted?" Morgan asked, voice growing louder as Libbey and her gun moved away from Nick again. "For me to hug you and call you *Mommy?*"

"It would've helped." Libbey drew her head back and stood a little straighter, sweat glistening on her brow. A muscle beside her right eye twitched. "I gave everything up for you."

What the hell? "You gave up shit," Morgan muttered, taking another step toward her mother as the older woman flinched. "You abused and neglected us, tried to *murder* us. What the hell'd you give up? Ten minutes of smoking your damned dope?"

"I was going to work with horses," Libbey said, gun shakily rising to point at Morgan's chest. "I used to sneak off to the stables to volunteer to help muck stalls. I begged to walk them. I'd do anything for the horses. *Anything.* But no one let me."

Morgan tried not to gape. *Horses again?*

Libbey didn't seem to notice Morgan's shocked disgust. "Then a guy offered to show me Arabians if I sucked his dick. Lipizzaners if I took him up the ass." The gun shook in Libbey's hand and tears welled in her eyes. "I was just a kid. I'da done anything for the horses, but all I got was knocked up with you!"

Libbey rubbed her forehead again, hard, above her right eye, and sagged. Morgan sidled a half-step closer.

"You took away everything I wanted, every goddamn dream I ever had," Libbey muttered. "I turned tricks because of you. Sold dope. Sucked dick. You were supposed to love me, but all you did was shit your pants and scream."

Morgan slid closer. *C'mon. Get distracted. Just one little moment. C'mon.*

Libbey took a shaky breath and snapped her head away from her palm as if the jerk would leave the pain behind. The movement sent her stumbling aside, toward Ranger, still writhing on the floor. "You're my biggest fucking mistake and I've hated you since your first breath."

Libbey tried to turn toward Morgan again but her heel hooked Ranger in the gut and she tripped. "Get out of my way, you fucking dog!" she yelled, arms flailing.

Morgan lunged, palm-heels forward. One slammed Libbey in the gut, the other below her jaw, and she knocked the older, heavier woman off her feet.

Libbey fell backwards, squawking her surprise. Morgan followed, momentum carrying her forward.

Morgan punched her in the throat, the face, even as Libbey clawed at her hair and eyes and hit her head with the gun. "I was a little kid! Mothers shouldn't hurt their kids!" Morgan pummeled her mother, hands closing around her throat. "You were supposed to protect us!" She lifted Libbey's head and slammed it back, grunting as Libbey's gun slammed hard alongside her skull. Her vision faded to washed-out black and white.

"You're finally dead, fucking ungrateful bitch," Libbey snarled. Morgan felt metal press against her armpit and she shoved herself backward, hands still clenched on Libbey's throat and yanking her from the floor.

The gun went off, a deafening sear that screamed along Morgan's inner arm, but she reached for it anyway, burning her hands on the metal, her elbow repeatedly slamming into Libbey's face. It went off again as they fought for it. Again when Libbey lurched up to bite Morgan's hand. Then one last time between them, leaving Morgan with a high-pitched scream in her ears but no additional pain.

Libbey fell, gasping, but Morgan couldn't hear. Both still held the gun until Morgan wrenched it free. She shoved it under her mother's blood-streaked chin and smelled her flesh sizzle. "I should just kill you," she said, barely registering her own voice over the screaming whistle in her ears.

Libbey said something, her mouth moved at least, and she struggled weakly before she spat in Morgan's face.

Snarling, "Shut up!" Morgan clocked her on the forehead with the butt of the gun.

Libbey's eyes drifted half-closed and she fell limp.

Gasping, gun clenched in her hand, Morgan rolled off Libbey and she panted, staring at her living room ceiling. Blood had speckled the fresh paint and plaster dust fell like gritty snow from a hole above her.

"Oh, God," Morgan gasped, sitting, still unable to hear anything but a high-pitched whine over the frantic slam of her heart. A window had nearly shattered and the couch sported a fluffy divot not four inches from Nick's neck.

"Nick!" she cried, crawling to him. He was limp, blood drenching the lower half of his shirt and his lap, but he was breathing. "Nick, please wake up," she begged, reaching for his face. She saw the gun in her hand and screamed, flinging it aside as if it would bite her, then she held Nick's head. Kissed him. "Please, please wake up!"

He sagged, and she flinched, shaking her head. Ranger twitched not far from her feet, his legs working, trying to crawl to her while blood leaked from his mouth. His eyes were pained but acutely aware.

"Oh, buddy, oh Ranger boy," she said, reaching for him and stroking his fur. His breathing was erratic. Labored. "Shh. Shh now," she said, bawling. "It's gonna be okay. Somehow, it's gonna be okay."

She felt footsteps on the porch and she turned, one hand on her dog, the other on Nick's ankle, as the screen door flew open. *The sheriff! Thank God!*

A heartbeat later, Morgan yelped, cowering under her arms. Guns drawn, deputies kicked her door open and, despite her struggles, forcibly dragged her from the house.

TWENTY NINE

"I NEED TO SEE NICK!" Morgan demanded for surely the hundredth time, but no one cared.

She'd been taken to the hospital then stripped, poked, prodded, swabbed, and photographed, both clothed and nude, especially the bullet-burn on her arm. Which they bandaged after she bled all over herself because some pervert of a photographer split open the wound while getting a close-up that surely included her left boob. When she'd complained—and demanded, again, to see Nick— they'd made her dress in crappy scrubs and paper booties. They let her keep her undies, but took her bra, the bastards. After they dragged her to a tiny, private room, two rough-handed orderlies had strapped her wrists and ankles to a hospital bed and left her there to stew.

Probably because she'd managed to kick the photographer in the balls.

"Where's Nick?" She struggled against the binds. "You bastards better take me to see Nick!"

No one came.

He'd been alive when they carried him to the ambulance, pale with his shirt off and an EMT running alongside carrying an IV bag, but that had been an eternity ago. And he'd lost so much blood.

And Ranger. What about Ranger? He was still in the house when the cops had driven her away, kicking and screaming and demanding to go to the hospital with Nick. Was her man dead? Her dog? Her psycho-bitch mother? Why wouldn't anyone talk to her?

Why hadn't they come to question her at least?

"And where's my fucking lawyer?" she yelled at the empty room, the low auditory squeal faded yet still muffling her world. "I demand my lawyer, and I demand to see Nick!"

The door swung open a few heartbeats later, both detectives strolling in while Hildebrandt flipped through a clip of papers. "You have quite the set of lungs, Miss Miller," she said. "You're lucky they didn't sedate you."

"I *run*. Miles and miles. My lungs haven't even started getting tired yet. Where's Nick?"

Morgan's lawyer pushed past, wearing a suit and carrying a briefcase this time. "No reason to bait her, Jill." He stood beside Morgan and opened the case. "I want all of her previous comments stricken," he said, plucking a paper from the case.

"And I want to see Nick!"

Hildebrandt flipped another page and scowled. Out in the hall, a nurse dragged a teenage boy past. The boy's multi-pierced face was blotchy and streaked with tears. Kramer closed the door.

"She was Mirandized," Hildebrandt muttered, "right there at the scene by the deputy who hauled her out of that mess."

Biddermahn tapped the paper. "She couldn't hear because of the gunshots. Your own examination noted severe ringing in her ears. I've filed a motion. Her previous statements are all off record as is anything else she says until you re-read her her rights."

Hildebrandt shrugged and managed to smile. "It's not like she said anything useful. All she did was holler for her boyfriend and tell us to quit touching her or she'd sue us. You have the transcript."

"I do, and your department will face charges for sexual assault first thing tomorrow." He leaned forward. "She's an assault *victim*, so you stripped her to her skin, forcibly arranged her for lurid photos, *then* you took her bra, for Christ's sake, all without getting her permission?"

"We asked for her permission. All she did was scream."

Hildebrandt sat, sighing. "Two people in her home were shot and her fingerprints are on the weapon. She was covered in evidence including gunshot residue and at least one other person's blood. She fought the responding deputies on scene, she fought the lab and photographer, and she fought all the way in here and into that bed. They had no idea she's had problems with a stalker or is a victim. They only knew a deputy brought in a combative suspect covered in evidence of a shooting, so I now have two guys getting stitches and one in the ER because his vasectomy scar split open. All because we needed her clothes for testing."

"You should've asked," Morgan snarled. "And you should have taken me to see Nick."

"We did ask, Miss Miller. Your response was to demand to see your boyfriend and to kick medical personnel." Hildebrandt sighed, nodding, and Kramer read off the particulars of Morgan's right to remain silent.

Morgan fumed, hands balled into fists. As soon as Kramer finished, she snapped. "How's Nick?"

"Honestly, Miss Miller, we don't currently know anything about his state other than he was brought here in an ambulance. You've wasted all that energy, and all our eardrums, for information we don't even have. You'll just have to wait until we know more."

"Untie me! I have to see him!" Morgan snapped despite her lawyer's quieting hand on her arm.

"What happened, Miss Miller? Between the time we left your house with your phone, and the *astonishingly short* six minutes when the first report of gunshots came in?"

Willing her voice to stay level, Morgan took a breath and looked Hildebrandt in the eye. "I wanted to leave right after you did, but Nick, he had to get the computer backups. Said it'd just take a few minutes. I was nervous, pacing, so he sent me and Ranger to say goodbye to Frank and Jannis. Mostly so my pacing wouldn't drive him crazy, I think."

Hildebrandt checked her notes. "Your neighbors to the south?"

"Yes. They were working in their yard and I was just gone a minute or two. Ranger and I came home through the back..."

She explained, carefully and slowly about the smell, Ranger getting shot, and Nick bleeding with a gun to his head. "Everyone thought she was Mrs. Parson's daughter. But she wasn't. She's... she's my mother. She came to kill me." Morgan swallowed. "Again."

"Mrs. Parson lives to your north?" Hildebrandt asked.

Kramer's phone rang and he excused himself, stepping to the hall and closing the door.

Morgan nodded, gaze returning to Hildebrandt. "Yeah. Cranky old lady. She got sick, and her daught... No, Libb..."

Morgan's eyes widened and she struggled against the straps. "Did she hurt Mrs. Parson? Kill her too? No one's seen her for weeks. You have to find her!"

"It'll be taken care of, Miss Miller," Hildebrandt said. "What happened then?"

Hildebrandt wrote a few notes, and listened while Morgan explained how she and Libbey had argued, then fought. The gun, the plaster, the blood.

"I couldn't wake up Nick. And Ranger, he was in so much pain," Morgan said, struggling not to cry. "When the deputies came in, they dragged me out to the car and locked me in." Pleading, she said, "I have to know how Nick is. And Ranger. Are they both dead?

Please tell me they're not dead."

Hildebrandt asked a few more questions, then looked over as Kramer returned. He slipped her a note, and she stood, handing him her papers before walking to Morgan.

"Someone's come to take you to your boyfriend," Hildebrandt said as she unfastened Morgan's wrists. "We'll have more questions later, but, for once, can you not scream at everyone as you cross the hospital?"

"I'll be as quiet as a ghost as long as I get to see Nick."

* * *

Scott waited in a room down the hall. "Where the hell are your clothes?" he asked.

Morgan accepted a quick hug and followed him down a deserted hall. "They took them. Evidence. How's Nick?"

Scott paused. "No one told you?"

"No, no one told me," she managed, clasping her hands so they wouldn't shake. "How is he? Is he…"

"Still in surgery, when his folks sent me to find you," he said as he pushed a door open to a service hall. "The shot missed his liver, thank God, but went through his stomach, part of his intestines, and clipped his spleen. His guts are an infected mess from the punctured bowel, and they had to give him a *lot* of blood." They reached a bank of elevators and Scott pushed the up button.

Morgan struggled not to cry. "Is he going to be okay?"

"We don't know yet. His cancer… They said the spleen's part of his immune system, which the cancer tore up." He glanced at Morgan and said, "They just don't know."

* * *

By the time they arrived, Nick was out of surgery and moved to a private room. His family and friends milled about in a huge clot outside, talking in low worried voices. Bailey cried openly and two struggling nurses failed to get the crowd to move to the waiting room. Morgan hurried to them and Nick's mother grabbed her, hugged her, and drew her aside.

"How is he?" Morgan asked, frantic. "Is he gonna be okay?"

"We think so. The surgeon said the shot tore the hell out of his gut, and they had to remove his spleen, but it's all repaired now and should heal. I saw him in recovery and he knew me and asked about you, so that's great news. The big worry is infection and how he'll tolerate eating, when they let him. They just brought him up not five minutes ago, and they're getting him settled in. We all can see him then."

Donna squeezed Morgan's hand. "He's going to be fine. Sore. Weak for a while. But just fine."

Morgan's breath fell out of her, shaking, and her knees felt weak, but she managed to nod and murmur her thanks. "It's my fault," she said, almost babbling. "All my fault."

"No," Donna said, arm around Morgan's shoulder as they walked down the passageway. "It was that awful woman's fault. She's the one who shot Nick, not you. And Nick should have just got in the car and left while the police were still there. We know you wanted to go right then, but he had to get his backups and files and things. That's just how he is."

"But—" Morgan started, but Donna cut her off.

"It was not your fault, sweetie, and we all know it, so stop blaming yourself. Mark was on the phone with Nick when he answered the door, when that evil woman barged in demanding to see you. He heard the shot, you coming back, the whole thing."

Morgan stopped and blinked at her. "All of it?" She thought of the things she'd said—the horrid words, the threats and taunts, and how violent, insane Libbey was her mother. Morgan looked away and murmured, "You must think me an awful person."

"No," Donna said, hugging her. "Only an incredibly brave one."

Footsteps hurried toward them and they turned to see Trish waving them back to Nick's room. "What are you two doing clear out here? He's awake!"

They rushed back and pressed into the room despite a nurse insisting most of them had to leave because he needed to rest. Firemen and their families apparently refused to listen to such nonsense.

Morgan heard Nick mumble, "You sure she's okay? Last I remember, that bitch had a gun to her chest."

"I'm here, and I'm just fine," she said as she reached the foot of his bed. Ken stepped back to give her room to squeeze past.

A long tube ran from an IV into Nick's forearm, and a short, capped tube spouted out of his chest near his shoulder. Yet another tube curled out of his belly to a little bag beside him on the bed. Morgan grasped his hand and tried not to notice the tubes, instead she looked only at his eyes, so happy and thankful to see her.

* * *

Half an hour or so later, the crowd had thinned to Morgan and Nick's parents. She sat beside the bed, holding Nick's hand as he dozed. Mark sat in the corner reading a battered home decorating magazine, and Donna whispered with other nurses just outside the room.

Mark closed the magazine and sighed. "You sure you don't want me to run you home for some clothes? You can't be comfortable in that."

"I'll be all right." Morgan smiled at Mark and stretched her back without releasing Nick's hand. "Do you know if they did anything to help Ranger? If..." She winced and looked away, unable to speak her worry that whoever came for him simply put him to sleep, if he'd managed to live long enough to get found at all.

"I'm sorry, kiddo," Mark said, Morgan's heart clenching as he reached into his pocket. "I haven't heard. But I'll call Frank and see if he knows anything."

Morgan's free hand pressed against her chest to slow her heart's frantic slam. "Thank you," she said, trying to not let her hopes get too high.

Mark talked a few moments, relaying Nick's status, then he asked, "Hey, do you know anything about their dog? He was—" He shifted in his seat, listening. "Really? Good, I'll let her know."

Morgan bit her lip and held her breath. *He said good!*

Mark covered the phone with his hand and whispered, "He was still alive when animal control arrived. Jannis called the vet and insisted they take him there. So he's at the vet's, but that's all we know."

Morgan closed her eyes and whispered a quiet prayer. *That is good. Amazing. At least he has a chance.*

Mark returned to the call and asked, "Can you guys do us a favor? The kids need some clothes, especially Morgan. She's been sitting here in disposable scrubs."

"You don't have—" she started, but his stern glare cut her off.

He listened a moment then said, "Yeah, they'd supposedly packed to come to our house, so there ought to be a bag downstairs somewhere. If not, I'm sure it's okay to just get something out of the closet. Underwear, socks, the whole bit."

Mark thanked Frank then closed the phone before returning to his magazine. "They're still examining the crime scene, so Jannis is going over there now to tell them she needs some things from the house. If they won't let her in, she'll call me right back and I'll drag you to the mall myself, if I have to."

He turned a page in the magazine with a snap. "I'll be damned if I let my future daughter-in-law go about half dressed."

Morgan covered her chuckle with her hand as Donna came in, lips pressed tight.

"Morgan, honey, can you come with me for a sec?"

Mark looked up, but Donna shook her head. Morgan stood and swallowed back the worried taste in her mouth. "Is there a problem?"

"No, of course not," Donna said, motioning for her to follow quickly. "Just need to show you something."

Morgan followed Donna down a flight of stairs to the second floor. They paused at the stairwell door and Morgan saw Donna's hand shake. She took a breath and winced. "Maybe I shouldn't have brought you."

"What's going on?" Morgan asked.

"That woman... Your mother... She's on my ward," Donna said. "The shot went upwards through her lung. She'll live, but she'll have problems breathing for the rest of her life. I thought, maybe..." She shrugged and struggled to smile. "I thought you might want say something to her before she gets taken to jail in the morning."

"She's awake?" Morgan asked, astounded that her voice was calm and even.

"Medicated for pain, but yes, she's awake. She's also handcuffed to the bed." Donna touched Morgan's arm. "If you don't want to see her, it's okay, I understand." She smiled sweetly. "I'd personally like to rip her throat out, but it'd ruin my pension. And any chance I'd have to see my grandkids."

Morgan clenched her back teeth and nodded. "I have a few things to say, yes."

* * *

Donna beside her, Morgan stood watching Libbey doze for what seemed like a long time. She, too, had tubes coming in and out, plus oxygen hissing at her nose. Her skin was pale, sagging, and, even in her early forties, speckled with age. A deflated alien hag, so different from the memories that haunted Morgan's dreams.

But no one looks the same after twenty years, Morgan told herself as she crept closer. *Even folks who aren't crazed, drug-addict prostitutes.*

Libbey's eyes opened, giving the merest hint of bored acceptance. "If you come looking for an apology, you ain't getting one," she said, her voice a low, rattling sigh. "You ain't worth apologizing to."

"I don't want an apology," Morgan said. "Just an explanation. Why'd you do this? Why'd you hunt me down after all these years? Why kill Darcy at all?"

"I told you," Libbey said, head rolling so she looked at the far wall instead of Morgan. "You kept me from my horses."

Morgan struggled to keep her voice level. "Fine. You blame me for being born and ruining your career mucking stalls even though you could have given me up for adoption or any of a hundred other responsible things. Okay," she said, shrugging. "Whatever. You were a shitty, abusive whore who killed Bret and Cas and Nori, and tried to kill me, because we didn't let you play with some damn horses." Morgan forced her fists to unclench. "That was more than twenty years ago and you were strung out on God-knows-how-much crack. You were nuts. Still are. All that I can, somehow, accept."

Libbey's head rolled back and her eyes glistened aware and cold.

"But what I can't accept, or understand, is why, for God's sake, *why* did you come back after twenty goddamn years? Why kill Darcy? Why shoot Nick? Hadn't you done enough back then to ruin my life?"

"It's your own damn fault," Libbey said. "I was still locked up when you contacted *me*."

"I *never* contacted you. *Never*. I used to pray you'd die."

"Deny it all you want," Libbey said, shifting in the bed. "But I got the letters. I got the proof," she said, the 'oo' stretching out in a long whoosh.

"No you don't," Morgan said. "I never, ever wrote to you, not once, not even when those damn therapists told me I had to, that it'd help me heal."

"Oh, I have them," Libbey spat. "Letters and letters about your life, your adopted family, and how you didn't really love them because you knew I was your mom, your only mom, and you loved me because I obviously loved you very much since I let you live." She glared at Morgan and spat out, "You signed every goddamn one 'Morgan, the only daughter you love'. 'Bout made me fucking puke."

"I never..." Morgan started, but she swallowed and asked, "Is that how you met Darcy? Because of the letters?"

Libbey grimaced. "Crazy bitch. Came to visit me, claiming she was you. Like I don't know what my own fuckin' daughter looked like. Your daddy was a horse trainer from fuckin' Brazil, not some mashed-faced piece of trash. She got all upset, ran out cryin' that first time, but it didn't stop her from visiting, or insisting I call her Morgan."

Libbey shifted again, eyes narrowing. "I don't know what you paid her to fuck with me, but when she showed up at the crazy house to take her mommy to lunch, I shut her up. Shut her up good."

"I never paid her anything," Morgan said. "And she *was* your daughter."

"No she wasn't," Libbey said, looking away. "I never had no drugged up kids. Just you and those three I killed."

Morgan's hands clenched again. "How many babies did you deliver. Are any of them still alive?"

"I never had no deformed druggie babies!" Libbey said, face growing red as she struggled against the cuffs. "All of my babies were pretty and I killed 'em all, every damned one, except *you*, Morgan, goddamn ungrateful bitch!"

Donna stood beside Morgan and laid a comforting hand on her arm.

"That crazy bitch knew you, knew where you were, I fucking saw it. So I tracked her ass down, found her address, even paid her a couple of visits, but she wasn't ever home. Then when you came in, came to see that one-legged wretch, I knew it was you."

Ryder? You saw me visit Ryder?

Morgan choked back a gasp as Libbey glared, tongue flicking out to clear foam from her slobbery lips. "I snuck a look at your sign in, and you lived in the same damn house! I got to Minneapolis and traded my car for a gun, ready to do what I shoulda done all along, but you weren't home. That old cunt next door saw me, so I stuffed her into a freezer and decided to wait and watch. Every damn day I saw you there, with your nerd and your dog and your pretty little house. Fuck that shit."

She tried to sit, but the straps held her down. "You're not supposed to be *happy*, Morgan, not after you ruined my life!"

THIRTY

TWO MORNINGS LATER, Morgan carried a perky dieffenbachia through a muddy, misty cemetery with Jannis. Eight mourners stood beneath the awning, all watching a young and nervous minister preparing to say a few kind words about Mrs. Parson. Morgan stood with them, head lowered, as he struggled to craft a hopeful service out of such a miserable day.

After, as folks left their plants and cards and hurried into the drizzle, a timid middle-aged woman approached. "You're Morgan, from next door?" she asked.

"Yes." Morgan accepted the woman's offered hand and said, "I'm so sorry about your mom."

"Thank you," the woman said, barely meeting Morgan's gaze. "I know mom wasn't easy to get along with, but I tried to call her every weekend. Well, most weekends."

Morgan managed a consoling smile. "That was very nice of you."

"I, I just wanted you to know that Mom found you, well, fascinating. I'm sorry," Mrs. Parson's daughter said, blushing, "but, after you returned her dog, she told me, 'How can she run around in shorts all the time? Doesn't she know about sweat suits?'"

"Excuse me?" Morgan asked, confused.

The woman rummaged in her massive purse. "After she said that, she insisted she was by-God going to march over to your house and give you this." She pulled a bulky, shimmering velour warm-up suit from her purse and took a cleansing breath before presenting it to Morgan. "She'd been a cheapskate my whole life, always convinced people were trying to swindle her, and it's the only thing she ever said she'd give anyone. She didn't have a will, or friends, or anything. But you made enough of an impression on her that she was going to give you this."

Bright red. With white racing stripes down the sides.

Morgan laughed and embraced Mrs. Parson's daughter in a quick hug. "She was quite the rascal, wasn't she?"

The woman smiled. "Actually, she was pretty much a bitch, but thank you. And thank you, too, for taking in her dog after she died."

"I was happy to help however I could. Did you want to pick up Chauncy? No rush. I know you have a lot to deal with right now."

Mrs. Parson's daughter wiped at her eyes. "Yeah, that stupid dog was the one good thing about visiting Mom. Thank you again for looking out for him, but I'd love to have him back."

"Absolutely. Come get him as soon as you're ready." Morgan hugged her again and thanked her for the clothes. "Jannis and I were going to have a bit of lunch before we pick up my Ranger from the vet," she said. "Do you want to come along?"

"I think I'd like that," Mrs. Parson's daughter replied, beaming.

* * *

The following June found Morgan at the courthouse, sitting on a bench as she waited for Nick to finish his testimony. She moistened her lips and tried to still her shaking hands. *I only have to look at her this one last time, then never again.*

"Mrs. Hawkins?" a deputy said. "It's time."

Morgan stood, nodding as she smoothed her dress over the bump low in her belly. She took a breath and straightened her spine as the deputy opened the door.

The witness bench was a step above the main floor and she steadied her quaking knees before climbing up. She looked at the jury as she was sworn in.

Once she'd sat, she held her hands together to quiet them, and answered every question clearly and simply, as Biddermahn had instructed her, had practiced with her. Libbey slouched in her seat across the room, a can of oxygen at her side. When Morgan insisted that Darcy was Libbey's daughter as well, Libbey stood and protested the accusation.

But the prosecutors had proof, and copies of the letters they'd found in Libbey's room at the mental health facility, and, perhaps most damaging of all, the phone calls left on Darcy's machine. All were brought up as reminders of previously-entered evidence to quiet Libbey's objections.

Morgan let out a sigh of relief when they finally thanked her for her time and released her. She fought the need to run in a desperate escape through the door to the fresh air outside of the courtroom, and managed to keep herself to a fast walk.

Nick waited for her, pacing near Biddermahn, hands stuffed in his pockets. His face lit up when he saw her. "You're done?" he asked, rushing to her.

"It's over. Finally."

Nick kissed her and held her close. "I'm so glad that's done," he sighed, lips caressing her forehead.

"Yes, well, there's still judgment and sentencing," Biddermahn said, smiling. "But the prosecution has a pretty tight case. I doubt the jury will let her get off for two murders and a shooting, let alone the rest. And insanity is off the table. This time, she'll be locked up for the rest of her life. Congratulations."

Nick's arm came around Morgan as he reached out to shake Biddermahn's hand. "Thank you. For everything."

Biddermahn laughed. "Remember that when you get my bill. It's not often a defense attorney gets to coach for the prosecution." He gave them a wink and walked toward another courtroom and a scrawny tattooed guy in chains.

Nick held Morgan, breathing her in. "Did you want to stay and see the end of this?"

"I already have," Morgan said. "Let's just go home."

Hand in hand, they turned to leave the courthouse, but stopped as Detective Hildebrandt walked up to them, an envelope in hand.

"No," Morgan sighed, shaking her head. "Not another warrant or court order or—"

"Nothing like that," Hildebrandt interrupted. "The county attorney subpoenaed your mother's records from Wisconsin. I thought you might want to see some of them."

"I don't want to see anything of hers," Morgan said as she turned to go.

"You have two brothers," Hildebrandt said, and Morgan jolted to a halt before turning back. "One, his brain and body were so damaged from her drugs, he's, well, a vegetable. But, the other was born about eight months after your siblings' deaths. No trace of drugs in him when he was born. He's fine."

A brother? "Really?"

"Really," Hildebrandt said, handing her the envelope. "He's a marketing major at Wisconsin State and said he'd like to meet you. That's his contact information." She gave Nick and Morgan a friendly nod and wished them a good afternoon before walking away.

Morgan's hands shook as she opened the envelope. Adam Freddenberg, nineteen years old, from Canton, Wisconsin. At the bottom of a tense but eager note expressing his excitement and hope to meet her, he'd listed snail mail for home and school, a website, email, even a cell number. *And* he included a photo of him on a dorm couch, playing video games.

Morgan's heart clenched. He looked amazing, young and brilliant with a whole life of promise ahead. He had Darcy's eyes.

Nick flipped open his phone and Morgan turned, confused. "Who are you calling?"

"My folks, to tell them to feed Ranger since we're going to be out of town for a few days." He grasped her hand, leading her toward the door.

"What?" she asked, slightly fuddled.

"We're going to Wisconsin to meet your brother. It's about time you had family worth claiming."

Yeah, I guess you're right. Laughing, Morgan squeezed Nick's hand and walked out with him to a gorgeous Minnesota day.

THE END

Thank you for reading!
Be kind and review. I value your feedback.

Other Books by Tambo Jones:

Ghosts in the Snow Series:
Weight of the Castellan's Curse
The Lord Apparent's Razor
The Linen Maid's Choice

Threads of Malice Series:
Rabbits and Wasps

Winter of Ghosts Series
(Author's Vision of Ghosts in the Snow):
Weight of the Castellan's Curse
Protection of the Holy Knights
The Seer of Truth
The Killer's Lair
The Sourge of Demon Metal

Stand Alone Novels:
Spore

Short Stories:
Fire (A Lars Hargrove Story)
Endorphins
SID

ABOUT THE AUTHOR

Tamara Jones started her academic career as a science geek, earned a degree in art, and, when she's not making quilts or herding cats, writes tense thrillers as Tamara Jones and the award-winning Dubric Byerly Mysteries series (Bantam Spectra), as Tamara Siler Jones. Despite the violent nature of her work, Tam's easy going and friendly. Not sick and twisted at all. Honest.

Find her online at http://www.tambojones.com/